LINDA CRAIG
Mysteries

LINDA CRAIG

The Palomino Mystery
The Clue on the Desert Trail
The Secret of Rancho del Sol

———————————

Anne Sheldon

This edition published 1994 by Diamond Books
77–85 Fulham Palace Road
Hammersmith, London W6 8JB

The Palomino Mystery
© Stratemeyer Syndicate 1962
First published in USA in 1962 by Wanderer Books
First published in the UK in Armada in 1982

The Clue on the Desert Trail
© Stratemeyer Syndicate 1962
First published in USA in 1962 by Wanderer Books
First published in the UK in Armada in 1982

The Secret of Rancho del Sol
© Stratemeyer Syndicate 1963
First published in USA in 1981 by Wanderer Books
First published in the UK in Armada in 1992

The Author asserts the moral right to be identified
as the author of this work

Printed and bound in Great Britain

ISBN 0 261 66419 0

LINDA CRAIG

The Palomino Mystery

ANN SHELDON

Illustrated by St Ward

Linda Craig and her palomino pony, Chica d'Oro . . .

Glossary

Adobe   Sun-dried bricks used for building in California, Mexico and Arizona.

Barker   A fairground stallholder who attracts customers by shouting to passers-by.

Billfold   Wallet.

Bosal   Noseband.

Box canyon   A three-sided canyon with vertical or almost vertical walls.

Bronco   A wild or partially tamed pony of the western plains of the U.S.A.

Brownie   A piece of flat, nutty chocolate cake.

Burro   A donkey – especially one used as a pack animal.

Butte   An isolated, steep-sided, flat-topped hill.

Chaparral   A clump or thicket of thorny trees and shrubs.

Cinch   Girth.

Chuck hole   A hole or rut in the ground.

Concha   A shell.

Corral   A pen for cattle or horses.

Cottonwood   A name given to several kinds of North American poplar. The seeds are covered with cottony hairs.

Cutting horse   A horse trained to "cut" cattle out from a herd.

Demi-john   A large, short-necked bottle with wicker case and handles.

Diamondback   A type of large rattlesnake with diamond-shaped markings.

"End of the Trail" statue   A famous statue of a tired Indian pony.

Frontier pants   Western riding trousers.

Faucet   Tap.

Gopher   A burrowing squirrel native to North and Central America.

Greasewood   A spiny shrub that yields an oil used as a fuel.

Ground-hitch A word used when a horse is trained to remain stationary with its reins left dangling.

Hacienda The main house on a ranch.

Hackamore A bit-less halter made of rope or rawhide.

Joshua tree A tree-like desert plant found in the south-western United States. It has sword-like leaves and greenish-white flowers.

Lariat Lasso.

Latigo A strap used to adjust the saddle girth.

Mojave Desert A desert in Southern California, south of the Sierra Nevada.

Morgan An American breed of strong, light trotting horse.

Post To mark a place by erecting a signpost.

Quarter horse A small, powerful breed of horse, originally bred for sprinting in quarter-mile races in Virginia in the eighteenth century.

Saddlehorn The pommel of a western saddle round which a lasso can be looped.

Slaw Coleslaw.

Spell To take turns with someone in doing a job.

Tarp Tarpaulin.

Tennessee walker A type of American horse bred for its stamina and trained to move at a fast running walk.

Tinhorn Slang for a fool who has delusions about his importance or cleverness.

Trail horse A horse which is able to keep a steady pace for long distances over rough ground.

Truck bed The open part at the back of a truck.

Wash A channel made by running water.

Whitewing Chaffinch.

Yucca A plant of the lily family which has stiff, sword-shaped leaves and a white flower. It is found in Latin America and the south-western United States.

Mysterious Lights 1

"Come on, Speedy!" Linda Craig coaxed the sleek bay horse. "Nod your head!"

The slim, sixteen-year-old brunette, dressed in blue shirt and tan levis, moved a cupped hand toward the nostrils of the horse. But the cue failed. Speedy jerked his head aside, wheeled in the corral, and trotted off a few steps.

With a sigh, Linda turned to her tall brother Bob, eighteen, seated on the top rail of the corral fence. His sandy hair and a sprinkling of freckles indicated the two Craigs' Scottish background, while Linda reflected their Spanish ancestry.

"Bob, I'm doing exactly what I read in the training manual," Linda insisted. "I guess Speedy'll never be a trick horse!"

Bob grinned. "Maybe Speedy should learn to read the book."

Linda laughed. Dark eyes flashing mischievously,

she tossed her wavy hair. "What would you suggest, Brother dear? Sending him to school?"

"You'll have to ask Cactus Mac," Bob answered. "He's the expert here on Rancho del Sol."

Bob tilted his cowboy hat forward to shade his brown eyes against the May sun, and scanned the ranch for a sign of Cactus, the foreman. Rancho del Sol, better known to Southern Californians as Old Sol, stretched for acres on all sides of the main house.

Linda's eyes, too, roved over the pasture where horses and cattle grazed on the lush grass. Presently her gaze turned toward the hacienda, the long, low ranch house lying in the shade of six giant oak trees. Patches of sunlight glinted off the white adobe walls and red tile roof. Beyond stood the water tank on high stilts with a windmill beside it. Nearby was the barn.

"I love it here," Linda said. "Oh, there's Cactus Mac now," she added, pointing to a bandy-legged man who strode briskly from the barn. "Cactus, please come here!" she called.

The foreman hurried over and listened to Linda's complaint about Speedy.

"Wal now," Cactus drawled, "let me tell you something about Speedy thar." The foreman ran his tongue across his lips. "He's one of the best cuttin' horses I've ever known. Just turn him loose in a herd, and he'll cut out a good beef whether thar's a rider directin' him or not. That's what he was

trained to do, and it makes sense to him. Forcin'
Speedy to nod his head up and down for no purpose
don't appeal to his savvy."

"I guess what you really mean," said Linda, "is
that I'm not a very good trainer."

"Didn't say that," Cactus Mac replied quickly.
"You shouldn't expect any horse, no more'n any
person, to do all things. If you want to teach a horse
tricks, you get yourself a pleasure horse, and it'll
plumb love doin' tricks."

As the foreman went off, Linda turned to Speedy,
took off the halter, and gave the animal a pat. She let
down the bars into the pasture. "Go cut out a beef
for yourself!"

Speedy eyed the opening, then bolted through it
to freedom. He kicked up his heels, arched his back
in a leap, and galloped off to join the other horses.
Linda draped herself over the corral fence and
looked into space.

"What are you thinking about?" Bob asked her.

"A golden palomino of my very own," she answered dreamily. "A young one that I can teach to
do tricks."

"Why a palomino?"

"Because that's a Spanish breed," Linda replied.
She clasped her hands earnestly. "It'll understand
me and I'll understand the pony. I guess that's the
Spanish in me."

Linda's and Bob's great-great-grandfather, Don
Fernando Perez, and his beautiful wife Rosalinda,

had come from Spain as bride and groom to this California ranch. The oldest daughter in each generation since then had been named Rosalinda. But Rosalinda Craig had been nicknamed Linda.

To her secret delight, she looked just like pictures of her famous great-great-grandmother, but unlike her furbelowed ancestor, Linda always wore simply styled or tailored clothes.

As she stood mulling over the idea of owning a palomino, the ranch's coyote-shepherd dog, Rango, began to bark. Linda and Bob looked up. Coming along the lane to the hacienda was a lone horseman.

"High stepper," Bob commented as the glistening golden-chestnut Morgan approached, head erect, its gait in perfect rhythm.

"Looks like a show horse," Linda replied.

In a few minutes the strange rider came toward the corral. He was about thirty-five years old, had clean-cut features and a pleasant smile.

Bob had already swung his long legs over the top rail of the fence and dropped to the ground. "May I help you?" he asked the stranger.

"I'm looking for my friend, Mr. Tom Mallory," the tall, gray-eyed caller stated with a smile. "Is he here?"

"Not at the moment," Bob replied, and introduced himself and Linda. "Bronco went into town this morning, but he expected to be back by now."

"Bronco?" the rider inquired with a grin.

Linda laughed. "Our grandfather has had that

nickname since childhood, when he tried to imitate the antics of the ranch's broncs."

"I see," the rider said. "I'm John Davis, on vacation up here from Los Angeles. I have a mystery for your grandfather to solve."

Mystery! Linda and Bob were alert at once to hear it. But they were forced to wait. The sound of a jeep announced the arrival of Bronco Mallory.

The jeep stopped with a squeal of rubber and Tom Mallory stepped out. He was a big man, whose sombrero made him look even taller than his six feet. He had iron-gray hair, a ruddy tan face, and friendly blue eyes.

Bronco grinned and pumped his friend's hand. "Johnny, you jet birdman, where'd you come from?"

"Ditched my plane for a couple of weeks to roam around on this horse. Prince Brownlee, meet *Bronco* Mallory and his granddaughter and grandson."

The horse shook his head and snorted. Linda thought, *He* knows how to respond to commands.

John Davis said he was browsing around the countryside to get the feel of ranch life again. "I'm staying at the Brownlees and borrowed this prize-winner from them."

Linda walked around the horse, noting its regular breathing, good conformation, and sound legs. She liked the way he pawed the ground with his right front hoof, shaking his head at the same time.

He must be used to taking bows, Linda thought.

Bronco asked Linda and Bob to water Prince Brownlee and tether him in a shady spot by the barn. While they were gone, Tom Mallory led the way to the house.

"Linda and Bob have come to live with my wife and me," he said. "Their parents were killed in an accident a few months ago."

"Not your daughter Rosalinda?" Johnny asked, shocked.

"Yes." Tears glistened in Bronco's eyes. "It unnerved all of us. Her husband was a major in the army. The children fortunately had always spent their summers here, so this is a second home to them. They're excellent riders and Linda is sure daft about horses. Bob attends engineering college. He's real handy at repairing tools and machinery."

Johnny expressed his sympathy, then asked, "How are you and your wife?"

"We're both well, thanks. Let's go up to the house, Johnny."

Linda and Bob were coming from the barn as John Davis called to them. "I want you to hear about the mystery. Perhaps you can help solve it."

The four seated themselves in sturdy redwood chairs on the shaded patio, and Linda leaned forward eagerly to hear the story.

"As you know, Tom, my plane run takes me over the desert. For some time, on moonless nights, I've seen green, red, and purple lights strung out just beyond your extra grazing lands."

This acreage was part of a ranch once owned by Bronco's father. His son had retained part of the lush pastureland near distant Fossil Mountain and used it for his cattle during dry seasons.

Mr. Davis went on, "Each time the lights have vanished suddenly, as if somebody did not want them to be seen. Does anyone live there?"

"No," Bronco replied.

"Since it's close to your fence, I thought you might want to look into it," John said.

"Thanks for the tip, Johnny. Maybe someone's helping himself to my land. I'll ride out to see what's going on."

"Oh, Bronco," Linda cried excitedly, "may Bob and I investigate with you?"

Bronco smiled and gave John a wink. "I figured I'd have two enthusiastic helpers."

John Davis advised that they not go for a few days. "Not until the moon rises late," he said. "I've noticed that unless the night is very dark the lights don't appear."

"That's strange," said Bronco. "I'll do as you say, Johnny."

At this moment, the genial Mexican housekeeper, Luisa Alvarez, appeared, bearing an antique silver tray with tall cups, a slender pot of cinnamon-spiced hot chocolate, and a silver plate of home-made cookies.

"An old family custom when callers come,"

Bronco explained. "My wife likes to use the Spanish silver."

Linda was already pouring the hot chocolate. "Doña—that has been Bob's and my nickname for Grandmother since we were very little—is out riding, or she would join us."

As soon as John Davis had finished his drink, he stood up and announced that he must leave. "Let me know how you make out."

Bob hurried off to bring Prince Brownlee, and soon the pleasant caller was waving a last farewell from far down the road.

Bronco looked into Linda's eyes and said, "I've brought news of my own. For some time, I've thought that there's no horse on Old Sol exactly right for you. While I was in town I heard of a man who has a fine young palomino for sale. How would you like to ride out to his ranch tomorrow and see it?"

"Would I!" Linda exclaimed. "Oh, Bronco, how wonderful of you!"

The rancher chuckled. "Don't praise me. Thank your grandmother. She said if I ever came across a horse especially suited to you, I was to look into the matter."

Linda's eyes became dewy. "How lucky I am to have Doña for a grandmother! She's just the grandest person in the whole world. And that goes for you, too, Bronco!"

"It sure does," Bob said with a grin.

Linda was so happy she wanted to share her good news with everyone. She ran to tell Luisa, then Cactus Mac. Both expressed delight. Next, Linda telephoned one of her best friends, Kathy Hamilton, who lived nearby.

"A palomino of your own!" Kathy cried. "Linda, how marvelous! I hope you'll find one soon."

Just before dinner time—and dinner time at Old Sol followed the Spanish custom of being late in the evening—the telephone rang. Luisa came to tell Bronco that Mr. Brownlee was calling.

After a few moments, Linda heard him exclaim, "Johnny Davis has disappeared! He's long overdue? Yes, yes, we'll go out and hunt for him pronto!"

Bronco put down the phone and called the bunkhouse. He requested Cactus Mac to saddle up his chestnut Morgan, Colonel, and go with him on the search.

Then Grandfather Mallory turned to Linda and Bob. "I'm sure you both want to be in on this," he said. "Linda, put a first-aid kit in your saddlebag. Johnny may have been thrown from his horse or had some other accident."

The Runaway 2

As Linda hurried to the tack room in the barn with Bob and Bronco, she asked, "Do you think John Davis had a natural accident?"

"What do you mean?" Bronco said, puzzled.

Linda answered slowly, "If the people who are using the strange lights he was talking about are breaking the law and knew he had reported them—well, they might have attacked him."

Bob whistled and Bronco's forehead took on a deep, worried frown. Quickly Bob remarked, "In that case, the mission we're going on in a couple of days will probably be a dangerous one."

Cactus Mac was told about the lights and insisted upon accompanying the group when they were ready to look into that mystery.

The riders strung out, Linda on roan Gypsy, Bob astride Rocket, a bay quarter horse, and Cactus Mac on Buck. The four looked intently to the left and right of the long lane that led to the main road for signs of the missing John Davis. They found a horse's hoofprints, but Johnny was not in sight.

"Ted Brownlee said he had looked all along his lane," Bronco reported, "so I'm inclined to think Johnny took a shortcut."

"Might 'a been the one that's half a mile down the road," Cactus spoke up. "Not much more'n a dry streambed, but mighty direct."

"Let's try it," Linda urged.

The heavily wooded shortcut proved to be very rocky and full of tiny but treacherous gravel pits. The riders guided their horses with constant, careful skill, pausing many times to gaze around them. There was not a sound.

Finally Linda said, "If Johnny Davis came this way, he covered a good distance. How far are we from the Brownlee ranch?"

"We're on their land," Bronco answered, "but several miles from the ranch house."

Suddenly Linda said, "Listen!"

Everyone reined up and sat motionless. From their left came a rhythmic thumping sound.

"Thar's no animal around here what makes a noise like that," Cactus Mac said, puzzled.

Instantly the riders dismounted and plunged into the woods toward the strange thumping which continued. A few seconds later Bob, in the lead, cried out, "Mr. Davis!"

The others rushed forward and saw the missing man, tightly bound and gagged, lying on the ground. He had raised his legs to pound with his boot heels against the trunk of a cottonwood.

In a flash, the rescuers had him unbound and on his feet to stretch his cramped limbs. Johnny grinned ruefully. "Hello, everybody. And thanks."

"Who did this to you?" Bronco stormed.

"A couple of your 'friendly' neighbors. Get me some water and I'll tell you the rest."

Bob dashed back to his saddlebag and brought a canteen. As Johnny drank from it, Linda tried without success to spot the show horse he had been riding. "Where's Prince Brownlee?" she asked.

"Gone! Stolen!" was the astonishing reply.

"By the men who tied you up?"

"Yes. This is what happened. When I reached a spot near here, two masked men jumped out at me from among the trees. They ordered me to get down. When I refused, they dragged me off. There was a fight—which I lost. Then the men tied me up and dragged me to this spot."

"And if you hadn't been found," said Linda indignantly, "you might have died!"

Johnny grinned at her. "Oh, I'm pretty tough!"

Bronco spoke up. "Horse thieves! They probably had a van waiting some place to haul Prince Brownlee away. Which direction did they take?"

"That's the funny part of it," Johnny said. "They led the horse on up the shortcut right toward the ranch house."

Cactus Mac, silent up to this time, snorted.

"Them hoss thieves'll prob'bly hide the Prince and try to collect a big ransom from Mr. Brownlee."

"It's a logical guess," said Bob. "I wonder how soon we'll know."

"Right now the most important thing is to get Johnny home," said Bronco. "Do you feel strong enough to ride with me on Colonel?"

"Sure." Johnny walked with the others to the horses. Bronco borrowed one of the two blankets on Linda's horse, swung it across Colonel's hips, and the two men got astride.

When the riders reached the Brownlee home, the owner and his wife rushed outside, relief showing on their faces. Linda and Bob were introduced to hearty, gray-haired Mr. Brownlee and his pleasant, slightly stout wife. Then Johnny Davis told his story.

Mr. Brownlee's face turned red with anger. "This sounds like the old West! Our peaceful community invaded by horse thieves! We'll soon stop that! I'll phone the sheriff right away!"

The group from Rancho del Sol said good-bye and hurried back to a very late dinner. Grandmother Mallory, who always insisted her family dress properly for the evening meal, awaited them in a fashionable, long-sleeved black dress. Her dark, graying hair was pulled back into a knot and held in place with a high tortoiseshell comb. She was a beautiful woman, slender and dignified, and had a warm, ready smile. Her olive skin was set off by an emerald necklace and earrings, family heirlooms. Mrs. Mallory was considered an excellent horse-woman—one of the most accomplished in the West.

"Tell me, did you find Mr. Davis?" she asked.

"Yes, Roz," Bronco replied and told the circumstances briefly.

"How unfortunate!" Grandmother Mallory said. "But at least we can be thankful he's safe now."

The searchers excused themselves and quickly changed for dinner. Conversation throughout the meal was lively. Linda felt that never in her life had so many exciting things happened to her in such a short time. The report of mysterious lights in the desert; horse thieves and the loss of a valuable show mount; and the promise of a fine palomino of her own!

Presently Bronco said, "Why don't we combine our trip to see Linda's palomino with a hunt for Prince Brownlee? Those thieves may be hiding him somewhere in the desert. We can head for Indian Charlie Tonka's cabin, which is near my grazing lands, then go on to investigate the strange lights."

"It sounds marvelous," Linda said enthusiastically. "Indian Charlie's one of the guards for the pipeline, isn't he? May I go, Doña?"

Grandmother Mallory smiled understandingly. "Of course you may go."

Linda threw her grandmother a grateful smile and said, "Thank you."

The Mallory household was up at dawn. Yet by

the time Linda reached the barn, she found Cactus Mac nearly ready to leave.

"It's rugged country we'll be riding through, and dangerous, too. Got to be well-prepared," the foreman warned.

He said that he had checked the latigo leathers on the saddles, taken down a couple of pack saddles from a shelf, and four bedrolls from a cupboard.

"And the hosses have been curried and brushed."

"Cactus, you're spoiling us!" Linda laughed. "Well, at least we can help load the packhorses."

Bob joined her and together they strapped on a small hamper of lunch, cans of food, a supply of water, a two-way radio set, the sleeping paraphernalia, and extra clothes.

As Linda swung into her saddle, the girl's exhilaration was beyond words. Bob sat mounted and ready. Bronco was beside Linda, a .45 revolver in his gun belt. Cactus Mac carried a rifle in his saddle boot.

"For stray mountain cats or rattlesnakes," the foreman said, grinning.

With Bronco leading the way, and the two packhorses on a string behind Cactus's saddle at the rear, the ranchers rode east into the Mojave desert. Its undulating surface, dotted with cactus, juniper trees, and spiny, bent-arm Joshua trees, spread out distinctly in the clear morning sky. In the distance, wrinkled, rocky hills rose abruptly from the desert floor.

"It's beautiful!" Linda said, gazing at the scene of which she never tired. Nevertheless she was aware of the weird, weighty silence so peculiar to deserts and thought, I'll be glad to hear some whitewings cooing.

Her wish was fulfilled a moment later as two of the birds flew from a tree, giving their plaintive call, and landed on a rock to continue their song.

Bronco angled the riders' trail, and touched ranch country again. Eagerly, Linda watched for the palomino her grandfather had mentioned. She was first to see a weathered sign nailed to a fence post, announcing horses for sale.

"There are some palominos!" she cried.

As she and her companions rode up to them, Linda's spirits fell. The animals were too light in color, and one had a Roman nose, which she knew was not desirable for a show horse.

I want a palomino the color of a freshly minted gold coin, Linda thought, with a white mane and tail, and four white stockings!

The ranch owner, who was mending a fence, came to speak to Bronco. "The palomino you want to see is in the barn. I'll get him."

The horse proved to be a sleek gelding. Linda gasped. He looked exactly like her dream horse!

"How old is this palomino?" Bronco asked.

"Just going on five. Old enough to have good sense and young enough to have plenty of ginger."

"May I try him out?" Linda asked excitedly.

The rancher saddled the palomino. Linda mounted quickly, and turned out of the gate to work him on a clear spot of desert floor.

She rode around twice in a big circle. The horse had nice easy action. Then she attempted to put him through a figure eight, with little success. It took tugging to bring him about, so Linda knew he was hard-mouthed.

That toughness isn't good in a horse, she told herself.

Linda turned the palomino on a straightaway for a canter. Suddenly, he took the bit in his mouth and sped out over the desert. This was an unexpected move. Linda pulled hard on the reins, yet all her strength was not enough to stop the horse's headlong dash or even to haul him around. Going this fast, she did not dare throw herself off.

If this crazy horse keeps running, Linda thought desperately, I'll be lost in the desert!

Search in the Desert 3

Linda knew that her best hope of survival on the runaway palomino was to stick with him, praying that he would not slam a hoof into a gopher hole and throw her.

The palomino veered so sharply that Linda nearly lurched off. Then, before it could pick up speed again, her brother's lariat snaked out. The loop settled over the horse's head, bringing the animal up short.

Bob gave Linda a quick glance to be sure that she was all right, then grinned. "Nice ride?" he teased.

"Not exactly what I had in mind," she panted. "Thanks, Brother." They walked the horse back to the ranch, and Linda slid off him.

Bronco clapped Bob on the leg. "Good figuring, Bob, riding to cut them off instead of chasing straight after that horse. And a splendid catch."

"Just lucky," Bob muttered modestly.

"A fine horse," the owner said enthusiastically as

he patted the heaving palomino. "You going to buy him?"

Bronco looked into the animal's mouth, and replied curtly, "This horse's worn teeth indicate he's at least twelve years old. No, he's not the palomino for us."

"I wouldn't want him anyway," said Linda. "He's mean!"

She and Bronco and Cactus Mac mounted their horses and the four callers rode silently away from the abashed rancher. Linda was still recovering from her scare.

A short distance beyond, Bronco suggested that they stop in the shade of a few oak trees. While Linda unpacked the lunch, unable to forget her disappointment about the palomino, Bob and Cactus watered the four mounts at a little spring.

Bronco sensed the girl's mood. "Don't give up hope," he said. "We'll find just the right horse for you yet." Her answer was only a smile but it indicated the confidence she had in her grandfather.

When Linda and the men settled down under the trees to eat, Bob brandished a fried chicken leg and asked, "*This* is what you call roughing it?"

"It'll get rougher at supper time," Bronco promised him with a chuckle, "when you get your turn with a frying pan over an open fire."

After lunch, the four rode on to the mouth of a red granite canyon, where Cactus thought a horse thief could conveniently hide. As they wound along between its high walls, the shadows were deep and sounds reverberated. There was no sign of any animals.

Bronco grinned. "Kind of weird in here," he said. "Note the rock formations." He pointed out well-known ones and asked Linda, who had never been here before, to guess what they were.

"Cathedral and woman-at-an-organ," she spoke up presently. "Oh, I see an eagle, and a donkey's head!"

When they were deep in the canyon, Bronco gestured to a sloping pinnacle above them. "Bandit Rock," he said. "There's a pocket in back of it. Years ago, the famous outlaw Vasquez used to lie in wait there for people he intended to rob."

Linda felt a tingle up and down her spine. "A good place for horse thieves to hide Prince Brownlee," she remarked. "They could be up there right now, spying on us!"

"Yes," agreed Bronco. "You and Bob stay here and guard the rocks from the front. If anyone comes, yell! Cactus and I will investigate the rear."

Cautiously, the two men began to climb the slanting crags. Presently they disappeared. Linda and Bob waited with bated breath, hoping not to hear any shots to indicate a fight. None came and no strangers appeared.

Fifteen minutes later Bronco and Cactus Mac

returned. "Not a sign of Prince Brownlee," Bronco reported, "nor of any thieves."

The riders went on through the lengthening shadows. Finally they emerged from the canyon into the open, where dark, bushy junipers and sweet-smelling greasewood trees grew.

"Camping site just ahead," Bronco announced.

Soon the group reached a small ravine with a scant flow of water. After unsaddling the horses, Bob and Cactus Mac rubbed down their backs, then hobbled them so they might move about and graze.

Cactus Mac, who had never camped with Linda and Bob, watched with interest as they prepared supper. First Bob scooped out a narrow oval in the sand, built a fire in it, and rimmed it with large rocks.

On these Linda put the kettle, a skillet with bacon, and a pan of canned tomatoes. Bread and apples rounded out their supper.

"Wal, what you know? You sure can cook. The grub couldn't be better," the foreman declared, finishing the meal with a second cup of coffee.

Linda scoured their dishes with sand and paper, wiped them with a damp cloth, and put them back into the clean oat bag out of the dust.

As a big yellow moon rose over the dark, uneven skyline to the east, the weary travelers laid out their bedrolls. Bronco took a rough hemp rope from his saddle, and made a wide circle around the campers.

"What's that for?" Linda asked.

Bronco laughed. "No rattlesnake is going to crawl over that. The rope prickles its skin."

The campers pulled off their boots and slipped into the bedrolls. Linda watched the moon float higher and turn paler. Around her the bushy junipers shone like silvery ghosts. She lay awake drinking in the eerie beauty, and wondering about the mysterious lights, her dream horse, and the missing Prince Brownlee. But her eyes would not stay open long. Soon she snuggled down and went to sleep.

Linda and the others rose in the cool of the dawn. After a quick breakfast, they swung into their saddles and again looked intently for Prince Brownlee. They had no luck.

"I'm dreadfully worried about him," said Linda.

Bronco led the way to the fertile valley at the edge of which lay his grazing land. To left and right were majestic mountains.

Mr. Mallory and his grandchildren looked in every direction. There was no sign of a person, cattle, horses, or any type of equipment for lighting up the area. Finally the riders went on.

"We may be able to see the strange lights from Charlie's," Bronco remarked. "Then we'll know where to look for them."

It was mid-afternoon when they arrived, hot and tired, at the top of the mountain to the left, where

Inside was a little palomino filly . . .

Indian Charlie lived. Under the shade of planted acacia and elderberry trees, they saw his log cabin. On the far side of it stood a shed barn. Between the buildings was a corral.

Linda suddenly straightened in the saddle, reined up, and pointed at the enclosure. "Look!" she cried.

Inside was a little palomino filly daintily prancing in excitement at the visitors' approach. The graceful creature, tossing its white mane and tail, trotted to the fence and whinnied.

"Oh!" Linda breathed softly, unable to say more. "Oh, oh, oh!" she repeated in delight. Swiftly she jumped from the saddle and ran to get a closer look. "Gold!" the excited girl exclaimed happily. "Pure gold, and four white stockings!"

Bronco, Bob, and Cactus Mac exchanged grins. As they dismounted, Charlie Tonka came running from the cabin.

"Señor Bronco! Señor Bronco!" he exclaimed, and flung his arms around the big man.

"What luck to find you at home!" Bronco said smiling, and shook the Indian's hand. "You know Cactus Mac. I'd like you to meet my grandchildren," he added proudly. "Linda and Bob Craig."

Hearing her name, Linda pulled herself away from the palomino and joined the men. Charlie grasped her hand, then Bob's in welcome. The Indian was lean and bony, and the tight skin of his face shone like polished copper. His black hair, with a little gray in it, was brushed straight back and cut square across the nape of his neck.

"Can you stay long?" Charlie asked, beaming.

"As long as we need to clear up a little mystery."

"Ah, good!" said Charlie. "What do you want to solve?"

Bronco told about the strange lights near his grazing grounds. "Have you ever seen them?"

"Lights? Near your grazing fields? No, Señor Bronco. You think there is funny business going on?"

"We don't know exactly."

The horses were taken care of and turned into the section of the corral where Charlie's black Tennessee walker, Jim, welcomed them with nosing and nickering. Then Bob and Cactus carried the visitors' belongings into the cabin.

Linda yearned to stay with the little filly, but went along. I wonder if the palomino could possibly be for sale, she asked herself.

The interior of the cabin was rectangularly shaped—clean, neat, and bare. Cots flanked each long wall. There was a gas cookstove and cupboards at the far end of the room. In the center was a plain wooden table and four chairs.

"I'll have my own bed out under the stars," Cactus Mac announced.

The other end of the room had been partitioned off into a narrow section for storage of provisions.

"Linda, you sleep with the food," Charlie said,

grinning, and dragged one of the beds into this section.

As soon as Linda had set her bundle of clothing beside her bed, she slipped outdoors and hurried to the corral. Quietly she opened the gate and stepped inside.

The filly raised her head. Linda stood still. For a moment the two looked at each other. Then the palomino snorted lightly and shifted uneasily. Linda walked toward her, talking softly, and in a moment laid her hand on the silky, golden nose. Unknown to Linda, the men had followed and were watching her over the fence.

"You like my young'un?" Charlie asked, coming into the enclosure.

Linda's heart sank as she saw him gently stroke the horse's mane. She felt sure he would never want to part with his pet.

"Where did you get her?" Linda asked.

"One day I found her mother in the brush. She was a fine sorrel Arabian," Charlie informed the girl. "She was badly torn by wild animals. I brought her to the corral. She foaled this little golden filly. In a few days, the mother died. I fed young'un with a bottle. She is over two years old now."

The Indian chuckled. "Young'un very smart. Too smart sometimes. She slides the bolt on the gate." He squinted his eyes. "I think maybe her mother did the same thing. That is how she wandered off and got lost."

Charlie went on, "Her little one learns fast. Watch this." The Indian said "How!" and the filly raised her dainty right foreleg to "shake hands."

"Oh, you darling!" Linda cried softly, wrapping her arms about the golden neck. "I wish you were mine, you lovely creature!" Then she laughed. "If you were mine, I'd call you—well, I'd call you Chica d'Oro—little girl of gold!"

"That's a good name," Charlie agreed. "You call her that." But he did not say a word about selling the pony to Linda.

The next morning the Indian set off on his duties as guard for the cross-country gas pipeline. He planned to stay that night in a hut at the other end of the range.

"You make yourselves at home," he called from the walker's back as he rode off.

Bronco gave Linda a steady gaze, then asked, "Do you want to stay here while Cactus, Bob, and I scout around for some clue to the mysterious lights? Or would you rather come along?"

Linda was torn between two desires—helping to solve the mystery, and trying to teach the palomino a trick.

Her grandfather, guessing that she wanted to work with the pony, answered the question for the undecided girl. "If there's a horse thief around, that palomino ought to be protected, I suppose. Tell you what, Linda. See that bell on the post? If there's any trouble, ring that, and we'll come running."

"All right," Linda agreed, happy at the arrangement.

In a few minutes, she was alone. Taking several slices of bread in her hand, Linda hurried eagerly to the corral. Chica d'Oro promptly trotted over to her. The filly was used to having Charlie give her pieces of bread for a treat. Linda broke off one corner of a slice and put it in the pocket of her shirt. The palomino tried to pull it out with her soft lips.

"Good girl," Linda praised her.

Linda wrapped the bread in her handkerchief, tucked it in the pocket with the corner dangling, and Chica pulled it out. Soon the horse was pulling the handkerchief out whether there was bread in it or not.

"Oh, you wonderful pony!" Linda said affectionately.

When Bronco and Bob rode in at noon with Cactus Mac, she had them watch the trick.

"That horse has sense," Bronco said in praise.

Bob told his sister that they had found nothing in the area of his grandfather's grazing land to indicate any trespasser—the fences were intact. But as soon as the four had eaten, the men took off again on a more extensive search for a clue to the mysterious lights. Linda began clearing the table in a hurry so she could get back to Chica d'Oro.

Suddenly she heard the filly begin to prance and whinny shrilly. Dropping the spoons she held, Linda ran outside and was almost to the corral fence when she stopped short. A harsh, dry rattling sound was coming from the enclosure.

A rattler—a deadly rattler! Linda thought in terror. Chica d'Oro's in danger!

Trembling, she forced herself to walk quietly to the gate and look over it. In front of the distraught pony was coiled a big diamondback, its head erect and its tail warning of an attack.

Linda froze. If Chica strikes at the snake, it'll bite her! The pony might die!

Burro Trap 4

Quick as lightning, Linda grabbed a sharp rock near her feet and hurled it with all her strength at the rattler. The stone hit, but rolled off. The reptile had been hurt, however. It recoiled and started to slither out of the corral. Linda ran for a shovel she saw leaning against the barn. Hurrying up behind the snake, she ended its life with one blow.

Oh, Chica d'Oro, you're safe! she thought in relief.

For a moment the girl leaned weakly against the fence. Then, knowing the poisonous snake should not be left around, she swiftly scooped the dead reptile up in the shovel and buried it among some nearby bushes.

Too bad that had to be done, Linda thought. Rattlers have their use keeping down rodents. But right now I'd prefer a rat!

Finally she went into the corral and petted the palomino, whose chest was heaving from fright.

"What a scare!" Linda said. "You poor thing!"

When Chica d'Oro was calm again, Linda talked to her for a long time. The pony responded with nuzzles and head shakes. "I'm pretty crazy about you," the girl said excitedly. "Oh, what can I do to make Indian Charlie sell you to me?"

When Bronco, Bob, and Cactus Mac returned, she told them about the rattler and they praised her quick thinking. Bob, noticing that his sister was still shaken, and hoping to tease her into smiling again, offered to bring her the rattles from the snake.

"No, thank you!" Linda stated positively. Then seeing the twinkle in his eyes, she added, "Okay, Brother, I get it. But don't you dare dig up that beast!"

"You do not want your trophy? Now what do you think of that, Señor Bronco?" Cactus Mac asked, imitating Indian Charlie. At this they all burst into laughter, and Linda felt better.

"Tell me about your trip," she urged the men. "Did you learn anything about the lights or about Prince Brownlee?"

"No, sorry to say," Bronco replied. "We'll look again tomorrow."

The next day brought no better results. Early that evening, Bronco put Chica d'Oro in the barn away from snakes and marauding animals and Linda joined the men in a short ride to meet Indian Charlie. It was dusk when they saw him in the distance and spurred toward the Indian.

As they drew close and reined up, Linda exclaimed, "Look!" She pointed down to her right. "Hoofprints!" As they all scanned the ground, she added, "They're only in one place, though. How could that be?"

Bronco had a ready explanation. The horse had been ridden to the spot over an outcropping of smooth rocks that extended for some distance then disappeared into a woods.

"Pretty hard on the poor horse," Linda said sympathetically.

A moment later Charlie caught up to them. He dismounted and examined the ground. "Fresh print," he told them. "Made sometime today."

There was speculation as to whether or not an innocent rider had been in the locale, or perhaps the rider was one of the horse thieves.

"The horse *could* have been Prince Brownlee," Linda suggested.

She and the others made a search of the area but did not find the missing show horse. No one was around, and finally they went back to Indian Charlie's cabin.

After supper, the group walked out onto the grassy promontory beyond the cabin from which, by daylight, they could survey the ranches and valley for miles around. Silhouettes of trees and bushes stood out like black ghosts. Suddenly, in the distance, several varicolored lights flashed on.

"They must be some of the lights John Davis was

talking about!" Linda exclaimed tensely. "Oh, Charlie, is there any way we can get down the mountain and find out?"

"No good at night. You would break a leg. Go tomorrow with horses. I have a couple days off—I will come with you."

Linda felt impatient at the delay, but could do nothing except wait. She and her companions tried to place the exact spot of the strange sight. Charlie gave a clue. "The lights are on the other side of the valley at the edge of Fossil Mountain. You will find it easy."

An hour later the lights, which had blinked on and off intermittently, vanished completely.

"We'd better get some sleep," Bronco said, yawning.

In the morning, Cactus Mac elected to stay at the cabin, while the others rode off to find the lights. This time Bob brought up the rear. Linda was just ahead, calling back speculations about what they would find.

It suddenly occurred to her that Bob was not replying. She turned in her saddle and gave a gasp. Her brother and his mount had disappeared from sight! It was as if they had been swallowed up by the earth!

She heard a muffled cry and thought in terror, Bob's been hurt!

With a sharp sense of danger, she reined Gypsy back. Suppose Bob were in trouble greater than she could cope with? She spun around, at the same time shouting frantically, "Bronco! Charlie!"

At Linda's outcry, the two men stopped abruptly and galloped back to her.

"Something has happened to Bob!" she exclaimed, pointing to where he had been. "He's gone!"

They all made for the spot, and came to the edge of an oblong pit that had been covered over with brush.

"Help!" came a plea from below. "Rocket broke through!"

With a leap Linda, Bronco, and Indian Charlie were off their mounts and leaning over the edge of the opening.

"Bob, are you all right?" Linda called down frantically.

They could dimly see the horse, but Bob was not in the saddle. "Yes, I'm all right. Just examining Rocket's legs."

"Is he hurt?" Linda asked anxiously.

"Don't think so," Bob replied. "One leg may be sprained some. But how are we going to get him out of here?"

"We will get you out," Charlie shouted. "I will go to the cabin for a spade."

"Who made this trap here—and why?" Linda asked, perplexed.

"Some tinhorn fixed it up to catch a wild burro," Bronco replied, angrily kicking aside the brush. "It would never catch a burro—they're too smart. But it could kill a rider!"

Linda did not comment. She wondered if the trap might have been made for some other reason. Perhaps by the horse thieves or even the people with mysterious lights.

As soon as Charlie returned, he energetically began scraping away the salty earth at one end of the pit. Bronco spelled him, and shortly they had made a steep incline.

The rancher threw down one end of his rope to Bob and called instructions. "Fix a loop around Rocket's rump and mount up. When you hear me yell, boot him out of there."

Bronco now fastened his end of the rope to his saddlehorn, swung onto Colonel's back, gave a yell, and sent the horse hard ahead, away from the pit.

When Rocket felt the tightening rope around his rump, it annoyed him. With Bob's boot heel urging him on, he decided to come up the steep ramp in leaps and bounds.

"Whew!" exclaimed Bob. "That's the roughest ride I ever had. And I guess I'll have to give up the trip. Rocket's limping."

"We'll all go back," Bronco declared.

Charlie filled the pit with loose boughs and brush. Then the four sleuths started for his cabin, with Bob walking beside Rocket.

Once back there, the Indian gave Bob a bottle of liniment which he applied to Rocket's sprained leg.

The following morning it seemed slightly improved and Bob again rubbed the leg with liniment.

"He will be good as new in two days," Charlie assured him. "Then we will make the trip to the lights."

Again Linda was sorry for the delay but she decided in the interim to give her attention to Chica d'Oro and went to the corral. Running her hand lovingly over the palomino's mane, she murmured to it caressingly.

"You like my little young'un, eh?" Charlie beamed.

"More than any animal I've ever known," replied Linda earnestly. Then she asked, "Is Chica broken to the saddle?"

"No, but last month I broke her to hackamore," Charlie answered.

Linda was pleased. The hackamore's gentler than a bridle, she thought. It's constructed the same, except it has no bit. The bosal, which passed through the cheek straps, Linda knew, effected control.

"Would you like to ride her around the corral?" Charlie asked. "It would be good for her."

"I'd love to," Linda said excitedly.

Charlie went to the barn for the trappings. When he returned, Linda noted with relief that the braided rawhide bosal was well padded underneath. It was brought to a knot under the chin, and finished with a red tassel.

She chuckled. "It looks cute on Chica d'Oro—she's so dainty."

Charlie smoothed an Indian blanket over the horse's back and fastened it on with a surcingle. This leather band, which went around the horse, had a leather hand grip on top, and a couple of dangling stirrups.

"You ride all right like this?" Charlie asked Linda.

She nodded. "I've been riding around the ranch bareback. Takes less time to jump on that way than to saddle up," she added, laughing, and pulled herself easily onto Chica d'Oro's back.

The palomino danced sideways, but Linda gathered her in with the reins, and got her to heading straight in a few moments. Chica d'Oro was coltish and green, but settled down more and more to Linda's gentle guidance.

The pony began to respond nicely. Soon she was turning promptly in the direction indicated by the touch of the rein on her neck.

Not wanting Chica d'Oro to become nervous or jumpy from too prolonged a workout, Linda stopped her at the barn in about thirty minutes. She removed the trappings, and with a piece of clean sacking, rubbed down the pony's golden back until it shone.

"You're such a beauty," the girl said admiringly.

Late that afternoon Linda, Bob, and Bronco were leaning on the corral fence absorbed in watching

49

Charlie and Cactus Mac, who were in the enclosure.

Presently Bronco said, "I remember, Charlie, the times you and Cactus Mac put on that stunt of yours at some ranch rodeo. You'd send the bunch into stitches. How about showing it to Linda and Bob?"

"Oh, please do," Linda begged.

"We-ell now, I don't know about that." Cactus hesitated. "How about you, Charlie? You as spry as ever?"

Charlie straightened. "I am spry," he replied with offended dignity. "I will get the smoke bomb."

He hurried into the kitchen and returned with a large pan of flour. Cactus Mac had saddled up and mounted his horse Buck. Now he took the pan and announced in a barker's stagey voice, "Lady and gentlemen, I be introducin' the great humbug, Perfessor Galoot, and Chief Hog-Um-Gold."

Linda and Bob burst into laughter, then watched in fascination as the act began. Charlie, on foot, pretended to run off to the corral gate. Cactus promptly lassoed the Indian and brought him back.

"Tell me whar that there rich vein o' gold is located in yonder old Humpy Mountain, or you die!" proclaimed Cactus.

"I not tell," growled Charlie. "I not die."

"Perfessor Galoot" loosened the rope from Charlie, and started riding about in a close circle. "You

50

tell or sure as shootin' I'll call on many demons to skin you alive!"

"I no tell. You no know demons."

"You tell or I'll make you disappear."

"I no tell. I no disappear."

"Ho!" shouted Cactus Mac, riding around Charlie faster. "Yippee-ki-oo, and a good-bye to you!"

Then he slammed the pan of flour in front of Charlie, and galloped to one side. When the white cloud subsided, Charlie was gone!

"What happened to him?" Linda cried in real amazement.

Bob stared with an astounded grin. "That's a real disappearing act, if ever I saw one!"

"But where is he?" asked Linda.

"Maybe he went through a trapdoor into the ground," Bronco suggested. "Cactus, you'd better make Charlie reappear in a hurry, or you'll have to ride herd on his pipeline."

As the foreman from Rancho del Sol grinned, Charlie dropped to the ground from the far side of Buck. He had leaped there, grasped the stirrup leather with both hands, and had been holding his body parallel to that of the animal.

The Craigs applauded and howled with laughter. Then Bob said, "That's a great trick. The only one I know with flour is making a cake disappear!"

For hours after supper, the group watched for the strange lights across the valley. But they were not turned on.

After breakfast next day, Charlie asked the men to go with him on an inspection trip. They also would keep a sharp lookout for clues to Prince Brownlee. "You take care of the young'un?" the Indian asked Linda. "She is in the corral."

"Indeed, I will," she answered, delighted at the thought.

As Linda tidied the cabin, she heard the palomino whinny shrilly. The girl froze. The horse's cry was not one of terror as at the snake. It showed the nervous excitement Chica d'Oro had displayed when the visitors from Rancho del Sol had first ridden up to the corral.

There must be a caller, Linda thought.

She clenched her hands tensely. Who was out there? The horse thieves? With a knot in her throat, she ran to the window and peered into the yard.

The Fossil Clue 5

Linda gasped at the sight of an unshaven, dusty rider by the corral. She stood frozen, watching and hoping that he would ride away.

But when he dismounted with an old rope halter and tie rope in his hand, and started to open the corral gate, Linda rushed out. He's going to steal Chica! she thought in dismay.

The man stopped and regarded the girl in surprise. It was apparent that he had thought nobody was on the place.

"What are you doing here?" Linda demanded. "What do you want? What's your name?"

"Luke Poe," the man said in a slurred tone. "I'm a friend of Charlie Tonka's. I take care of his horse when he's gone."

Linda was speechless for a few moments, thinking it odd that Charlie had not mentioned this. She was sure that the Indian had said he always put the palomino in the stall with plenty of food and water when he went away.

Now the man asked curiously, "Who're you?"

"I'm visiting here with a group from Rancho del Sol," Linda replied coolly.

"Where's everybody else?" he inquired.

"They'll be back any second," she said and decided she had better run and ring the alarm bell. But she changed her mind as Luke Poe, with a sneering smile, pushed open the corral gate and went inside.

"I'll take the horse out for some exercise," he said boldly.

As he entered the corral, Chica d'Oro danced back and forth, nickering uncertainly. When Luke Poe reached up to put the dirty rope halter on her, she pranced away from him.

"Come here, you!" he said roughly, and jumped after the pony.

He threw the end of the tie rope over Chica's neck to hold her, and quickly slipped on the halter. He fastened it, then started to lead the palomino out of the corral.

Instantly Linda slammed the gate shut. "You're not taking that horse out of here!"

"Get out of my way, girl!" the man ordered. Reaching through the rails of the fence, he pushed Linda so hard that she fell to the ground.

He mustn't steal Chica d'Oro! Linda thought in panic.

Suddenly, as Luke started to open the gate, Chica d'Oro reared with a high squeal, striking at the man with her hooves and pulling the rope from his hand. He grabbed for it with one hand, while attempting to pull open the gate with the other.

The palomino rose up on her hind legs again and once more went at Luke with her flailing front hooves. One of them struck his arm, tearing the sleeve of his coat.

Linda jumped to her feet and cried, "She'll kill you!"

As Chica d'Oro went up in the air again, a look of terror flashed across Luke Poe's face. He quickly clambered over the rails, jumped on his horse, and galloped away.

Linda calmed down at once. She leaned over the fence, saying, "Everything's okay, young'un. Don't be frightened any more. You and I had a good scare, but that horrid man is gone."

Nevertheless, it was ten minutes before Linda felt it was wise to enter the corral. Then she hugged Chica d'Oro, pressing her cheek against one side of the palomino's head. The pony nickered softly as Linda took off the halter.

On the ground lay a handkerchief. Luke must have dropped it, Linda decided.

Realizing she should keep it as a possible clue to the man's identity, if he had given a false name, Linda picked it up. Then she noticed something which lay beneath it—a hard, round, slightly concave shell.

Luke must have dropped this, too! she thought.

After another reassuring pat for the palomino, Linda took the two clues into the cabin and put them on a shelf. All this time she was mulling over several ideas. "Perhaps Poe knew Chica d'Oro's Arabian mother! He traced her colt here to Charlie's and waited for a chance to steal her! Maybe he's even one of the men who took Prince Brownlee!"

Linda went out to feed the filly, then returned to the cabin and started supper. In a little while, the men returned.

At once, Charlie asked, "Who has been here? There are strange horse tracks outside."

Linda told them of Luke Poe and his rough actions.

"I know nobody by that name," Charlie declared. "I did not hire him or anyone else to take care of young'un."

"This must be reported at once," Bronco declared.

He tuned in their two-way radio to Rancho del Sol and talked to Grandmother Mallory. After learning that affairs were running fairly well at the ranch, he asked his wife to report the attempted theft to the sheriff.

"Linda will give you the man's description," he said. "She had a good look at the fellow."

"Oh, Linda dear," her grandmother said, after hearing the story, "this must mean you were in great danger. Perhaps you should come home?"

Linda laughed. "The scare is over, Doña. And I must stay here to help solve the mystery of those queer lights. We've spotted their location."

Mrs. Mallory begged her granddaughter to be careful.

"I will," Linda promised and chuckling, added, "I'll tell Bob and Bronco to watch their step, too!"

After the conversation was finished, Linda showed the men the handkerchief and shell she had picked up in the corral. Charlie examined the articles with interest.

"This ancient clam shell is from Fossil Mountain over there," he informed them. "High, jagged. It is full of old shells. Smart men say thousands of years ago it rose up out of the ocean."

"I'm familiar with that peak," said Bronco. "The rocky soil is crumbly and treacherous to travel on in some places."

Cactus Mac spoke up. "Pokin' around, it's dangerous business, sure enough."

"If that's true, not many people would be prowling around there," Bob observed. "It would be a good place for a hideout."

"And if Poe came from there, then he probably is in hiding," Linda guessed.

"Very possibly," Bronco agreed.

"That fellow left a good trail when he took off,"

said Bob. "How about our riding out tomorrow morning, Linda, to see how far we can follow it? Rocket's okay now."

"Yes, let's," she replied eagerly. "We might even find that Luke has Prince Brownlee there! I'll pack a lunch in case we get hungry."

"Good luck!" said Bronco. "And promise me you won't try to make a capture alone. Come back to report it over the radio if you see this Luke Poe."

Linda promised, then said, "In the meantime, you take good care of Chica d'Oro." She wagged her finger playfully.

The men looked at one another guiltily, then Bronco admitted they had all planned to ride off. "Mac's going back to the ranch, and since Charlie needs a little help on the pipeline, I was going with him."

Linda's forehead puckered. "But we can't *all* go. We don't dare leave the palomino."

"I will put padlocks on the corral gate and stall door," Charlie offered.

"Those wouldn't do a bit of good if anyone is determined to steal Chica d'Oro," Linda said worriedly. "The thief would break in."

"You're right," agreed Bronco.

"I know of one solution," Linda offered brightly. "If you wouldn't mind, Charlie, I could ride Chica d'Oro."

"Sure, why not?" Bob asked. "Since apparently it's only the palomino someone wants to steal, the other horses, which are branded, won't be bothered."

The Indian grinned. "Okay, Linda. You ride the young'un. But she has no shoes. It will break the edges of her hooves to walk on pebbles."

Linda was crestfallen. "And there is no blacksmith anywhere around, is there?"

Charlie saw her disappointed expression. "I will put on shoes," he said quickly. "I will do it now."

"Oh, wonderful!" Linda exclaimed, happy again. "Is there anything you can't do, Charlie?"

"I did not find who has those funny lights in desert," he answered. "Maybe bad people."

"Don't worry. We'll solve the mystery," Linda assured him.

Charlie took the bright gasoline lantern from its hook in the ceiling and went out to the barn, trailed by the others.

"Where are your forge and anvil?" Bob asked.

"I do not have any," answered the Indian. "I shoe cold."

"I didn't know that was possible," said Linda, surprised.

"It's the way cowboys do it on the range," Bronco informed her. "They either shoe that way or they're likely to find themselves afoot or with a permanently lame horse."

Charlie went about gathering together different sizes of iron horseshoes, nails, knife, clippers, and a rasp. He said to Linda, "You get young'un."

Chica d'Oro had been put in her stall for the night. Linda haltered her, then led the horse into the center of the barn.

Charlie had been keeping her feet trimmed, so she promptly lifted a hoof for him to fix now. As he worked, Linda stood at Chica d'Oro's head, holding the halter rope and talking to her. The palomino nuzzled the girl and made no fuss while Charlie fitted the correct size of horseshoe to her hoof and nailed it on.

Bob watched every move intently, praised Charlie, and said to Linda, "You sure have a way with horses."

When the job was completed, Charlie said, "Turn young'un loose in the corral so she will get used to shoes."

Linda did so, and Chica d'Oro danced coltishly off into the enclosure. Finally she settled down to the feel of her iron shoes, and started walking about, bending her knees and picking her feet up high.

"Look at her, Bronco!" Linda gasped. "She's just like a full-fledged parade horse!"

Silently the girl pleaded, *Charlie, please, please let me have Chica d'Oro for my very own.* But there was a big ache in her chest because she felt sure he would never do it.

Linda managed to shake off the mood when Bob asked her to walk out onto the promontory and look for the mysterious lights. They did not appear and two hours later he said with a yawn, "John Davis told us the lights came on only when it was very dark. But maybe not on all dark nights."

Early the next morning Linda rushed out to the barn to see Chica d'Oro, who was chomping on her breakfast hay. Charlie and Bronco had gone out earlier to feed all the horses.

Linda held up the hackamore for the palomino to see. "Do you want to go on a long ride today? Someplace you've never been before?"

Chica d'Oro threw her head back and whinnied.

"You do know what I say to you, don't you?" Linda asked her softly.

The pony whinnied again through a mouthful of hay.

"Horses like to be talked to," Charlie said, walking over to Linda. "They know what you mean by the sound of your voice. You ask a question, it is instinct to try to answer. You give a command, a horse stands at attention. She wants to please." He laid a fond hand on the palomino's rump. "If a person acts mean like Luke Poe, the horse feels mean, too. Strikes with hoofs. You saw yourself."

Linda nodded. "Now we'd better go in and eat our breakfast, Charlie. Bob is fixing it. And I have lunches to pack."

"You spoil me." Charlie grinned. "How am I ever going to like dry bread for lunch again?"

"I'm glad you're spoiled," Linda answered, smiling, as they went into the house.

Bob, with a dish towel tucked around his middle,

was spooning rounds of pancake batter onto one griddle, and turning bacon on another. Bronco and Cactus were already eating. Linda and Charlie joined them, followed by the cook.

When they had finished, Cactus Mac rode off. The other men tidied the cabin while Linda prepared a stack of sandwiches from canned meat. She made four oblong packages of sandwiches, brownies, and prunes, and wrapped each in a clean piece of tarp for tying behind the cantles of the saddles.

Since she could carry nothing on a surcingle, she had packaged her food with Bob's. Next she filled the four canteens with water, to be swung from saddle strings. Charlie and Bronco carried the lunches and other gear out to the horses.

Before leaving, Linda tied a new red bandanna around her neck, and tossed a blue one to Bob. The neckerchiefs would serve to pull up over their faces as protection from stinging sand in case of a windstorm.

Bob fastened a hunting knife in a leather scabbard to his belt. Then, grabbing a lariat to hang over the pommel of his saddle, he strode out the door behind Linda.

Charlie and Bronco were ready to go and waved good-bye. The latter cautioned Bob and Linda.

"Just follow the tracks. Don't get into a tangle with any ruffian. Come back here and radio for help."

"I hope we learn where Luke Poe hangs out, and what he's up to," Bob said. Then he grinned. "Don't worry about us."

Chica d'Oro was so excited and fidgety that Linda had difficulty getting the surcingle fastened firmly. The palomino managed to dance close enough to Rocket to reach out and flutter her lips along his neck. The older horse stood still, and gave the flighty young animal a tolerant side look from soft, wise eyes.

When Bob and Linda started off, they found it was easy to follow Luke Poe's trail. It led directly toward Fossil Mountain.

"Just as we thought," said Bob. "And we have Chica to thank for the clam shell clue, giddy equine though she may be."

With a tender laugh, Linda reached out to pat the filly's neck. "Don't you pay a bit of attention to him, baby," she cooed. "He's only kidding."

Chica d'Oro apparently did not mind the aspersion. She minced along gaily, mostly concerned with keeping nose to nose with Bob's mount.

"Speaking of clues," Linda went on, "do you think there is any connection between the horse thieves who took Prince Brownlee, and Luke Poe?"

"Could be," her brother replied slowly.

The hemmed-in valley had begun to shimmer with heat, and the riders were relieved when Poe's trail led into a shady gap in the mountain. The chaparral growth on the side walls was grayish green, and the erosion patterns were like rippled satin. Many little ravines branched off from the trail Poe had taken, filled with lush undergrowth dotted with red Indian paintbrush. Apricot mallow grew riotously in spots.

"There must be water near the surface here," Bob commented.

"But it doesn't last all the way to the top," Linda remarked, noting the small pines scattered here and there far above them. "Where do you suppose the fossils are, Bob?"

"On the peak above the timber," he replied. "We'll take a good look at it, but won't risk riding up."

Suddenly a young deer bounded into their path and stopped still in surprise. Startled, Rocket jumped to one side. Chica d'Oro reared, then bolted off like a shot!

When Linda finally pulled her in among a dense flat of pines, she spoke to the palomino in a low, quieting tone. "You're all right, golden girl. That was only a little deer, and a deer never hurt anyone." She stroked the pony soothingly along the neck.

When Chica d'Oro's quivering subsided, Linda said, "Come on now, let's get back to Bob," and gave the pony a flick with the reins. At this, the filly balked.

"Oh, come on now," Linda urged. "You have to learn to be a good trail horse." The palomino still stood stiff-legged. Linda clicked the animal's sides with her heels. Finally, Chica d'Oro resentfully dogged ahead among the trees.

"That's the girl," Linda said.

In a few minutes, she was sure they were not going in the right direction. They were riding deeper into the woods instead of toward the trail where Bob was waiting. Linda felt panicky. She was lost on Fossil Mountain!

No Trespassing 6

Linda reined up and sat still to think. Which way should she go?

I mustn't panic, the young rider told herself. Then a sudden thought came to her and she leaned forward to caress Chica d'Oro.

"You knew this was the wrong way, didn't you?" she said. "And I wouldn't pay any attention to you."

Linda turned the palomino around, and gave the pony her head. But she did not move. With a sinking sensation, the girl realized Chica d'Oro did not have the slightest idea which way to go.

Sharply Linda called, "Bob! Bob!" But her voice did not seem to reach far. Worse yet, if her brother had come looking for her, he might have taken a different course through the dense pines. She would have left no trail on the soft carpet of dry needles.

"Well, let's head out this opposite way," Linda said to the pony, and urged her on.

But Chica d'Oro stopped so abruptly that Linda nearly sailed over the palomino's head. Her ears were pricked forward. Linda heard a noise in the underbrush.

She tensed and her heart pounded. Was someone hiding there? Luke Poe, maybe? Had he been following her and was now waiting in ambush? Linda sat still and strained to listen. A large bird rose from the brush and winged away.

Linda laughed softly. "Chica, you'll have to get used to such things." Then she called again, "Bob! Bob!"

Her hands tightened on the reins, and her fear of being lost was imparted to the horse. Chica d'Oro began prancing in one spot.

Instantly Linda released the reins, and with studied control pressed a hand on the pony's neck. "Quiet, baby," she said. "Someone will find us eventually."

Eventually! Not for days, maybe! If anything happened to Charlie's "young'un," Linda was sure the Indian would never forgive her. And she would never forgive herself.

Under her steadying hand, the palomino had settled down. In fact, the filly seemed to be enjoying herself here among the pines. She held her head high, moving it about, and seemed to be pleasurably sniffing the aromatic scent.

Then, on her own, the horse started trotting confidently in another direction. Linda was amazed, but figured that the animal had picked up a familiar scent—perhaps Rocket's—and she let Chica d'Oro go on weaving among the pines.

In a few minutes, through an opening among the trees, Linda caught a glimpse of the trail. The palomino turned toward it, and found her way down through the ravine. She emerged at the spot where Bob sat waiting on his horse, concern on his face.

"What were you two doing?" he asked.

"I was lost," Linda admitted sheepishly. "But Chica knew the way."

"Horse sense," Bob commented. "And *you* have been trying to teach *her* tricks!"

"Just the same," Linda declared, "I am going to buy a compass to carry when I'm riding."

"That goes double," Bob agreed. He squinted up at the sun. "Almost noon," he said.

"What do we do now?" asked Linda.

"Well, we lost Poe's trail," he replied. "It doesn't show up on this tufty rock floor. The scoundrel could be holed up anywhere in this wilderness. We might just as well keep riding, and see what we can discover."

They rode on among the trees, catching glimpses of the valley and the mountain opposite where Indian Charlie lived. At one point, they forded a narrow creek that tumbled down the steep slope.

A little farther along Linda pointed. Nestled among the trees part way up the side of Fossil

Mountain was a large rustic building of split logs that might have been a lodge or a hotel.

"Do you suppose that could be where Luke Poe lives?" Linda asked. "And look! Hoof marks! The same as the ones we were following!"

"Yes," Bob agreed. "But right now there isn't a horse in sight. Let's scout around!"

He and his sister eased their way down the mountainside in a zigzag manner to keep from slipping.

"I think Chica d'Oro is getting tired," Linda remarked. "It'll be good to give her a rest."

"We'll shade up over by that log building and eat our lunch," Bob replied.

"And keep our eyes open!" Linda added.

A short distance from the lodge stood another building, a large, gray, frame structure built against the mountain. Over the door was a sign: MINERAL SPRINGS BOTTLING CO.

"I guess this must have been the office for a health resort," Linda suggested absently, noting that there were hoofprints crossing and recrossing the area. "I wonder why a lot of horses have been here lately."

Bob shrugged. "Now don't tell me some of these prints belong to Prince Brownlee!" He went on, "A drink of that mineral water would taste good right now. Let's see if there's a spring around back."

They dismounted and Bob told Linda, "Wrap Chica's reins around my saddlehorn. Rocket ground-hitches." He dropped the bay's reins to the earth.

As Linda and Bob started forward, the office door was flung open, and two middle-aged men stepped out. They were well-dressed and clean shaven, but had a glowering manner.

"Get out, you snoopers!" commanded one, and the other said harshly, "This is private property!"

Bob and Linda stood speechless. Finally Bob bristled and was about to speak when Linda touched his arm. It had occurred to her they might learn something about the horse thief if they showed no resentment.

Quickly Linda said, "We're sorry. We didn't mean to trespass."

Bob controlled his anger and said firmly but politely, "We thought the place was deserted. Otherwise we'd have asked permission to get a drink of your mineral water."

"We planned to eat our lunch here." Linda pointed toward the log building. "Under those nice shade trees. We didn't mean any harm," she assured the men gently.

They were taken aback and exchanged quick glances. Then the taller one said with forced affability, "If we spoke a little rough it's because we've had prowlers. We don't want anyone breaking in here and causing damage."

"Oh, we understand," Linda replied. "There's been a prowler, too, at the cabin where we're staying. His trail led toward this mountain. Maybe he's the same one who has been bothering you."

The other man, a squat, powerful fellow, spoke up. "What did he look like?" he asked, squinting steadily at Linda.

"He was medium in height and thin," she answered, "and had a brown, fuzzy stubble on his face. He was poorly dressed."

"That description fits the fellow we've seen around here," the man said.

"And did his horse leave all these hoofprints?" Linda asked, trying to sound naïve.

The other one nodded, then turned toward the frame building. "Well, since it is only a drink of water you want, come on in."

Linda and Bob followed the man into a room furnished with a couple of pine desks, two plain wooden chairs, a faded-looking daybed, and a small wood-burning stove in one corner. A bottle of water stood on one desk, with a tin cup beside it.

In the back wall was a wide sliding door. It was open, revealing a large yard in the rear, between the building and the mountain. In it stood several big glass demijohns, crates, and a pickup truck for hauling the bottled water away.

"We're Bob and Linda Craig from the Rancho del Sol in the San Quinto Valley," Bob said.

The taller man cleared his throat and said in return, "I'm Worley, and this is my partner, Mr. Garrant." Then he poured out a cup of water and handed it to Linda. She sipped it experimentally, and exclaimed, "Why, this is good!"

While Bob was drinking his cup of water, Linda stood at the wide open door and looked up the side of the mountain into the dark, yawning mouth of a cave.

"My goodness!" she exclaimed. "Do some sort of wild animals live up there?"

Bob joined her, looking about intently.

"No animals," Mr. Garrant said with a small, clipped laugh. "That's where the mineral springs are."

"Thank you," said Bob, putting down the cup. "We appreciate this. If you have no objections, we'd like to eat our lunch by that log building. Then we'll ride on."

"Go ahead," Garrant said.

Mr. Worley put in hastily, "If you two young folks would like to try a shortcut out, I can show you one."

"That would be a good idea," Linda said, "My horse is pretty tired."

"Come outside, and I'll point the way," said Worley, stepping to the front door. "Zigzag down the mountain from here. Cut directly across the valley and go up that low butte in the distance. Ride along the crest until you see the highway which runs parallel to it for a short distance, then turns northwest. That's where you turn directly west. Is that clear?"

"Quicksand" Linda screamea

"Yes, it is, and thank you again," Bob said. "Come on, Linda."

They walked their horses to the lodge, found a faucet in the back and an old wooden tub in which they put water for the thirsty animals.

While their mounts rested, Linda and Bob settled under a sycamore, and Linda laid out the lunch. As Bob picked up a sandwich, he remarked, "I can't figure out those men."

"They struck me as rather odd," Linda said. "And they weren't telling the truth about the hoofprints. *Several* horses have been here."

"I see what you mean. The horse thieves could have brought stolen animals through this spot— even Prince Brownlee. The question is, where did they take them? The trail seems to end here."

Linda and Bob could find no answer and felt it was unwise to ask Worley and Garrant any further questions. They finished the lunch and Bob insisted they go at once.

"I have a feeling it isn't safe for just the two of us here. We'll come back next time with Bronco and Charlie."

His sister agreed but was reluctant to leave the mystery of Poe and the horse tracks unsolved. As she went to get Chica d'Oro, Linda was relieved to find that the palomino was as sprightly as ever after her brief rest.

With Bob in the lead, they rode down the mountain, crossed the valley, and went up on the butte which stretched out in a long, silty elevation. The going was precarious and the horses kept losing their footing on the loose earth. After a while, the two riders sighted the highway in the distance.

"It isn't so near as that fellow indicated," Bob said in disgust. "And it doesn't run parallel to this ridge."

"But we are headed out all right, aren't we?" Linda asked anxiously.

"Oh, sure," Bob called back. "But I certainly would never come on this silty, dangerous butte again. Take it easy!"

Just then the edge of the ridge near Linda gave way. Chica d'Oro and her rider went sliding down the slope onto a flat of sand. There she floundered for a moment, then began to sink.

"Quicksand!" Linda screamed.

The Pony's Warning   7

Linda threw herself off the pony and grasped a limb of chaparral on the fringe of the treacherous spot. In a moment, she had pulled herself to safety.

At Linda's cry, Bob had looked back. Instantly he slid his horse down the slope, building a loop with his rope at the same time. He pulled up short at the edge of the quagmire, and flung the noose about Chica d'Oro's neck. Then he fashioned a wider loop, and hurled it about her body, tightening it under the rump. Quickly he fastened the end of the rope to the toughest scrub root at hand.

"Oh, thank you!" Linda said in relief.

"I don't know how long this will hold," Bob said tensely. "Linda, ride Rocket to the highway for help," he ordered.

Linda mounted hastily, and galloped off. She reached the highway and waited anxiously. Tourists were the first to come along in a car. Frantically she waved for the driver to stop. But misunderstanding her gesture, the man waved back and continued on his way.

Tears sprang to Linda's eyes. The next car was a convertible holding a couple of grinning teen-age boys. It screeched to a stop.

"Hi, Annie Oakley!" one sang out.

Irked by their flippancy, Linda said shortly, "We have a horse down in quicksand over there. Please get someone to bring boards and help us."

"Sure, beautiful, at your service," the driver said and sped away. Linda's heart sank. The boys probably had no intention of finding help.

Linda tried not to picture the rope around Chica d'Oro fraying strand by strand, and the beautiful palomino sinking out of sight. She felt sick and grasped the saddle horn until her knuckles were white.

Suddenly at high speed came a jeep from which protruded several wide boards. The car was marked BENTLEY'S GARAGE, RUDDVILLE. The driver stopped and called out, "I'm Bentley. You the girl those boys said had a horse in quicksand?"

"Oh, bless them!" cried Linda, sorry she had mistrusted the boys. "This way!"

She turned at a gallop to lead him. With the jeep bumping along behind her, Linda pounded ahead, hoping against hope that she would not be too late. When she caught sight of Chica d'Oro, her heart leaped in relief. The filly seemed to have sunk but a fraction more in the quicksand.

"Good work, Linda!" Bob praised her.

The man in the jeep knew exactly what to do. Together he and Bob shoved boards under the pony's belly and laid them on each side of her to ride on should she topple over. Then Mr. Bentley fastened ropes to a piece of tarp he had brought along.

He gingerly stepped out on the boards and secured the tarp as a sling around the palomino's rump. Next he fastened each rope end to the back of the jeep, got behind the wheel, and inched ahead.

Chica d'Oro started thrashing up with her front hooves, and finally landed them on the firm fringe outside the quagmire. In a few minutes, she was standing beside Rocket, shaking herself and wearing a baffled expression.

Linda hugged her close. "I didn't put you in that place on purpose, baby," she explained. If the pony had had any such thoughts, she had already forgiven Linda, for she began to nuzzle the girl affectionately.

Mr. Bentley said, "We must post this quicksand. Kids hunting rabbits could get into it." He wrote QUICKSAND with his black crayon pencil on one of the boards and erected it on the bank.

"Ought to have a bright red rag on this so's it would attract attention," he murmured.

"Here," Linda said, and snatched off her red bandanna.

Mr. Bentley fastened it on top of the board. Bob

then attempted to thrust four one-dollar bills, the whole amount he carried in his pockets, into the hand of the jeep driver.

"Naw," protested the garage man, "I wouldn't take money for saving a horse's life. Drop into my place some day when you're in town and say hello. It's on the edge of Ruddville."

"We'll do that. Thanks again," Bob replied.

"You'll never know how much this means to me," Linda said warmly, brushing the sandy muck off Chica d'Oro.

"Just glad I got here in time," Mr. Bentley answered, and climbed into his jeep.

After he had driven off, Linda and Bob mounted and set off parallel to the highway. They rode in silence for a while. Both the Craigs were thoughtful and Linda was pale. At last she asked, "Do you think those men Worley and Garrant sent us out on that trail deliberately to—well, to get rid of us?"

Bob's face muscles tightened. "They were so familiar with the trail, they must have known about that bad spot."

It was late afternoon when Linda and her brother arrived at Indian Charlie's. Bronco and Charlie had returned and were inside the cabin. They listened attentively to the story of the mineral water company and the quagmire.

The two men looked serious. "Mineral Springs Bottling Company changed hands last fall," Charlie informed the others. "The old owner ran the hotel and water company. Many people went for cures." The Indian shook his head woefully. "The new owners are unfriendly. Closed the hotel, and do not want anybody around. Why do they not want to make money from the hotel?"

"That does seem odd," Bronco commented.

Linda nodded. "I want to go back there with you. But right now, Bronco, will you come out with me while I put the pony in her stall?"

"Sure, honey," he replied. As soon as they were outside he asked, "Well, what's on your mind?"

"Chica d'Oro," Linda replied. "I just *must* have her for my very own. How do you think I could get Charlie to sell her to me?"

"You might try asking him," Bronco said with a grin. "If he isn't interested in a cash sale, dangle a horse trade. There are a couple of fine young quarter horses down on Old Sol that may prove hard for him to refuse."

"Oh, thank you, Bronco, thank you," Linda said softly and hugged him.

By the time she had put Chica d'Oro into her stall, it was sundown. Linda prepared supper, then addressed Charlie.

"I thought I'd get Chica used to the saddle, if you don't mind."

"You do that," he replied.

"Charlie," she continued earnestly, "I'd like to own Chica. Will you sell her to me?"

The Indian gave the girl a long, stoic look. He said, "Never thought to sell young'un."

Linda swallowed. "Bronco says I may offer a couple of fine young quarter horses in trade for her. Would you like those, Charlie?"

A flicker of interest shimmered in the Indian's eyes. "Um-m, quarter horses. I will think about it."

After that, he would say no more. During supper, the group discussed the stolen Prince Brownlee, Luke Poe, and the men at the bottling company.

"I'm positive," Linda said, "that Fossil Mountain holds the answer to those mysteries. And maybe the secret of the lights. Shouldn't we go on a thorough search there?"

"We'd have to make it overnight," Bronco replied. "But your idea is a good one. If Luke Poe is a horse thief and he's hiding out near the mineral springs, maybe we can catch him in that vicinity."

While Bronco planned the trip in detail, Linda arose to get the men more coffee. Suddenly she gasped and pointed out the open window, whispering, "I saw a man's shadow!"

They all rushed into the moonlit yard. A man jumped up from a crouched position near the shed barn, flung himself onto a horse, and galloped away. The group realized it was useless to follow. By the time they could saddle up, he would have outdistanced his pursuers.

"I wonder if that was Luke Poe again," said Linda.

"Whoever the man was, I'll bet he was eavesdropping and heard our plans to go scouting on the mountain," Bob said.

"And you mean he may plan to ambush us!" Linda said worriedly as they reentered the cabin.

"We'll certainly have to be on the alert," Bronco remarked grimly. "Everybody up early and get your horses ready."

Linda looked at Charlie. Should she or should she not approach him on the subject of Chica d'Oro? Finally, taking a deep breath, she said, "Charlie, have you decided whether you are going to trade me young'un for the two quarter horses?"

The Indian did not answer at once and looked at the girl noncommittally.

Worry shadowed Linda's face. "I'm afraid something dreadful will happen to her when we're not here any more and you have to be away on the pipeline."

Charlie's black eyes regarded Linda steadily. Then he said slowly, "I have two grandsons living on a small ranch in the next valley. They are getting to be big boys. Should have horses."

Linda held her breath. A slight smile creased the Indian's face.

"I will trade."

"Charlie, oh, Charlie," Linda cried, "How wonderful of you!" She shook his hand vigorously. Then she did a spin in the middle of the floor and ended by hugging Bronco so suddenly and hard that he grunted.

"As soon as we return to Old Sol," Linda said in earnest enthusiasm, "I'm going to start trying to establish Chica's bloodline so I may obtain registration papers on her."

"How will you do that?" Charlie asked.

"Through the registration book of the Arabian Horse Association," Linda told him. "I'll check on each entry. Maybe I can find the owner of Chica d'Oro's dam."

"Which will take just about from now till you're an old lady," Bob said skeptically.

"Go to it, honey," Bronco encouraged her. "You may be lucky right off."

"I will. I just know I will," proclaimed Linda. "I feel it."

She went to bed too happy and excited to sleep. Chica d'Oro was hers! For hours the girl lay listening to the rain drum on the aluminum roof, but at last her eyes closed. When she opened them again it was Sunday morning and the sky was clear.

As soon as Linda could dress she ran out to the barn. Hugging her new possession, she told the pony softly, "You're mine, mine, all mine!" Then she added with a laugh, "Well, almost!" The filly nickered and nuzzled the girl's neck.

Linda gave the palomino a small can of oats, then laid a thick pad, an Indian blanket, and a saddle on her back. Chica d'Oro only turned her head curiously, touched the stirrup with her nose, and finished the oats.

Her new mistress cinched up the saddle and led the horse outside. She mounted and rode Chica d'Oro about the corral. The filly seemed to feel as good as Linda did. She tossed her mane and picked her dainty feet up high.

When Linda returned her to the barn, she found Bob, Bronco, and Charlie feeding the other horses. Linda unsaddled the pony and gave her a flake of hay, as Bronco strolled over to the stall.

"Get along all right?" he asked.

"She's the most wonderful horse in the world," Linda said firmly, her eyes shining. Grandfather Mallory smiled and patted the girl's arm.

In a short time, Bob, Linda, and Bronco were on their way. They took only one packhorse to carry the bedrolls, leaving the other behind as company for Gypsy. Along with canteens, the riders carried some of the food and a few accessories in tight packs on their saddles.

Linda noticed that Bronco was not taking the most direct route to Fossil Mountain. She asked why.

Bronco gave her a broad smile. "Since we can't get to our own church today, I'm going to take you and Bob to Cowboy's Church. It's on the outskirts of Ruddville."

"Cowboy's Church?" Linda repeated, puzzled.

"The preacher holds morning services outdoors," Bronco explained. "Riders come from all around and sit on their horses during the service. The horses stand as quiet as mice. After the service the ladies sell lunches to help pay off the mortgage on the church building."

"I'd like to go," said Linda.

"Me, too," Bob added.

The Ruddville Community Church yard was pleasantly shaded with blooming acacias under which were a few picnic tables. There were thirty horseback riders present, and as many people seated on folding chairs.

The minister officiated from a truck bed which also held the choir and a piano. He was a zealous young man with a commanding delivery and sense of humor, and preached an excellent sermon.

Mr. Bentley, who had helped rescue Chica d'Oro, assisted with the collection, and nodded, pleased, when Bob dropped into the plate the four one-dollar bills the garageman had refused at the quicksand pit.

Afterward Linda, Bob, and Bronco bought sandwiches, slaw, cherry pie, and milk from the church ladies, and enjoyed eating with the friendly congregation.

By early afternoon they were on their way again, approaching Fossil Mountain from a different direction to the one Linda and Bob had taken before. Near the foot of it, Bronco called a halt, took his rifle from the bedroll pack, and slipped it into his saddle boot.

"You must expect trouble," Bob remarked.

"One never knows," Grandfather Mallory replied. "I'd rather be safe than sorry."

They rode on again and came to a canyon of huge boulders and steep granite walls with fissures and rimrock caves.

Near the entrance, Linda stopped. Before her was a magnificent, creamy-white, single yucca, growing against a big, pinkish-red granite rock. She gazed at the tree-like plant in admiration. Oh, how I'd love to paint that! she thought.

Suddenly Chica d'Oro endeavored to back away, whickering uneasily. She pranced up and down, tossing her head. Linda looked sharply about the ground for a snake, but saw none.

Bob and Bronco rode up, and her brother asked, "What's eating Chica?"

"I don't know," Linda replied, troubled.

The two men circled, looking about. "There doesn't seem to be even a rabbit track around here," Bronco said. "Sometimes a strange scent from far away will cause a horse to gallivant a bit."

The rancher rubbed his chin as he looked at the big rock. Then he cast his eyes up the canyon. "There's a narrow cut ahead to the left. Beyond is a trail up the mountain. Let's move!"

As they rode into the ravine, single file, the palomino settled down to her easy gait. "Chica's all right now," Linda announced. "I think she was trying to tell us about something or someone behind that red rock."

"I think so, too," Bronco admitted. "But I didn't want to scare you by saying so."

"Why not?" Bob asked indignantly. "We could have caught the fellow."

"The fellow?" Bronco smiled wryly. "Half a dozen scoundrels could have been hiding in back of those rocks. We're not taking chances on being outnumbered."

"I didn't think of that," Bob admitted. "But we'd better keep a sharp eye out in case we're followed."

As they rode through the cut, the three riders stopped often to look back and listen for sounds of a person following them. But they saw no one. At last they came out of the ravine at a steep trail. It was some distance from the place where the mysterious lights had been seen. The riders climbed up and up.

"The lodge and Mineral Springs Bottling Company are around this curve to the right," Linda said finally. "But the frame building is so close to the mountainside you don't see it until you are right on it."

"Good!" Bronco exclaimed. "If Worley and Garrant are there maybe they won't see us either. We'll stay on this side of the cave and make camp in a secluded spot."

"Let's keep our eyes open for any clue to the horse thieves," Linda suggested, as the little group turned left. But they did not spot anything.

After they had climbed a little higher, they came to a creek. Bronco beckoned for them to cross it to a place on the far side enclosed by thick, bushy laurel and trees.

"This creek must be the same one we forded before," Linda said to Bob.

"It's the overflow from the dam above here," Bronco said, adding, "We can see the bottling company from this spot but no one can see us."

Although it was only five o'clock, the shadows were deep around the campers. In the growing dusk, they took care of their horses and fastened each to a bush with rope long enough so that they could move about. Contentedly the animals began to crop their supper of grass, seasoned with tufts of sage.

Bronco made a low fire of bark chips that soon became hot, but gave off very little smoke. Bob opened three cans of spaghetti and meatballs, and put them against the heat. Linda opened a can of green beans which they ate cold. There also were brown-bread sandwiches and apples.

Afterward Bronco said, "How about crawling in now and getting up at daylight for some early-bird detective work?"

"Let's," Linda agreed. "I'm tired." She checked Chica d'Oro, pulled off her boots, and snuggled down inside her sleeping bag.

Linda was awakened by her pony nuzzling the

side of her face and nickering plaintively. "How did you get loose?" she asked a bit crossly. "This is no time to play." With a sigh, she felt in the dark for her boots.

Chica d'Oro gave the girl a hard shove with her nose, whickering in terror. Then with frenzied screams, she took off up the side of the mountain.

"Bronco! Bob!" Linda cried as she heard a loud roar.

The two men awakened. They jumped up and began pulling on their boots.

"Run up the mountainside, Linda!" Bronco ordered. "The dam's given way!"

The other horses were threshing at their tethers, and whinnying in terror. While Bronco and Bob released them, Linda scrambled up the slope to Chica d'Oro. With the roar coming closer, the two men led the bolting, struggling horses up the silty slope. Bronco kept tight hold of Colonel's tie rope, knowing the other horses would follow him. By grabbing at scrub growth, he and Bob hauled themselves up the treacherous hill.

In a few seconds, Linda saw a high wall of water come crashing down through their camp with a deafening roar. The horses screamed in fright at the onrushing tumult.

Suspicious Cans　　　　　8

The flood boomed past the feet of Linda and her companions, wetting them with its spray, but leaving them safe.

How long can this last? the girl thought as the minutes dragged into hours.

Badly shaken, the group clung to their precarious footing for the rest of the night. As dawn broke, Linda, Bob, and Bronco looked down on a desolate scene. They shuddered at the devastation and shivered in their damp clothes.

Their camp spot was a shambles of mud, debris, and broken branches. The sleeping bags, cooking equipment, saddles, blankets, and bridles had been swept away.

"Oh!" Linda gasped. "Everything's gone!"

"Well, we're not!" Bob exclaimed cheerfully. "Thanks to that yaller young'un of yours."

"Come on, let's get down," Bronco urged, and began a sliding descent.

Linda and Bob followed, while the horses tagged along with Colonel. The Craigs picked up the ends of their horses' tie ropes to keep them from dragging through the mud.

Holding up one of them, Linda exclaimed, "Look, Bronco! Chica d'Oro chewed through the rope to get loose!"

"She must have felt the vibration of the dam giving way and sensed the danger, even before she heard the roar," Bronco said. "You have an intelligent, finely bred piece of horseflesh there, Linda."

Bob grinned. "For my money, she's the queen bee from now on."

In spite of their predicament, Linda gave him a warm smile. But in a moment she looked troubled again. "What do you think caused the dam to break, Bronco?" she asked. "Was it getting weak?"

"That was a well-built dam," he answered flatly. "Dynamite broke it."

"Dynamite?" Bob cried out.

"Yes."

"But who," Linda said, appalled, "would blow it up? And why?"

"Somebody who wants to get rid of us," Bob answered. He had been looking toward the Mineral Springs Bottling Company, untouched by the flood. "Maybe Worley or Garrant. After all, they ordered us off the place the first time we came here."

"And they sent us home by the quicksand route," Linda reminded the others.

"I wonder what their game is," Bronco mused. "Something big and illegal, I'd say, the way they're trying to keep it secret."

"Do you suppose *they're* responsible for the strange lights?" Linda surmised.

"Possibly," her grandfather agreed. "If those men are up to something crooked, they might be using the lights as a signal."

"Since Bob and I have seen both men and can identify them," Linda continued, "maybe that's why they want to get rid of us." She glanced about uneasily. "Do you think they know we weren't drowned?"

Bronco's forehead puckered. "Perhaps," he said. "One of them—or a henchman—must have followed us through the ravine yesterday and known we were camping here. The same spy might be watching in this direction now for signs of life."

"But why don't they just shoot us if they want us out of the way?" Bob asked abruptly.

"They want it to look like an accident," Bronco replied, "so the deaths can't be traced to them. Come on!" he ordered. "Let's go!"

Linda begged him to wait. "We came here to check on the bottling company," she said, "Please let's do a little sleuthing before we leave."

"What kind of sleuthing?" Bronco demanded.

"Will you stay with the horses while Bob and I tiptoe up and around the lodge and the office to find out what we can?" Linda proposed. "Yes, we'll be mighty careful," she answered the question she knew was coming.

Grandfather Mallory closed his eyes a few seconds as he mulled over the request. Finally he gave his consent. "Bob, whistle like a song sparrow if you need help and I'll come running."

Linda and Bob hurried forward, darting among the trees to escape detection. There was no evidence that anyone was around.

Just then Linda's attention was attracted to a heap of rubbish, evidently the dumping ground for the bottling company. Her eyes noted an empty gallon can of black dye.

Funny, she thought.

"What would they use black dye for at this place?" she asked Bob, who strode over to the pile. In it were several other empty cans of brown or black dye. "Worley and Garrant must be in the secret business of dyeing wigs!" he quipped.

Linda did not take time to laugh at her brother's remark. She said excitedly, "Bob, do you think they are in the secret business of dyeing horses?"

"You mean stolen horses?"

"Yes. Horse thieves change an animal's appearance and then sell it," Linda replied. "Why, Bob, if that's what happened to Prince Brownlee, we may never find him!"

She and her brother looked for more signs of the suspected nefarious business. They found two more cans, but nothing else.

"Let's take some of this evidence along," Linda proposed.

"Okay," Bob agreed, "but you know this may be only a wild guess."

"Let's call it a hunch," Linda countered as they each picked up a can.

The grounds yielded no further clues, and no one appeared from either building. Linda and Bob returned to Bronco, who was very interested in his granddaughter's theory.

"Are the horses brought to the bottling company for a dye bath," he speculated, "then taken away?"

"There's no place here to stable a horse," Linda spoke up. "Of course there *could* be a hideaway." But none was in evidence.

The puzzled trio decided to set off. Before leaving, Bob whipped out a jackknife and cut his horse's tie rope in two for a pair of reins. After unraveling a couple of ends, he fastened them to each side of Rocket's halter. Then he did the same for Chica d'Oro. He and Linda swung onto the horses' backs. Bronco, also riding bareback, led off, guiding Colonel in Indian style with his knees.

The bedraggled riders plodded their way carefully down the slope—a good distance from the creek. Reaching the bottom, they kept close to the foot of the mountain through an arid sandy area, and finally crossed the valley and headed for Charlie's cabin.

When they arrived, the Indian was not at home.

Hastily the visitors rubbed the hungry horses down, grained them, and tossed some hay into the feeding troughs.

Linda lingered in the barn for a few moments beside her pony. Gently she stroked the mane of the filly, who looked up from her food.

"Thank you," Linda said earnestly. "You saved our lives."

She now hurried from the barn and followed Bob and Bronco into the cabin. After they had changed into fresh clothes and washed up, Linda put on the coffee pot and made a quick breakfast of creamed chipped beef on toast.

While they were eating she asked, "What is the next step to find the missing Prince Brownlee?"

"I have a suggestion," said Bob. "Suppose I take those empty dye cans into Ruddville—even if I have to ride bareback. I'll find out, if possible, where they were purchased and by whom. That might help us locate the horse thief."

"A splendid idea," Bronco agreed. "And while you're in town buy us each a saddle, bridle, and horse blankets. You can arrange to have Linda's and mine sent out in the morning, when Charlie picks up supplies in his jeep." He signed a blank check and passed it over to Bob.

"What are you and Linda going to do?" Bob asked.

Linda smiled. "I'm going to teach Chica d'Oro some tricks."

"Well, good luck," Bob remarked.

Linda put several pieces of bread in her pocket and went to the corral. The pony greeted her with joyous nickering and a tossing of her mane.

"Would you like to do a few tricks, baby?" Linda asked her. She flipped out her handkerchief, and then stuffed it back into her shirt pocket with the corner sticking out.

Chica d'Oro immediately snatched it and waved the handkerchief up and down, proving that she did not forget her lessons. Then she received the first bread tidbit.

"Very good," Linda praised her. "Now let's see how smart you are at learning to nod yes."

She put the palomino through the same process as she had Speedy, the cutting horse. After half a dozen tries, Chica d'Oro responded perfectly to the cue. When Linda moved her cupped hand toward the filly's nose, the animal nodded her head up and down.

"Wonderful!" Linda said excitedly. "But you can't always be a yes horse. How about learning to say no?"

She tickled the inside of the pony's ear with the end of her finger to simulate a crawling bug. Chica d'Oro vigorously shook her head back and forth to get rid of the annoyance. After only a few tries she recognized the movement of Linda's finger toward her ear and shook her head automatically.

"That's great!" Linda said, feeding the filly her

expected treat. "How about giving me a good old horse laugh?"

Chica d'Oro looked at her young mistress expectantly with shining eyes. Linda took a bobby pin from her hair and gently pricked the horse on the bottom part of her upper lip. The pony raised her head, curled back her lip, and stuck out her lower one. Linda repeated the training until the horse "laughed" when the girl merely pointed her finger toward Chica's mouth.

"That's enough for today, sweetie," Linda said, and fed the palomino the remaining tidbits of bread. "Next time I'll teach you how to bow, to sit, to lie down and pull a blanket over yourself, and to pose like the 'End of the Trail' statue. Then we'll have a show, take up a collection, and buy a silver concha!"

Chica d'Oro whinnied. "Oh, you doll!" Linda exclaimed, unmindfully pointing a finger toward her pet. The horse rolled back her lip in a laugh!

As Linda walked toward the cabin, she met Bronco coming out. Both heard a whirring noise in the sky and looked up.

"A whirlybird!" Linda remarked. "I wonder where it's going."

She and Grandfather Mallory watched as the helicopter came closer. To their amazement, it began to settle down on a level spot near Indian Charlie's cabin.

"Who can it be?" Linda asked. "Someone from the pipeline company to see Charlie?"

Bronco did not reply. As Linda looked at him, she noticed that his jaw was set and his brow furrowed. This means he's worried, she felt.

Suddenly Linda thought, Could the 'copter contain men who have come to harm us? The same people who have tried it before?

California Windstorm 9

As Linda and Bronco waited tensely, the helicopter set down. The blades ceased to spin and the side door opened. Framed in it stood John Davis.

"Hello there!" he called.

Grins of relief spread over the faces of Linda and her grandfather, who cried, "Good to see you, Johnny! What brings you here?"

"I'm doing a little hedgehopping with this bird," Mr. Davis answered. "Went to Old Sol and heard you were here. Well, Linda, I have a surprise for you." He jumped down, then reached up a hand to assist a passenger.

"Doña!" exclaimed Linda, and as soon as the woman's feet touched the ground her granddaughter threw both arms around her.

Before she could say more, John Davis was lending a hand to a second passenger. Again Linda cried out in amazement. "Kathy! This is just marvelous!"

Kathy Hamilton, with honey blond hair and an apricot-tinted complexion, was sixteen and full of fun. She and Linda had known each other since childhood and recently Kathy had been a great solace to Linda.

"This is the grandest surprise ever," Linda said, hugging her attractive friend.

John Davis explained that he could stay only a short time. Mrs. Mallory would go back with him, but Kathy had permission to stay if there was room in the cabin.

"She wants to help solve the mysteries—unless they've already been solved," he explained.

Linda shook her head. "We haven't found Prince Brownlee, but we have a possible clue. Bob has gone to town to check on it."

"And the lights?" John Davis asked.

Bronco said, "We have a theory they're being used for some illegal purpose. But none of us has been able to find out what or by whom."

"I just thought of something," said Linda. "Do you suppose the lights are removed when they're not in use? That's why we can't find them?"

Bronco slapped his thigh. "I believe you have a point there, Linda."

Doña Mallory had started for the cabin. Linda ran after her, apologizing for her lack of hospitality. "May I get you some hot chocolate?" she asked.

"Yes, dear."

The whole group had cookies with the hot

chocolate while the Craigs' experiences were related. Mrs. Mallory sighed, then said to Kathy, "Are you sure you want to stay here?"

"I'd love the adventure," Kathy replied. "And I promise not to take any crazy chances."

Mrs. Mallory smiled. "I'll tell your mother that."

"Come see my wonderful surprise," Linda begged and led the visitors to the corral. "Look! Isn't that a beautiful palomino? She's mine! My very own!"

Linda's grandmother smiled. "She's a fine-looking pony. Tell me about her."

Kathy and John Davis admired Chica d'Oro as Linda briefed them all.

"Oh, I'm so happy for you," Kathy said enthusiastically.

Mr. Davis added his praise, then said he must leave. Kathy's extra clothes and blankets were brought from the helicopter, and a few minutes later the pilot and Grandmother Mallory took off.

"Would you like to go for a ride—bareback?" Linda asked Kathy.

"Bareback? Well—"

"That won't be necessary," Bronco spoke up. "I came across an old saddle of Charlie's. It will fit Gypsy." He led the way to the barn and showed the well-worn black leather saddle to Kathy. "Could you manage with this?"

"Oh, yes, and I'd love to go. Maybe we can do some detective work, Linda!"

Her friend grinned. "I'll take you to the spot where there's the most beautiful yucca I've ever seen." As Kathy looked puzzled, Linda went on. "Near it is a huge rock. Chica d'Oro shied away from it the other day. Maybe somebody was hiding—and left a clue."

Bronco looked intently at the girls. "Don't forget your promise to Doña. In fact, I think I'd better come along."

"Please do," Linda said. "I'll fix some lunch to take with us."

Grandfather Mallory rode Colonel bareback with no halter, while Linda put the hackamore on Chica d'Oro. The three riders set off, with Linda leading the way. By taking a shortcut, they arrived at the beautiful yucca in less time than the day before.

As they approached the entrance to the gorge, a sudden sharp explosion echoed within its rocky walls. The riders reined up.

"That sounded like a shot!" Linda exclaimed. Seeing Kathy's uneasy expression, she added, "But it might have only been someone hunting game."

"Just the same," Bronco said, "I'll ride up first and have a look. You two wait here."

The girls watched until he disappeared around a distant bend in the gorge. They walked their mounts over to the yucca in front of the red rock.

"Isn't it lovely?" Linda exclaimed.

She and her chum sat for a few minutes admiring the creamy color of the bloom. Then Linda's eyes fastened on the rock. She decided no one was hiding behind it because Chica d'Oro was not acting worried the way she had the day before.

Nevertheless, Linda looked again at the red rock, wishing that she could see through it. In a moment, curiosity began to exceed caution.

Linda said to Kathy, "Let's take a look back there."

The girls dismounted and slowly went toward the rock, scarcely breathing. When they reached the back of it, Linda and Kathy gave sighs of relief. No one was there, but Linda found a cranny just big enough for a horse to stand in, and there were horseshoe prints visible.

As she looked closer at them, Linda noted something else and picked it up. "A purple electric light bulb!" she cried.

"What a wonderful clue!" Kathy exclaimed.

Linda was elated. She said excitedly, "This must have been dropped by someone connected with those strange lights. They're probably strung on wires and laid down when needed."

"But where," asked Kathy, "would you get any current way out here?"

"Powerful batteries," Linda answered, "or even a generator. But don't ask me where *that* is. It may be stationary or the portable type carried on a truck."

Linda put the light bulb in her pocket, and the two companions fell silent, each trying to guess the meaning of the strange lights.

"I wonder what's taking Bronco so long," Kathy said uneasily.

"We ought to ride after him and find out," Linda replied, plainly tempted to do so.

"But he ordered us to stay here," Kathy said, "and he's the trail boss today."

"You're right," Linda conceded with a grin. "Let's get out the lunch. He ought to be back soon."

The girls unpacked the sandwiches and tomatoes. As they ate, Kathy remarked how still it was. "Even the horses aren't moving."

"Unusually still," Linda said. "The horses should be foraging the growth. I don't like it."

Suddenly alarmed, the girls became aware of a current of air against their faces. The yucca began to sway, and the dangling rope reins on Chica d'Oro's halter started to swing. A sound like agonized wailing came from around the rocks.

"We must find Bronco and get out of here!" Linda cried.

At that moment, the girls heard a faint shout in the gorge and saw Bronco galloping around the bend. "Ri-ide—home!" he called, waving his arms to them to go ahead. "A windstorm's coming!"

Kathy had no trouble mounting her horse, but Chica d'Oro proved to be a problem. The wind, sand, and eerie sound had spooked the pony. She sidled away and circled, tossing her head and whinnying, when Linda started to swing onto her

Linda galloped toward Charlie's cabin . . .

back. Linda pivoted the pony fast twice, and in the following moments, while Chica d'Oro stood confused and quiet, the girl managed to mount her. She galloped after Kathy toward Charlie's cabin.

That was where Chica d'Oro now wanted to go, so Linda kept only one hand on the reins. With the other, she pulled her slipping kerchief over her face and held it there against the stinging, gritty dust.

Suddenly one of Chica d'Oro's hoofs went into a chuck hole and she crashed down on her knees. Linda was thrown violently over the pony's head. The breath was knocked out of the girl, and she lay stunned.

Linda was conscious, however. With her face down in her arms, she began gasping for breath. When the anxious girl opened her eyes a slit, she noted that her sleeves were torn. The wind, dust, and sand were a swirling fury by now. She could see nothing around her.

"Chica d'Oro!" Linda called weakly. "Baby!" But she could scarcely hear the sound of her own voice.

Linda pulled herself to her knees, but had to keep her head bowed against the stinging gale. She pulled her kerchief down to unmuffle her voice, and desperately called her pony again and again.

Finally she heard a plaintive whinny. Linda kept calling to direct the palomino to her, and in a few minutes there came the soft, blessed nuzzling against her neck. At the same moment, she heard Bronco's voice behind her.

"You all right?" he shouted over the storm as he dismounted.

"Y-yes. Just a spill."

Bronco helped the girl to her feet and she caught hold of Chica d'Oro's mane to steady herself. Linda pressed her face against the warm flesh of the pony's neck, grateful that she was not badly hurt and had stayed with her.

As Linda adjusted the kerchief over her face again, Kathy rode up. "Linda!" she cried. "Are you hurt?"

"I'll be all right," Linda insisted.

Bronco helped her mount. "Linda, go first!" he called over the wind. "Stick together!"

The girl gave Chica d'Oro a loose rein. The palomino started off as if she knew the way, but at a slow gait, limping badly. Linda was unhappy at having to add her weight to the little horse, but she dared not dismount in the raging windstorm. Frequently she reached out a hand to Chica d'Oro's neck, petting her gently, and felt an answering quiver of flesh.

Suddenly the filly slid down a nearly perpendicular embankment. Linda grasped hard at the handhold to keep from plunging over the horse's head. They landed in a wash, however, and the sides provided a little protection.

Bronco, who had followed with Kathy, said this was a longer way home, but a more sheltered one. After following the gully for a while, the riders emerged close to a trail leading to Charlie's cabin.

When they were almost there, Bob crossed their path, fighting his way back from town. At his dumbfounded look, Kathy's eyes sparkled sideways at him across the top of her kerchief. "Hi!" she called. "I came to join your detective force."

"Great!" said Bob.

Further conversation was impossible until the riders reached Charlie's barn. Then there was a quick exchange of stories. Bob said a Ruddville hardware man had told him the cans of dye were not sold in Ruddville, but probably had been purchased in Los Angeles.

"There was no identifying mark to any store," Bob went on, "so I guess it would be impossible to trace the cans to a particular place. When I suggested to the hardware man that the dye might have been used on horses, he remarked, 'It wouldn't be the first time horse thieves have used that method of disguise in their underhanded business.'"

"Then we might be on the right track!" Linda exclaimed. "If so, I only hope Prince Brownlee hasn't been shipped so far away we can't find him."

"If he has been dyed a different color," Kathy interposed, "how could you recognize him even if you saw him?"

"I'm sure I could," Linda said. "Every horse has certain characteristics, just like a person. No dye is going to change that. Prince Brownlee was a high stepper. He held his head erect and his gait was in perfect rhythm. When I went up to him, he shook his head and snorted."

During this conversation, Bronco had brought out some of Charlie's horse liniment and was applying it to Chica d'Oro's leg. When he had finished, they all went into the cabin and the girls closeted themselves in the supply room.

"We'll have to sleep together without moving," Linda said with a grin, "or one of us will fall out of bed!"

Linda applied ointment to her own scraped skin. "Now I know exactly what a lemon must feel like on a grater," she said, laughing, and put on a fresh blouse.

A little later, when Charlie came home, the cabin was filled with the aroma of frying steaks. While Linda and Kathy set the table, they told him about their afternoon adventure and the light bulb Linda had found.

The Indian frowned. "I do not like that. Those men are too close."

He said he would examine every inch of ground as he walked the pipeline to see if he could pick up any suspicious tracks made by Luke Poe—or others.

When the group arose the next morning, they noted that both Charlie and the jeep were gone. He drove in just as they were finishing breakfast, and everyone hurried outside to help him unload the riding equipment and groceries he had brought. When Bronco reached the car, Charlie handed him a telegram.

"It came to the Ruddville office just before dawn," he said.

Bronco opened the envelope as Linda, Bob, and Kathy watched in silent concern.

Mr. Mallory scanned the message quickly and scowled. "This is from Cactus Mac," he announced, and read aloud, "Bad trouble here. Return pronto."

Ranch Trouble 10

Bob and Linda exchanged worried looks.

"Trouble?" Bob said, taking the telegram from Bronco. "What kind of trouble? Why didn't Mac say what it was?"

Bronco smiled dryly. "You all know Mac. He'd rather tell you the whole story himself with all the dramatic details."

"But what do you suppose is the matter?" Linda asked anxiously. "And why didn't Cactus Mac use the two-way radio to tell us?"

"Probably he couldn't get us," Bronco answered.

"Or the telegram might not even be from Cactus Mac," Linda suggested. "The Fossil Mountain men could have sent it. Perhaps we're too close to finding out what they're up to—especially if they're tied in with the horse stealing."

Bronco rubbed his chin and squinted his eyes in speculation. "Maybe, maybe not. But if it is a scheme to pull us off the scent," he said firmly, "we're not going to fall for it!"

He strode into the cabin and turned on the shortwave set. He could get no reply from Old Sol.

"Either these batteries are gone or else those in the ranch set." He turned searching eyes on Linda and Bob. "I believe you had better start for home at once and take Kathy with you. Find out if anything did happen, or whether this message was a hoax."

"And what about you?" Bob asked.

"I'll stay here as guard," Grandfather Mallory replied, "in case something peculiar takes place in this area."

"How will I get a message to you? By telegram?" Bob questioned.

"Good idea. Wire me tomorrow. Charlie or I will ride into Ruddville and pick it up."

All this time Linda had been silent. She was worried about Chica d'Oro. Finally she said, "But Bronco, I can't go today. My pony is too lame to ride and I'd be afraid to leave her. Something might happen to her when you and Charlie are away."

"Don't you worry about Chica d'Oro, honey," Bronco said. "I'll take good care of her. It'll be good for her sprained leg to give it some easy exercise— keep it from getting stiff—so I'll take her with me if I go out of sight of the cabin."

"Well, all right then," Linda agreed. "When shall we leave?"

"Better start as soon as possible," Bronco replied. "Ride one of the packhorses and take the other one along. You have no sleeping bags or cooking equipment, but you can ask one of the ranchers to put you up for the night." He took out his billfold and passed several tens over to Bob.

"I'll pack my things and fix a lunch for us to take," Kathy offered.

When Rocket, Gypsy, and the other two horses were ready for the journey, with packets of food and canteens filled, Linda turned to Chica d'Oro. Despite a limp, the filly had been dancing around Linda, expecting to go along. Now the girl led her into the stall and hugged her close.

"I'll be back soon for you," she told the pony, "or else you'll be coming to me."

As Linda rode off, Chica d'Oro whinnied jealously, kicked at the door, and limped back and forth behind it. Poor baby! her owner thought.

Bob had noted landmarks on the ride up to Charlie's: an exceptionally large, twisted Joshua tree, an abandoned mine shaft, a Mojave desert shack, and rock formations, so he had no trouble finding the route home. Nevertheless, he and Linda consulted their new compasses frequently.

In the evening, they stopped at a ranch to ask for lodging, and the pleasant owner was glad to have them. There was a fenced-in shed yard for the horses. On the big screened porch in the back, along with laundry tubs and an ironing board, two cots were set out for Linda and Kathy. Bob would sleep on hay in the barn.

After the riders had joined the family for a hot, boiled ham dinner, they went to bed early and slept soundly. At dawn, they were in the saddle again.

It was forenoon when they drew near to Old Sol. Linda said huskily, "I sort of have the whim-whams coming back here now. I wonder what we'll find."

"We'll know soon enough," Bob replied grimly.

In a few moments, Linda, Bob, and Kathy mounted a low rise and looked down into the shallow basin where the ranch house and main buildings lay in a cluster. For a second, they stared, astonished.

"The windmill's gone!" Linda exclaimed.

Together the three riders spurred down toward the corral. Bales of hay were lying around it, some of them broken open. As the Craigs dismounted beside a damaged water trough, Grandmother Mallory came hurrying from the ranch house to greet them. Cactus Mac emerged from the barn.

"Thank goodness you three are here!" Mrs. Mallory said. "Where's Bronco!" she inquired just as Cactus Mac joined them and asked the same question.

Bob explained. "Bronco thought that whoever made the trouble here might have done it to get us away from Charlie's place, so he stayed there to keep his eye on things."

"Those varmints must want to keep you away

from there pretty bad," Cactus Mac growled. "Just wait till you see the damage."

"We noticed that the windmill is down," Bob said.

"And the fences are cut. Come on, I'll show you," Mac offered.

Linda had been looking around. "Wait a minute!" she said. "Where's Rango? He's usually here to welcome us."

"He's gone," Cactus Mac blurted. "Disappeared the same time the damage was done, I guess."

"Oh, no!" Linda breathed in dismay.

"But how could anyone walk close enough to Rango to get hold of him?" Bob asked. "He always barked loudly when anyone came around."

Cactus Mac could not answer this. "They got him away somehow before he could sound an alarm," the foreman declared. "Maybe they gassed him and then shot one of those new tranquilizer drugs at him—the kind they give wild animals when they want to bring 'em back alive."

"And then they carried him off!" Linda wailed.

"If Rango is not dead, he'll try to come home," Mrs. Mallory assured the girl, patting her arm.

"How about our water supply?" Bob asked.

"Fortunately the tank was full," Cactus Mac replied, "and I've got an old jack pump workin'. It'll do till this windmill can be repaired and stood up again."

"Some of the vanes of the wheel are broken," Linda observed, frowning.

"Worse'n that," Cactus Mac said, "the varmints cut fences near the house. The cattle ready for shipment wandered out along the highway," he went on bitterly. "Three good steers were killed before we could round up all the strays."

The Craigs went with him to the fences. Bob noted that a hasty mending job had been done by twisting wires together. "We'll have to get new wire strung in these spots," he said.

"Yup," Cactus Mac agreed, "and a real tough job that is, too. We'd better start on it first thing in the morning."

"Was the sheriff notified of the damage?" Linda asked.

"Right away," Cactus Mac replied. "The sheriff and a deputy came out that same night and looked the place over. Later they picked up two suspects, but they weren't the ones."

"Did you find anything that someone might have dropped or did you see any tracks?" Bob asked.

"No footprints," Cactus Mac replied. "But over by the windmill were tread marks from the tires of a pickup truck. It was used to pull the windmill over. In the middle of the night, we heard the mill go down. I ran out as the truck was speeding off."

The conversation was interrupted by the sound of the metallic triangle being beaten to call the ranchers to lunch. The young people followed Mrs. Mallory to the house and went through the kitchen. Luisa stopped the Craigs. She held the two slender young people off at arm's length and exclaimed in her Mexican tongue. "*Delgado!* So skinny! You eat a lot of Luisa's pork pie. That put some fat on those stick-out bones."

"Don't you worry!" Bob declared with a grin, sniffing the delicious aroma. "We'll eat plenty. Just bring it on!"

Besides the steaming pie, Luisa served crisp green salad, corn bread, and apple dumplings for dessert. Kathy declared she had never enjoyed a meal more.

When they finished, Bob went at once to the two-way radio and tried to contact his grandfather. He failed, so sent a telegram.

A little later Kathy said she must go home and Bob offered to take her. He saddled one of the horses for her and brought it to the ranch house door.

"Let me know, Linda, what happens," Kathy said as she mounted.

"I will," her chum promised, and stood gazing after the couple as they trotted down the lane. Kathy's parents operated the Highway House, a restaurant and souvenir shop on the main road. They lived in a rambling, split-level dwelling alongside it.

When Kathy and Bob were out of sight, Linda

began a bit of sleuthing around the ranch house grounds to see if she could figure out anything about the mysterious saboteurs and in what direction Rango might have gone.

The question is, did they take him, or after he woke up, did he pick up their trail and follow them? she asked herself.

Linda got down on hands and knees to examine the ground thoroughly. There was a crisscrossed confusion of tire tracks, horseshoe prints, and boot marks. But finally the girl was able to make out the dog's toeprints.

Now where do they go? she wondered, following them slowly back and forth between the house, the corral, and the barn. She traced the marks to the rear of the stable. Here they ended.

That proves Rango was stolen. Linda's eyes blazed. I don't know who is worse—a horse thief or a dognapper!

Cactus Mac found her staring into space and asked what was on her mind. When he heard, the foreman said, "You got a good right to be hoppin' mad. Thar ain't any kind o' thief what ain't a sneakin' wretch." After a moment he added, "I'm goin' to jeep into Lockwood. Want to go along and clear that thar brain o' yours?"

Linda smiled. "Mac, you're an old darling. Yes, I'd love to go. I'll run in and tell Doña."

When they reached Lockwood, Cactus Mac said his errand would take half an hour. A sudden idea came to Linda, who said she would get out and meet him later in front of the deputy sheriff's headquarters.

She walked a couple of blocks, and entered the office. Linda introduced herself to Deputy Randall and asked him whether any trace had been found of the shepherd dog Rango.

"Not a thing yet, Miss Craig," he replied kindly. "But we have a broadcast out on him. We'll let you know just as soon as something comes in."

"Thank you," Linda said, unable to keep the disappointment out of her voice.

She explained to Deputy Randall that she, her brother, and grandfather were working on the theft of Prince Brownlee, and told about the cans of dye.

"Good detecting," the man commended her. "I'll get in touch with the sheriff up there and talk it over."

Linda spoke of the damage at the ranch and was dismayed to learn that the authorities had no clues yet to the identity of the perpetrators. "We're working on it, though," the deputy assured her.

Linda thanked him and left, wondering how long it would be before the enemy might strike again. She and Cactus Mac reached home in the late afternoon.

During dinner that evening, Linda said to Bob and Grandmother Mallory, "Don't you think we should stand watch tonight in case any men come to cause more damage?"

"Yes," Bob agreed. "I'll do it."

Grandmother Mallory shook her head. "Not all night," she said. "Cactus Mac can spell you."

Linda wanted to offer her services for part of the time but knew Doña would never permit this. It was arranged that Bob would be on duty until midnight, then Cactus Mac would relieve him.

That night Linda slept fitfully. She kept waking up to wonder what was happening outdoors. Finally, at eleven-thirty, a faint noise brought her to the window on a run. Linda listened intently.

Then, hurriedly, throwing on a robe and slippers, she slipped outdoors and along the back patio which ran the length of the house.

The noise came from the barn, she thought. It sounded like an animal, but it could be a trick by those marauders to ambush Bob and do more damage.

Staying in the shadows of the oak trees, she moved cautiously. Nothing was in sight. Linda ran around to the rear of the barn and came up the far side of it. At the front corner, she stopped. Flattening herself against the side wall, she peered around.

Where's Bob? she thought, worried, then looked straight ahead.

In the moonlight shining onto the barn door, stood Rango. Scarcely able to move, he came limping toward the girl with a couple of weak yelps.

Linda ran to him, sat down, and gathered the dog

into her lap. "Oh, poor fellow!" she exclaimed. "Poor Rango! You're hurt! Bob! Bob!" she called.

Almost instantly her brother appeared, racing across the yard. "Linda, what are you doing here? Well, I'll be—" He leaned down to pat the dog. "So you came home, old fellow."

Bob explained that he had been on his way back from a quick patrol of the fence when he heard Linda's cry.

"Rango has been injured," his sister said. "Let's carry him into the house."

Bob carefully shifted the big dog into his own arms and took him into the kitchen. Quickly Linda brought a pan of milk. As Rango stood, trembling, lapping it up, they watched him anxiously. "Look at those ugly marks on his legs," Linda said.

"He's been trussed up," Bob remarked angrily.

"How did he ever get loose?" Linda asked.

Bob shook his head, equally puzzled.

While Rango finished drinking, Linda quietly got an old blanket to make a pallet on the floor, and a pan of warm water and a sponge.

When the milk was gone, Bob stretched Rango out on the pad to wash his wounds. Deftly Linda took off the pet's collar.

"Bob!" she said a moment later, "I think there's a note wrapped around his collar!"

She removed the piece of tablet paper from the leather band. "It *is* a note, but oh, Bob, the message is dreadful!"

"What does it say?" Bob demanded.

Tears had sprung to Linda's eyes. "It says—it says, 'We have your palomino. If you want the horse back, get five hundred dollars for us and follow instructions!'"

Strange Orders 11

Linda and Bob sat back on their heels, too stunned to speak for a moment. Then Bob said, "They can't have Chica d'Oro. Bronco said he'd take good care of her. I believe this is just a trick to get money."

"Maybe," Linda said soberly, trying to make herself believe this. She read on: "Put fifty ten-dollar bills in outside mailbox by closed-up hamburger stand at junction of Ridgecrest and Vallejo roads at ten o'clock tomorrow morning. Palomino will be left at Silver Sage Ranch."

"I still think it's a trick," Bob declared confidently. "We should ignore this except to tell the sheriff."

Linda was not convinced. "Suppose Bronco was overpowered," she suggested ominously.

"Maybe. We'll have to find out," Bob replied with a taut face.

"Let's call Deputy Randall right away," Linda urged.

Bob agreed and hurried into the living room to

telephone. Meanwhile, Linda found a tube of ointment and gently applied some to the raw marks on Rango's legs.

When Bob returned, he said, "Deputy Randall talked with the sheriff in Charlie's county. He'll send one of his deputies out in a jeep to Charlie's right away, to see whether Bronco and he and Chica d'Oro are all right."

Linda looked up at the kitchen clock. "It's past midnight. It'll be morning before we hear anything."

At this moment, the kitchen door opened and Cactus Mac walked in. He was dumbfounded to hear the turn of events. "Guess I've lost my job as guard," he said.

"We're not sure the people who sent the note are the same as those who tried to wreck the ranch," Linda told him. "I think you'd better watch, and we'll let you know the minute we hear from the sheriff."

The foreman nodded and departed. As Linda and Bob went to their rooms, they were glad that Doña had not awakened. She was up at sunrise, however, to answer the ringing telephone. Her grandchildren flew to her side.

"Deputy Randall?" they heard her say. "Yes, Bob is here. I'll let you talk to him."

The conversation was short and ended with Bob's saying, "We'll be in Lockwood at eight."

After hanging up, he explained to the others,

"Bronco is all right. But three masked, armed riders surprised him and Charlie Tonka last night, and took Chica d'Oro at gunpoint." He paused, seeing Linda's stricken look.

Bob put his arm across her shoulders and went on, "We're to follow the instructions in the ransom note. First we're to go to Deputy Randall and give him the note. Then he'll accompany us to the bank in Ruddville. Bronco has arranged with the president to give us the money."

Mrs. Mallory stood up very straight and said, "I hope those lawbreakers will be caught soon and severely punished." But her voice trembled ever so slightly, indicating to Linda and Bob that she was worried about her husband's safety.

By eight o'clock, Linda and her brother were walking into the deputy's office. He greeted the Craigs affably. Bob took the pencil-scribbled ransom note from his pocket and handed it over.

"We'll have this checked for fingerprints," Randall said, giving it to a man at the desk. "And when we get the money, I'll have the bank make a record of the serial numbers, and keep a set here. By the way, your grandfather also said to tell you to have Cactus Mac load a couple of three-year-old quarter horses into the trailer. Take them with you to the Silver Sage Ranch and then bring the horses on to Charlie Tonka's place."

"And where is the Silver Sage Ranch?" Linda inquired.

"About fifty miles out on the Sierra Highway," the deputy informed her. "You can't miss it."

"Do you think the ranch folks are in cahoots with the horse thieves?" Linda asked him.

"No, I don't believe that," Randall replied. "I know them—people by the name of Larsen, and a real nice couple. Board horses and rent pasture. I think that they are just being used."

Deputy Randall went on. "We can start for the bank at once." He took his ten-gallon hat from its hook. "The sheriff is putting a man in the hamburger stand where you're to leave the money, and staking out a couple on the hills behind it."

"I'd like to call home before we go," Linda put in quickly, "and tell my grandmother to have everything ready."

"Go ahead."

"Use this phone," the man at the desk said.

Linda talked to Mrs. Mallory, who was relieved to know deputies would be hidden at the ransom spot, but alarmed about the task ahead of the young people. She warned them to be cautious and promised to give their message to Cactus Mac.

Linda and Bob went to the bank with Randall and took care of the money transaction with the president. Finally Linda and Bob returned to Old Sol. Cactus Mac had the two chestnut quarter horses loaded in a three-horse trailer hitched to the pickup.

"That third stall's for Chica d'Oro," he said hopefully.

"Oh, yes." Linda smiled, wishing she were as certain as she sounded.

Hurriedly she and Bob changed from town clothes into riding jeans. As they climbed into the truck beside Cactus Mac, Mrs. Mallory admonished them, "Just put the money in that mailbox, pick up the horse, and leave the catching of those bounders to the sheriff." Her grandchildren consented.

After a long drive down the sun-baked highway, Cactus Mac turned off on a dusty side road. He had no trouble finding the closed hamburger stand and mailbox at the junction of two little-used back-country dirt roads. The surrounding terrain was barren and rough.

Quietly Bob slipped the packet of money into the box. Then the three drove back toward the highway.

"There was supposed to have been a deputy in that shack, and two more hidden on the hills behind it," Linda remarked. "It gives me the creeps to think that we were being watched."

"Don't forget there was probably at least one of the horse thieves spying to make sure we left the money," Bob reminded her.

"Yup," added Cactus Mac, "and *he* was being watched by them thar deputies."

After they had swung into the main road, two

highway patrol cars passed them at intervals, going in opposite directions.

"I have an idea they too are on the lookout for your palomino," Bob said.

"How will the thieves get her to the Silver Sage without being seen?" Linda asked. Then a dreadful thought came to her. "Maybe they dyed Chica d'Oro! If the authorities are looking for a palomino, they might not recognize her!"

"If those hoss thieves did that," said Cactus Mac vehemently, "I'll tar an' feather 'em!"

An hour and a half later, when they drove up to the Silver Sage Ranch, Linda and her companions saw a group of neat buildings and white corral fences enclosing squares of pasture. Different sizes and types of horses were nibbling contentedly. In a riding ring, a dressage group of eight were practicing a formation drill with their gaited mounts.

As Cactus Mac brought the pickup to a stop, a tall, rawboned, sandy-haired woman in tan frontier pants and a cream shirt strode toward them with a pleasant smile.

Linda jumped out excitedly, saying, "Are you Mrs. Larsen?"

"Yes, I am," the woman replied. "What can I do for you?"

"I'm Linda Craig. We've come for the palomino that was left here for me."

"Well, a palomino was left here today," she said

kindly, "but not for you. It came in a rental trailer from the city for a Helen Andrews."

"Maybe they gave the wrong name," Bob suggested.

"Would you know the horse?" Mrs. Larsen asked.

"Oh, yes," Linda replied.

"Follow me then," the woman said, "and see if this is the one."

All of them went with her as she led the way to a box stall with a private paddock. Inside, stood a palomino mare with her ribs showing.

"She needs fattening up," Mrs. Larsen commented.

"That isn't Chica d'Oro," Linda said sadly. "My horse was stolen. We paid a ransom and she was to have been left here."

"Could our pony have been put somewhere around the place without your knowing it?" Bob asked.

"We'll just see about that," Mrs. Larsen said, and led the way to the big barn.

Chica d'Oro was not there. Nor was she in any of the two long rows of box stalls, the pastures, or the huge feed shed, packed to the rafters with hay.

"We've been duped, Linda," said Bob.

"I'm sorry, young lady," Mrs. Larsen told the girl, who was pale and silent. "But I'm certainly obliged to you for warning me of horse thieves on the loose. I'll post an extra guard."

Cactus Mac put in, "Thank you, ma'am, for your trouble. We'll be gettin' along."

Discouraged, the searchers drove back to the hamburger shack mailbox. The money was still in it. A deputy sheriff showed himself at the door of the boarded-up stand.

"My horse wasn't left at the ranch," Linda told him.

"Better take your money then," the deputy replied. "We'll stay on guard tonight and pick up anybody who comes around."

Cactus Mac buttoned the packet of money inside his shirt, and headed back to the highway. They stopped at a roadside restaurant for a belated lunch, but despite Bob's urging, Linda was not able to eat much.

"We'll follow this highway to a spot close to Charlie's," Mac told them as they climbed back into the truck. "Then you two can cut cross-country to his place on horseback."

Ahead of them the road wound around the foot of a high hill. Linda's eye caught something small and white waving on the hilltop. What can that be? she wondered, puzzled.

As they neared a sharp bend, Linda saw that the curve of the highway paralleled a deep ravine on their right. Seconds later a car zoomed around the bend in their lane!

Cactus Mac turned the truck out of the way so sharply to avoid a head-on collision that the horse

A car zoomed around the bend in their lane . . .

trailer nearly rocked over. For a moment, it seemed to Linda that they would surely go off the highway into the chasm. She clapped her hand over her mouth to stifle a scream.

But Cactus Mac held the truck and the trailer to the road. He proceeded slowly around the curve and stopped. The foreman nervously mopped his perspiring face.

"Oh, Mac, you're a marvelous driver," said Linda. "We and the horses might have been killed!"

Bob agreed. "If it hadn't been for the way you handled the outfit, Cactus," he said soberly, "that crazy driver might have put us at the bottom of the ravine."

"Do you think," Linda asked, "that he might have done it deliberately? Just before we came to the bend I saw something white waving on top of the hill. It could have been a signal to that car to say we were coming."

"Maybe this whole horse-thieving setup was just a ruse to get us out here and pull off another 'accident,'" Bob said worriedly.

"That's right," growled Cactus Mac and pointed to a small dirt road which led out of a stand of trees onto the highway. "Varmints could've been waiting right thar."

Bob swung down from the truck and hurried to the rutted path, with Linda directly behind him. "Here are tire marks," he said triumphantly, "and they don't go any farther down this road. It looks as if a car only drove in and turned around."

Suddenly Linda said, "Look! Boot prints! One of the men got out. Bob, let's remember these left and right prints—size, shape, and— Oh! There's a star mark on the bottom."

Bob whipped a piece of string from his pocket and measured the length and width, tying knots to indicate the dimensions. He and Linda hurried back to the truck and requested Cactus Mac to report the whole incident to Deputy Randall, give him the string, and mention the star trademark.

"I'll do that," he agreed. "But if I can lay my hands on that thar road hog, I'll give 'im a lickin' on my own account!"

Cactus Mac drove on and at last pulled over to the side of the highway, where they unloaded the horses. Bob and Linda saddled them. As they waved and rode off toward Indian Charlie's, Cactus Mac headed the truck and trailer for Rancho del Sol.

When the two riders arrived at the cabin, Bronco and Charlie were waiting for them. "I'm glad you made it safely," said Grandfather Mallory. "But where's Chica d'Oro?"

He was told the story of the double cross. Then Linda asked, "The men who attacked you—did they leave any kind of clues, like boot prints?"

"Come to think of it, they did. But they looked like anybody else's—nothing special about them."

Linda said she would like to see them, just the

same. When she and Bob looked at the prints, Bob exclaimed, "They're just like the ones we saw. See the star mark!"

"Which could prove a lot *or* a little," Bronco remarked philosophically. "We'll tell the sheriff first chance we get. One of the things the horse thieves did was to take my two-way radio set."

"So that's why we couldn't get you," said Linda. "Any more trouble here?"

"No. I'm convinced the thieves are taking only blooded stock," Bronco decided. "For that reason, Charlie's horses are safe and we needn't stay here. I believe I'm needed at home. By the way, those mysterious lights haven't been turned on once since you left."

"Do you think that's because we're here?" Linda asked.

"Perhaps." Grandfather Mallory added, "I forgot to tell you something. When the deputy drove me back here from Ruddville, we picked up Charlie and followed Chica's tracks to Fossil Mountain, but lost them there."

"Sheriff is sending another jeep for the search tomorrow," Charlie put in.

Linda was excited at this information. "Please, Bronco, may Bob and I stay here and try to pick up their trail?"

"That's a great idea," Bob said. "On horseback we can get into some of those rocky spots on the mountain where even a sheriff's jeep can't go."

Bronco gave his consent but requested, "If you find something, leave a note here for the sheriff's men. They're going to check up on these premises each morning until the palomino is found."

Linda was thrilled at the prospect of action but still sobered by the loss of her pony. She prepared a tasty supper in silence. At the end of the meal, she turned to the Indian. "Anyway, Charlie, we brought the two horses for your grandchildren."

"No deal," Charlie declared. "Not a fair trade. You have no horse."

"The trade was made before the palomino was stolen," Bronco stated with finality. "You take the horses to your grandchildren."

After a pause, Charlie gave in. "I will go tomorrow, and be back next morning."

"Maybe we'll have Chica by then," Bob said hopefully. "We're going to keep on searching."

The following day everyone was up for an early breakfast. Soon afterward the group separated. Charlie went in one direction with the quarter horses from Rancho del Sol. Bronco headed for home. Linda and Bob, using two of Charlie's mounts, went more slowly to follow Chica d'Oro's tracks.

It was easy to pick up the hoofprints of the four horses, and to distinguish the filly's from those the three thieves were riding. Her prints were slightly smaller.

The marks, instead of going up a pass in Fossil

Mountain, as Linda and Bob rather expected them to do, swerved right into rough terrain of rocky mounds.

"This is where Bronco and the deputy lost the thieves' trail, I guess," Bob said.

He and Linda rode on, but it became almost impossible to pick up a single track. Finally they stopped to look around.

Linda was bewildered. "Which way shall we go? Straight ahead or up the mountain?"

"It's anybody's guess, but let's try the mountain in the direction of the bottling company."

They started to climb.

After a few minutes, Linda spotted Chica d'Oro's tracks, and those of one other horse, then lost them again. She and her brother assumed the thieves had separated. Linda and Bob hunted fruitlessly and finally came to the foot of a steep, narrow trail.

"Maybe your pony was taken up here and maybe not," Bob said, sighing. "It's too gravelly to see prints."

"Let's try anyway," Linda urged, and they started up the steep path.

Suddenly she gave a little cry and pulled her horse to a stop. Linda slid off, picked a red object from brush beside the path, and held it up triumphantly.

"It's the tassel from Chica d'Oro's hackamore!" she cried jubilantly.

Mountain Tunnel 12

Linda clutched the tassel in her hands. "You know," she said happily, "I believe Chica d'Oro scraped this off on the bush so that we could follow her!"

Bob smiled. "Maybe. Anyhow, we know now that we're on the right track."

"We'd better go ahead cautiously," Linda advised. "We may be riding straight into that bunch of horse thieves!"

Bob was worried too. "Perhaps we'd better go back to town and notify the deputy sheriff."

"But my pony could be tied up near here," Linda protested. "Why don't we try to rescue her and make a run for home? If we don't, Chica may be taken farther away."

"I guess you're right," Bob conceded, dismounting. "But before we move on, I want to take a look around here. The thieves or their mounts may have left other clues."

Linda stood lookout while he examined both

sides of the trail, then went off it, into the brush. She could hear him poking among the bushes. For a few minutes, there was silence. Then she heard Bob's long, low whistle.

"He wants me." Linda jumped off her horse and hurried toward the sound. She broke through the brush to a clearing to find her brother kneeling and scooping loose dirt and leaves away from one spot.

"What are you searching for?" Linda asked, rushing over to him.

Bob pointed. "Not searching for something. Locating something. Look!" he cried excitedly. Lying exposed were several colored electric bulbs attached to a cord.

"The mysterious lights! You've found them!" Linda gasped.

Bob nodded. "I almost tripped over them. Whoever is using these as a signal doesn't remove the lights—just keeps them camouflaged by the leaves and dirt."

Brother and sister excitedly decided to follow the bulbs. "This must be part of the line and it starts at the edge of the valley," Bob noted. "That explains how we could see some of the lights from Charlie's cabin."

A sudden thought struck Linda as she and her brother, leading their horses, started off. "You know, if stolen horses *are* being hidden somewhere in this mountain, the thieves might be using these lights after dark to guide them here! Oh, Bob, that could mean this string of bulbs will take us to Chica d'Oro!"

"I hope so," said Bob. "We'd better be on our guard, though, every minute."

He and his sister concentrated on keeping track of the light bulbs. Using sticks, each poked dirt and leaves away from the cord at intervals. Progress became increasingly difficult, since the trail of light bulbs did not follow any well-defined path. The route took the Craigs gradually up the wooded mountainside, around boulders, and through tangled brush.

Finally, Bob offered to hold both horses, while Linda went a little distance ahead to uncover the string of bulbs. This made the going somewhat quicker. But at one spot of especially rocky terrain, she lost the line completely.

"We'll have to backtrack," Bob said, "and start again from the last spot uncovered."

Chafing over the time they had lost, Linda determinedly moved her stick back and forth until she relocated the trail. The eager searchers pushed through the heavy brush, with Linda exposing the electric wire inch by inch.

"Goodness, will we ever come to the end?" she murmured, stopping at last to catch her breath.

"Better take it easy for a minute," Bob advised.

They had just sipped cooling water from their canteens when they heard a crashing through the underbrush.

Linda gasped. "Someone's coming!"

"Down!" Bob ordered. "Behind that bush!"

Linda complied, but whispered fearfully, "They'll see you and the horses!"

Bob remained calmly beside the horses, ready to fend off an attack. The crashing grew louder. The next instant two mountain goats bounded into view. The animals, evidently startled at the sight of Bob, stopped dead for a moment. Linda, with a relieved giggle, stood up quickly. At this, the goats leaped away.

Linda gave a great sigh. "I'll love goats the rest of my life!" she declared.

"I sort of welcomed them myself," Bob said with a grin. He looked up the mountainside. "We're nearly halfway to the top," he observed.

"Let's keep going!" Linda urged, refreshed by the short rest. "We must find out the secret of these lights—and Chica d'Oro!"

"Lead on!" Bob, between the two horses, once more swung into step behind his sister. Her eyes were glued to the ground as she resumed the tedious search for the bulbs.

The minutes seemed like hours, but the weary pair trudged on doggedly. The string of light bulbs snaked around a dense growth of brush and led upward.

"This is certainly a zigzag path," Linda said.

"Probably an old Indian trail," Bob surmised.

Carefully the girl negotiated the steep ascent.

Behind her, Bob had all he could do to keep his own footing and retain his grip on the horses' reins. Presently the searchers approached a heavy growth of bushes directly ahead. Linda skirted them and came to an abrupt halt.

"Bob!" she whispered, astonished. "Look!"

Behind the screen of brush was an opening in the mountainside.

"A tunnel!" he exclaimed. "Maybe an old mine entrance."

"Yes!" returned Linda, shaking with excitement, "and I'll bet the light bulb cord goes into it!" They scratched eagerly at the earth around the entrance and in a few moments Linda held up the cord in silent triumph.

The young sleuths were elated at the discovery. Eagerly they pushed aside several bushes and peered into the yawning black cavern.

"The horse thieves use this tunnel!" Linda guessed. "These lights are a guide to them to bring the stolen animals here at night and hide them inside!"

"Wonder where it leads?" Bob said.

"Let's explore and find out!" Linda proposed, hopeful that the passageway might take her to Chica d'Oro.

"All right," Bob agreed, sensing his sister's thoughts.

Quickly they walked to the wooded growth opposite the tunnel, tied their horses to the trees, and went back to the tunnel. Bob turned on his flashlight and was about to step inside, when Linda grabbed his arm.

"Did you hear that? Horses whinnying!"

"Not in the tunnel?"

"No, somewhere to our left and below us."

Linda and Bob stood still and listened. For a few moments there was silence, but presently the whinnying came again.

"There are horses down the mountain all right," Bob said. "They must have caught a scent of our animals."

"Let's go look at them!" Linda said eagerly. "They might be stolen horses—and Chica d'Oro with them!"

She started off on a run in the direction of the sounds. The whinnying grew louder. At the foot of the mountain, Linda and Bob came face to face with a completely different terrain. Monstrous crags sawtoothed along each side of a crevice.

"The horses are in *there!*" Linda said.

"But this area is patrolled by air. Why weren't the horses seen?" Bob asked.

Linda was already running along the crevice, with Bob in close pursuit. All the while the whinnying noises became steadily more persistent. The excited Craigs raced around a bend. The next instant both skidded to a dead stop at the entrance to a small box canyon. With pounding hearts, they stepped warily inside.

A dozen horses were standing side by side . . .

"Bob!" Linda cried. "Over there! Horses! All purebreds."

Brother and sister stood staring at a dozen horses standing side by side beneath a huge overhanging cliff. Their halters were attached to long iron stakes imbedded in the rock wall.

"What a marvelous hiding place!" Linda exclaimed. "No wonder the horses couldn't be seen from the air. That overhang screens them completely."

"Let's have a close look," Bob urged. "Linda, do you realize how much these horses are worth? Thousands of dollars!"

Quickly scanning the area to make certain no one was around, Linda and Bob cautiously approached the group of handsome animals.

"Easy, boy," Linda said softly, going up to one. She was fearful that the sudden presence of Bob and herself might panic the horses. But they remained calm.

Linda's eyes flitted over the animals and beyond them, hoping to spot Chica d'Oro. But the golden pony was not in sight. Every horse was bigger than her palomino.

Oh, dear, what have they done with her? Where is she? Linda wailed inwardly.

Suddenly she noticed in particular a dark bay Morgan. He has the same wonderful conformation as Prince Brownlee, he holds his head erect, and— Excitedly she drew her brother's attention to the

Morgan. "Bob, I have a strong hunch that's Prince —and he's been dyed! And these other horses too. They've all been stolen."

"I agree. But how can we find out for sure?"

Without hesitation, Linda went up to the Morgan. "Hello, Prince Brownlee," she said. "You remember me, don't you?"

The horse's response was immediate. He shook his head and pawed the ground with his right front hoof.

"Exactly what Prince did the first time I saw him!" Linda exclaimed. "Oh, if only we can get him out of here, and take him back to Mr. Brownlee! But first I must find Chica d'Oro!"

"You think she's still hidden somewhere around here?" Bob asked. "She may have been sold."

Linda refused to accept this suggestion. "I think she's nearby, and we must rescue her!"

They speculated on the possible whereabouts of the palomino. Linda had an idea. "Maybe she's at the spot where the thieves dye the horses," she suggested. "I think we ought to go back and investigate the tunnel—perhaps that's the place."

"It's worth a try," Bob conceded.

As they turned to go Linda paused and looked around her, puzzled. "Do you see any running water here?" she asked.

Their eyes scanned the canyon for a spring or a stream.

"No," replied Bob. "How are these horses watered?"

"That's a good question," Linda said. "Let's hurry up to the tunnel and see if we can find some answers."

Bob agreed. "Besides, we'd better get out of this canyon before someone sees us," he warned.

Linda stroked Prince Brownlee's nose. "We'll come back for you and your friends as soon as we can."

She and her brother climbed quickly up the mountainside to the tunnel entrance.

"All set? Let's go!" Bob clicked on his flashlight and led the way inside. Linda, beaming her own light, tiptoed close behind. They found themselves in a medium-sized, rock-walled cavern with an earthen floor. Along one side ran the telltale electric wire, with bulbs attached at intervals.

The Craigs looked about for a light switch, but saw none. Suddenly Linda tensed and pointed to the ground. "Horseshoe prints! They're about Chica's size!"

Bob bent down to study the marks in the hard dirt. "You're right. Those thieves must bring the horses here—and dye them somewhere in the tunnel."

The pulses of both raced. Was the stolen Chica d'Oro within close range?

"Come on!" Linda urged, seeing a passageway ahead.

Deep silence prevailed as the two moved stealthily forward. The light from Bob's flash caused eerie shadows to leap and dance over the walls.

Presently the space became narrower. "Ugh! It's weird!" Linda shivered. "Poor Chica—in a place like this!"

In another few seconds, Linda and Bob were brought to a sudden halt. Ahead of them was a door of heavy planks banded by iron strips, with huge iron hinges fastened into the solid rock of the wall. The door handle was a big ringbolt.

"Oh, I hope we can get through!" Linda said in a low voice.

"We'll soon find out," said Bob and stepped up to the huge ring.

He grasped it and strained to open the door, but could not budge it. Linda grabbed the ring with him and pulled. But even their combined strength was not enough to move the door.

"That's odd," Linda remarked. "I just realized there's no lock—the door *should* open, unless it's bolted on the inside."

"It's extremely heavy, and the hinges are rusted," Bob replied. "Maybe that's the trouble."

"I know! Why don't we try horse power?" Linda suggested. "We can tie one end of our lariats to the ringbolt and the other end to the horses, and make *them* pull."

"That's a bright idea!" Bob said approvingly. "But

we'll probably never get them in here. Walking in a dark room is something horses won't do."

"There's always a way of getting a horse to do what you want it to," Linda declared cheerfully. "Once in New York I saw a mounted policeman try to ride his horse into a dark, narrow passageway between buildings. When it wouldn't head in, he backed it in. Let's try!"

"What are we waiting for?" Her brother grinned.

He and his sister hurried outside and took their lariats from the saddles. Bob carried them inside the tunnel. Deftly he knotted an end of each securely to the ring. This done, he gave a low bird call.

Upon hearing the familiar signal, Linda turned her horse around with its rump directly at the entrance. She stood in front of the animal and commanded firmly, "Back! Back! Back!" stepping foward herself as she did so.

The horse obeyed the order perfectly until it was a few paces inside the narrow passageway. Then, suddenly conscious of the black interior, it balked.

"That's far enough," Bob said, and brought the rope ends over. He held Linda's horse until she had backed in the other one.

Swiftly and skillfully the Craigs fastened the lariats securely to the saddle horns and led both the horses forward. Eager to get out into full daylight again, the animals strained full force at the ropes.

Linda watched hopefully while Bob trained his light on the heavy door. The horses continued to tug toward the entrance. At last there came a long, drawn-out grating sound.

"That did it!" Linda exclaimed. "The door's moving!"

In another moment, Bob had untied the ropes from the horses. "We'll take them back outside," he said, "before they get nervous and make a noise."

After fastening their mounts once more to the trees, Linda and Bob retraced their steps to the plank door. It stood open about three inches. Bob now turned off his flashlight as a safety precaution, and when their eyes had become accustomed to the darkness, he slowly pulled back the door.

Linda and Bob peered around it into a pitch-black interior. For a full half-minute they stood motionless, listening for sounds that would indicate a person's presence.

But there was absolute stillness. Linda nudged her brother as a signal to enter. Noiselessly the two slipped into the unknown area beyond the door. The atmosphere felt cold and damp. Not yet wishing to risk a light, Bob and Linda groped their way along, feeling walls and floor with their hands and feet before each step.

"It's all of stone," Linda told herself.

The next moment her hand touched a different substance—glass. Curious, she stooped and ran her fingers over the large object.

I'm sure it's a bottle of some kind, she thought, but what's it doing here? "Bob!" she called softly.

Bob joined her and Linda guided his hand to the bottle-sized object. "Reminds me of a water jug— like those demijohns we saw in the bottling company yard."

He decided to take the chance of turning on his flashlight. The beam stabbed into the blackness and swept over the rugged rocky interior of the tunnel. A demijohn stood on a ledge.

They kept going. Presently there was dim daylight ahead. Trickling from one wall into a pool below was sparkling water. The Craigs looked around and were astonished to see not one, but row after row of heavy, water-filled glass jugs standing near them.

"Bob!" Linda whispered, startled. "We're in the cave behind the bottling company!"

Trapped! 13

Excitedly the Craigs looked around the huge rock chamber at the rows of glass demijohns.

"Here's the water for the horses!" Linda exclaimed softly.

"Of course!" said Bob. "The thieves could fill the jugs here and store them, then carry them down to the box canyon as they're needed."

"Those men Garrant and Worley were lying," Linda went on excitedly. "They're not in the mineral water business. All those jugs and crates and the truck we saw in their yard were a cover-up. Horse stealing is their game!"

"I think you're right," Bob told her. "But we'll have to prove it."

"To think we were talking to them! I wish I'd known then!" Linda said vehemently. "And that awful Luke Poe probably *is* in league with them. Come on," she pleaded. "Let's keep going. We might find Chica d'Oro outside!"

"Not much farther," Bob warned. "We've been lucky up to now. Even the horses' whinnying didn't bring anyone."

Just then his flashlight picked up another tunnel which ran from the cave wall opposite the pool. Linda wanted to investigate it but Bob shook his head.

"We must notify the authorities. We can't wait any longer," he insisted.

"I suppose you're right," Linda said slowly. "But I'd certainly like to know what's in that other tunnel. Please, Bob, just shine your flashlight into it. Then I'll go."

The tunnel was narrower than the other one. It curved sharply a short distance ahead, so nothing was visible beyond the bend. There were small, sharp jutting rocks on the side, and as Bob threw the beam of light on them, Linda gave an exclamation. Quickly she picked a tuft of long white horse hairs from one rock.

"From Chica's mane!" Linda whispered excitedly.

Bob held his light close to the hairs. "That pony sure is bent on being found."

"We're coming, baby!" Linda murmured tensely.

Excited by their discovery, the two went ahead. Presently they came to an enlarged place in the second tunnel, from which ran two branches.

"Now which way?" Linda asked.

"We'd better stick to the main one," Bob answered. "There was most likely a pocket of ore in this spot, and the other two tunnels were dug to bring it all out. They probably don't go deep."

A little farther along Linda whispered, "Listen!"

There were faint echoing noises as if some sort of machine were operating. Then they heard the indistinct sound of voices.

"Let's get out of here!" Bob urged.

They turned back, stepping as lightly as possible. It seemed a long time before they closed the iron door and emerged into the sunlight on the exterior of Fossil Mountain. Their horses stood with locked joints, contentedly dozing.

"Shall we go to the deputy sheriff at Ruddville?" Linda asked, as she and her brother swiftly untied their mounts.

"Too far," Bob replied, swinging into the saddle. "Let's ride to Charlie's."

They started downhill, following the path of the electric wire they had uncovered. "We can make our report to the jeep patrol which is searching for Chica d'Oro, or leave them a message," Bob said.

It was late afternoon when Linda and her brother arrived at the cabin. They had seen nothing of the patrol. Bob took the Indian's binoculars outside and scanned the area.

"The jeep isn't in sight," he told Linda, as he came back into the cabin.

"Maybe they've quit and gone into Ruddville for the night," she suggested.

"Possibly," replied Bob. "But Charlie said the deputy would check here in the morning. We'll leave him a note and a map." Then Bob asked suddenly, "Are you as hungry as I am?"

"Is that a hint?" his sister said with a grimace.

Linda cut slices from the ham that they had brought from home and put them in the oven with canned yams, heated a can of green beans, and opened another containing pears.

When they had finished eating, Linda brought out a large piece of wrapping paper, and with Bob's help started to draw a map on it. They sketched the approach to the narrow mountain trail and showed the line of light bulbs running along the side of it to the tunnel entrance.

Then Linda put in the mineral-water cave of demijohns, and the smaller passageway where they had heard voices. Bob made a drawing of the side of the mountain, showing the water-bottling building with the cave in the slope above it.

"This is pretty terrific," Linda said. "Anyone could follow it."

"Let's leave it tacked on the door so the deputy sheriff will be sure to see it," said Bob.

"Do you mind riding out at dawn?" Linda requested. "I want to try again to find Chica."

Bob nodded. "You bet."

The next morning was a pleasant one, sunny but crisp. Below the cabin, the mountainside was abloom with small, white, starflowers, and the brush was full of tiny, twittering sandpipers.

The Craigs reached Fossil Mountain. As their horses climbed up the steep trail toward the tunnel, Linda took a deep breath. "It's so beautiful and peaceful out here, it's hard to believe wicked people are using the old mountain for mean and dishonest business."

Suddenly Bob raised a quieting hand and pulled his horse off the trail into the brush. Linda followed closely with a questioning glance.

"Someone's up there," Bob murmured. "I saw him move."

They could not distinguish the tunnel entrance, but they knew exactly where it was. As Linda and Bob held their eyes on the location, the figure of a man came into view again.

"They've posted a guard," Linda said in a low voice. She strained to see better. "Maybe he has Chica with him."

Bob pointed to a rock formation among the trees just ahead. "We'll leave our horses behind it and go on foot. Bronco said not to tangle with the men, and I can't let you take any unnecessary chances."

Linda threw her brother a grateful smile. "Okay. We'll see what to do when we get up to the tunnel."

Sister and brother climbed stealthily to the entrance, keeping well to one side of the electric cord trail. When they finally crouched in the brush close to the opening, Linda and Bob saw that the man was Worley.

"I wish we were in that tunnel instead of out here," Linda whispered. "Then we could keep going through to hunt for Chica d'Oro."

"That gives me an idea," Bob said. He picked up a big rock and hurled it toward the path. The rock went crashing down the mountainside through the brush. Worley immediately ran toward the trail to investigate the noise.

"Come on!" Bob whispered, grabbing Linda's hand, and they sprinted quickly into the tunnel. "Don't use your flashlight," he said in an undertone. "Then if Worley comes in here, he won't be able to spot us. We'll have a head start."

Linda followed the suggestion and they managed to get to the iron-hinged door, which now stood open, before turning on their lights. They went ahead quickly.

When they entered the cave back of the bottling company, Linda and Bob stopped and listened. Again, down the tunnel which branched from it, they heard the faint noise of a machine.

"I believe it's a generator," said Bob, "but I'd like to get a glimpse of it."

"And I want to see if my palomino is there," Linda added.

They inched along past the two smaller branches, and then noticed radiance from beyond the curve.

Peering cautiously around it, they saw that the tunnel ended in a large rock chamber. In one corner of the brilliantly lit spot stood a squat power generator. It was making the noise Bob and Linda had heard. Strung across the ceiling and on the walls were rows of high wattage electric light bulbs.

Near one side, Garrant was seated at a table, writing. Luke Poe slouched against the wall behind him and watched. He was as unshaven and poorly dressed as the day he had tried to steal Chica d'Oro.

Garrant said with a self-satisfied smile, "We've got just about enough buyers' names now to make a nice haul."

"How many more horses do we have to sell?" asked Poe. "I'd like to get out of this squirrel hole."

"You just sit tight in your skin," snarled Garrant. He tapped his head. "I'm the brains. I say what we do."

"Sure, you're the big brain," Poe replied, "but I got you the water-bottling works to hide behind, didn't I?"

Garrant gave him a condescending look of appreciation. "Of course, it takes a team to work a deal like this."

With a rough guffaw, Poe slapped his knee. "I'm laughing at old Worley out there, scraping dirt off and on those colored lights."

Garrant grinned with amusement. "My master stroke. Since there's nothing showing above ground unless we want it to, nobody's going to catch on to our little scheme. Who'd guess it's to guide the horses to this spot at night after we've stolen 'em?"

"And whose idea was it to dye the horses?" Poe asked. "Mine!"

He pointed with pride to the opposite side of the chamber. There lay a spray gun, next to several large black-stained paint containers.

Linda and Bob nudged one another. *This* was the place for dyeing the horses!

Garrant scowled. "Yeah, but you could have brought the law down on us when you went after the yellow horse."

"That animal was worth money," the slouching man retorted. "If I could pick it up for nothing, who's to say I'm not the smartest one?"

"You're not," Garrant snapped, "because you fumbled it. When I took you and Worley to steal the horse we not only succeeded, but made the theft serve a purpose."

"Sure, you had Gus and Ed take the pickup down to the ranch with the dog and the ransom note the same night. That really got the law after us," Poe replied sullenly.

"The law is out in the valley picking daisies," said the leader smugly, checking off the last item on a record sheet.

"And why did you and Worley steal that chestnut Morgan in daylight when he had a rider on him?" Poe needled. "Was that the smart, quiet way to do the job?"

"We have the horse. That's all that matters," Garrant answered shortly.

"We also have the girl and her brother on our trail," Poe retorted.

"We're rid of the Craigs," Garrant said icily. "They're so busy looking for the palomino they have no time to look for us."

Under the ringleader's cold eyes, Poe shifted. "Worley better not catnap guarding that entrance," he muttered.

Linda and Bob glanced at each other with a quick grin.

"How's the water supply?" Garrant asked. "Many full jugs out there?"

"Couldn't say right off," the henchman replied. "A lot, I guess."

"Guessing isn't good enough," Garrant said harshly. He picked up a flashlight from the table and tossed it to the other man. "We'll go count. And don't turn on any lights."

With Garrant close behind, Poe started to shamble across the room toward the Craigs.

"We must get away from here," whispered Bob.

"Into a branch tunnel!" Linda replied quickly.

They skimmed to the junction on tiptoe, and hurried into the black opening on the left. Not daring to use flashlights, they felt their way along until they saw a dim light which came from beyond a curve.

Stepping gingerly, they investigated. Suddenly Linda almost cried aloud.

Before them, in a small lantern-lighted dugout, they saw Chica d'Oro tethered to an iron stake driven into the dirt floor!

The palomino recognized Linda and Bob at the same time and gave a joyous whinny. Linda rushed up to her and held one hand over the horse's nose, saying, "Quiet, baby! Quiet!" Chica d'Oro kept up a soft nickering as she nuzzled her owner's head and neck.

Suddenly Linda and Bob heard running footsteps in the tunnel. As the Craigs whirled, Poe and Garrant burst in upon them.

"I told you a horse doesn't talk to itself," Garrant exclaimed to his henchman. A look of amazement changed to a cold, calculating smile directed at the girl and boy. "So your palomino led you into a trap!" he gloated. "Fine! Fine! This time you don't get away from us!"

For a moment, Bob and Linda faced their two captors in shocked silence. Chica d'Oro, however, snorted and pawed at the hard dirt floor with a forefoot. From the instant Luke Poe and Garrant had entered the dugout, she had quivered nervously, tossed her head, and switched her tail.

Linda remembered well the day Poe had attempted to steal the palomino, when the horse had reared and struck at him with her hooves. Now the filly was well tethered down so that she could not repeat the onslaught, but as Garrant took a step toward her, she whinnied shrilly.

Linda's dark eyes snapped. "The pony doesn't like you," she told the ringleader, and Bob added, "You must have tried to hurt her."

"She remembers me all right," the man replied grimly. "She'll follow my commands or I'll beat her."

Linda drew in her breath, and wrapped her arm tightly around the palomino's neck.

"She'd kill you if you ever struck her," the girl said hotly.

Disdain twisted the man's face, but in his eyes was a flicker of fear like Linda had seen the day Chica d'Oro had fought Poe off.

Both men are afraid of her, Linda thought; they know that if she ever gets free she'll strike at them.

With a chill, she remembered that the men had carried guns when they stole the palomino from Bronco. If they could not control the animal, they might shoot her! Linda's concern for the pony was so great she had no thought of her own predicament.

"Hand over those flashlights!" Garrant ordered.

As Linda and Bob obeyed, the sound of hurrying, stumbling footsteps along the main tunnel drew their attention. The two men listened sharply for a moment.

"Worley," Garrant said.

"We're in here," Poe called out.

Worley burst in upon them with a worried look. Then he stopped short and stared bug-eyed at the sister and brother. "How'd they get in here?"

"That's what you'd better tell us if you want to save your skin," said Garrant icily.

"I found a couple of horses out there," explained Worley. "Didn't know whose they were. They're different from the ones these two rode here from the ranch. Thought some mounted deputies might have come this close. I rushed in to warn you."

Garrant turned to Bob and demanded, "How did you get in here?"

The boy replied evenly, "The same way those daisy-picking deputies are going to!"

"You know too much," growled Poe.

"We know that Garrant is the leader of you horse thieves," said Linda.

"How'd you find that out?" asked Poe, surprised.

"You just told me," she said triumphantly. Garrant scowled at Poe angrily for being so gullible.

"How can you prove it?" Worley asked Linda.

"Lots of ways," she answered. "Strings of colored electric lights, cans of dye, a spray gun, and a box canyon—"

The men's mouths dropped open in astonishment. Finally Poe collected his wits and asked, "What are we going to do about these two snoopers?"

"They're evidently on to our whole scheme," Worley declared.

Garrant swaggered a bit and said harshly, "It doesn't matter what they know because they are never going to get out of here alive!"

Linda's heart sank. Bob, however, stood steadfast, his crackling brown eyes straight on the ringleader.

"You're too late," he said. "Before we came out

this morning, we left a note for the sheriff's deputies, who are due any minute. We also left a map showing exactly how to get here, the location of the cave with the full water jugs, and the generator and dyeing equipment in the rock chamber."

"I'm getting out of here," blurted Poe.

"Don't move!" barked Garrant, drawing a revolver from a shoulder holster. "These two kids are lying. That was just a try to save their skins."

"We're not lying," Linda retorted. "We've been here before."

"You hear that?" Worley exclaimed.

"It doesn't matter," snapped the ringleader. "We'll get those horses out of the box canyon and take them down through the woods. Nobody will see us. Let the sheriff's men have this place."

"Have you gone loco?" Poe spoke up. "We'd better let those horses in the canyon loose and scram as fast as we can! We don't want to be nabbed with stolen goods."

"I'm not going to get caught," Garrant declared. "The deputies won't make it here this early. First I want to clean out all our records, starting with my desk. Poe, you go down to the canyon and bring three horses up to the mine entrance. I'll meet you there and load the papers into the saddlebags. We'll ride those three mounts and lead the others. Worley, you stay here and guard these two prisoners of ours." He turned sharply and went into the tunnel, followed by Poe.

His forehead beaded with sweat, Worley pulled an empty box up to the entrance and sat down. "How come you two didn't fall into that quicksand?" he asked in a surly tone.

"We did," said Linda, hugging Chica d'Oro, whose nervousness had ebbed as soon as Poe and Garrant had left. "But we got out."

"You're too smart for your own good," growled Worley.

"Why did you do all that damage at Rancho del Sol?" Bob asked. "What did you expect to accomplish?"

"It was to get you two and your grandfather back to the place and keep you there taking care of it," replied Worley.

"Why didn't you pick up the five hundred dollars we left in the mailbox at the hamburger stand?" Linda questioned him.

"Aw, I wanted to," Worley admitted, "but Garrant found out there were sheriff's deputies staked out all over the place. We weren't going to be taken in for chicken feed when we can make hundreds of thousands of dollars." He looked at Linda and Bob curiously. "How come you didn't give up looking for that yaller horse when it wasn't left at the Silver Sage Ranch?"

"Because I love her," Linda replied. "I would never give up looking for her."

"She's just a horse," mumbled Worley. "You could have got yourself another one."

"There isn't another Chica d'Oro and you know it," Linda said angrily. "Otherwise you wouldn't have stolen her."

"She's been more trouble 'n she's worth," Worley grumbled. "Poe saw her first, one day when he was passing the Injun's cabin, and he made up his mind to have her. After that, he spied on the place for days, looking for a safe chance to take the horse. He was up at Charlie's that Sunday when you arrived. That's when he heard you say you'd come to investigate the lights and look for the Morgan horse."

"So you decided to get rid of us."

Worley nodded. "Garrant decided the best way was to see that you had an accident. So Poe and me dug the burro trap. If that didn't work, we figured to try something else."

"Was that you," Bob asked, "who tried to run us off the road in a car?"

"Sure. I waited on a side road and Poe signaled me from the hilltop when you were coming." Worley laughed. "Guess that shook you up, didn't it?"

"You were pretty careless to leave your trademark in the dust there and in Chica's corral," Bob said.

"What do you mean?" the man asked resentfully.

"The star mark on your boot sole," Bob replied, "or was it your companion's?"

Quickly the man looked at the bottom of his boot. "I didn't know it was there," he said gloomily.

"What's in that other branch tunnel?" asked Linda.

Worley looked at her sharply and set his lips. "I'm through talking," he declared.

"He doesn't know, Linda," Bob said quickly. "Garrant apparently doesn't let the little fish in on everything."

"Not so fast," Worley protested. "Garrant isn't holding anything back on me. We're all in this together. Poe and I are just as smart as he is." Worley chewed his under lip, then blurted, "Sure, I know what's in the tunnel. No harm in telling you, because you're not getting out of here. There's a dugout like this one with bags of oats in it. Don't dare leave 'em where they can be seen."

"I'm tired of standing up," Linda said a few minutes later. She pulled one of the empty boxes up against the side of the dugout behind Chica d'Oro.

"Don't you try to pull anything, or you'll be sorry," Worley warned her.

"I just want to sit down," Linda answered with a sigh.

"That's a good idea," the man said. "You sit down and stay down. You too, young fellow."

Both Bob and Linda sat on the box. The girl leaned her head back wearily. Then her eyes widened. In the silence, she could faintly hear the sound of the electric generator.

She turned her head, and saw in the dimness that planks, not dirt and rock wall, were behind her.

Through a hair-wide crack between the boards, she now noticed brighter light.

Bob was sitting forward with his hands clasped in front of him, pondering their situation. Linda touched his arm and motioned for him to put his ear against the plank partition.

He said in an undertone, "This dugout is next to the rock chamber." Then he leaned forward again and called, "Say, Worley, why did they board up the end of the dugout?"

"The tunnel made a bad draft. We were afraid of fire." Then the man asked suspiciously, "Why do you care?"

"Just curious," Bob replied casually.

Linda murmured to her brother, "We must get out of here! But how?"

"I know," Bob replied softly. "We'll stand up and stretch. Leave the rest to me." He stood up.

"What are you trying to do?" barked Worley.

"Just stretching," Bob replied, and yawned. "I'm getting stiff."

"Me, too," said Linda, rising.

"Hey, look at that dirt!" Bob cried suddenly. "It's coming down fast! Look at it, Worley, over on the side. There's going to be a cave-in. We'll be buried!"

Worley, who had regarded the boy suspiciously at first, now stood up, asking quickly, "Where do you see it?"

"Over there," Bob exclaimed, pointing.

The man took his glance off the prisoners just long enough for Bob to snatch the box he and Linda had been using and hurl it at Worley. The box struck the man broadside, and he lurched back a step against the crate on which he had been seated. He lost his balance and went down with a crash which knocked him unconscious. Worley's gun had dropped from his hand. Linda kicked it hard and the weapon skidded behind a coil of rope.

Quickly Bob grabbed up a length of the rope. He tied Worley's hands behind him and bound his ankles securely together. Then he took out the man's kerchief and tied it tightly over his mouth so he could not call out when he regained consciousness.

Linda turned to Chica d'Oro. "We'll be back for you soon, baby."

"Come on!" Bob urged, grabbing his sister's hand.

They ran out of the branch tunnel into the main one, across the mineral springs cave, and into the longer tunnel that led to freedom. A moment later the Craigs could hear men pounding in pursuit.

As Linda and Bob sprinted faster down the dark passageway, Garrant suddenly loomed up in front of them. He made a grab for the sister and brother, catching each by an arm. His fingers were like steel vises. The men called Gus and Ed panted up and also seized them.

Garrant eyed his captives and laughed shortly. "Surprised you, eh? I just packed one load of papers on my horse. Lucky I had to return for another batch, wasn't it? Gus, Ed!" he barked. "Take these kids back!"

Followed by the ringleader, the two men hustled Linda and Bob to the small dugout. Worley was now straining at his bonds and making sounds in his throat. Garrant threw him a contemptuous look as he tossed a rope to Gus and one to Ed.

"Tie up these kids!" he ordered. "Make it fast!"

As the men obeyed, Chica d'Oro began to move around fretfully. Garrant cast her an uneasy look.

Just then Poe came in. "Hey, Worley," he said, "the horses are all . . ." He stopped short and stared at the trussed-up man.

"Get him free!" commanded Garrant.

Poe jumped to oblige.

"Hurry!" Garrant snapped nervously. "We've got to move!"

Linda and Bob, bound hand and foot, were pushed down on the empty box where they had been before.

"You're not leaving the palomino, are you?" Poe asked Garrant.

"I am," the leader snapped. "There's no time to bother with it. Follow me. I have two more jobs before we go." The three men hurried off.

"Sorry, Linda," Bob whispered. "I thought Garrant was still in the office and we could manage Poe alone if we met him."

"Never mind," his sister replied. "Let's try to

hear what the men are saying. They're doing something in the next room!"

She and her brother pressed their ears against the board partition and heard Garrant's voice. "There are two jeeps full of sheriff's men heading across the valley in this direction. They'll be arriving before long. We'll set a stick of dynamite to cause an earth slide in here, and then run."

"Let's go out the cave entrance," Poe said anxiously. "It's closer."

"Of course," Garrant replied. "We'll go around the mountain and pick up our horses at the mine tunnel. Poe," he ordered sharply, "set this charge with a good long fuse so we can get away before the explosion goes off."

Linda and Bob were horrified. "If I could just get at my knife!" gasped Bob, struggling against his bonds.

The weapon was clasped to his belt in a leather case. Linda tried to work it loose with her tied hands. She could reach the case but could not move her fingers enough to pull open the latched-down flap of stiff leather.

"Oh, I can't do it!" she wailed softly. Then Linda exclaimed in a whisper, "I know something else to try."

She hopped to Chica d'Oro's head, saying, "Untie the rope, golden girl. Untie my hands." She pushed them up against the pony's nose.

The filly nuzzled them. Then, feeling the rope,

she started working at it with her nimble lips and strong biting teeth, as Linda had seen her do playfully.

"Hurry, baby, hurry!" Linda begged.

Suddenly they heard Poe say sharply, "All set, boss."

"Cut off the generator!" Garrant commanded. The humming noise ceased and the thread of light between the planks went out.

"Let's go!" said Garrant.

Linda and Bob heard the men running from the rock chamber and knew that the fuse had been lighted.

"It will burn fast!" Linda cried in panic. "Oh, Chica d'Oro, hurry, hurry!"

An Arabian Princess   15

Linda trembled as Chica d'Oro's teeth picked at the rope around her wrists.

"Is she getting it?" Bob asked unsteadily.

"I—I think so," his sister answered.

Then it seemed to Linda as if the rope had loosened a little. Next Chica got a firm hold of a strand with her teeth and shook her head. The girl thought her wrist was cut in two, but in the next instant the rope fell away and her hands were free.

"Thanks, baby," she gasped and hop-jumped over to Bob, quickly drew out his knife, and cut his hands and feet free. He grabbed the lantern and bolted from the dugout.

Linda freed her own ankles and severed her pony's tether. "I'll be right back for you," she promised the filly and groped her way after Bob.

She hurried down the branch tunnel and up the other passage into the big chamber. She could hear the fuse sputtering and on the rock wall across from her was a flickering glow. In the eerie light, Bob knelt beside the generator.

"It's here!" he called. "Bring the knife!" Linda handed him the blade and he swiftly sliced off the burning tip.

The girl heaved a long shuddering sigh. Bob leaned back against the wall, rubbed his hand over his forehead, and croaked, "Whew!"

After a moment, he fumbled for the generator and the room was flooded with light. Less than two feet away lay sticks of dynamite. Just then Bob and Linda heard hoofbeats in the tunnel. Chica d'Oro had followed Linda in spite of the darkness.

"In here, Chica," she called, "in here!"

At that instant, Garrant dashed in from the tunnel. He pushed Bob and Linda aside, grabbed for the fuse, and gave an exclamation of relief at seeing it out.

Then he turned on them with a wrathful face. "You've got the lawmen swarming around this mountain," he said bitterly. "They nabbed the others, but not me. I'm getting away! First, though, I'm going to even the score with you."

As he took a threatening step toward the Craigs, there was a shrill whinny behind them. The palomino had entered the rock chamber! In her intelligent brown eyes flashed the hatred she held for him. Now she reared and struck the man a stunning blow. He fell to the ground.

Swiftly Linda and Bob knelt beside the motion-

The palomino reared and struck Garrant.

less Garrant. "He's unconscious," Bob said.

Linda hugged Chica d'Oro and murmured praises to her. Suddenly she and Bob heard men's voices and hurried footsteps in the main tunnel. A few moments later Charlie Tonka and a couple of deputies came into the rock chamber.

Charlie spotted Garrant on the floor and darted to the Craigs. "You all right?" he asked.

"Yes," Bob replied, "but it was close." He held up the fuse and pointed to the dynamite.

"Chica saved our lives," Linda declared and told what the horse had done. The deputies looked at the filly with wonder.

"Good young'un," Charlie said, patting her.

Just then Deputy Wilkins strode in from the tunnel. "Who's that?" he asked, seeing the unconscious man.

"His name's Garrant," Bob said. "He's the mastermind of this ring of horse thieves."

Wilkins spotted a jug of the mineral water standing in a corner. He picked it up and hurled the full contents into Garrant's face. The man rolled his head back and forth, groaning.

"On your feet," Wilkins commanded.

Under the deputy's firm urging, the captive groggily stood up. His smoldering eyes fell on Linda and Chica d'Oro. "You!" he snarled.

Wilkins snapped bracelets on his wrists and gave the prisoner a push. To the others he added, "You all come along, too. We want to get some matters cleared up for the record."

He marshaled Garrant into the tunnel, and a few minutes later the Craigs and Charlie followed with Chica d'Oro at their heels.

"Good thing you left the note and map," the Indian said. "Two deputies checked at my place the same time I got there. They used a two-way radio to call Deputy Wilkins in Ruddville. He brought his men here through the cave mouth. He told us to go around to the other side of the mountain and come in through the mine entrance. We sped in the jeep to the bottom of the hill, climbed the trail, and hurried fast into the tunnel."

"Garrant saw the deputies coming down the valley. That's what started the fireworks," Bob said.

Charlie cocked his head with a sly smile. "Señor Bronco will be very proud when he hears what you did."

Linda smiled at Charlie. "Now you can go back to riding your pipeline without strange lights and horse thieves to worry you."

The Indian's face turned glum. "It will be dull."

"But now that you've given the horses to your grandsons," Linda continued enthusiastically, "you can have the boys with you sometimes."

A quick, happy smile wreathed the Indian's face. "That will be okay. They are fine boys. I will show them how to be good riders."

When the group came out of the cave mouth, they saw below three jeeps and several sheriff's deputies outside the water-bottling building.

Linda let Chica d'Oro's tie rope loose so that the horse could get down the steep slope in her own way. She chose to slide on her rump. Linda followed on the narrow foot path, slipping on her boot soles most of the way, as did the others.

They went in the wide back door of the building. Poe and Worley sat glumly on the daybed, manacled together. Next to them were Gus and Ed. Garrant sat opposite in a straight chair. The prisoners were advised of their legal rights but they agreed they did not want counsel.

Deputy Wilkins, standing before the men, said, "You might as well talk. We know that you, Garrant, are a wanted horse thief in many states. We have your picture on file."

The three men sat in stubborn silence as Wilkins went on, "Now then, the dam was government property. Which of you blew that up?"

"I didn't have anything to do with it," Poe blurted out.

"I didn't blow it," growled Garrant, as Gus and Ed shook their heads.

"You?" the officer asked Worley.

The tall henchman was quaking. "He gave the orders." He thrust out a finger toward Garrant.

"I gave no orders to blow up the dam," snarled the ringleader.

"You said to get rid of the snoopers," Worley babbled.

"Talk!" the officer ordered. "It will go easier for you."

A young deputy seated at the table was taking rapid notes in shorthand.

Worley shifted uneasily. "After we found out these kids were on our trail, Poe and me took turns spying on the Injun's cabin. One night I sneaked up to an open window and heard the Craigs talk about camping on the mountain. Next day I hid behind a big granite rock and saw them riding past."

"And followed us!" Bob exclaimed.

Worley nodded. "With my binoculars I saw them bedded down on a slope a mile below the dam. So I blew it. They ought to have been drowned." He turned, sour-faced, to Linda and Bob. "How come you got away?"

"Chica d'Oro awakened us," Linda replied. "She saved our lives."

"That horse again!" Garrant grumbled.

Linda had let the filly loose to nibble about in back of the building. At the moment, Chica d'Oro stood at the door, looking in curiously. Linda blew her a kiss. The pony nickered and turned back to her foraging. As she did, a tall deputy came in the front door, carrying a pile of papers.

"What did you find?" asked Wilkins.

"Garrant and his gang have been living in the Mineral Springs Lodge," the man replied. "They had a file there of all their operations, with the names of the owners and the stolen horses listed."

Garrant groaned. "I was going to clean out that file, but didn't have time."

"Was Prince Brownlee one of the horses?" Linda asked quickly.

"Yes," the tall deputy replied.

"I knew it! I've seen him. He's been dyed!"

"We've seen a number of purebreds," Bob added. "They're hidden not far from here."

"What!" Wilkins exclaimed.

Linda told about the box canyon with its overhanging rocks, under which the horses were prisoners.

Wilkins turned to Garrant. "You're going with us to identify those horses."

The thief tried to protest but was prodded along. Linda led the way back through the tunnel with Bob, Charlie, Wilkins, and Garrant following. The excited girl ran most of the way down the hill, through the winding crevice, and into the box canyon.

At once, the captive horses began to caper, rear, and snort. Linda thought, I'll bet they recognize this horrid horse thief!

She, Bob, and Charlie tried to soothe the panicking animals. It was not until Linda walked up to the Morgan, once golden chestnut, now dark bay, and said, "Prince Brownlee, boy, I'm going to take you home," that he quieted down. His example seemed to calm the other animals.

"The capture of these thieves was a fine piece of work on your part, young lady, and yours, too, Bob," said Wilkins. "And now, Garrant, who are the owners of the other horses?"

The thief tried to bargain. "Will you guarantee me a light sentence if I tell you?"

"If you don't tell, we'll find out anyway," was the curt reply.

Garrant hesitated a moment. "All right," he said grudgingly. He pointed to the nearest horse. "From Hilltop X ranch in Nevada. The next is from the Bide-a-wee Stables—"

As he droned on, Linda went over to Prince Brownlee and untied him. She caressed his neck and laid her cheek against it. Finally she said, "Bob, help me up, will you? I'm going to ride him to meet Chica d'Oro."

Bob offered his hand as a stirrup and Linda swung onto Prince Brownlee's back. The horse did not move until the rider nudged him with her knees. She guided him up the hill, across the top of the tunnel, and down to the front of the bottling company plant.

The others had cut through the tunnel and were waiting for her. She noted that all the prisoners were manacled and ready to be driven off to jail. Linda was told that the sheriff's men would take

181

care of the other stolen horses until their owners could come for them.

"Charlie," Bob added, "will pick up his horses near the mine entrance where we left them. He'll ride one and lead the other back to the cabin. You and I can take Chica and Prince Brownlee. Are you ready to go?"

Linda dismounted. "After all this excitement, I'm starving. Is there any food here?"

"Plenty," said Wilkins. "Help yourselves. The gang won't be needing it!"

"Thank you," said Linda, and found cans of biscuits, meat, and juices in the kitchen of the former hotel.

After she and Bob had eaten a snack, they rode back to the cabin. Early the next morning the Craigs packed their gear on the horses and said good-bye to their Indian friend.

"We'll come back to see you, Charlie," the girl called.

With Linda mounted on Chica d'Oro and Bob on Prince Brownlee, they made the long ride back to Rancho del Sol. Bronco strode out to greet them with Doña Mallory right behind him. He hugged Linda and exclaimed, "By jump, you found your horse and Mr. Brownlee's too, and solved the mystery of the strange lights!" Then he shook hands proudly with Bob while their grandmother beamed on the two and kissed them.

"Deputy Randall called," said Bronco, "and gave

us the news. Wilkins had phoned him. Now Mr. Brownlee is waiting to hear from us. I'll give him a ring at once."

The best stall, which opened out on a large fenced paddock of permanent pasture, awaited Chica d'Oro. It had been heaped with clean bedding straw, and Linda made the filly comfortable there before she hurried into the house.

A short time later the very grateful Mr. Brownlee arrived. He was dismayed to see that his prizewinning horse had been dyed, but remarked that the artificial color would gradually disappear.

Everyone gathered in the living room to hear Linda and Bob tell their story, including Cactus Mac and Luisa, who stood in the doorway with a mixing spoon in her hand.

When the account was finished and all questions answered, Linda added, "But now I have a greater mystery to solve. I just must find out Chica d'Oro's lineage so that I can have her registered."

Bronco rubbed his chin. "That might prove tough, but go to it."

The next day, as soon as the family was up, representatives from the press, a newsmagazine, and photographers arrived. Once again Linda and Bob recounted their adventures and the part the golden horse had played.

There were no more visitors until the middle of the afternoon. Linda was with her pony in the paddock when she saw a station wagon drive up beside the corral. In it was Mrs. Larsen from the Silver Sage Ranch. The tall, handsome woman strode over to Linda, smiling.

"I heard on the radio about your adventure," she said, "and thought I'd come to invite you to enter Chica d'Oro in the Parade Class for the Perpetual Trophy in our next horse show."

"Oh, I'd love to," Linda answered excitedly. "Tell me more about it."

"The trophy has to be won three times in succession in order to keep it," Mrs. Larsen explained. She smiled. "It's a handsome, engraved silver tray."

"Of course I'll enter Chica d'Oro," Linda replied. "I'd love to!"

"Fine." Mrs. Larsen took a small notebook and pencil from her purse. "Now if you'll just give me the names of her dam and sire for publicity, I'll sign you up."

A shadow fell over Linda's face. "I don't have the names yet. But I'm going to get them."

"Oh, dear," Mrs. Larsen said. "I presumed that the horse's registration had been taken care of. I'm sorry, Linda, but the class is open only to registered parade horses." Then she said pleasantly, "Later some time, when you have had it done, let us see you at the Silver Sage show."

"Oh, you will," the girl assured her.

After the woman left, Linda stroked Chica

d'Oro's neck with a tender hand and told her, "I'll get you registered, baby, don't you worry!"

Linda obtained a copy of the registration book from the state Arabian association, and started the long check-out. She began writing to each owner of Arabian horses, asking if he had lost a mare at the time Charlie had found Chica's mother. Answers came in, but they were always no.

Linda thought of almost nothing else until diverted one day by a visit from Mr. Brownlee. She had not seen him ride in, but was called to the living room to meet him.

"I've brought a present for that golden horse, who I think deserves high honors," he told her and led the way to the back patio.

There Cactus Mac held Chica d'Oro, who was standing like a golden statue, adorned with a gleaming silver saddle, martingale, and bridle. At sight of Linda, the filly whinnied joyously, tossed her mane proudly, and tapped the brick floor with a dainty forefoot.

Linda was almost breathless with excitement, but managed to exclaim, "How absolutely beautiful! Oh, Mr. Brownlee, how can I ever thank you enough?"

The caller was smiling but held up his hand. "I have something for Bob, too. Guess you can use this at college."

The gift proved to be an electronic traveling clock

that would keep perfect time under all conditions. Bob was as overwhelmed as his sister.

While all this was going on a car pulled into Rancho del Sol. A big square-jawed man stepped out and introduced himself as Tom Wister from Nevada. He came to the point at once.

"I've read the accounts of your remarkable palomino with great interest. I believe she is the colt of an Arabian mare in foal that was stolen from me a little less than three years ago."

Linda listened breathlessly.

"It's possible," Mr. Wister continued, "that my horse was brought to California, then escaped her captor. She could open almost any latch. Ranashi was her name. She came of a fine Arabian blood line, and the sire of her foal was Golden Supreme, my famed saddlebred stallion. Now, if I can see the filly, I think I can verify my claim. Every colt of Golden Supreme's has a jag in the blaze between the eyes."

"She has! Oh, she has!" Linda said aloud, but thought in panic, He'll claim Chica d'Oro!

With a sinking heart, she led Mr. Wister and the others to the paddock. Linda watched the big man's eyes narrow when he saw the pony, and he nodded. There was silence as he stroked the filly's nose gently and nodded again.

"She's the one, I'm sure," he said. "Looks just like her dam except for the jag. But I wish we had positive proof."

Linda took a deep breath. "You'll sell her to me, won't you?" she asked.

"No," the man said quietly. "No." He looked from the horse to Linda. "She's yours. You've earned her."

Suddenly Bob excused himself and raced off. He was gone only a few minutes. When he returned, his face wore an expansive smile. "I have proof!" he exclaimed. "Chica d'Oro's dam *was* Ranashi. I asked the sheriff to look in Garrant's records of stolen horses. The name was there. Garrant and his gang operated for a while in Nevada. They brought Ranashi down here, but she escaped from them. When they found the mare, she was badly hurt, so they abandoned her."

"And that's when Indian Charlie found Ranashi!" Linda exclaimed.

The whole group was exultant and made a great fuss over Chica d'Oro. Mr. Wister pulled a registration blank and the address of the palomino registry from his pocket and handed them to Linda. "I like to keep track of my stock," he told her. "If you would just send me a picture of this horse some-time, I'd appreciate it."

"I will," Linda promised with tears of happiness in her eyes. "Thank you. Thank you."

As Bronco and Grandmother Mallory escorted the visitors back to the house, Linda waved the registration blank before Chica d'Oro's eyes.

"We've won!" she sang out. "We've won!"

LINDA CRAIG

The Clue on the Desert Trail

ANN SHELDON

Illustrated by St Ward

Linda had won the magnificent trophy . . .

Glossary

Arroyo   Stream.

Bluff   A steep bank formed by river erosion.

Buckskin   A horse that is greyish-yellow in colour – literally, the colour of a "buck" or male deer.

Burlap   A coarse-textured cloth made of jute, flax or hemp.

Burro   Donkey.

Butte   An isolated, steep-sided, flat-topped hill.

Chaparral   A clump or thicket of thorny trees and shrubs

Charros   A Mexican snack.

Cholla   A spiny cactus grown in the south-western United States.

Chuck wagon   A wagon to carry provisions and cooking utensils.

Cinch   Girth.

Corral   A pen for cattle or horses.

Cutting horse   A horse trained to "cut" cattle out from a herd.

Diamond hitch   A type of knot.

Enchilada   A Mexican dish consisting of a fried *tortilla* (pancake) filled with meat and served with chilli sauce.

Freshet   Stream.

Frijol   A type of bean (similar to a kidney bean) cultivated in Spanish American countries.

Gunny   A coarse fabric made from jute.

Hacienda   The main house on a ranch.

Joshua tree   A tree-like desert plant found in the south-western United States. It has sword-like leaves and greenish-white flowers.

Lariat   Lasso.

Leery   Wary.

Mesquite   A spiny tree with sugary, bean-like pods which can be eaten by cattle.

Mojave Desert   A desert in Southern California, south of the Sierra Nevada.

Parade Class An exhibition in which high-stepping horses and fancily-dressed riders lead a parade.

Peon Farm labourer.

Pepper tree A tropical or sub-tropical evergreen tree with yellow-white flowers and ornamental red fruit.

Petroglyph A drawing or carving on rock — often prehistoric in origin.

Pumpernickel Coarse, dark bread made of unsifted rye.

Quarter horse A small, powerful breed of horse, originally bred for sprinting in quarter-mile races in Virginia in the eighteenth century.

Railroad tie Railway sleeper.

Rockhound Someone who searches for and collects precious and semi-precious stones which can be cut, polished and set as gems.

Saddlehorn The pommel of a western saddle round which a lasso can be looped.

Sashay To move around.

Scallion A type of onion — similar to a spring onion.

Spot A dollar bill. A "five spot" would therefore equal five dollars.

Stake Class A competition with high entry fees and large cash prizes. Literally, a competition with high stakes.

Tamales A Mexican dish of crushed Indian corn mixed with finely chopped meat and oil and highly seasoned with red pepper.

Tostadas A Mexican toasted snack.

Toxicity The degree of strength of a poison.

Trail Class A "handy horse" competition in which horse and rider have to negotiate various obstacles at speed.

Wranglers Show A show with calf-roping and steer-wrestling.

"Trail Class Ride In!" 1

"What a romantic old marketplace!" exclaimed Linda Craig, her brown eyes sparkling with excitement.

The pretty, dark-haired girl and her friend, honey blond Kathy Hamilton, threaded their way through crowded Olvera Street, the oldest in Los Angeles. A jumble of voices mingled with guitar music, while the aroma of chili spiced the morning air.

The two slim sixteen-year-old girls, on a visit from ranch country, had been looking over the colorful shops of Mexican wares. Now they paused at a pottery booth displaying rows of small clay animals.

"Look!" Linda cried out in delight. "Horses!"

"Leave it to you to find horses," Kathy said with an affectionate grin. Her eyes roamed over the street while her companion chose one of the ceramic pieces to buy.

As Linda paid the man, Kathy suddenly clutched her friend's arm. "We're being watched," she said softly.

Linda smiled. "Should we be flattered?"

"Not by him," Kathy murmured. "I don't like his looks."

Linda whirled and gazed straight at the staring man. He was small and swarthy-faced, and had hard, calculating eyes.

"He—he may be a pickpocket," Kathy whispered, as the stranger, knowing the girls had spotted him, ducked his head and sidled away.

"We'd better grip our shoulder bags," Linda advised. "And let's have lunch before we meet Bob and Larry at the horse show."

As the two girls walked up the street, they were a striking pair. Kathy, whose skin was tanned to a soft apricot glow, wore a yellow knit suit. Linda, in a pink skirt and sweater which set off her glossy black hair and creamy-textured skin, had inherited her beauty from her Spanish forebears.

Her great-great-grandmother Rosalinda had come to the New World as a bride from Spain. Linda, like her mother and grandmother, had been named for this first Rosalinda.

The girls paused a moment to breathe in the flower and spice scents from the candlemakers' shop and again to listen to the lively strains of a Mexican orchestra strumming in the *La Golondrina* restaurant.

Linda and Kathy came to an open-air Spanish snack bar and seated themselves at a small table. They ordered enchiladas and hot chocolate. While they waited, Linda took the statuette from its bag and placed it on the table.

"I wanted this one because it looks just like Chica d'Oro," she said, referring to her own beautiful palomino.

There was a deep bond of love and understanding between the filly and Linda, who spent a great deal of time on horseback. Kathy had a pinto named Patches and liked to ride with her friends, but there her interest in horses ended.

The girls had come into Los Angeles the day before for the big Wranglers' Show at the Western Stockyards. Linda was entered in the Trail Class event.

"Speaking of Chica," Kathy said, "what time is your performance?"

"I have to be in costume and ready to ride at one o'clock," Linda answered.

Kathy glanced at her watch. "You have just one hour." Her gray eyes lighted warmly. "I just know you and Chica will win the trophy."

"Cross your fingers," Linda cautioned. Then her excitement bubbled through. "Wouldn't that be wonderful, though? We'd better hurry," she added. "The boys will worry if we're late."

Linda's eighteen-year-old brother Bob and his friend Larry Spencer had driven to Los Angeles with the girls, who had spent the night at the home of Kathy's married sister, Helen Brewster. Since it was customary for men participants in the show to sleep at the stockyards, the boys had stabled their mounts and put down their bedrolls in the horse trailer they had brought.

Hoping to pick up some prize money, Bob had brought along Speedy, the best cutting horse on his grandparents' ranch, where he and Linda had lived since the death of their parents a few months before. The Craigs had been in various foreign countries where Major Craig, of the army, had been stationed. As a result, Linda and Bob spoke several languages fluently and felt very much at home among the Spanish-speaking people of California.

While Kathy finished her hot chocolate, Linda paid the bill. Then she picked up the clay horse to return it to the bag. Linda noticed that carved on the underside was an arrowhead with a short, curved shaft.

"What an odd mark!" she commented. "I wonder what it means?"

Kathy took the figurine. "Maybe it's just a trademark," she suggested, standing the clay horse on the table.

"Perhaps it is," Linda agreed.

Out of the corner of her eye she saw the small swarthy-faced man who had stared at the girls before. He suddenly darted to the table, snatched the statuette, and sped off through the throng of tourists.

"Stop!" cried Linda, jumping up to take after him. Kathy followed.

Dodging around people, Linda caught up with the man and grabbed his arm. The clay horse flew from his fingers and shattered on the tile pavement. Instantly the stranger jerked free and fled.

Linda stared in dismay at the fragments. Quickly she stooped and picked up the horse's head, which was still in one piece, and dropped it into her purse.

"Well, for goodness' sake!" Kathy exclaimed indignantly. "If that man wanted the horse so much, why didn't he buy it himself?"

"He probably didn't have as much as two nickels," Linda replied. "Come on, I'm going back to buy another horse statuette."

The girls returned to the ceramic booth and quickly looked over the rows of figurines. "There isn't another like it," said Linda. "The one I had was unglazed."

Kathy bobbed her head. "Yes, all the rest are shiny."

Linda was disappointed. Sighing, she said, "Well, we'd better go."

They caught a cab at the end of the street. As they rode along, Linda mused, "Since it was the only horse of its kind, maybe it was a special one."

"What do you mean?" Kathy asked.

"That strange little arrowhead on the bottom may have been a sign to somebody," Linda replied.

"Who?" Kathy asked. "And what does it mean?"

Linda smiled wryly. "Those are questions we'll never know the answers to, I guess."

In fifteen minutes, the girls reached the Western Stockyards with their long exhibition building, big arena and grandstand, extensive stock corrals, and rows of barns. The horses being used in the show were stabled closest to the arena, so Linda had their cab driver take them inside the grounds to Barn Number Two.

There the Rancho del Sol station wagon and trailer were parked in front of Speedy's and Chica's stalls. The palomino nickered joyously at sight of Linda, and the girl ran over to give the filly a hug.

When Linda had been visiting at Indian Charlie's in desert country several weeks before, she had seen the beautiful horse, which had been foaled there. It became hers and she had named the palomino Chica d'Oro, Spanish for Golden Girl. The filly's native intelligence and response to Linda's tireless training were already causing her to be an outstanding entry in the horse-show rings.

Speedy's stall was empty, so the girls knew that

the stake classes were being run off. Bob must be there now.

"Kathy, you'd better run into the arena and let your sister and Larry know we're here," Linda said.

"Sure you don't need any help?"

"No, thanks, I have everything organized, and I can manage better alone."

"Okay, then," Kathy replied. She kissed Linda on the cheek. "Good luck! We'll be rooting for you." She hurried off toward the grandstand section reserved for families and friends of the participants.

Linda threw her shoulder bag on the front seat of the car and locked the door. Then she unlocked the dressing room in the horse trailer and slipped on a long denim smock. Next she brought Chica over to the trailer and fastened her tie rope to the metal loop on the side, planning to brush her.

The palomino was so clean she needed little brushing. Linda put a carved-leather Western saddle and bridle on the pony, instead of the beautiful silver equipment she used for the Parade Class in a formal horse show or parade riding.

"I'll leave the saddle cinch loose, baby," she told the filly, "until I'm ready to mount. You'll be more comfortable."

As she turned away from Chica, Linda stopped short. A swarthy face was peering at her around a parked car. The next instant it was gone.

That man again! Linda thought. With a surge of

anger, she started after him, determined to find out what he was up to. But she was stopped by the blare of the loudspeaker. "Trail Class—stand!"

Quickly Linda turned back to the horse trailer and stepped into the dressing room. Bob had picked up her badge and left it there for her. As she pinned the seven on the back of her shirt, Linda was relieved that she did not have to work first. But she would have been happier if her number had been three. Chica was inclined to become nervous if she had to stand too long before showing.

Quickly Linda put on her sage green gabardine riding suit, white boots, and white-felt hat. She looked beautifully trim and attractive.

As the young rider stepped from the trailer, she saw Larry Spencer running toward her from the arena. He was a tall, sun-bronzed eighteen-year-old.

"Hold it!" he called out. "Stand right there by Chica's head." He stopped a short distance from her, took a small camera from his pocket, and snapped the girl's picture.

Suddenly Linda saw the mysterious, swarthy fellow behind him. "That man!" she exclaimed. "He's been following us." Bright flags of anger flamed on her cheekbones. "I'm going after him and find out why."

She turned, stepped into a stirrup, and swung up into the saddle. It slipped down over Chica's side.

Instantly Larry leaped, slid to the ground under Linda, and caught her as she fell. Chica crow-hopped, and whinnied frenziedly.

"Quiet, Chica!" Larry commanded. "Stand!"

The well-trained horse did so, but stood quivering and looking around at the young people with panic in her soft brown eyes. Larry untangled Linda's foot from the stirrup, and stood her up.

"Thank you," she said, and added with a shaky laugh, "I forgot to tighten Chica's saddle cinch."

"Lucky I was here," Larry replied, his brown eyes showing concern.

As he resaddled Chica, Linda gently ran her hand down the filly's neck. "It's all right now, baby," she said quietly. "Easy now. Easy." The palomino began to settle down.

In a few minutes, Larry had the saddle securely in place.

"I'm going after that man," Linda declared as she mounted.

But again she was interrupted. The loudspeaker blared, "Trail Class ride in!"

A Determined Thief 2

Linda looked in dismay at Larry.

"Forget that snooper for now," he told her. "If he comes back, we'll go after him."

From the arena came the music of a Western band and vocalists. Chica tossed her mane and sidled in excitement. Her young owner laughed and tingled with anticipation.

As Larry walked with Linda and Chica toward the arena, he saw Bob coming out on Speedy. Linda's brother rode with the easy grace of a lifelong ranch hand. Visitors to Rancho del Sol were often surprised to learn that when summer was over he switched to engineering studies at college.

"How did you do?" Linda asked eagerly, as he approached.

Bob pushed back his hat, revealing tousled, sandy hair, a hint of his paternal Scottish ancestry. "I picked up fourth-place money," he replied with a laugh. His clear brown eyes glinted humorously. "Speedy got a little rattled by the crowds." He gave the horse an affectionate pat on the neck. "He's just a country boy, you know."

"I watched you work," Larry said. "You had tough competition. I'd say you did all right. Congratulations."

"Thanks," Bob replied. "I'll take care of Speedy and get back in the grandstand to watch you, Linda."

"Wish me luck," his sister called, as he rode off.

"You'll do all right," said Larry, and left her to return to Kathy and her sister in the grandstand.

Linda lined up with the rest of the contestants at the end of the arena. It was an open class for sixteen years of age or over, and contained six women and five men, all experienced show participants.

Linda looked over the course and drew in her breath. They were the most difficult Trail Class obstacles that she had ever seen.

There were tires for the horses to walk through, railroad ties to step between, and a bridge to cross which had high, thickly leafed branches nailed to the sides. After that came a right angle of spaced rails to back through, a gate to go through, and a mailbox where the rider was to dismount while ground-hitching the horse. At the end lay a calfhide to walk over, and a trailer to lead into.

The horse of the first contestant, a middle-aged

man, refused to go over the calfhide for so long that he was ordered around it. The second horse grabbed a mouthful of leaves off the bridge, which was a fault. Another broke its ground hitch at the mailbox. Two others went around the course all right, but took a long time opening and closing the gate. Number Six clicked the railroad ties with its hooves.

Linda picked up a good tip from careful watching. The contestants, she thought, had brought their horses to the obstacles too quickly.

When her name and number were called, Linda collected Chica firmly, held her a moment before the tires, and then gave her an easy rein. The filly picked her dainty hooves up high, and went through the tires without touching them. Applause followed.

As obstacle after obstacle confronted Chica, she made her way faultlessly through the course. The spectators expressed their recognition of Linda's expert horsemanship by thunderous clapping.

The last four contestants, with the exception of one whose horse refused to walk into the strange trailer, managed to get around the course without faults, but Linda thought that they had not given very smooth performances.

Finally all the contestants were ordered to ride in and line up. Linda's heart thumped as she waited to hear the results. With a surge of pleasure, the girl from Rancho del Sol heard Number Seven called as the first-place trophy winner.

"Oh, bless you, Chica!" she murmured softly

The presentation was made by Hal Crawford, the rugged, handsome Western star of screen and television. He and Linda held the trophy while pictures were taken. Then Crawford shook the girl's hand and congratulated her. Linda was thrilled, but she managed to say, "Thank you," in a clear and steady voice.

The trophy was a magnificent, two-foot mahogany standard rising from a golden half dome and topped by a golden saddle horse. On the front of it was an engraved gold plate and on each corner of the base was a golden horse.

"It's beautiful!" she said excitedly.

When Linda reached the arena exit, she was met by Bob, Larry, Kathy, and Helen Brewster. She leaned over happily amid their congratulations and was kissed by everyone. She handed the big trophy to Bob to carry, and they all went back to the trailer.

There Linda dismounted and gazed at the trophy while stroking Chica's silken mane. "Thank you, baby," she told her, "for such a wonderful performance!"

The palomino nickered softly, her brown eyes gleaming.

Kathy asked with a laugh, "Linda, how could you keep from swooning off your horse when Hal Crawford shook your hand?"

"It was pretty thrilling, all right," Linda admitted with a grin.

As she turned to lead Chica to her stall, Linda glanced into the front seat of the station wagon. She gave a sharp cry. "My shoulder bag! It's been opened by someone."

The others hurried over to look at the contents of the bag, strewn across the car seat.

"This vent window was forced open!" Larry pointed. "Then someone reached in and unlocked the door."

"The clay horse head is gone!" Linda cried out. "The thief must be that man who stole the figurine in the first place!"

"What is this all about?" Bob asked.

"Yes, please tell us," Helen Brewster said, looking worried.

Quickly Linda and Kathy related their adventure in Olvera Street. Linda added that the same man had been lurking around the trailer before she went into the arena.

"That horse must contain something pretty important," Bob declared. "Maybe contraband."

"I'd better go back to the shop and find out everything I can about where the statuette came from," Linda said.

Bob agreed. "Meantime, I'll rub Chica down and feed both horses. But hurry," he cautioned her. "Remembered, we have to drive back to Rancho del Sol tonight, and be ready to leave there again at dawn."

"So early!" Helen Brewster exclaimed. "Where are you going?"

"Out on the Mojave Trail," Linda replied. "Grandfather has ordered twenty-five head of Black Angus cattle from the Scotsward Ranch across the desert from us."

Bob spoke up. "We thought it would be fun to bring them back over the old Indian trail instead of going to the expense of trucking them the long way around on the highway."

"It sounds like a real adventure!" Kathy's sister declared. "As soon as you're ready, Linda," she added, "I'll drive you girls to Olvera Street and then go on home. You don't mind taking a cab back here?"

"Of course not," Kathy assured her.

Linda hastily changed to her pink skirt and sweater. In a short time, she and Kathy were in the old marketplace. The crowds had thinned, so the man who ran the ceramics booth was not very busy.

Linda described the broken horse to him and said she would like to purchase another just like it. "Do you have one in stock?" she asked.

The proprietor slowly shook his head. "Why no,

miss. It's a funny thing about that horse. A fellow ordered it especially from the same pottery in Mexico where I buy my things. He was going to collect it here, but he never showed up." The man shrugged. "So I put it out for sale."

"Could you tell me the name of the man and where I could find him?" Linda asked.

"His name is Rico," the shop owner answered readily. "But where he lives, I don't know. He said he was a traveling salesman, and because he had no permanent address, wanted to have the horse sent here."

"If he comes in now, what will you tell him?" Kathy asked.

"That I do not hold goods forever," replied the shopkeeper brusquely. "He should have paid for it beforehand, then I would have laid it away for him."

"I'd like another horse just like that one," Linda informed him. "If one comes in from Mexico, would you send it to me? I'll pay you for it now. Will you give me a receipt, please?"

"Sure, I'll do that for you," the owner said. "But that kind of statuette isn't likely to come in unless it is specially ordered. I'll have to wait until the pottery salesman calls to do that. It may be quite a while."

Linda wrote her name and address on a paper for the man and gave him the money. The girls hailed a cab and returned immediately to the Western Stockyards. They found the boys eating frankfurters and drinking sodas.

"What did you find out?" Bob asked eagerly.

Linda told them about Mr. Rico who was to have picked up the clay horse at the shop, but had failed to do so.

"Maybe Rico was the name of the fellow who snatched the horse in Olvera Street and was lurking around here," Larry suggested, "just waiting for a chance to steal the head."

"I'm certainly sorry to have lost it," Linda said, "especially if there was a mystery connected with it."

"Just the same," Kathy declared, "this means he'll let us alone, and I'm glad to be rid of him. Ugh! He had an awful face!"

Bob remarked soberly, "Linda, I think you and Kathy had better go to the police and report this whole affair. Meanwhile Larry and I can pick up the supplies I promised Bronco I'd bring back." Bronco was Grandfather Mallory's nickname.

Linda and Kathy took a taxi to police headquarters. When they informed the desk sergeant that they had information about possible contraband, they were ushered into a small council room Immediately they were joined by a plainclothesman who introduced himself as Detective Carson.

Linda carefully told him all that had happened

from the time she purchased the clay horse to the interview with the shop owner about Mr. Rico.

"We'll question the proprietor," the detective said, "but he may be only the innocent middleman. Rico is the one who knows the answers."

"Do you think he is a smuggler?" Kathy asked.

"It sounds as if that horse's head contained contraband of some sort," Detective Carson replied. He gave Linda a piece of paper. "I want you to draw the symbol that was on the bottom of the statuette."

Linda sketched the sign of the arrowhead with the short, curved shaft.

The plainclothesman studied it for a few moments before he spoke. "Since the suspect who followed you got the horse's head, it isn't likely he will be seen again at the ceramic booth, but we'll stake out a man nearby anyhow. And if you do receive another clay horse with this arrowhead symbol on it, notify us immediately."

"I'll do that," Linda promised. Detective Carson thanked the girls for their report and they left.

When Linda and Kathy arrived at the stockyards, the boys had not yet returned. The girls strolled over to the chuck wagon at the entrance to the arena to buy hot dogs and soda. They brought them back to eat inside the dressing room of the trailer and as they ate, they talked about the mystery of the clay horse.

30

"I'm glad the police have taken over," Kathy concluded with relief, "and that we're out of it."

A few minutes later the girls heard a scraping noise near the door. Linda flung it open and looked out, Kathy behind her. A man was running away from the trailer! He was not the swarthy stranger —he was taller.

"I wonder what he wanted?" Linda said.

"Look there!" Kathy exclaimed, pointing to a piece of paper thrust under the door handle.

Linda pulled it out and unfolded the sheet.

The scrawled message said: BEWARE. STAY AWAY FROM C. SELLO.

Beneath the word *Sello* was sketched an arrowhead with a short, curved shaft.

Mysterious Poison 3

"The arrowhead! It's the same sign that was stamped on the clay horse!" Kathy whispered in dismay.

Linda nodded soberly. "C. Sello," she said. "Who could that be?"

"Maybe it's Mr. Rico, using another name," Kathy suggested.

"I don't think so," Linda replied. "The man who left this note and ran off was larger than the one who followed us."

"Anyway, we don't know for sure that the man who stole the horse's head is Mr. Rico," Kathy reminded her friend.

"That's true," Linda agreed with a sigh. "There's a lot we don't know."

"Sello," Kathy murmured with a puckered forehead.

"That's a Spanish word," said Linda. "*Sello* means

a seal or a stamp, but the initial *C* before the word *Sello* puzzles me. That seems to indicate it's somebody's name."

"Whatever it is, I surely intend to beware," Kathy declared. "If I see that arrow sign again, I'm going to run the other way."

"We'd better turn this note over to Detective Carson right away," Linda said. "But I hate to leave Chica d'Oro and Speedy unprotected."

"Oh, the boys should be back before long," Kathy said. "I think your horses will be quite safe in their stalls. After all, there are guards on duty."

"I guess you're right, Kathy."

After leaving a note for Bob and Larry telling what had happened, the girls hurried to the street, hailed a cab, and rode to the police station. In a short time they were again closeted with Detective Carson. Linda gave him the note and related what had happened.

When she had concluded, the detective looked very serious. "It might be advisable for you to return to your homes as quickly as possible," he said.

"Are we in danger?" Kathy asked.

"Perhaps," the plainclothesman replied. "Since we don't know what this mysterious warning means, you must take no chances."

"We're going tonight as soon as we get the horses loaded," Linda told him.

33

"Good," the detective answered. "Be careful."

As the girls were leaving headquarters, Linda paused in the lobby and said, "I would still like to know if C. Sello is really a name."

"Let's look it up in the phone books," Kathy suggested.

Several telephone booths stood against a wall. Beside them was a long counter holding all of the directories for the different parts of the big city.

The girls hurried over to consult them. They found only three Sellos listed. One was a Franklin Sello, a doctor in a suburb; one a Karl Sello, whose address was in the wholesale district; and another was listed as Sello, palmist, with an address on a side street not far from the police station.

First Linda called Dr. Sello. She asked him if he knew a C. Sello. The physician informed her that he had no relatives with that initial and knew of no one else by that name.

Next she called Karl Sello, hoping he might still be there, although it was past closing time. Linda found him at his desk.

"You want something special?" asked Karl Sello with a guttural accent.

"I would like some special information," Linda replied. "Would you please tell me if you have ever spelled your first name, Karl, with a C?"

"Ho, not me, not ever," Karl Sello said with a laugh. "I was born with that K, and I'll die with it."

When Linda asked if he knew of a C. Sello, he said he did not. She thanked him and hung up.

"Well, now for the palmist," Kathy said with a sigh.

"Why don't we pay that one a visit?" Linda suggested. "She's only a few blocks from here."

Kathy agreed, but when they reached the area five minutes later, she lost her nerve. The two girls had turned down a street of old, shabby, frame dwellings. The number they were looking for was on one of the dingier buildings. Beside the front door was a row of mailboxes with the names above them.

"Here it is!" Linda exclaimed. "C. Sello, palmist! We've found C. Sello!"

"Let's get away from here," Kathy begged uneasily. "Remember that warning message."

"Now that we've found the name," Linda said firmly, "we ought to investigate. After all, this may not be the C. Sello mentioned in the note."

Linda entered the dimly lit hallway with Kathy close behind her. They climbed three flights of stairs to a door that also had a sign, C. SELLO, PALMIST, with ENTER under the name.

As Linda cautiously opened the door, a bell tinkled. The two girls stepped into a tiny room with a table and two chairs. The only light came from a dirty skylight.

Kathy grimaced silently at the stale smell of

cabbage she detected. "I don't like this," she whispered.

They heard a chair being moved in the next room, and from behind the red drapery hanging at the doorway came an old woman. Her straggly white hair was banded by a strip of folded red cotton cloth. She wore red felt bedroom slippers, a faded, flowered cotton dress, and a black, crocheted shawl which she clutched together in front of her with bony fingers.

She welcomed her callers with a toothless smile and said in a raspy voice, "Good day to you. I see you have come to Carmelita to learn your future."

"Are you C. Sello?" Linda asked.

"That I am, child," replied the crone hoarsely. "Carmelita, the famous." She seated herself in one of the chairs. "Sit right down there now, and cross my palm with a dollar."

Linda hesitated a moment, then sat down, paid her dollar, and laid out her palm. "Do you see any strange sign in it?" she asked. "Like an arrowhead, maybe?"

The old woman looked at her belligerently. "You let Carmelita tell what she sees with her own eyes." The woman peered along the lines of Linda's hand, and then brightened a little, exclaiming, "I see—it is here—you will meet a wanderer, a vagabond who will lead you into some dark mystery."

Carmelita beamed into Linda's face, pleased at

her divination, and then went on, "Aha, there is a dark-haired man." Her voice became ominous. "Look out for him, young lady! Beware!"

Kathy let out a little squeak at that word, and then clapped her hand over her mouth.

"Just tell me this," Linda asked. "Why did you have a man leave a note on our horse-trailer door warning us to stay away from you? What does the arrowhead sign mean?"

The old woman's confusion and blankness were too genuine to doubt.

"I know nothing of what you are saying," she replied. "As for me, I haven't been farther away from this street than the corner grocery for ten years."

"Thank you," said Linda, standing up. She and Kathy walked to the door.

"B-but—the other young lady," pleaded Carmelita plaintively. "I have good things to tell you!"

"Some other time, perhaps," Kathy told her, and they left.

Down on the street Linda sighed. "We certainly drew a blank on that C. Sello clue."

Kathy nodded and glanced at her watch. It's almost eight o'clock," she exclaimed. "We'd better hurry. The boys may be worrying about us."

"They're probably worrying about their dinner," Linda returned with a grin. "Those hot dogs they had were only a snack."

The girls had to walk back to the main street before they were able to catch a cab to the stockyards. When their taxi reached Barn Number Two, the girls found that Bob and Larry had just arrived. They were taking the supplies they had bought out of their station wagon. Speedy's brown head tossed over the half door of his stall with pleasure at the familiar faces, and he gave a joyous whinny.

"Where's Chica d'Oro?" cried Linda, running to the filly's stall. Kathy followed. "Oh, dear, she's lying down," Linda said with sudden concern, "but not sleeping. Her eyes are open!"

"Bob! Larry!" Kathy called urgently.

As the boys hurried over, Linda quickly slipped back the latch and dropped to her knees beside the horse. "Chica, Chica," she cried softly, "what has happened to you?" Linda stroked the filly's neck.

Chica weakly turned her head, then dropped it back again to the straw.

"She's sick," Linda said breathlessly. "Someone get a vet, quick!"

"I'll call one!" Bob offered, hastening away.

"Let's try to get Chica on her feet," Linda said. "We must keep her blood circulating."

Together the two girls and Larry attempted to get Chica up, but she refused to respond.

Suddenly Kathy picked up something near the filly's head. "It's a lump of sugar," she announced.

"I thought you never gave Chica sweets."

"I don't," replied Linda, "I always give her pieces of carrot or bread for treats."

"Let me see that," Larry said. He peered at the sugar closely and sniffed. "This has been poisoned!"

"Oh no!" Linda cried. Her eyes filled with tears. "Who would do this to you, baby?" she whispered.

Larry knelt and put a comforting arm across Linda's shoulder. "The vet will fix her up, I'm sure," he said encouragingly.

"At least she didn't eat all the sugar," said Kathy comfortingly.

"Do you think that Sello gang did this?" Linda asked.

"Maybe," Larry replied. "But I think somebody tried to give Chica the sugar before the show to knock her out of competition. It was probably still damp with poison and bitter, so she spit it out. Later, when it dried, she must have picked up a bit in her stall and eaten it."

Bob had gone on a run to the arena office to phone. The show was over and nearly everyone had gone. But fortunately the veterinarian who had been retained by the Wranglers was still there, having coffee and chatting with a couple of men.

"We have a very sick horse over in Barn Two," Bob broke in.

Dr. Saunders tossed his half-filled paper cup into a refuse barrel and said, "Come on, let's go!"

He and Bob jumped into his fully equipped car and shot over to the barn at high speed.

Linda stood up as the veterinarian and Bob hurried in. "Save her!" she begged the doctor. "Do everything possible to save Chica d'Oro!"

Larry handed Dr. Saunders the sugar cube. "We found this in the stall. I think it contains poison."

The veterinarian gave the cube a quick, close inspection. "That's it, all right," he snapped. "Good to know this. It will save time."

He hastily prepared a long needle and gave Chica a shot for toxicity. Then he prepared another and administered it to her for a stimulant. Next he mixed an antibiotic drench and forced a quantity down the filly's throat. For about an hour the doctor worked over the palomino while the four young people watched anxiously. Finally Chica began to give an occasional grunt.

"She's starting to respond," Bob said to Linda.

"Well, I've done all that I can for your horse," Dr. Saunders finally remarked. "Twenty minutes' delay and she would have been gone."

"She'll be all right now?" Linda asked shakily.

"She should be," replied the veterinarian. From a jar he shook out a half-dozen pills the size of a quarter and gave them to Linda. "Give her one of these in an hour and one every hour thereafter," he ordered.

He also handed Linda a pill gun, a long contraption to reach to the back of the horse's mouth, so she might shoot the pill far enough in for the animal to swallow it. "Let her be quiet for another hour," he said, "and then get her to her feet and keep her walking. Someone will have to stay with her all night."

"I'll do it," Linda declared.

"We'll take turns at that," Bob told his sister.

"I'll stop by early in the morning," the doctor informed them and drove off.

"I'll go call the ranch and tell Bronco what has happened so he and Doña won't be looking for us tonight," Bob said. Doña was the name he and Linda had called their grandmother since early childhood.

While he was gone, Larry and Kathy went across the street to a lunch stand and brought back a belated dinner of hot roast-beef sandwiches and milk for all of them.

"That was a close call for your horse," Larry remarked to Linda, "but she looks pretty good now."

In about two hours the four friends managed to get Chica on her feet and begin walking her easily in a circle outside the stall. The boys cleaned out the empty stall next door, put down fresh hay, and brought in their sleeping bags. Linda and Kathy slept there while the boys stayed with Chica. The girls took second watch while Bob and Larry slept.

By 6 A.M., Chica was bright and chipper, but the four young people were exhausted!

Dr. Saunders came by and picked up his pill gun. As Bob paid him, Linda thanked the veterinarian earnestly for saving Chica.

"Good care helped," the doctor replied with a smile, and left.

The young people went over to the lunch stand for breakfast. Then they loaded the horses and gear and headed for Rancho del Sol.

Bob turned on the car radio to keep himself alert. In a little while, the news broadcast came on. A daring bank robbery had been successfully pulled off in West Los Angeles, and the bandits were believed to be fleeing on Route 99. Roadblocks were being set up.

"That's this highway!" Linda exclaimed.

"You don't suppose they'll want to hijack a couple of horses to head for the hills on, do you?" Kathy asked drowsily. Her tired companions did not answer.

Bob automatically glanced into the rearview mirror. A blue convertible was speeding straight toward them. Faster and faster it came. Could it be the robbers' car?

"Hang on!" Bob cried to his companions and swerved sharply, as the convertible careened up close behind them.

The Rescue 4

Jolted by the sudden motion, Linda and Kathy saw a speeding convertible with several occupants zoom past. It shot to the edge of the highway and was suddenly braked, while the driver tried to swing into a turn. The car rocked badly for a few seconds, then went over the steep embankment.

"Oh!" cried Linda in horror.

Immediately Bob pulled to the side of the road and stopped. The four jumped out and looked over the edge of the bank into a meadow.

The convertible had turned upside down, pinning its occupants beneath it, with the exception of one girl who had been thrown clear. She lay without moving, a slim, dark-haired figure in yellow slacks and poncho top.

"How dreadful!" murmured Kathy, feeling faint at the sight. "How can we help?"

"First we must get that car off those people!" said

Linda. "Oh, I hope it won't catch on fire. Bob, maybe we could use the horses and our ropes to lift the car."

"Yes!" Bob agreed. Quickly he took a couple of lariats from the station wagon and handed one to Larry. "We'll tie these ropes to our car and slide down them. Then, Kathy, you untie the lariats and throw them to us."

"I'll get the horses," Linda offered, hurrying to the trailer. "Bob, look at that poor girl when you reach the wreck."

As Linda led the animals out, her brother called, "She's alive. Just blacked out."

At this moment, a sheriff's car drove up and stopped a distance ahead, where the embankment tapered off. Two deputies ran into the meadow.

Kathy looked relieved. "I'm glad they're here," she said, untying the lariats. She threw them down to Bob, then joined Linda.

At a place where the bank sloped gently, the two girls took Speedy and Chica down, and ran with the horses toward the wreck.

When they reached it, Bob, Larry, and the two deputies were attempting to force open the jammed doors, but neither one would budge. The convertible had bedded deep in the soft earth.

"No use," declared one officer. "We can't right it."

"Help!" came a cry from inside.

The horses strained on the ropes . . .

"We'll have you free in a minute," Linda called, thankful that at least one passenger was alive.

Bob picked up the lariats and tossed one to Linda. With deft hands, sister and brother fashioned harnesses of them. As Linda placed hers around Chica's shoulders, Larry fastened the end of the rope to the far front wheel of the convertible. Bob quickly harnessed Speedy and did the same to the rear wheel.

"Linda," Bob ordered, "you and Kathy take the horses hard ahead when I give the signal, and we four men will lift up at the same time." He ran around the car, and was joined by Larry and the deputies. "Go!" he commanded.

Linda and Kathy held the horses' halters. "Come!" ordered Linda, abruptly jumping ahead.

Both horses leaped to follow, straining on the ropes with all their strength. In a few moments the car was righted.

Linda freed the ropes, and the girls moved the horses away from the car. The deputies, Bob, and Larry immediately started to free the passengers, then carried them to the shade of an oak. There was a small red-haired girl, who was crying, as well as two brown-haired boys of about seventeen. One was unconscious. The blue eyes of the other were filled with fright and pain.

One of the officers remarked, "I radioed for an ambulance. It will be here soon."

Linda and Kathy tied the horses to an adjoining oak and ran over to see what aid they could administer. At once, Linda dropped to her knees beside the unconscious boy, and sought his pulse. "It's a little weak, but regular," she said.

The girl who had been thrown clear suddenly sat up and looked about as if dazed. The grassy, spongy meadow had prevented her from being badly injured. She grasped her face in her hands as if to shut out the whole scene.

Kathy went to her and gently wiped the grime off the girl's face with clean tissues from a little case she carried in her pocket. "Everyone will be all right," she said.

"I'm relieved to hear that," the accident victim said simply. "That other girl is Shirley. I'm Mary —Mary Sutton." Kathy assisted her over to the others.

"Thanks, you people, for stopping to help us," the blue-eyed boy said with effort. "I must've been crazy to drive like that."

"Don't try to talk any more now," admonished Linda. "The ambulance will be here any moment."

"I've always loved horses," said Mary quietly, "but never had much chance to be around them. I'll remember yours as the most beautiful I've ever seen. May I pet them?"

"Of course," Linda said with a smile.

Mary limped over to Chica d'Oro and Speedy,

and stroked the neck of each. Then she pulled thick bunches of succulent green grass and fed them to the horses. Eagerly the animals extended their muzzles for more.

"They'll never forget you," said Linda, who had followed Mary over.

Just then Chica spotted the gay, flowered handkerchief in Mary's poncho pocket and snatched it out with her lips, waving it up and down.

"Oh, you wonderful creature!" Mary said warmly. "So you want my hanky? I'll gladly give it to you." The linen square was perfumed with a spicy scent.

Mary took the handkerchief from Chica's lips and knotted it to the horse's mane. The filly nickered softly.

"Oh, I wish I could learn to ride," Mary said with a sigh.

Linda liked the girl. "If you'll come to our ranch sometime, I'll be glad to teach you to ride," she offered. "We live at Rancho del Sol."

"Oh, I'd love that," Mary exclaimed, "and I know where your ranch is."

Larry had joined them. "You two girls look almost like twins," he said. "The same size, same black hair and brown eyes."

After the ambulance had arrived and gone off with the accident victims, Linda, Kathy, and the boys took the horses back to the trailer. In another half hour they were on their way home again. When the station wagon pulled into Rancho del Sol, Mr. and Mrs. Mallory stood by the corral, anxiously awaiting their grandchildren's arrival. Rango, the large coyote-shepherd ranch dog, barked a greeting.

Bronco Mallory swept off his felt hat and strode over to the station wagon. He was a robust man, over six feet tall, with a shock of iron-gray hair and keen blue eyes.

"Glad you all made it safely," he said.

His wife, a slender, olive-skinned woman, and the owner through inheritance of the ranch, was a few years younger than Bronco. She wore her long, black hair high in a braided crown. Though there was an air of proud reserve about Rosalinda Mallory, her deep brown eyes were warm and full of concern as she greeted Linda, Bob, and their friends.

"I have been alarmed about you," she said.

"We're all right, Doña," Linda assured her quickly. "And Chica d'Oro's fine."

As Rango leaped about, showing off, Cactus Mac, the bandy-legged foreman in his middle fifties, came out of the corral. Immediately he unloaded Chica and gave her a quick inspection.

"As fit as ever," he announced with a grin. "And how'd you folks come out in the show?"

Linda smiled and proudly showed her trophy.

"Um, that thar's pretty fancy," Mac said.

Linda and Bob chatted gaily as they all walked toward the attractive, sprawling, Spanish ranch house. Large trees shaded the building and bright-colored flowers grew in profusion near its white stucco walls.

Luisa, the genial, plump Mexican ranch cook, had a hearty pork-pie lunch waiting, so they all went in to the table and did the rest of their talking as they ate.

After the four friends had told all the events of the past week in detail, Bronco pushed back his chair and cleared his throat. "Well now, I've had some rather bad news from the Scotsward Ranch," he announced. "There has been an outbreak of anthrax among cattle near there. We'll have to get those Black Angus away from Scotsward at once. That means you young folks must leave early in the morning." He looked at them solicitously. "Think you're up to it after all you've been through?"

"You bet!" exclaimed Bob.

"Of course," Linda said, smiling.

"I'm raring to go," Larry declared with a grin. "But I promised Dad I'd help him finish a saddle for delivery tomorrow." Mr. Spencer had a leather goods and saddlery shop in Lockwood. Larry went on, "I'll meet you the next day at the Ghost Town crossroads. I can take a shortcut."

"That's okay," Linda said, "but we might not get there until the third day out."

"I'll take my bedroll and some grub on the back of my saddle, and just camp until you arrive," replied Larry good-naturedly.

"We want you to come along too, Kathy," Bob said.

"Oh, I'd love to go, if I wouldn't be in the way," she replied with glowing eyes.

"You'll catch on," Bob said, grinning.

"And pep Bob up," Larry teased.

Bob ignored the gibe and said, "Right now we have to get you and Kathy home. I'll drive Kathy. You ride Gypsy and use her for the trip, Larry. Kathy's dad can bring her and Patches over here at five A.M."

The Hamiltons lived on the main road next to the Highway House, which they owned. It contained a fine restaurant, a souvenir store, and a shop where Mr. Hamilton, a lapidary, cut, polished, and sold semiprecious stones.

After Larry left and Bob had driven off with Kathy, Linda went out to check Chica d'Oro. She took Mary Sutton's bright handkerchief off the filly's mane and held it before her.

"Here is your present from Mary," she said with a laugh.

Chica bobbed her nose against it, sniffing the strong, spicy fragrance. Linda tied the linen square in a corner of the pony's stall, then returned to the house and went to her room.

A pile of mail lay on her bedside table. She began opening it. There were letters from friends in Mexico and Honolulu, advertisements for riding clothes and equipment, and an official-looking long, green envelope.

It contained a cordial invitation to ride in the Cherry Blossom Fiesta the following weekend at Santa Carita, south of Los Angeles. The blossoms would be beautiful, Linda thought, and the pretty little Spanish town would be gaily decorated.

The young rider was excited. What fun it would be! she thought.

From talk Linda had heard around the horse shows, she knew that only the best entries were invited to participate in the big parade.

I'm flattered, she told herself.

There would also be a pit barbecue after the parade on Saturday. This would be followed by a big bonfire and sing that night in the walnut camping grove.

On Sunday, a six-hour trail ride was arranged through the lush cattle-ranch country, with lunch at a cow camp beside the stream that wound its way along the trail.

Linda took the invitation to show her grandmother. She found Mrs. Mallory in the big beam-ceilinged living room. "Doña, isn't this exciting?" she cried.

"What an interesting and fine time you could

have," her grandmother said. "But will you be back from the cattle drive in time to go?"

Linda shook her head soberly. "I'm afraid not."

Bronco had entered the room in time to hear most of the talk. "I'll take you and Chica d'Oro down there, if you would rather go to the fiesta than on the Mojave Trail ride."

"Oh, but I wouldn't," Linda declared without hesitation. "I've never been on a cattle drive." Bronco smiled his appreciation.

A little later, right after Bob returned, a long-distance call came for Linda from Los Angeles. It was from the owner of the little ceramic shop in Olvera Street.

The man spoke crisply and Linda thought she detected a note of anger in his voice.

"Without my ordering it, another one of those yellow clay horses—like your broken one—came in yesterday afternoon. I mailed it right out to you. But," he drew in a hard breath, "late last night, after the shop was closed, someone broke in and smashed the heads off every one of my pottery horses. If you know who did it, you'd better tell quick!" he growled.

"Oh, I don't know," Linda gasped. "How dreadful! You must get in touch with Detective Carson at the police station at once, and tell him about it. He may have the solution."

Immediately the shop owner hung up, perhaps to

follow her instructions. Linda reported the startling news to Bob, Doña, and Bronco.

"Why do you suppose all those beautiful little horses were smashed?" she asked, bewildered.

Midnight Intruder 5

"Such evil work sounds as if some vicious person had a grudge against the pottery-shop owner," Doña said.

Bob frowned. "There may be more to it than that."

"Suppose the man who stole the head of my statuette found it didn't contain what he was looking for," Linda said thoughtfully. "He might have smashed every other clay horse trying to find it."

"Sounds reasonable," Bronco agreed.

Linda's eyes widened with excitement. "The second yellow horse that's being mailed to me might hold what he's after!"

"But you won't be here to receive it," Bob said.

"I shall send it to you at Scotsward Ranch," Doña offered.

"Do that," said Bronco, "just as soon as it arrives.

Someone may have found out about the figurine being sent here and come after it!"

"One of that Sello gang, you mean?" said Linda with a little shiver.

Doña looked at the girl a moment, then said firmly, "We have talked enough about this unpleasant mystery. You three must pack for your trip tomorrow. But first I want to tell Linda and Bob about some strange signs to watch for on the trail."

"What kind of signs?" Linda asked curiously.

"Rock writings," her grandmother replied. "Religious symbols of the Mojave Indian tribes which once inhabited the desert."

"Picture writing!" exclaimed Linda. "How fascinating!"

"You will also see the three crosses of Cortez," Doña continued. "There are two crosses the same size with a taller one between them. Where you see that sign, you will know that Hernando Cortez and his men passed that way four hundred years ago."

Meanwhile Bronco had been thumbing through a shelf of historical magazines. Now he pulled one out. "Here's what I was looking for. It's a recent article on the disappearance of a valuable collection of Cortez relics owned by a well-known historian in Mexico City."

Bob scanned the illustrations. "They'd be hard to dispose of," he commented.

"Maybe the thief intends to demand money for

the relics before he'll return them," Linda suggested.

"That's a good guess," said Bronco. "Your Mexican statuettes brought the article to my mind. I suppose you young folks know the story of how this Cortez, for the glory of Spain, landed in Mexico with his soldiers and burned, pillaged, and tortured the Indians until he conquered them and made the country a colony of Spain."

"Yes," said Linda. "And he took all their gold to use in buildings both there and in Spain."

"Not all of it." Bronco smiled. "As soon as the Indians caught on to the scheme, they began to hide their precious possessions."

"Good for them!" Linda said vehemently. "I just can't stand people who help themselves to others' property!"

Doña smiled and gave her granddaughter an affectionate pat on the shoulders. "Keep your high ideas always," she said in her low, musical voice.

The little group talked about the stolen relics for a few minutes, then Linda and Bob hurried away to get their packs and gear together. Linda brought out a little camera to put in her saddlebag, and Bob added a small transistor radio to his supplies.

Cactus Mac had laid out the sleeping bags to air, and was busy with the pack saddles and equipment. He raised a hand in greeting and went on with his work. His big buckskin, named Buck, was already in the barn corral. Bob and Linda went to the pasture to bring in Rocket and three packhorses.

In the kitchen, Luisa was busy getting food ready for the trip. Groceries were piled on the table. When Bob came through with another load for his saddlebag, he grimaced at the stack of small cans of green beans and tomatoes. "Those again!" he cried out, and clutched his stomach as if he had dreadful indigestion.

"They are good for you!" Luisa retorted firmly. "Makes healthy!" Bob grinned and went out the door.

During the preparations, Rango sat on his haunches close by the corral, bushy tail thumping and every nerve and muscle tensed with eagerness to go along. Only his brown eyes showed he was resigned to staying home.

"Hey, Rango!" Bob said suddenly. "Don't look so hangdog. You're going along!"

Rango observed Bob for a split second of incredulity, and then leaped into the air in a wild flurry of yellowish tan hair.

"What happened to him?" asked Cactus Mac.

"He just found out he can go along," Linda replied with a laugh.

She had finished her work and now hurried over to Chica d'Oro's private stall and large paddock. "Do you feel like starting out on the trail, baby?" she asked.

From across the paddock, the palomino whinnied a greeting, did a coltish circle and buck at the pleasure of seeing Linda, and then loped up to her.

Linda patted the filly's neck and scratched her gently behind the ears. "How about earning your supper tonight by learning how to bow? You must start some time."

Chica tossed her mane in readiness for whatever was coming. Her young owner went to the tack room for a length of soft cotton rope and a handful of rolled oats, which she put in her pocket.

"Now we're ready," she said.

Linda tied the rope loosely around Chica's left front pastern. The horse nosed it curiously.

"You'll soon know what that's all about," Linda said with a laugh.

She took a handful of oats from her pocket and let the filly smell it. Just as Chica d'Oro reached for the oats, Linda moved her hand down a little, and then a little farther, before giving the horse the treat.

Linda took out more oats and this time moved her hand down and back between Chica's forelegs, at the same time gently lifting the horse's left foot with the cotton rope. This caused the pony to ease down on her knee. When she did, Linda gave her the oats.

"Good work, baby!" her young trainer said.

Chica d'Oro soon learned to move her head down and back. Then Linda stopped, aware that too long a training session can do more harm than good. She knew it would take a lot of time and patience to teach the horse to bow on cue.

As Linda gave the filly her ration of evening hay, she thought, I'll stow the cotton rope in my saddlebag so I can work with Chica on the trip.

Once having started to teach the horse a trick, it was not wise, she knew, to stop working until the animal had learned to perform perfectly.

Mindful that she would have to be up before dawn, Linda went to bed early. In the middle of the night, the family was startled out of deep sleep by Rango's fierce barking. Linda went to her window and in the white moonlight saw the dog leap at a man. The intruder broke loose, however, and sped away.

Linda quickly donned robe and slippers and joined Bronco and Bob, who had rushed outside. Mr. Mallory held a piece of dark-blue, coarse cloth that Rango had torn from the intruder's clothes.

"Good boy," praised Bob, patting him rewardingly. Rango thumped his massive tail and held his head as if balancing a halo.

"Who do you suppose that fellow was, and what did he want?" Linda asked, perplexed.

Bronco cleared his throat to disguise his concern. "Just a wanderer, probably," he said. "Looking for a soft sleep in the hay. Everyone to bed." But he made a point of bringing the scrap of material into the house, saying he would turn it over to the sheriff.

With the first rays of the rising sun, Kathy's father drove in with his daughter and Patches. Mr. Hamilton kissed Kathy good-bye and wished her a good trip. She waved until the car and trailer disappeared.

Then Kathy immediately went about saddling her horse. She fastened on the roomy, cavalry-type saddlebags, packed with her personal needs and canteen. Mr. Hamilton had laid her sleeping bag alongside the Craigs', to be loaded onto a pack-horse.

A few minutes later Linda, Bob, and Cactus Mac came hurrying out the kitchen door. They had not been able to get past Luisa until all had eaten a hearty breakfast.

"Hi, Kathy!" called Linda and Bob, and Mac said, "Mornin', ma'am."

Quickly they saddled up their own mounts and arranged the baggage on the packhorses. Cactus Mac inspected each diamond hitch on the packs, and found them perfect.

"One of these days I'm going to lose my job running this ranch to one of you young whipper-snappers," he drawled wryly.

"You never will," protested Linda fondly.

Rango, who had expended his excitement the previous night, stood by in important quietude.

"Come here, you, Rango," called Cactus Mac. Instantly Rango trotted alertly over to the foreman. "Everybody does his job on this here trip," Mac stated firmly. "Yours'll be to guard the horses and gear. *Guard horses!* Understand?"

Rango's eyes gleamed with intelligence and he gave a short, affirmative bark.

"Get your collar," Linda ordered.

Rango darted into the barn, stood on his hind legs, took his collar with the attached license tag off a nail with his teeth, and brought it out to her.

Linda put it on him. "Now you're ready to go," she told him. Rango happily licked her hand.

Soon the riders were mounted. Doña and Bronco waved and wished them luck. Bob raised his hand, called out, "Scotsward, ho!" and led off with Rango leaping along at his side, followed by Linda and Kathy. The three packhorses were on a line behind Buck, and brought up the rear.

After an hour's riding the little group had left the green trees and square fields of the ranch country behind, and the desert unrolled far ahead like beige carpeting.

Cactus Mac, who knew his way about the Mojave with his eyes closed, pulled ahead now. He crossed the southeast strip of the sandy waste, and headed into a rugged gorge with towering rock walls.

"They call this here place Jawbone Canyon," he called out. "It'll lead direct to the old Mojave Trail between the Calico Mountains and the Mojave River."

As they rode, Linda and Kathy noticed that the crooked, spiny-armed Joshua trees were in bloom as well as the small hedgehog cactus. Each short, prickly stalk wore a huge, silky, yellow blossom.

"Oh, here's an odd beauty I'd like to get a closer look at!" Linda exclaimed. She came to a halt near a pale green, fluffy-looking bush.

"Keep well back from that thar pest!" warned Cactus Mac. "It's a teddy-bear cholla, one o' the worst o' the jumpers. They throw thar spines right into your flesh if you get too near."

"You've changed my mind about getting closer," Linda said with a grin.

Suddenly Kathy cried in alarm, "Ooh, I think the heat must be getting me! Those rocks are walking!"

Linda followed her gaze and asked, "Cactus Mac, what's happening? It certainly *does* look as if those rocks are moving across the sand."

The foreman and Bob had a good laugh. Then Cactus Mac drawled, "Those are just three old desert tortoises takin' the week off to cross the road."

"Okay, have your laugh. Call me a desert tenderfoot," Linda retorted.

At noon, the riders stopped for a picnic lunch at the Chuckwalla well. Nearby, Linda and Kathy discovered disks of earth ringed by rocks.

"What are these, Bob?" Kathy asked. "You seem to know all the answers."

Bob confessed that he did not know and appealed to their guide.

"Those," Cactus Mac explained, "are Indian house rings. Ancient Indian tepees stood thar."

"Very clever way of making their houses stay in place," Bob remarked.

A short time later the travelers were in the saddle again.

Late that afternoon they reached Cuddleback Canyon, where Cactus Mac called a halt for the night. Flash floods had washed out huge caverns.

"These are known as shelter caves," he said. "We'll be snug inside. Besides, the Cuddleback well is the last water hole for some distance."

The horses were unsaddled, rubbed down, hobbled, grained, and then left to graze on runty desert-floor growth, which they seemed to find palatable.

Bob built a fire. Linda and Kathy got out the food they needed from one of the packs and cooked supper. Soon afterward they were all glad to crawl into their sleeping bags in the quiet, roomy cave.

Always a light sleeper, Linda suddenly awakened with the impression that she had heard the tinkling of a bell. Then, some distance away, she heard a sharp bark from Rango, followed by the soft whinnying of Chica d'Oro.

Hastily pulling on her boots, Linda wondered what had caused the palomino to shuffle off so far away from the other horses. She was glad Rango was doing his guard duty and had gone with her.

Outside Linda looked around anxiously. Then she heard Rango bark and, though the night was moonless, Linda thought she spotted Chica and the dog some distance away. They stood beside a pile of huge boulders beneath a bluff.

Linda ran to them. As she drew close, the astonished girl saw a dark figure behind a rock. Rango growled.

Vagabond 6

Linda stood silent, her heart pounding hard. Who was the person behind the rock? Should she demand that he come out?

Rango barked furiously, but to Linda's amazement, Chica d'Oro nickered softly and stepped toward the dark shadow beyond the boulder.

"Wait, baby!" Linda cautioned, and caught hold of her pony's mane.

She listened tensely, but no sound came from behind the rock. Rango continued to growl and bark. It seemed like ages before Bob and Cactus Mac came running up.

"What is it?" Bob asked. "What's the matter with Rango?"

"Something there," Linda whispered, pointing toward the boulder.

Cactus Mac shone his flashlight beam in that direction.

"Oh!" Linda cried in surprise. "Why, it's only a burro!"

Rango went yip-yipping around the rock.

"What's the poor little thing doing way out here alone?" Linda wanted to know. She went to it and Chica d'Oro followed her. The palomino touched her nose gently to the burro's and nickered.

"What's wrong with the burro? Why is it hiding here?" Bob asked.

The little gray animal was pressing up against the boulder, holding its neck and jaw immobile across it.

"He's wearin' a bell," Cactus Mac said, "and he's pressin' it against the rock to keep it from jinglin' so he won't be found."

"A stray!" Bob exclaimed. "Do you suppose he ran off from a pack train?"

Cactus Mac was running his flashlight over the burro and now said, "Look thar, on his rump!"

The others bent their heads closer and saw the words *Follow Sign* and an outlined arrowhead in a fresh, raw brand.

"What a cruel thing to do!" exclaimed Linda.

"Looks as if this here little fellow was intended to be used as a messenger of some sort," Cactus Mac remarked soberly.

"And he wants no part of it," declared Bob.

"The poor burro's eyes are full of hurt and reproach," Linda noted.

"That's a fact," Cactus Mac agreed. 'This here jack is feelin' very mistreated. He'd drop where he stands from thirst and hunger rather'n let that thar bell jingle again, announcin' his whereabouts to the person who branded him."

"What kind of person would do such a thing?" Linda asked indignantly.

"Could be an old-timer of sorts," replied Cactus Mac. "In the pioneer days, this method o' brandin' some animal to bring help was occasionally used by a lone cowboy or prospector in trouble. I recall a story told around the ranches when I was a young fiddlefoot signin' on for only a season o' ridin' at a time," he reminisced.

"In the early days, thar was a mighty good cowhand by the name o' Buzz workin' on a big ranch near the Owl Creek Mountains in Wyoming. One day he disappeared, and no one ever did see hide nor hair o' him again. Then two years later a wild cow was flushed out o' the brush with the scrawled brand on her hip: *Indians 5–17–1872 Buzz.*"

"How sad!" said Linda. "Do you suppose this is an SOS message?"

"Whatever it is," said Bob, "we'd better try to figure this brand message out. Someone might need help."

"First I'm going to get this little fellow out of his

trouble," said Linda, reaching for the buckle of the bell strap.

All this time Chica d'Oro had been standing with her neck across the burro's.

"Sure looks as if Chica intends to claim this here burro for her own pet," Cactus Mac remarked, grinning.

"She did find him," said Linda. "Chica must have heard the bell when I did, and came out to him. She probably sensed he was in trouble."

Linda took the bell off the burro's neck and held the clapper to keep it from tinkling. She turned to her pony. "Do you think you can persuade your little friend to trot back to the cave with us? Come on!" She walked off with Cactus Mac and Bob.

The palomino started to follow, then gently nudged the burro on the back and nickered quietly. When Chica d'Oro started off again, the burro trotted close to the filly's side.

"There's an animal who recognizes a friend when he's been found by one," Bob said with a laugh.

Kathy stood at the entrance to the cave. "What happened?" she asked anxiously. Then noting the burro, she exclaimed. "Oh, I see! Something new has been added."

"Looks like it," Cactus Mac said. "If Chica d'Oro wants to keep the little fellow."

"Whose is it? Where did it come from?" Kathy asked.

"He's just a vagabond," Bob told her.

"Vagabond," Linda repeated. "Let's name him that!"

"Linda!" Kathy exclaimed. "That Madame Sello, the palmist, predicted you'd meet a vagabond."

Bob laughed. In a high, girlish-sounding voice he said, "Goodness me, I was looking for a man and all I get is a burro!" Kathy threw him a dark look.

Linda was gazing closely at the mark on the burro's hip. "It's an arrowhead," she said thoughtfully, "but not like the one that the Sello gang uses."

"You kids are moonstruck," muttered Cactus Mac. "Right now I'm goin' back to sleep."

"We'd better go, too," said Linda. "But first I want to do something about that raw brand on Vagabond."

She got a tube of insect-bite ointment from her first-aid kit, and applied a thick layer over the brand marks. Then she scooped up some of the loose, tannish gray earth, just the color of the burro, and patted it on top of the ointment. It made the writing completely indistinguishable.

Bob brought Vagabond a bucket of water and a small pan of grain. After the burro had drunk thirstily and ravenously licked up the grain, he waved his long ears back and forth and brayed in high glee.

"I certainly hope that if anybody's out hunting him, he didn't hear that!" Kathy said with a laugh.

Linda led Chica d'Oro over to the other horses at the side of the cave. They were standing with locked joints, contentedly snoozing. They roused at the return of the filly with the burro close at her side, but paid them little heed. They had all been on trail trips with pack burros, so Vagabond was no novelty to them.

Rango, now feeling that he had discharged his guard chore in good manner, curled up on a horse blanket beside the gear and went to sleep.

The next morning when the horses were given their grain, one of the pack animals nosed into Vagabond's ration. With a shrill whinny, Chica d'Oro butted the moocher away, and stood between it and Vagabond until the burro had eaten his last oat.

"I'll sure feel sorry for anyone who tries to mistreat that little guy from now on," Bob declared.

After a quick breakfast, Cactus Mac gave the order for the riders to mount.

"Remember to watch along the trail for that arrow sign," Linda said.

When they had been riding for a while, Bob came upon big mud disks with rims about a foot or two high. Here and there they were frosted with sparkling crystals.

"What are they?" Kathy asked.

"Salt saucers," Cactus Mac answered.

"The salt crystals look like hoarfrost!" Linda

exclaimed. She took out her little camera. "I want a picture of those."

"There's lots o' funny sights in this here desert," Cactus Mac told the others as they rode on. "Later you'll be seein' haystacks."

"In the desert?" Kathy asked incredulously.

"Yes'm. Rows and rows o' small eroded mounds o' marsh mud. Back in 1880, the Chinese coolies what came here molded up the mud with shovels so the borax they were after would leach out."

"Salt saucers and haystacks!" Kathy exclaimed with a laugh.

"But no arrowheads," Linda reminded her.

They sat in the shade for a long noon hour against Pumpkin Butte, whose deep-orange soil explained its name. The slopes bristled with colorful, weird stone formations.

"I've heard of this place," said Bob. "It's a mecca for rockhounds, and the water trough is maintained by the county in a niche at the base of the butte."

While the riders waited for cooler traveling, Linda brought out the cotton rope and gave Chica another lesson in bowing. Vagabond watched the beginning of this training with evident disfavor, not sure whether the horse was being mistreated.

Realizing that Chica d'Oro enjoyed it and was winning Linda's praise, the burro stood spraddle-legged, watching intently. Then he started imitating the palomino, putting his head up and down.

72

"Look at those rocks!" Linda exclaimed.

He finally ended by going down on both knees and falling over.

"Good try!" cried Linda.

Then while everyone laughed, she gave Vagabond and Chica each a handful of treat.

"I can tell you one thing," Linda said, putting away the training rope. "If we do meet Vagabond's owner, we're going to have to buy the burro for Chica d'Oro."

Kathy giggled. "A sort of horse pen pal?" Then she curled up for a siesta.

Linda, Bob, and Cactus Mac climbed to the top of the butte to get a good view of their surroundings. Arid desert was all they could see.

"I hope there's a water hole ahead," Bob said worriedly.

"None out thar," drawled Rancho del Sol's foreman, "but we'll have water all right where we're beddin' down."

"Where will that be?" Bob asked.

"At old Hungry Homer's deserted ranch," replied Cactus Mac. "We'll head that way by skirtin' around those dunes to the right yonder."

Linda had been turning about, gazing down at the desert floor. Suddenly she exclaimed, "Look at those rocks!"

The two men squinted in the direction Linda was pointing. Then Mac said, "They look like they been put thar in the shape of an arrowhead."

"That's what I thought," said Linda excitedly. "Let's have a closer look at them."

The three descended the slope and walked out toward the formation of rocks.

"Everything's always farther off in this here desert than it seems to be," Cactus Mac grumbled as they plodded along.

When they reached the arrowhead formation, Bob led the way around it. The riders carefully checked for any clue to explain its presence there.

"On the ground, one wouldn't notice the formation," said Bob. "We'd have missed it if we hadn't seen it from above."

"That's why I think it means something," said Linda, who had been examining an area a short distance away. "Come over here!"

"Did you find a clue?" Bob asked.

"Hoofprints," his sister replied. "In the direction the arrowhead is pointing."

Bob gazed at them. "Three horses and a burro," he concluded.

Eagerly the group followed the prints a short distance. Then the hoofmarks dipped into a rocky arroyo and disappeared.

"Maybe they belong to the riders who sent out Vagabond," Bob suggested.

"It's a possibility," replied Cactus Mac. "The riders might have been rockhounds or hunters, and all three got hurt and had to send out their pack burro."

"How fresh are the.e prints?" Linda a.ked, wondering whether she should explore fu.:her.

"They could be two or three days old," Mac answered. "Guess we'd better be gettin' back."

When they reached Kathy, Linda told her about the discovery. "How amazing!" Kathy said. "But you didn't find out whether those riders were good or bad people. Well, if they're dangerous, I'm glad you didn't find them!"

Rango was stretched out full length on a spot of damp sand beside the watering trough.

"Hey there, Rango!" exclaimed Cactus Mac. "Why weren't you along, scouting with us on the hot desert? We may have needed your help."

Rango cast a baleful eye at the foreman without moving a hair.

"You told him his job was to guard the horses, remember?" Linda reminded Mac with an impish smile.

The rancher grinned sheepishly. "That's right. And trust that bone burier to remember it when he has to make his own choice o' lyin' in a cool spot o' shade or paddin' it out on the hot desert."

They saddled up and rode off again around the primrose-sprinkled dunes. Ahead, as far as they could see, the ground was carpeted with lemon yellow desert dandelions.

In the late afternoon, they arrived at the vast forest of Joshua trees in the midst of which was Hungry Homer's abandoned ranch. It consisted of a shack with the windows broken out and a tumbledown shed. A rusty plow stood to one side, and an old flat-bed wagon on the other.

Under a Joshua tree was a weathered board marker with dim printing on it that read: HERE LIES HUNGRY HOMER WHO NEVER LIKED TO WORK. HE NEVER GOT ENOUGH TO EAT.

"Some epitaph!" Bob laughed.

There was a good well on the place with a pump handle and wooden bucket. The ropes on the bucket were fairly new, and Linda remarked about this.

"That's 'cause the government takes care o' this watering place for desert adventurers," Mac explained.

The horses were attended to first, with Bob vigorously pumping water for them.

Linda stood looking at the spike-limbed Joshua trees with the clumps of creamy blooms at the ends. "These are the weirdest trees I've ever seen," she remarked.

"This here is the only place in the world you'll see 'em," Cactus Mac told her. "They're native to the Mojave Desert."

"How did they get their name?" Linda asked.

"I know," put in Kathy. "It was given to them by

the Mormons during their westward journey because it seemed to them that the branches pointed to the promised land."

"Of course," said Linda. "It was Joshua who led the Israelites into the promised land of Canaan."

Vagabond knew about the value of the Joshua trees. He was busy going from one to another, devouring the juicy clumps of blooms that he could reach.

Suddenly Bob whistled and called the others over to the tree where he was standing. "Here is another sign," he said, pointing to the ground. Little rocks had been arranged to form a small arrowhead. "And there's a footprint," he added. "The arrowhead is pointing in the same direction as the other one," Cactus Mac noted.

Linda said, "The footprint looks sort of slurred, as if the person's leg was dragging."

"Someone could be hurt all right," said Kathy.

"I certainly wish we could find whoever it is and help him," said Linda with concern.

"All we can do is keep watching for the signs," Bob told her.

"No use worrying now," declared Cactus Mac. "It's time to swing the skillet!"

A fire was built and supper prepared. After the meal was over, the young people sat by the fire, singing and watching the moon rise over the Joshua trees.

"Let's take a stroll," Linda suggested. As the three young people wandered off a little way, they came to a rocky grotto and stepped inside.

"I've found another symbol!" Kathy called out excitedly, pointing to the moonlit marking.

Crash on Stage 7

The Craigs whirled to see the symbol Kathy had discovered. Carved in the rock near the entrance to the grotto was the sign of Hernando Cortez—the three crosses.

"To think," Kathy said, "that Cortez himself may have stood on this very spot! It gives me the shivers."

"I wonder," said Linda, "if he was hiding here with his soldiers. At that time California was part of Mexico."

"If it wasn't Cortez, I'll bet it was one of his generals," Bob added. On the way back to the cabin, he said, "I suppose Larry is sacked down over in Ghost Town."

Kathy shuddered. "I surely wouldn't want to be there all alone."

"He'll probably have a ball with the ghosts." Bob laughed.

In a little while, the travelers inched into their sleeping bags. Chica d'Oro and Vagabond stood so close together as they slept that in the shadows they appeared as one figure.

In the morning, Linda took a couple of snapshots of the grotto. Then as soon as they were on the trail again, she asked Cactus Mac, "About what time should we reach Ghost Town?"

"Midmorning, I'd say."

A couple of hours later the foreman led the procession up a small butte.

"What's the reason for this?" Bob asked.

"Never ride into an unlikely place without lookin' it over first, son," Cactus Mac replied soberly. He dismounted and took out binoculars from one of his saddlebags.

Linda and the others went for theirs. For a few minutes, everyone silently strained eyes at the few ramshackle remains of buildings far in the hazy distance.

Finally Linda said, "It gives me a funny feeling to think that a lot of people once lived in Ghost Town, and now nobody does."

"Ten thousand of 'em," said Cactus Mac. "But that's the way it goes with a gold strike. Folks flock where 'tis and leave when the veins run out. Then thar's no other way left to make a livin' so the town dies. Yes'm, at one time a lot o' gay elegance was takin' place over thar."

Kathy was moving her glasses about. "I don't see any sign of Larry," she said.

"He's likely shaded up beside a building," Cactus Mac told her.

Suddenly Linda exclaimed, "Look to the far side of town!"

As they gazed, two riders left the town and began to climb the hill on the far side.

"Maybe someone does live there now," said Kathy.

"I doubt it," Bob said. "Probably they're just passers-through like us."

In a moment, the two men had disappeared in a northeasterly direction, and Cactus Mac said, "Let's get along!"

It was almost two hours before the group arrived in the sandy main street of Ghost Town.

"It's deserted, all right," said Kathy in awe. They called Larry's name, but there was no answer.

"He isn't here," stated Linda flatly. "Perhaps he was one of the two we saw riding out."

"But who was with him?" Kathy asked.

"Could have been a companion from home who had just come this far with Larry for the ride," Bob said. "Maybe he got tired of waiting."

"Larry would have waited," Linda declared, "unless—unless he had been forced to ride out."

"Now, Sis, don't worry about him," Bob said.

"Larry can take care of himself." But Linda detected concern in her brother's tone.

"We'll tie our horses back o' this buildin' in that wide spot o' shade," Cactus Mac told the others, "and scout around on foot. But be careful about goin' inside the buildin's. They could tumble down on you. Besides, they'll be full o' rats' nests."

Rango was given a pan of water. Then he stretched out in the shade by the horses.

The group started walking through the dilapidated town to see what they could find.

At the end of Main Street, Bob stopped. "Here are the tracks of the two riders," he said.

Cactus Mac scrutinized them carefully. "I don't believe any o' those belong to Gypsy, the horse you lent Larry," he concluded. "Her hooves are slightly smaller."

"Then where is Larry?" persisted Linda.

"Something could have hindered him from coming," Bob replied.

"Yes, I suppose so," Linda mumbled, disappointed.

The four ambled about the ruins until they came to the far end of town.

"Here are a lot of tracks together!" exclaimed Linda.

There were plain prints of three horses leaving town toward the west. Beside them were tracks of only two of the same horses returning. Cactus Mac declared they were the same animals which had recently gone northeast.

"That third rider!" Linda exclaimed. "Could he have been Larry? Did he meet with foul play?"

"What do you think, Cactus?" asked Bob. "Could one of those three horses have been Gypsy?"

Cactus Mac shook his head. "Nope, not Gypsy," he declared.

"You aren't saying that just to make me feel better, are you?" Linda asked tensely.

"Honey," drawled Cactus Mac, "if one o' those sets o' tracks belonged to Gypsy, you think I'd be standin' here jawin'? I'd be in the saddle and after her!" Linda smiled her thanks.

Close to the hoofprints were the ashes of a cook fire. Toeing around it, Linda uncovered a crumpled piece of paper that had not burned.

She smoothed it out, then announced excitedly, "I've found something!"

The others crowded around to look at a crude map of the ghost-town area.

"And here's an arrowhead like the brand on the burro and the rock formations!" Linda cried. "They point northeast!"

"That's the way the two riders we saw were going," Kathy said.

"The state highway is about twenty miles in that direction," Cactus Mac remarked.

"Somebody could have been waiting there for those two riders with a horse trailer," Linda suggested.

"The main question," said Kathy, "is, where's Larry?"

"Might be that he hasn't got here yet," Cactus Mac suggested.

"We'll leave him a note if he's not here by the time we move on," Bob said.

"I'll write it on an old board with a black grease pencil I have in my sketching kit," said Linda. "Then weather or animals can't destroy it."

"I'd like to poke around the inside of these old buildings some before we go," Bob said. "How about you, Cactus?"

"I'll go along on that," said the foreman. "But I suggest the young ladies wait here at the Royal Hotel." He grinned and pointed across the street to the tottering structure with its weathered, peeling sign.

When the men had gone off, Linda said to Kathy, "I can't just sit here. I think I'll bring Chica d'Oro over to practice her bow. Do you think you could keep Vagabond back with the other horses? He distracts Chica too much."

"I'll tie up Vagabond," Kathy replied, "and give him a good currying down. He sure needs one and it will make him feel better."

Chica d'Oro, working alone with Linda, went

through her bowing routine much more smoothly than before.

"We're ready now for the next step, baby," Linda told her pony as she mounted.

But Chica was hesitant to go down on one knee with Linda on her back. She would, however, pick up her foot on cue.

"You're doing beautifully," Linda praised her, "but it's going to take a lot of practice."

As the rider dismounted, Kathy rejoined her. "I left Vagabond tied up, feasting on a weed," she said. "Ooo, this is a spooky place to be alone in."

The girls sat together on one of the steps of the Royal Hotel, wondering what could have happened to Larry. They came up with no new guesses. Before long, Cactus Mac and Bob returned.

"We'd better ride on till evening," said the foreman. "Thar's a stock-waterin' tank a few miles farther along. We can sack thar."

With Linda leading Chica, they walked back to the building where the horses and Rango had been left.

"Where's Vagabond?" asked Bob, looking around.

"Tied over there," answered Kathy, then cried, "Oh, my goodness, he *was* tied over there!"

Now only a short piece of rope greeted their eyes.

Linda examined the end of it. "The little rascal

chewed himself free," she said. "I'll bet he wanted to find Chica d'Oro."

"Sure, that's it," said Bob. "Come on, let's round him up." But the search revealed no Vagabond.

It was Linda who noted the door of the opera house swinging half-open on one hinge. "That wasn't open when we came here," she declared.

The searchers peered into the tumble-down theater. At the end, on the stage, stood Vagabond.

At sight of Linda and the others, the burro gave a series of high-pitched brays. The onlookers laughed.

"What a fancy tenor!" Kathy exclaimed.

Then Vagabond added to his act by giving a couple of gay bucks, a jarring routine that the rickety old stage could not bear. With a splintering crash the burro disappeared from sight!

Kathy gave a horrified scream and started to rush in, but Bob held her back. "Step very easy, everyone," he admonished, "or we're likely to bring this whole building down on us."

"I'm goin' for ropes," said Cactus Mac, turning back to the gear lot.

The others gingerly made their way to the stage and carefully peered into the black chasm beneath. They were just able to see Vagabond trying to shake himself free from some crossed boards.

"Easy, little fellow," Linda called down. "We'll get you out in a minute."

Vagabond gave a weak "yawp" in response.

"He sounds more scared than hurt," Bob commented.

"Oh, I hope so," said Linda.

When Cactus Mac returned, he had ropes, a horse blanket, and his flashlight. "You get down into this here hole with me," he said to Bob.

He handed the flashlight to Linda to keep a beam on them, and dropped his trappings below. Then he and Bob lowered themselves into the opening. They made a sling of the blanket, then pulled the ropes underneath Vagabond and threw the rope ends up to the girls.

Cactus Mac called to them, "Get down in front o' the stage and tighten up as hard on the ropes as you can when we lift."

Bob and the foreman raised Vagabond up and the girls pulled back on the ropes until the little burro was rolled on his side topstage. Linda and Kathy hauled him as carefully as possible to the edge of the platform. Bob and Cactus Mac helped to lift him down to the floor.

"Now you're all right," Linda told him soothingly, although she noticed that both of Vagabond's front legs were badly skinned.

At Cactus Mac's shouted instructions, Linda threw back a rope. Holding the end of it, both girls braced themselves against the stage as first Bob, then Cactus Mac clambered up out of the hole.

"Hmm," said Cactus Mac, seeing the burro's injuries. "By the time we get this here nuisance doctored up, it'll be too late to hit the trail today. We may as well plan on makin' camp in Ghost Town for the night."

"While there's still some daylight," said Bob, "I'd like to follow the tracks of those three riders who left town at the far end. Maybe we can discover where they were headed."

"I'm for that," Cactus Mac agreed.

"I'll take care of Vagabond," Kathy offered. "I'm the best bandager-upper ever graduated from three different first-aid classes."

"All right," said Linda. "While you're doctoring him, I'll put a few Rancho del Sol brand marks around town for Larry's benefit. In case he should ride in after we've left, he'll know we've been here and follow us. Then I'll bring Chica around in front of the opera house for another bowing lesson."

Linda hurried away to get the filly and also the black grease pencil from her sketching kit. She ground-hitched Chica d'Oro with her tie rope at the Royal Hotel, and went on to sketch a half-dozen sun brands in noticeable spots about town.

She had just returned to the hotel porch when a couple of riders came down the street from the northeast. One of the horses was limping badly.

They stopped in surprise before Linda. The men were in dusty clothes and had a day's stubble on their faces.

"Look who's here!" exclaimed one raspily. "A doll!"

Linda's spine tingled with apprehension.

"Say, girl, did you see a lone rider with a burro around these parts?" asked the other.

"No, I haven't," she replied, hoping desperately that Vagabond would not choose this moment to bray.

"Now there's a nice piece of horseflesh," remarked the other man, running gleaming eyes over Chica d'Oro.

"Looks sound as a dollar," said his companion.

"And me with a lame horse." His friend laughed. "I'll just make a switch." He started to dismount.

"Oh, no, you won't!" Linda cried.

She raced to Chica d'Oro. Snatching up the loose tie rope, Linda leaped on the filly's back and rode away furiously.

The man was gaining on her . . .

Landslide! 8

Glancing back, Linda saw the two riders in hot pursuit as she raced out of town. The lame horse was no threat, but the other one was gaining on her!

Linda strained her eyes for sight of Cactus Mac and Bob, but did not see them, and she was riding too fast to pick up their trail.

Suddenly, as Linda glanced back rapidly, she saw that the man on the fast horse had a lariat in his hand. He was going to try to rope her!

Linda urged the palomino toward a rugged rise of mammoth boulders. The man sent the loop snaking out and Linda veered sharply to the side. The rope missed her.

As her pursuer gathered in his rope, she gained a little distance and turned left around the boulders. It was fast growing dark, but the fleeing girl was able to see an arroyo ahead. Quickly she put Chica down the steep bank on her rump and slipped off her.

'The man, believing that she had continued round the boulder hump, went on that way. Linda pressed close against the bank of the gully. Then she heard the ruffians circling back. They stopped not far from her.

One said, "No use trying to find the good horse in these rocks tonight. That gal slipped through our fingers."

The raspy voice of the other barked, "Bad luck! I'm likely to be put afoot any minute with this horse. And if we don't catch that guy soon, the boss'll make trouble." Then the men rode off.

Linda sighed in relief and asked herself, Who's the person they're trying to catch? Could it be Larry? But why would they be after him?

She mounted Chica d'Oro again and the filly scrambled up the embankment. Not far off Linda recognized Bob and Cactus Mac returning on Rocket and Buck. She hurried to join them.

"What brought you out here alone in the dark?" Bob asked with sharp concern.

She told them what had happened.

"Horse thieves!" growled Cactus Mac. "I'd like to get my hands on 'em!"

"They sound like a couple of pretty rough characters," said Bob. "I hope Kathy is all right."

They found her seated by a campfire with Rango

on his haunches beside her. A pot of vegetable soup
was heating.

"Linda Craig, where have you been?" she demanded. "I've been so worried."

"I didn't leave you on purpose," her chum said.
"Wait until you hear about my adventure." Kathy
listened in amazement.

Bob asked Kathy with a twinkle in his eye, "Were
you scared, being here alone?"

Kathy gave a little laugh. "I wasn't a bit scared
with Rango beside me." She put one arm affectionately around the huge dog. "He's my protector."

As soon as the horses had been rubbed down and
fed, Linda and her friends had their own supper of
soup, cheese, crackers, and canned pineapple. As
usual, Bob turned on his transistor radio for a bit of
outside news and a couple of good tunes. Then the
tired travelers tucked themselves into their sleeping bags.

Before the group left in the morning, Linda wrote
a message with her grease pencil on the Royal
Hotel. Under the sun brand she wrote, LARRY: ON
TO SCOTSWARD. FOLLOW OLD SOL RIDERS.

"I hope he shows up soon," Linda murmured.

A couple of hours later she and the others rode
through Yucca Pass into a canyon of ancient cliff
dwellings. They stopped to stare up at the even
lines of holes in the canyon side which had been the
homes of Indians long before.

"My goodness!" exclaimed Kathy. "It sure would be bad if you took too big a step out of your front door!"

"It was too bad for any o' their enemies who got close," said Cactus Mac. "The cliff dwellers routed 'em good and proper by throwin' down rocks and spears onto 'em."

"I'd like to look into a few of those cave homes," said Linda. "We might pick up some relics for keepsakes."

"How do we get up there without wings?" Kathy asked.

"Off to the side yonder thar's a steep, narrow path," Cactus Mac informed her. He grinned. "You climb by diggin' in with your toes."

"Let's try it!" Linda urged.

They tethered the horses to mesquite bushes and began the slippery ascent. Linda and Kathy caught hold of the chaparral growing at the side for support, but Bob, followed by Cactus Mac, attempted the toe-digging method.

Halfway to the top, Bob shoved his toe under a ridge and pulled up a taut, buried rope. Instantly he saw that it was fastened to a large boulder high above them. He had loosened the rock, which came rumbling down at terrific speed.

"Look out!" Bob yelled, as a landslide of loose earth and boulders followed.

It was too late! The climbers were carried along, sliding on their heels. There were a few moments of fright before they landed at the bottom, fortunately with only slight bruises.

The noise of tumbling earth and rocks had thrown the horses into a panic. With frightened leaps, they had snapped the brittle mesquite branches and bolted from the avalanche. Rango, barking, leaped after them and caught hold of Buck's dragging reins, bringing him to a halt.

Linda, Bob, and Cactus Mac ran after the other horses and whistled. At the familiar sound the animals slowed, turned, and trotted back. Vagabond, next to Chica d'Oro, contributed a few weak brays. Cactus Mac took Buck's reins from Rango's mouth and patted the dog warmly.

Suddenly Bob exclaimed, "Where's Kathy?" She was nowhere in sight.

For an instant, the others stared in horrified shock at the great pile of earth and stones that had fallen. They threw their horses' reins down in a ground hitch and ran back to the slide. On the way, Linda called to the dog. "Rango, find Kathy! Get Kathy!"

Rango began sniffing around, while the others dug frantically in the loose earth with sticks and hands. The rubble caved in as fast as they scooped it out.

Suddenly the dog gave a series of small yelps and

pawed rapidly in the earth. Linda, Bob, and Cactus Mac ran to his aid and soon uncovered the missing girl.

"Kathy, Kathy!" Linda gasped, wiping the dust gently from her friend's face with a handkerchief.

Kathy's eyes opened. She blinked and then sat up, asking shakily, "What happened to us?"

"Not to us," Bob replied. "Just you, Kathy. You got caught under the landslide."

"Rango found you," said Linda.

The shepherd dog waved his tail and licked Kathy's face. This brought the girl out of her dazed state. She laughed. "Hey, cut it out! Thanks for finding me, Rango. But you don't have to keep on kissing me."

Linda pulled Rango back. "Can you stand up?" Bob asked Kathy, as he helped the girl to her feet.

"I'm all right," she assured him. Then she rubbed the back of her head. "A real goose egg! I guess my head must have hit a rock."

Bob frowned. "Someone set that devilish trap! All of us might have been buried or badly injured."

"Maybe the person's living up in those caves," Linda suggested, "and doesn't want visitors."

"And maybe not," said Cactus Mac. "That trap might have been set years ago. The rope looked old."

"Let's scout around up there anyway," Linda proposed.

D

The two men were willing, but Kathy said, "Not me. Rango and I will stay here with the horses in the shade of that brush."

As the others clambered back up the cliff, they found that the landslide had provided them with steppingstones.

Halfway up, Linda stopped the men, saying in a low voice, "Look at that end cave. There are a couple of empty food cans outside the entrance."

"Hmm!" Cactus Mac muttered. "I'll lead the way. Can't take a chance on your bein' hurt."

They climbed to a ledge which ran in front of the openings. Cautiously, and in single file, the searchers made their way along it to the end cave. They gazed inside. To their astonishment, they beheld a shaggy-haired old man in ragged clothing. He stood trembling.

"Go 'way!" he said raucously. "Most folks get scared and go 'way," the recluse went on. "What d'you want with Johnny Lee? I got nothing. I got no food till I go out and find me somethin'."

Linda and the men did not reply right away. Any anger they had felt against a malicious character began to ebb at the sight of the emaciated old fellow.

But finally Bob said, "You could have killed us with that rope device of yours."

"Not kill. Just scare," insisted the hermit. "It keeps away the rockhounds who keep comin' around these days pokin' holes in everythin'. And the others too."

"What others?" Linda asked quickly.

"Aw, there was a fellow here past Sunday," the hermit told her. "He was lookin' in the old rock grindin' holes where the squaws made flour out of their corn."

"Was he searching for a relic or did he have something he was trying to hide?" Bob asked.

"Can't say," replied the old man. "He sneaked up here without settin' off the rockslide, but I made sure to start one when he went down. That scared him off for good. Hurt him too. He went limpin' off to his horse and pack burro. Yep, he had a pack burro with him—looked just like yours." The recluse chuckled slyly. "I peeked down at you before."

The three exchanged significant glances.

Then Johnny Lee's expression became truculent. He asked, "What do you want here?"

"We were curious to see what these caves look like inside," Linda replied kindly, "and thought maybe we could pick up a relic or two."

"Ain't nothin' in 'em," said the hermit glumly. "You git, and let me be in peace."

"Sure," Bob said. "We'll leave. But first could you tell us which direction the man with the burro took?"

"He headed for Black Canyon," answered Johnny

Lee readily enough, eager to get rid of his unwelcome guests.

That's on our way, Linda thought.

The hermit went on, "The Black Canyon walls is covered with old Injun pictures and writin's. Mebbe you'll find relics there."

"I'm glad to know that," Linda said with a smile, and added gently, "We'll leave you some food down below."

The man's toothless jaw dropped open in unbelieving surprise and his eyes grew moist. The three thanked him for the information and began the difficult descent.

As soon as they reached the canyon floor, Linda said, "We must find that man who came with the burro. He may be seriously injured."

"Vagabond probably belongs to him," Bob surmised.

"Might be he's the one who sent this here burro for help," Cactus Mac offered.

While Bob told Kathy what had happened, Linda made up a pack of bacon, crackers, beans, and tomatoes and left it in the shade of the mesquite.

Soon the riders were on the trail again and heading for Black Canyon, hoping to locate the mysterious man with the burro. A sandy plain stretched ahead. Presently Bob and the girls exclaimed in amazement at the sight before them. In the distance, a white, tile-roofed mansion loomed imposingly, with green fields all about it and a sparkling lake in front.

"Whose magnificent estate is that?" Linda asked in awe.

Cactus Mac's eyes twinkled. "Sorry, friends. That thar estate just ain't thar. It's only a reflection."

"A mirage!" Linda exclaimed.

"I never saw anything look so real!" Kathy declared.

Suddenly Rocket bolted headlong toward it. Had he seen the mirage too and, being meadow-raised, had enough of desert-floor dry fodder?

Bob pulled back on the reins to hold in his mount, but realized immediately that it was no use. Rocket had taken the bit in his teeth and was intent on what lay ahead.

He'll run himself to death, Bob thought desperately. I must stop him.

The Desert Figure 9

As Rocket tore across the desert toward the mirage, Bob grimly noted the heavy growth of rabbit brush underfoot. If the horse tripped on it, he could crash down with Bob under him.

There's no way out. he thought. I'll have to stick with him!

Suddenly a big jackrabbit leaped from behind a bush directly in front of Rocket, who shied sharply to the side. Instantly Bob took advantage of the horse's fright to yank the bit back into the bay's mouth. He pivoted Rocket, then brought him to a standstill. The horse was lathered and quivering, and his eyes were wild.

Bob dismounted and said evenly, "It's okay, Rocket. I don't blame you. Those mirages are mighty deceiving. But from now on you let the boss guide you to green pastures."

His calm voice and manner settled the horse.

Although Rocket still breathed heavily, he stopped quivering and stood spent with his head dropped.

Bob broke off a piece of brush and scraped away some of the lather. Then he mounted and returned to the others at a slow walk.

"How did you ever get him stopped?" Linda asked, her face strained.

"One spry jackrabbit," Bob told his sister with a grin.

"And one rider who knows how to handle a horse," declared Kathy staunchly.

Cactus Mac sat back with a pleased expression on his face and nodded. "Fine control, Bob."

They rode on and at last entered the avenue of volcanic rock known as Black Canyon. There was no sign of anyone at the spot.

The visitors gazed at the jumbled black stones lining the cliff walls and garnished with prehistoric Indian writings and picture carvings.

"This is fantastic!" Linda exclaimed.

The riders dismounted and examined the engraved sketches of turtles, snakes, and other animals, as well as human figures. Also depicted were the sun, the moon, and ancient weapons. The writings were of many designs.

"These are all ceremonial symbols," Kathy informed them. She had picked up some archaeological knowledge from assisting her father in his lapidary business.

"Think of the talent and labor it took to carve these figures," said Linda. "Why would such an able race of people die out?"

"Wal now," drawled Cactus Mac, "the Survey Association of California has been workin' for years to unravel that thar riddle."

"I'm going to sketch some of these symbols," Linda declared. She leaned close to the rocks to look at the carvings, moving her hand across one.

Suddenly Bob exclaimed, "Watch out, Linda!" and gave her a push. Then he cried in pain, and snatched back his own hand.

Kathy gave a little shriek. "A scorpion!"

They all saw the straw-colored, crablike creature scuttle away. The narrow, barbed tail was jointed, and the scorpion had flipped it over its back with whiplike action to inflict a painful sting on the side of Bob's hand.

Cactus Mac said tersely, "It's not the deadly species. That sort has a longer, narrower stinger and two black stripes down its back."

"I'll bet your hand hurts just the same, Bob," said Linda, and quickly brought out the first-aid kit. Cactus Mac took it from her, saying. "Make a pot of strong coffee for your brother."

Kathy hurried off to build a little fire of twigs in a small circle of rocks in the shade provided by the canyon wall, and Linda put on the coffeepot.

Cactus Mac got Bob settled. Then he took the

small surgical scalpel from the kit and made a crosscut on the swelling, inflamed spot. He let the wound bleed for a few moments, swabbed off the blood, and poured ammonia into the opening.

Bob jumped. "Your cure is worse than the sting!" he declared.

Cactus Mac only nodded and stuck a large bandage over the discolored spot. When the coffee was ready, Linda brought the pot to Bob with a cup.

"Drink as much of that stimulant fast as you can," Cactus Mac ordered. To the girls he said, "We'd best stay around for a day, so Bob can keep kind o' quiet out o' the sun. Lucky thar's water here."

They had all noted the well just inside the entrance to the canyon. On it was a bronze plate stating that the well had been donated by the Sage Archaeological Society.

"What about the scorpions?" Kathy asked uncertainly.

"Just watch out for 'em," the foreman cautioned. "They're shy little critters and hide away in the crevices of the rocks in the daytime. They come out at night. But they won't bother *you* if you don't bother *them*. Linda and Bob must have upset that thar little fellow in his hideout."

"How about our having lunch now, even if it is early?" Linda asked. "Then we'll have a long afternoon to poke around the canyon."

Cactus Mac grinned. "The excitement's made me

hungry. I'll fix up the horses over by the well while you gals rassle up a bite of chow."

Kathy made sandwiches of canned lunch meat and pumpernickel bread, well wrapped in foil to keep fresh. Linda opened cans. "Same old tomatoes," she told Bob cheerily, "but I'm fixing them this time with sugar and vinegar."

With a wry grin, Bob turned on the radio, and the girls hummed along with the musical numbers being played as they prepared lunch. Suddenly the program was interrupted by a news commentator.

"Word has just been received," he announced, "that a girl has been kidnapped from Rancho del Sol in the San Quinto Valley. She is Mary Sutton."

"Oh, my goodness!" Linda exclaimed, as everyone froze and listened.

The commentator continued, "The young woman was calling at the ranch and was standing by the corral. Mrs. Rosalinda Mallory, the owner, was just coming from the house, when a man and woman boldly entered the ranch, pulled the young girl into their car, and drove away with her.

"Mary Sutton was an acquaintance of the Mallorys' absent granddaughter, Linda Craig. The two girls look very much alike. The sheriff believes that it was Linda the couple intended to kidnap."

"He's right," Linda said. "It must be the Sello gang." Her eyes filled with tears. "Oh, poor Mary!"

"Take it easy, Sis," Bob admonished. "The gang

must know by now that they have the wrong girl. They've probably let her go."

"I hope so!" Linda exclaimed. "Keep the radio turned on so we'll know what's happening."

"But if they have released her," Kathy added in a worried voice, "they'll come after Linda again."

The four sat listening to the music and waiting for further news. They ate without enthusiasm. After a while, Bob lay back and fell asleep.

"Best thing for him," remarked Cactus Mac. "That thar scorpion poison can make a man mighty sick." The foreman got to his feet. "Think I'll take a stroll up the canyon. I always like to know the lay o' the land 'fore I settle down in a place for the night."

As he disappeared around the bend, Linda rose and spoke softly to Kathy. "I'm going to climb up to the top of the canyon wall to see if there's any sign of Larry. Do you want to come?"

Kathy nodded assent. The two girls quietly stepped away, got their binoculars, and began the climb. When they reached the top of the cliff, both of them put the glasses to their eyes and scanned the desert.

"Somebody's out there leading a horse!" Linda exclaimed.

They gazed hard at the slow-moving figure in the distance. "He looks very much like Larry," Kathy said excitedly.

"He does," Linda agreed, "and I think he's in trouble."

As they peered anxiously the boy stumbled, fell and lay motionless.

"Come on!" Linda exclaimed. "We must go after him!"

Quickly the girls descended to the canyon. Bob was still asleep. Linda cast an anxious look at her brother's flushed face and decided not to wake him Swiftly and quietly she and Kathy saddled up and rode out.

They headed straight for the person who had fallen in the desert. When they reached the unconscious figure, Linda cried, "It *is* Larry!"

The girls dismounted and knelt beside him. While Linda held up his head and put her canteen to his lips, Kathy wet her handkerchief and bathed his face. After a few minutes he revived, and his rescuers helped him sit up.

"Don't try to talk," Linda said.

"I'm okay now," he replied weakly, and insisted upon struggling to his feet.

Together Linda and Kathy aided him to mount Chica d'Oro. Then Linda swung into the saddle in front of him and they returned to camp, with Kathy leading Gypsy. As they rode in, Cactus Mac came back from his walk and Bob awoke.

"Larry!" they both cried, and Bob added with a grin, "You an invalid too?"

The girls knelt beside him . . .

Kathy brought water from the well for him and Gypsy, while Linda quickly made him some lunch While he ate, Larry told them his story.

"Gypsy caught a front shoe in a buried root and we had a bad fall. The top was loose on my canteen, I guess, because all the water spilled out. Then I saw that Gypsy had pulled off a chunk of hoof wall along with the shoe, so I didn't think I should ride her." He sighed. "It was a pretty long walk without water."

"Lucky thing the girls spotted you," Bob said soberly. "I certainly was in no shape to help." He told Larry about the scorpion bite.

"Bad luck," said Larry, shaking his head. Suddenly he noticed Vagabond. "Where did you get the burro?" he asked in surprise.

"That's Chica's pal." Kathy giggled, and related the finding of the little animal and the mystery of the arrows.

Meanwhile Cactus Mac had been examining Gypsy's hoof. "Not too bad," he declared. "The break can be filled with a little wood dough. I'll put a new shoe on cold and she'll be ready to go."

"That's good news," Larry said in relief.

"But we have some bad news," Linda announced seriously. She told him about the kidnapping at Rancho del Sol.

When she had finished, Larry nodded and said, "You're the one they were after, I'm sure. It's because of that yellow clay horse from Olvera Street. Somebody wants it and will stop at nothing to get it."

"You sound positive," said Linda.

"Let me tell you why," Larry replied. "As soon as the package arrived at the ranch, your grandmother took it into town to mail to you at Scotsward. On the way, she noticed a dark sedan following her. When Mrs. Mallory reached the post office, a woman entered right after her, bumped against her, and tried to snatch the package away.

"The postmaster saw what was happening and dashed out to help your grandmother. The woman ran out, got in the car, and drove away. Later the mailman told your grandmother the same sedan followed him out to Old Sol at the time he delivered the package."

"Did Doña mail it?" Linda asked.

"Yes," said Larry. "It's on the way to Scotsward now."

"There certainly must be something of great value in that statuette," remarked Bob.

"Diamonds, maybe," suggest Kathy, "being smuggled in from Mexico."

"Did the woman see where the parcel was addressed?" Linda asked with a worried frown.

"Mrs. Mallory said that she could have," Larry replied soberly.

"Then we must hurry on to Scotsward right

away," declared Bob, "and pick up the parcel before someone else does."

"Oh, no!" protested Linda. "We can't ride until you feel better."

"I'm all right now," Bob replied. "The pain has nearly gone out of my arm."

"Package or no package," declared Cactus Mac sternly, "you don't ride till dawn tomorrow." That ended the argument.

Linda turned to Larry. "We had about given you up. Did you get a late start?"

"Dad had some extra harness-repair work come in, so I stayed to help him," Larry explained. "I was too late to meet you at Ghost Town, of course, but I read your signs and the note. You know," he continued thoughtfully, "I saw some odd tracks on the way here. They belonged to a burro and a horse with a broken shoe. After a while, the burro's prints went off in another direction, and the horse's continued straight ahead. Maybe that burro was Vagabond!"

"Very likely," Cactus Mac agreed.

Linda was thinking hard. "The horse with the broken shoe could belong to the man who was hurt by the rockslide," she said.

Seeing Larry's questioning look, she told him of their adventure at the cliff dwellings.

"Wow!" he said. "You had a ball."

As the afternoon wore on into evening, the

campers listened to the hourly news bulletins. They reported no contact had been made with the abductors of Mary Sutton. By the time the Craigs and their friends crawled into the sleeping bags, there still was no word.

"Then they haven't let her go," Linda said, deeply worried.

"They will," Bob insisted.

At dawn, the group listened again as they ate breakfast. Still no word. When the riders started off, Linda rode some distance ahead. She veered from one side of the canyon to the other, observing the strange petroglyphs on the walls.

Presently Cactus Mac took the lead and Linda dropped to the end of the line. About mid-morning, she noted horse tracks. One of his shoes was broken! she thought excitedly and followed the prints until they disappeared into a high, heavy growth of brush.

Cautiously Linda parted the branches and rode through. Before her was a huge pile of rocks. Chica d'Oro nickered uneasily. Linda dismounted and peered around the edge of the boulders. Tied to one of the rocks was a dusty, weary saddle horse.

As Linda stared at the animal, wondering where his rider was, she heard a deep groan.

Traveler in Trouble   10

Swiftly Linda led Chica out of the brush and signaled for her companions to hurry over. As soon as the riders came up, they too heard the groans.

"What is it?" Kathy asked.

"I don't know," Linda said.

"It could be a trap," said Cactus Mac. "Stay back!"

They all dismounted, and with the men in the lead went around the pile of boulders. In a brush-shaped depression beside the cliff lay an old man. The boot had been pulled off his right foot, and his pants leg was torn above the knee. His leg was discolored and swollen.

"Broke," guessed Cactus Mac.

The man opened his eyes a slit. "I heard horses coming. Hoped you'd find me."

"What's your name, fellow?" Cactus Mac asked him.

"Amos Trippe," the other replied. "And my leg's broke." He fingered some sticks at his side. "Aimed to tie it up in a splint, but—but—" his voice dwindled—"I couldn't make it."

"We found a burro with an arrow branded on it," Linda told him. "Was he yours?"

The old man nodded. "So you found the no-good, measly lil' beast?"

"We also found the rock arrow signs on the desert," Bob said "Where do they point to?"

"Don't know nothing about them," rasped the old man. "After I got hurt in a rockslide, I sent the jack right out, hopin' somebody would follow him and help me."

Linda said in an aside to Bob, "Chica d'Oro found Vagabond on Saturday, but according to the story that hermit told us, Amos Trippe didn't break his leg until Sunday."

"That's right," said Bob. "Trippe could be lying."

"He may be the man those two ruffians who chased me out of Ghost Town were trying to find," Linda suggested. Playing her hunch, she returned to the old man. "How did you happen to get separated from your companions?" she asked, giving him a drink of water from her canteen.

He slid her a suspicious look, then replied in a surly tone, "I got no companions. I been riding alone."

Bob and Linda exchanged unbelieving looks.

"What're we gabbing about?" fretted Amos Trippe. "Ain't you going to fix up my leg so's I can git out of here?" He attempted to sit up and fainted from the pain.

Just then, Rango, who had been doing some sniffing around a spot on the cliff, gave a series of sharp little barks. Linda and Kathy ran to investigate.

"What is it, Rango?" Kathy asked. "I don't see a single thing."

"Here, this is it!" Linda exclaimed, pointing to the body of a freshly killed rabbit nearby. "Some of the blood must have dribbled on the rocks there."

Kathy sighed. "Poor old man! He must have tried to fix that rabbit to eat."

Linda hurled it far away out of Rango's reach, in case it was contaminated. The two girls went back to the others, but the dog still sniffed and pawed about the rocks. "Come on away from there, Rango," Linda called.

The animal protested with a few whines, but did as he was ordered.

"What do we do now?" asked Kathy.

"Tie up Amos's leg the best we can with sticks and you girls' scarves," said Cactus Mac.

"We'll have to improvise some sort of a litter in order to carry Trippe out of here," said Bob.

"A travois would be best," Cactus Mac advised.

"We'll need two poles," Bob said.

"And a tarp to stretch across them," Larry put in. "I'll get mine." He hurried away to the horses and was back in a few minutes with the piece of tarpaulin.

"This kind of litter was once used by Indians, wasn't it?" Kathy asked.

"Yes'm," the foreman replied. "And it's still done the same way. You hitch one end to a horse and the other end drags the ground."

While he and the boys got to work on the contraption, Linda and Kathy carefully bound up Amos Trippe's leg. Then they poured some canteen water into the crown of a hat for the old man's horse and gave him a little grain.

When the travois was finished, Cactus Mac and the boys transferred the injured man onto it, and carried him out to the horses. Buck hauled the travois, while Bob managed the pack string. Larry brought along Amos's horse. The group rode steadily, eager to get to the Scotsward Ranch as soon as possible. They stopped only a couple of times to try reviving Amos Trippe with a little water, but he remained unconscious. Linda got out crackers and dry figs for the rest to munch on.

Bob kept his radio turned on. The Mary Sutton kidnapping was mentioned in every news broadcast, but there were no new developments.

"The kidnappers must know by now that they have the wrong girl," said Kathy. "Why won't they let her go?"

"Because Mary could describe them to the police," Linda replied.

"We're certainly going to keep our eyes on you, Linda," said Larry. "Since they still don't have the yellow clay horse, they may try again to snatch you and demand the statuette as ransom."

"Just let them try that!" said Bob vehemently.

The riders arrived at the Scotsward Ranch shortly after one o'clock. Lean, wiry Fred Scott and big, rawboned, hearty Mrs. Scott were waiting outside the rambling ranch house to meet them. The couple had been watching for the group and had seen them ride in.

Mrs. Scott barely exchanged greetings, as she eyed the old man on the travois. "Who is that, and what's the matter with him?" she asked in a deep voice.

"A lone desert traveler," said Linda. "His leg is broken. He's been unconscious all morning."

Mrs. Scott waved her hand toward the far wing of the house. "Put him in the first bedroom off the portico," she commanded the men. "You can move the redwood table from the patio into the room and lay the poor man on it, while I go call the doctor." She sailed into the house.

A genial-looking, white-haired lady with pink cheeks had come out. "I'm Angie, chief cook and bottle washer here," she said, smiling. "When did you folks last eat?"

"We had breakfast at dawn," Kathy replied readily. She was hungry.

"Oh, my!" Angie exclaimed. "I'll set a lunch right out."

"We don't want to be a bother," Linda said. "I'd love to help you fix it, if you ever let anyone in your kitchen."

"Young lady, you are sweet," Angie replied beaming. "You can come into my kitchen any time you want and fix anything your heart desires."

"I'll go peek in on Amos," Kathy offered.

"You girls take any room in that far wing you like," Angie said. "I expect you want to freshen up right off."

They thanked her, then Linda asked if any mail or packages had come for her.

"No, I don't think so," Angie replied.

Meanwhile Amos Trippe had been carried inside. In a few minutes, Cactus Mac, Bob, and Larry came back and followed Fred Scott to the barns with the horses. Linda and Kathy chose a plain but clean, neat room. They washed, combed their hair, and then went to look at Amos Trippe.

"Nothing we can do here," said Kathy, "but I'll

be glad to baby-sit. How about your helping Angie and hurrying up that lunch? I'm absolutely famished."

Angie had an enormous pan of sliced ham sizzling on the stove and a bowl of foamy, beaten eggs waiting to be scrambled. She was putting big, fluffy pan rolls into the oven to heat. "Would you like to make a salad?" Angie asked.

"Be glad to," Linda answered. After a few days of their trail diet, she yearned for fresh greens.

"Pick what you want out of the icebox," Angie said. "Dressings are here." She waved her hand toward a shelf.

Linda had never seen such a huge and abundantly stocked refrigerator. She cut up a large head of crisp lettuce, cucumbers, and scallions, and from the variety of dressing bottles chose an Italian one, flavored with a sharp cheese.

The five hungry trail riders sat down informally at the round table in one end of the big kitchen. They had just finished eating when the doctor arrived.

"Amos is semiconscious now," Kathy told him. "He was groaning when Mrs. Scott changed places with me a few minutes ago."

As soon as the doctor had examined the old man, he came to the kitchen and asked, "Can any of you assist me with the anesthetic?"

"I will," Kathy volunteered. As she followed the physician, Angie hurried away to phone a cousin who was a practical nurse to come and take care of Amos Trippe.

While Kathy stayed with him, the Scotts called Linda, Bob, and Cactus Mac out on the portico. "I have bad news for you folks about the cattle," Fred Scott announced. "The inspectors won't let you move any Black Angus out at this time. Anthrax has broken out."

"Oh, no!" Linda said. "Bronco told us about an epidemic near here, but we hoped it hadn't reached your ranch."

"How about your cattle?" Bob asked.

"Got a clean bill of health on them after yesterday's inspection," the ranch owner told him. "But the inspectors are quarantining them here for a spell until the vets are sure no infection is going to show up among them."

"How bad is the area?" Cactus Mac asked.

"Real bad in some sections," Scott replied. "They're trying to keep it from spreading."

"Suppose you folks stay on for a few days anyhow," insisted Mrs. Scott, "and get a good rest. The pond is real nice to swim in, and maybe you'd enjoy riding some of the quarter horses."

"Thank you," Linda said. "I'd love to—especially your Little Red. I guess he's the most famous quarter horse stud in Southern California." She arose. "I'd better phone Rancho del Sol and give Doña and Bronco the news."

Linda went to the living room and put her call through to the Mallory ranch. After telling her grandmother about the anthrax infection, Linda asked anxiously, "Is there any news of Mary?"

Doña sadly told her there was none, except that the sheriff's deputies had found the abandoned green kidnap car several miles south of Los Angeles. "I feel so sorry for that unfortunate girl."

Meanwhile Bob had asked the Scotts when the postman would arrive. He had kept his eyes on the RFD mailbox at the end of the long driveway, hoping the package containing the clay horse would be delivered.

"Around four o'clock," said Mrs. Scott. "He should be coming along any minute now."

Just as Linda hung up, Bob called from the portico, "Here comes the postman!"

Together the Craigs raced down the driveway. The man had already put a package in the box. Before Linda and Bob reached it, a compact car holding two men shot from behind a clump of trees at the roadside. The driver stopped, reached out, and took the package from the box. Then the car sped away.

"Thieves!" Bob exclaimed.

He chased after them, with Linda at his heels, trying to pick up the license number of the vehicle. They were unable to do so and returned to the house crestfallen.

"That was probably my package!" Linda said dolefully.

"If it wasn't, those two men are in for a surprise," Bob remarked. "In any case, we'd better notify the sheriff."

"Here comes the postman again," Linda said. "This is his last stop. He must have gone up the road to turn around. Maybe he'll remember something about the package."

At Bob's signal, he stopped. "Could you tell us," Linda asked, "if that package you put in the mailbox was from Rancho del Sol?"

"Why, yes, it was," the man replied. "It's a pretty name. That's why I recall it." Then he looked at the Craigs, bewildered. "You haven't taken it out yet?"

"It's been stolen!" Linda said, and explained the circumstances.

"The police should be notified," the postman declared. "That's a federal offense."

"We know," Bob replied. "I'll do it right away."

He and Linda went back to the house, where he called the sheriff's office. Bob reported the theft and gave a description of the car.

"We'll have the men picked up," promised the deputy who had answered, "and notify you."

Linda was so quiet during an outdoor barbecue supper which followed that Fred Scott, hoping to cheer her up, asked, "How would you like to take a look at my horses?"

"I'd like to ride one," Linda replied, trying to mask her deep disappointment at the loss of the horse statuette.

The wiry little man grinned mischievously. "Say," he said, "we have a couple that always race nose to nose. How would you and your brother like to take them around the ring, and see if you can bring one in a winner?"

"Great!" Bob exclaimed, and Linda smiled in anticipation.

A few minutes later Fred Scott snapped on the floodlights around the race track, and he and Cactus Mac went to get the horses.

The others gathered at the rail to watch, including Angie, who bustled up to Linda and whispered, "I'm rooting for you. If you win, I'll make you a chocolate cake."

"That's my favorite!" Linda exclaimed. "I'll do my best."

The horses were brought out. Brother and sister swung into their saddles and at the signal spurted around the ring. Linda thrilled to the speed of her horse, but although she rode her best, she and Bob pulled their mounts up to the finish line nose and nose.

"What a pair!" Bob exclaimed admiringly.

The riders gave the horses a breather, then took them around again. Once more they thundered across the line nose to nose.

As Linda stood to one side resting her horse, Angie called up, "You've just got to win that chocolate cake!"

Suddenly Linda's eyes sparkled and she smothered a grin as she thought of a way to please Angie. Reaching over the rail, she broke off a leafy branch of pungent silver sage.

As the race started again, Linda held the branch to her side. When the horses pounded into the home stretch, she leaned far along her mount's neck and extended the sage branch straight ahead. It was an irresistible morsel. The quarter horse stretched his muzzle for it. And won the race—by a nose!

Bob gave a cry of protest, then grinned wryly as the spectators laughed, whistled, and clapped. "Please forgive me, Bob," said Linda.

Suddenly over the noise they heard Vagabond braying. Everyone turned quickly toward the corral to see what was upsetting the burro. They caught sight of two men skulking away from the ranch house. The Scotsward men chased after them, but they disappeared into the dusk.

Meanwhile Linda and the others had hastened back to the house to see what the intruders had been doing there. They gasped in amazement.

All the guest rooms, including the one which Amos Trippe occupied, had been ransacked!

Smoked Out 11

When Linda and Kathy entered Amos Trippe's room, the old man began to stir and mutter.

Kathy placed her hand on his brow. "He's feverish," she said, as the others crowded in.

"Thank goodness he wasn't harmed," said Linda.

"Just look at this room!" Mrs. Scott exclaimed. "I wonder if those ruffians found what they were looking for?"

"What I want to know is where Rango has been keepin' himself all this time," Cactus Mac said in disgust.

A couple of sharp, high barks came from under the bed and the big dog's head emerged.

"Why, you scoundrel," Cactus Mac berated him, "hidin' like that from those snoopers! The jack's a better watchdog than you are." A growl came from Rango.

Linda stooped down. "He has something under

his paw. Come on out, Rango, and show us what it is," she urged.

Rango picked up the object in his teeth and wriggled out on his stomach. He waved his plume of a tail and looked about with glowing eyes.

Linda took a jacket button from his jaws. "This is from the clothes of one of those men!" she exclaimed.

Kathy smiled, "I guess it was Rango who ran the intruders off," she said, "And they left a clue behind."

"He surely protected Amos from them," Bob put in.

Cactus Mac regarded Rango with a sheepish grin. "Well, old fellow," he said, "I apologize." He gave the dog an affectionate thump. "You're all right."

Rango sat down on his haunches, draped his long tongue out of one side of his mouth, and assumed the silly, pleased expression he always did when praised.

With a laugh, Linda hugged him close. "You certainly *are* all right," she murmured.

"Well," declared Mrs. Scott abruptly, "it's no use standing here. I'm going to check the rest of the house to see if anything was taken."

As she left the room with Angie and Cactus Mac, Amos Trippe began to thrash about and blurt out incoherent words. One was "arrow." Linda, Kathy, and Bob remained to listen.

"I think he's hiding something valuable," Bob said, "but what?"

"And did those two men find it?" Kathy added.

"It's all connected somehow with the brand on Vagabond," Linda surmised. "Why else did he lie to us about when he branded the burro?"

"Listen," said Kathy quickly, "he's talking plainer now."

Linda leaned closer to the old man. Amos was muttering, "Rabbit—blood—sand—mortar—rabbit." He regained consciousness and moaned with pain.

"We won't learn any more now," Bob said. "He knows we're here."

Just then a pleasant voice spoke from the door behind them. "You young folks run along now. I'll take over." They turned to see a heavy, plain-faced woman with gray hair. "I'm Angie's Cousin Mattie," she said smiling. "The nurse."

The young people left, feeling certain that the old man was in good hands. While Bob went to look for Larry, who had joined the chase after the intruders, Linda and Kathy walked toward the corral.

"What do you make of Amos's words?" Kathy asked.

"Not much right now," Linda replied. "Amos did kill a rabbit and there was blood on the rocks."

They found Cactus Mac making a late check of

the horses and repeated to him what Amos Trippe
had blurted out.

"Probably just some event in that thar oldtimer's
life," the foreman answered. "Those old desert rats
have to rely on anything at hand in case of
emergency. With water so scarce, likely he had to
mix sand with rabbit blood at one time to make a
mortar to repair something."

Linda and Kathy exchanged significant glances
and walked on toward the house.

"Rango was sniffing and pawing at the rocks near
where Amos killed the rabbit," Linda reminded her
friend. "Maybe the old man made a mortar with
rabbit's blood and sealed something of value into
the cliff face there."

"It must be the very thing those men were
searching for tonight," Kathy suggested. "We ought
to tell the others and all ride out to look for it."

Linda said it might be nothing but a wild-goose
chase and they would be laughed at. "Suppose you
and I slip away early in the morning and investigate."

"Alone?" Kathy asked. Then she added, "All
right, if we take Rango."

The two girls were up the next morning at five
and went to the barn to feed Chica d'Oro and
Patches. Then they saddled the horses. Just before
they left, Linda put Vagabond in a stall kept for

stallions, where he could neither crawl out nor jump over the door.

"Sorry," she said, patting his head, "but you'd only be a nuisance tagging along this morning."

Linda and Kathy rode out quietly. Rango, having been roused from his bed in the hay and fed, trotted along beside the palomino with an important air.

The filly kept turning her head and whinnying. She seemed unhappy at being taken and her little friend, Vagabond, left behind.

"Quiet, baby, quiet!" Linda remonstrated in a hushed but firm voice. "This is a secret mission." She ran a soothing hand down the palomino's neck. "And it's time you learned that you can't always have Vagabond with you."

She gave an authoritative flip with the reins and pressed her knees against the horse's sides. As always, Chica d'Oro, wanting to please Linda, settled down now to an easy gait with her attention on the trail ahead. About nine o'clock, the girls arrived at the spot where they had found Amos.

Linda pointed to the rocks, commanding, "Rango, rabbit!"

The dog bounded off, sniffing, as the girls dismounted. Suddenly Rango gave a couple of yelps and started pawing at the spot. Linda and Kathy ran to him and saw a couple of large rocks mortared tight into a niche.

Excitedly they found sharp-pointed sticks and began digging out the mortar. Because it was not a hard-set substance, the girls soon were able to pull the rocks away from the niche.

For a moment they both stared speechless at the cache. Before them lay two stuffed canvas moneybags with the name of a Los Angeles bank stenciled on them.

"The bank robbers' loot!" Linda cried.

"I never would have suspected Amos Trippe of holding up a bank," Kathy declared. "He just doesn't seem the type."

"Maybe he didn't do the actual robbing," Linda mused. "But he certainly must belong to the gang. Otherwise how could he have gotten these two bags of money?"

"I guess only Amos can explain that," replied Kathy.

Just then Chica d'Oro bent her ears forward and whinnied. Rango bristled, barking furiously.

Linda and Kathy spun about and saw two riders rounding the big boulders. The men spotted the girls and bore down rapidly on them.

Linda snatched up the moneybags and tossed one to Kathy. "Quick!" she exclaimed. "Ride up into these rocks!"

Hastily the girls mounted, with Rango at their heels, and zigzagged up through the craggy rocks, which kept them out of sight of their pursuers. Suddenly Linda pulled up sharply and pointed to a high, narrow passage between the rocks.

"A cave maybe!" she exclaimed. "Come on!"

They rode single file through the narrow opening into a dark rock chamber. As they pulled up, there was the clatter of hooves outside and a hoarse voice shouted:

"Come out of there or we'll be in to get you!"

The girls froze, hearts pounding.

"All right," barked a second voice. "We know you're in there!" Rango growled deep in his throat. A moment later the girls heard footsteps approaching the cave. As a dark figure appeared in the narrow, sunlit opening, Rango snarled and leaped for it. The man fell back with a cry.

"Good boy!" exclaimed Linda softly. Rango growled and guarded the opening.

After a few tense moments, the hoarse voice called again, "Make it snappy or we'll smoke you out!"

Kathy turned a panicky look on Linda. "We'll suffocate in a few minutes if they try that."

Linda whispered rapidly, "Put the sacks of money in Chica's saddlebags, and we'll turn her loose. She'll head for Scotsward and Vagabond."

Quickly Kathy transferred the loot, while Linda tied the reins around the saddle horn. They softly called Rango away from the entrance. Then Linda commanded, "Go! Find Vagabond!" and gave the palomino a sharp slap on the rump.

The horse bolted from the cave and galloped away. The men let out surprised, angry cries.

Instantly Patches jerked her reins free from Kathy's hand and lunged after Chica d'Oro. But the men outside caught her.

"Now we're afoot," Linda whispered, dismayed.

Both girls turned pale as they heard chaparral being broken down and heaped at the cave entrance. Rango backed off and began sniffing his way to the rear of the small chamber. He disappeared around a crag.

"Let's follow Rango," Linda said.

Hastily the girls went after the dog and caught sight of a streak of light in the distance.

"It's a chimney through the rocks," Linda whispered in relief. "Rango smelled the fresh air. I hope the chimney's big enough for us to wriggle up."

With Linda's help, Kathy climbed into the chimney and pulled herself out on top of the roof of the cave. Linda boosted Rango up. Kathy caught hold of him and hauled the dog up. Finally Linda pushed and scrambled her way out.

"Whew," she breathed softly.

Cautiously the girls crawled to the edge of the rocks and peered down. The three horses stood directly below. The men were some distance away, in front of the cave entrance, where a good-sized fire was blazing.

Quickly Linda thought of a plan of escape and whispered it to Kathy. Silently Linda slid down, took the rope from Patches' saddle, and climbed up to the roof of the cave again.

Swiftly she built a loop. With Rango following, Linda and Kathy crawled to the edge of the rocks near the cave entrance. The men were right below them.

Taking a deep breath, Linda neatly dabbed her loop over the nearest man and pulled it tight, yanking him off his feet. The ruffian yelled in surprise and the second man stared up at the girls in amazement.

As he tried to pull the rope from his companion, Linda screamed, "Get him, Rango! Get him!"

Instantly the big dog sprang down at the man, knocking him to the ground. Then Rango stood with his jaws at the fellow's throat, growling.

The man's eyes rolled as he lay frozen with terror. Holding the rope tightly and reeling it in, Linda scrambled and slid down the rocks to the two men with Kathy right behind her. Hastily but thoroughly the two girls tied up the roped man first, while Rango snarled a warning to both ruffians. Then Linda cut the rope and they trussed up the second man.

The man was yanked off his feet . .

Linda rose to her feet and patted Rango with a trembling hand. "Good boy!" she said shakily. Rango switched his tail in appreciation, but did not relax his guard for a moment.

Still pale with fright, Kathy brought the three horses over to Linda and Rango. Swiftly they tied the third horse behind Patches and mounted the other two.

"You're going to leave us here on the desert like this?" the second man whined.

"Only long enough for the sheriff to pick you up," Linda replied. "We'll turn your horses over to him also."

"That's better treatment than you would have given us," Kathy added spunkily.

Linda noted that the fire at the cave entrance was nearly burned out. "There's no danger of it spreading," Linda remarked, "because there's no brush around the rocks and no breeze."

With that she called Rango, and the riders loped off for Scotsward. When they arrived at the ranch, they found the place in a tumult. Several deputies were on the patio. Everyone rushed up to greet the girls, firing questions at them.

Mrs. Scott's voice called for silence. "One at a time! One at a time!" she shouted. "Land o' Goshen, you girls are a better sight than a freshet in a sand dune. We were just ready to start combing the desert inch by inch for you."

"When Chica came back without you, we really got worried," Bob said to Linda.

"And after we found that thar bank loot in the saddlebags, we didn't know what to think," Cactus Mac added, his blue eyes still showing the strain of worry.

"I'm mighty glad Chica d'Oro made it," Linda said with a smile.

"And so are we," broke in one of the deputies. "Now, if we can just get a good line on the bank robbers, maybe we can bring them in. They're two of the worst."

"Your robbers are tied up near where we found the moneybags, waiting to be picked up," said Linda.

"Well, I'll be—" exclaimed one of the officers with a dumbfounded expression, as he scratched the back of his head under his hat.

"Tied up!" Bob was astounded.

"How did they get tied up?" asked Cactus Mac, amazed.

Quietly Linda and Kathy told their story. When they finished, the men looked at the girls in silent astonishment and Larry gave a long, low whistle of appreciation.

"Where is this place?" one of the deputies asked.

Linda gave them explicit directions, and they set off in their jeep. As the others broke out in excited laughter and congratulations, Linda pulled Rango to her side.

"This fellow saved our lives by leading us out of that cave those men were filling with smoke," she declared, an affectionate hand on the big, yellow-tan dog. Then she asked, "How is Amos Trippe? I'd like to talk to him."

"He's pretty good this morning," Mattie said.

The patio was just outside Amos's room. Now, as Linda went into it, the old man said, "I heard most of what you was sayin' out there. So you found my gold!"

"It wasn't yours, Amos," Linda said gently. "How did you ever happen to have it?"

Amos pressed his lips together in stubborn silence.

"Are you in partnership with those bank robbers?" Linda persisted. "Is that what you want us to think?"

Amos Trippe's expression changed a bit as he looked at Linda, then at the others around the bed. His eyes wavered and he ran his tongue around his cracked lips.

"Don't figure I want you nice folks to think that," he rasped. "Reckon I'll just tell you how I come by them bags of money."

Old-timer's Confession

12

"Wal," Amos began, "as I was havin' my flapjacks at the Green Corners Café—'twas the first meal I'd et in town for a year—a couple of fellows crowded me.

" 'You know this desert country good, old-timer?' one asked.

" 'With my eyes closed,' I told him, givin' the fellow a shove with my elbow for a leetle more room with my cutting tool.

"The other one blasted in my ear, 'Say, I think you're just the man we're lookin' for to help us find a nice, secluded spot out there in the desert for a dude ranch!'

"I give one man, then t'other, a good look. They didn't 'pear like the duded-up sort to me, with their day's stubble and mussed-up clothes.

"One caught on I wasn't bein' taken in. He laughed and said, 'We been roughin' it.'

"'It'll cost you,' I told 'em.

"'Sure thing, pardner,' one says real chummy-like. 'How much do you ask?'

"I figured a five spot would keep me goin' for quite a spell, but I wasn't for scarin' 'em off, so I says, 'Make me an offer.'

"'We'll pay you fifty dollars,' one o' them jaspers said.

"I like to choked to death on my last bite o' flapjacks. Wal, we got ready for the trip. They had a couple of stable horses they'd picked up, and I had my old horse and jack. I told 'em what grub to buy and they carried it in feed sacks swung over their saddle horns. They had somethin' rolled up in an old coat behind one of their saddles, but I reckoned it was spare clothes.

"I headed 'em out Ghost Town way, figurin' to drop them off by one of them rocky buttes beyond it, near a water hole.

"We made camp that first night at the south end of Ghost Town. While them two was finishin' their supper, I took a gander about. They didn't hear me come back behind 'em. They was laughin' and talkin' about what an easy time they had holdin' up the bank.

"I figured then what was in that roll behind one saddle and took a peek. Sure 'nuf, it was the bank loot. And I knowed then that all them two was aiming for was a safe place to hide out with the loot till the sheriff had stopped lookin' for 'em.

"I was sharp enough to know, too, that they wasn't goin' to let me go back to town to answer any questions about the pair of 'em. I'd end up a heap o' bleachin' bones for sure, soon as they had no further use for me.

"So when they began snorin', I shifted them moneybags onto my own saddle and slipped away from Ghost Town real quietlike.

"I knowed that the first thing next mornin' them two would tear all over that desert like wild critters, huntin' me. I started makin' rock arrows, all pointin' to the highway so's maybe they'd think I'd headed that way, and follow and get caught.

"I branded the jack with the arrow and turned him loose, hopin' they'd run onto him and know it was me, all right, who'd made the rock arrows.

"I lit right out for that cliff-dweller place to hide the money in one of them high caves."

Seeing the troubled look on Linda's face, the old man frowned and added, "Oh, I always knowed I'd have to give it back someday, but I was afraid just to take it to the sheriff for fear he'd think I was one of the gang. I needed time to figure out some way to return it without gettin' into trouble. Meantime it'd be in the cliff-dwellers' caves. I never knowed about that old hermit livin' up there and I got caught in his trap."

Amos Trippe gave a deep, quivering sigh. "There's no more to tell."

Mattie said, "You shouldn't talk any more." She fluffed the old man's pillow, straightened the bedclothes, and prepared a mild sedative.

The others drifted out to the patio. "Poor Amos!" Linda said. "I wonder what will become of him now."

"It's all settled," Larry said. "Fred Scott says Amos can stay here to help at the barns when he's well."

Angie appeared to announce lunch. "The dessert's that chocolate cake Linda won last night." Everyone beamed.

Late that afternoon two deputies returned to make a routine check. They told Linda and Kathy the bank robbers had been picked up and taken to jail.

"Could those two men be the same ones who stole the package from the mailbox?" Kathy wondered.

"I don't think so," Linda replied. "The men in the car didn't look the same as the bank robbers."

"Besides," said one of the officers, "their belongings have been thoroughly searched, and there were no signs of wrappings or contents of the parcel." He smiled. "By the way, a sport jacket among their things had a button missing. It matched the one your dog had, so apparently he saved the old man from them."

"Have you heard any news about Mary Sutton?" Linda asked hopefully.

"A news broadcast concerning her came in just a few minutes ago," the officer said. "There was a report that a girl answering Mary Sutton's description was seen in a car with a dark-haired woman and a blond man near Santa Carita."

As the officers drove away, Linda looked thoughtful. "Santa Carita," she repeated. "That's where the Cherry Blossom Fiesta is being held this weekend."

"You wanted to go and ride in the parade, didn't you?" Kathy asked.

"I still do," Linda replied. "And now for a double reason. Maybe I can find Mary."

"Why don't you go? There's still time," Kathy urged.

"Let's all go and ride in the parade," Linda proposed.

"What a wonderful idea!" Kathy's eyes sparkled, but a moment later she looked skeptical. "How could we get our horses there?"

"Mr. Scott has a big stock truck we might borrow," Linda replied. "Let's check with Cactus Mac first."

They found him halter-breaking some colts for

Fred Scott while Bob and Larry watched. Linda's proposal was eagerly accepted by the boys, but the foreman was leery. Finally he said, "Paradin's a little out o' my line, but so long as it ain't painful, I'll try it this once."

The girls hurried off to find Fred Scott, who gladly agreed to lend them the truck. Linda immediately wired the chairman of the fiesta committee at Santa Carita, requesting that a spot be assigned to them in the big parade Saturday morning.

Then she phoned Doña Mallory, who said, "Good luck to all of you!"

Swiftly and gaily the foursome loaded their gear and bedrolls into the truck. Then Bob and Larry led in the horses and burro, tying them crosswise, head to tail.

The cab was large, and the seat comfortably accommodated four. A foam-cushioned stool was put in with the horses for the boys to take turns using. Behind the seat was a wide ledge, to which Rango was assigned.

After warm thanks and good-byes to their hosts, and some money to Amos Trippe for the purchase of Vagabond, the Craigs and their friends left Scotsward in a merry mood. At the last moment, Angie had given them a big box of sandwiches and cookies with vacuum bottles of cold milk for supper along the way.

"How long will it take us to get there?" Kathy asked Cactus Mac, who was at the wheel.

"About six hours with this speed demon," he replied with a chuckle.

En route Linda bubbled with plans. "In the telegram, I said that we would enter the Family Class competition as the Old Sol group."

"Does that make you my kids?" asked Cactus Mac with a grimace and the others laughed.

"We'll have to fix up some sort of look-alike costumes," said Linda. "We all have white Western shirts and blue jeans, which we'd better wear. Then we can pick up some bright matching hats and ties. There will be a lot of fiesta stuff in the shops for sale. We can get some early in the morning and have the rest of the day to fix ourselves up."

"That will be fun," Kathy beamed.

Linda's dark eyes sparkled as she made plans. "We might get red Spanish hats, red ties, and red cummerbunds to wear."

"Great," said Bob dryly.

"Won't I look cute in a red sash?" grumbled Cactus Mac.

"Sure you will," Kathy teased. "You'll have all the ladies trying to date you!"

A few yards farther on, the truck was waved to a stop by a sergeant of the highway patrol, who stood in the middle of the road. Two cars with more officers were parked on each side.

"Looks like a roadblock," murmured Larry.

At Cactus Mac's quick stop, the horses began stomping. The foreman jumped out quickly and went around back to investigate. The officer gave the others in the cab a sharp appraisal as Larry, who had been seated on the stool, joined them.

"We're on our way to participate in the fiesta parade," Linda smilingly told him.

The sergeant gave her a penetrating look and started poking around the front. "Where's the registration card for this truck?" he asked.

The Craigs quickly looked about for it, but in vain. "Actually I don't know," Bob replied. "We borrowed the truck."

"Your driver's licenses, please," requested the officer.

The boys exchanged looks. "We don't have them with us," Larry said.

"If none of you can produce identification, you'll have to come along with me to the station." He peered at Linda again. "You fit the description of that girl who was kidnapped." At a signal, the other two officers joined him.

"I'm the girl who was supposed to have been kidnapped," said Linda evenly. Briefly she related the circumstances to the surprised patrolmen.

Just then Rango decided to have a stretch and leaped out the open door of the cab. He had been lying on several articles on the ledge.

146

Quickly Larry went through them: an old sweater, papers, a couple of stock magazines, and at the bottom a small, flat, black, zippered case. He opened it and produced the truck registration.

Cactus Mac came alongside. "Thought one of my horses might be down," he explained to the sergeant, "but they're all right."

"Your driver's license, please," the officer requested.

Cactus Mac slapped his pockets, then looked perplexed. Linda's heart sank. The group was under suspicion already because she looked like Mary. If the foreman had neglected to bring his license, they probably would be taken all the way to Los Angeles! And never get back in time to prepare for the parade.

Suddenly light dawned on Cactus Mac. He took off his hat and from the inner band produced the license!

The sergeant was satisfied and waved them on, as Rango jumped back in. But he gave Linda a last, lingering look. With the time lost, it was nearly midnight when the travelers arrived at Santa Carita.

"What a charming place!" Linda exclaimed. "And how fragrant!"

The long main street was lined with tile-roofed homes and shops of Spanish architecture. Among them and set back in a lovely old garden was a mission. On the side streets were cottages, all with little gardens, belonging to the Mexican and Spanish inhabitants. Everywhere cherry trees were in bloom.

"Over on that thar hill to the east," Cactus Mac told them, "are some mighty good-lookin' estates with big cherry orchards."

Although it was late, there were tourists in the street and some of the shops were still open. A smiling man, wearing an official badge, stopped the Scotsward truck, greeted the riders pleasantly, and directed them to the walnut grove at the edge of town where they were to camp.

The grove was dotted with little bonfires, aglow in circles of rocks. Many outfits were already there, and the people gaily called out "Hi!" to the newcomers as they slowly made their way through the grove until they found a cleared spot.

"I guess the horses will be glad to get out of that truck," said Linda.

Everyone helped to unload them and walk the animals around a bit to get their blood circulating. The men tied them to trees and fed and watered them, while the girls gave Rango his food.

"Now we'll go to town and get some supper," said Bob. They ate at one of the many attractive little eating spots.

There was little sleep for anyone in the grove that night, with outfits coming in and people making merry around the campfires. But the Old Sol group was tired after the long trip and managed to doze off in the comfort of their sleeping bags.

Next morning the place was abuzz with excitement and gaiety. The Craigs and their companions ate early, and as soon as the shops were open, Linda and Kathy went to buy their costume supplies at Fernando's.

They found five red Spanish hats in the correct sizes, red string bow ties, and good-looking, shirred red cummerbunds with sash ends. To these, the girls added a bolt of red satin ribbon to braid in the manes and tails of the horses; a few yards of Turkey-red cloth to cut for top saddle blankets; twenty yellow cotton tassels to fasten to each of the four corners, and several cards of safety pins.

Linda found a frayed, straw peon hat. "Let's put this on Vagabond," she said, and Kathy chuckled.

Feeling impish, Linda laid her pocketbook down and laughingly tried the hat on her own head. "Size is just right," she said.

Linda put the hat with their other purchases and reached for her bag to pay for them. It was gone!

Hacienda Sleuthing 13

"My pocketbook!" Linda exclaimed, dismayed. She looked about hastily. "I laid it right here!"

The salesgirl looked concerned. "A tall, dark-haired woman was standing here. She came in right behind you. I noticed her particularly because she had a leather shoulder-strap bag with some unusual Mexican silverwork on it."

Kathy ran to the door. "There she is!" she exclaimed. "Across the street."

Linda hurried to look and caught a glimpse of the silver-ornamented bag.

"Please hold these things for us," she called to the salesgirl. "We'll be right back!"

Staying on their side of the street, they followed the woman swiftly.

"She's going through your bag!" Kathy remarked indignantly.

"Let's cross over now and get it away from her."
Linda said.

As the girls started toward the woman, she looked
up and saw them. Snapping the purse shut, the
stranger quickened her steps. At the corner she
thrust Linda's bag into the hands of a policeman,
rapidly said something to him, and lost herself in
the crowd milling about the mission garden.

The officer shoved the slim tan purse into his
pocket, as Linda and Kathy hurried up to him. "I
think you have my bag," Linda said breathlessly. "It
was stolen at the store where I was shopping."

"I have a pocketbook," said the officer calmly.
"But the woman who handed it to me said that she'd
found it. What did yours look like?"

"It was braided straw," Linda told him. "It
contained twenty-five dollars, a compact, lipstick,
and my riding-club membership card with my name
on it, Linda Craig."

The police officer smiled and pulled the bag from
his pocket. He checked the contents, and then
handed the pocketbook over to Linda. "You're
lucky," he said. "Better keep a tighter hold on it
hereafter."

"Thank you, I will," Linda replied.

"Well, that was a happy ending," Kathy said on
their way back to Fernando's. "I wonder why the
woman didn't take your money? Even after she saw
us, she had time to do it."

"My guess is she wasn't after the money," Linda said soberly. "Do you remember, a news report said Mary was seen in a car near here with a dark-haired woman?"

Kathy's eyes widened. "You think this person was the one?"

Linda nodded. "She spotted me somewhere and followed us into the store. Because I look so much like Mary, she probably suspected that I'm the girl they intended to kidnap."

"But why take your purse?"

"To make sure by checking my identification."

Kathy looked puzzled. "I don't understand why they should be interested in you any more. After all, they have the clay horse from the mailbox."

"The kidnappers could be getting nervous with police hunting for them," said Linda. "Maybe the woman thought my being here was too much of a coincidence."

Kathy paled. "Then you're still in danger, Linda. They may try to get you out of the way."

"You, too, Kathy," Linda concluded quietly as they entered Fernando's. "The woman knows we both saw her."

The salesgirl was genuinely pleased that the bag had been retrieved. Linda paid her, then the girls gathered up their bundles.

On the way back to the grove, they stopped at the police station to report the pocketbook incident.

The officer listened to Linda's description of the dark-haired woman and agreed that she must be the one mentioned in the news bulletin.

"We'll step up the local search for Mary Sutton and her abductors," he promised, "now that we know the kidnappers are still here." He thanked the girls for their cooperation.

When they reached their camp, Linda and Kathy saw several children and a few adults gathered around Bob, Larry, and the palomino, who was untied.

"What are you doing with Chica?" Linda asked anxiously. "Is something wrong?"

"No." Bob grinned and looked at Larry. "Just showing her off to these kids."

Taking the boys and Cactus Mac aside, Linda and Kathy told them about the stolen bag and described the dark-haired woman. "The police are going to be on the lookout for her," Linda said, "and we should be too. She may lead us to Mary."

"Hmm, looks like we landed right in the middle o' the hornets' nest," Cactus Mac remarked somberly.

"We'll sure have to keep our eyes on Linda and Kathy," said Larry worriedly.

Just then Chica, who had been standing without attention long enough, to her way of thinking, gave a fretful whinny.

"All right, baby," Linda apologized. "I've been neglecting you." She took some pieces of carrot from her pocket. "How about showing me how nicely you can bow?" She stood to the side and brought her hand back in a signal.

With glowing eyes, Chica went down on her right knee in a perfect bow. Vagabond, who was nearby, wagged his head up and down, bent a knee, and pawed the ground.

The children clapped for the filly and laughed at the burro.

Linda slipped a treat to both animals and said softly to Chica, "That was a beautiful performance, baby. Please do as nicely in the parade."

"Show us some more tricks," the children begged.

"All right," Linda agreed. "Someone ask Chica a question."

A little girl piped up, "Do you like me?"

Linda gave a hand signal, and the filly shook her head up and down for yes.

"Do you like horseflies?" asked an impish little boy.

Again Linda cued the palomino and the animal shook her head violently back and forth for no.

"That's a clever horse!" exclaimed a man onlooker.

Linda quickly gave a signal and Chica lifted her head and rolled back her lips in a good horselaugh of pleasure at the man's compliment.

"My horse will do a trick, too," said an eager little

boy named Johnny. He was from the next camp and had his mount with him.

"Oh, please show it to us," Linda urged.

Johnny walked ahead with his small bay horse following, then stopped suddenly. The horse gave him a nudge in the back, pushing him a few steps, and repeated the shove every time the boy stopped.

Linda laughed. "That's a funny trick!" She turned to Chica. "Do you think you could do that?"

"Just you watch!" Bob exclaimed, and he and Larry exchanged winks.

Bob stood directly in front of the filly and began walking, with Chica following. Like Johnny, he stopped suddenly, but the horse gave him such a hard push with her nose that Bob Craig fell down.

"Hey, not so hard!" he cried, turning around quickly so as not to get shoved again. Everyone laughed.

"Bravo!" Linda exclaimed. "When did you teach her that trick?"

"While you were out shopping," her brother replied. "Johnny helped us."

"May we have a ride on your horse?" asked a couple of little girls.

"She's a bit too spirited to put children on her back," Linda replied gently. "But how would you like a ride on Vagabond?"

The youngsters jumped up and down in delight, crying, "We'd like that!"

"Here you go, then," Bob said. He lifted both little girls to the burro's back.

Vagabond's eyes went stubbornly glassy. He braced his legs and brayed.

"Come on, now," begged Larry, tugging at the halter rope. "Earn your hay."

Vagabond brayed his protest again and suddenly sat down. The two little girls slid off.

Linda ran to them. "Are you hurt?" she asked anxiously.

Both of them were giggling. "No," said one, jumping up. "That was fun!"

During this performance, Rango was having his own fun with the dogs who had come with other outfits. They went tearing through the grove or stopped now and then to grapple with each other, to everyone's amusement. It soon became evident that Rango had assumed leadership of the pack.

"I hope they don't get it into their heads to run off," remarked Cactus Mac, who had been enjoying himself in a talk with some of the other men. To avoid this "call of the wild," he ordered Rango to his side.

Meanwhile Linda and Kathy unpacked their purchases and gave the boys their outfits.

"Will I wow 'em!" said Larry with a grin.

Bob looked at his watch and announced he was going into town to see if he could get a gunnysack of carrots for the horses.

"I hope you can," Linda remarked. "They deserve a good treat for parading tomorrow." As he left she added, "We'd better start getting the parade things ready."

"I'll polish the gear," Larry volunteered. Cactus Mac joined the three to help.

There was a lot of equipment for the five horses. First the men cleaned it with saddle soap, then polished the leather to a high gloss.

Larry, slapping a polish rag back and forth assiduously, said, "Why didn't I think to go for carrots?"

"Thar'll be plenty left for Bob to do," Cactus Mac assured him.

"Our boots have to be polished," Linda said with an impish grin. "We'll set those out for him."

While the men worked on the gear, Linda and Kathy cut oblongs of red cloth to go over the hair pads under the saddles, and pinned a yellow tassel to each corner. Then the girls measured and cut pieces of red satin ribbon to braid into the horses' manes and tails.

They had just finished when Bob came hurrying into camp with a half-filled gunnysack over his shoulder. His expression was so disturbed that everyone gathered about him hastily with questioning looks.

"I think I saw that woman who took Linda's pocketbook," Bob told them. "She was tall and dark-haired and carried a strap bag with Mexican silver on it."

"It sounds like her!" Kathy exclaimed.

"Where did you see her?" Linda asked.

"In the old part of town," Bob replied. "As I came out of the feed store with the carrots, she was hurrying up a lane alongside it."

"Where did she go?" Larry asked.

"I followed her along the main street," Bob said, "but lost her in the crowd. The town is really packed now."

"Did you report it to the police?" Kathy asked.

Bob shook his head. "The police have all they can do without being bothered to run down such a slim tip. After all, I didn't see where she came from or went, and am not absolutely sure she's the woman they're looking for."

"We'd better forget her for now," said Larry, "and get ready for the parade."

Kathy said, "How about me giving all the ponies a treat of carrots?"

"Go to it," said Bob.

Linda's mind was on the dark-haired woman. Was she holding Mary Sutton a prisoner in this town?

I must try to find out, Linda told herself.

That evening while the men were busy with parade preparations, she asked Kathy to go to town with her for some sleuthing.

"The streets are so crowded I'm sure there'll be

no danger. If anyone tried to grab us, a scream would bring plenty of help."

"Okay," Kathy agreed.

They found the feed store easily. Its sign rose high above the low-tiled roofs around it. The girls turned down the lane. At the end was an old, walled Spanish hacienda with a courtyard. In front of it stood small cottages, with children and women holding babies, talking and laughing.

A splash of unusually beautiful yellow roses beside a cottage caught Linda's eye. She decided to come back early in the morning and try to buy some to decorate the horses' tails and manes.

The girls turned to the open gate of the courtyard and paused. Could the strange woman have come from here? Was Mary in the hacienda?

Quickly they crossed the paved enclosure to the big garden. At the far end of the tree-lined walk stood the house, its balcony deeply shadowed by a big blooming magnolia whose branches draped over it. There were no lights in the windows. Linda and Kathy wondered why. The late hour and heavy shade of the magnolia and pepper trees must have made the interior very dim.

Suddenly Linda's heart jumped. She had seen a movement on the balcony, and whispered this to Kathy. Staring hard into the darkness, they made out the figure of a girl.

Then a voice called faintly, "Help!"

The cry was sharply cut off. Straining their eyes in the fading light, Linda and Kathy could see nothing on the balcony now. They listened, hearts pounding. There was not a sound from the dark building.

Surprise Attack 14

Kathy had grabbed Linda's arm. Had they imagined the figure on the balcony and the voice calling for help? Was it a joke? Or could the person have been Mary?

The girls walked quickly toward the house, watching for any further movement and listening for the call to be repeated. A stairway on the side led up to the balcony.

"Kathy, you stay here on guard while I tiptoe up," Linda requested.

Cautiously she ascended. At the first window the draperies were partially open. Linda peered in. She was just able to make out the dark, carved furniture and a beautiful crocheted counterpane on the bed. The room looked unoccupied.

Quietly she stepped along to the next window. Inside was a neat bedroom, and there were articles on the dresser indicating that it was in use. Linda could see no one.

Her curiosity aroused, she rapped on the pane. No one appeared, nor was there any answer.

"It's hopeless," Linda thought and slowly went down the stairs.

"Any luck?" Kathy asked.

Linda shook her head. Then she boldly walked up to the front door and rapped. Her knocking echoed within the house. Still no answer.

Linda turned away with a strange feeling. The big home stood silent and apparently empty, but she felt as if the girls were being watched.

"Let's go!" Kathy urged. "We don't want to let our luck run out."

As the two friends made their way back to the main street, they decided not to mention their experience to the boys.

"They'll say our imaginations are running away with us," said Linda. "And maybe they are."

The girls returned to the grove and were not questioned. Apparently the men thought they had been visiting other campers. The boys had just finished their polishing.

"There!" exclaimed Bob, with a slap of his polishing rag. "That does it, and if anybody's equipment is in any better shape than ours, I'll eat one of my boots." He grinned. "I'm so hungry I might do it anyway."

"I'll settle for a good Mexican dinner," Larry declared. "How does that sound to you all?"

There were three enthusiastic replies, but Cactus Mac groaned. "You youngsters kin burn the linin' out of your innards with that thar hot stuff, but not me. I'll have steak."

Before they left, Linda asked about Rango.

"He's locked up in the truck," explained Cactus Mac. "Hurt his foot. I'm making him stay off it so he'll be okay for the parade."

"If anyone comes around," thought Linda as they walked off, "he'll bark and alert the neighbors."

The young people went to the El Toro Café near the grove, and Cactus Mac continued up the street looking for a good steak house.

At the El Toro, Linda and her friends ordered four combination plates with milk. In a short time the waitress brought platters of enchiladas smothered in melted cheese, fried frijoles, slim, sauce-covered beef tamales, and tostadas heaped with shaved lettuce and tomatoes.

"Looks marvelous," said Kathy.

Larry lifted his fork. "Well, here's to the fire food!" Everyone laughed.

"We'd better get some sound sleep tonight," Linda said later. "From the outfits I've seen, we're going to have stiff competition. The truth is," she added slowly, "we're outclassed in equipment and horses."

"You admit Chica d'Oro is outclassed?" Kathy asked incredulously.

"Not individually," Linda replied, "but our horses aren't matched. There's a family of four who have matching blacks. Then there's a couple with a little girl who have matching Arabians and silver equipment."

"Sounds as if there's not much hope for us to win a trophy," Larry commented.

"I don't think we'll win anything in the prejudging before the parade," Linda said frankly. "But we might pick up the winning points when we're judged for performance in the parade."

"How?" Kathy asked.

Linda thought for several seconds, then replied, "I think we should ride with Cactus Mac leading. Bob and I will follow—his bay quarter horse and my golden palomino will make a striking combination. Rango should be at Rocket's side, and Vagabond at Chica's, where they're accustomed to being. Then Larry will follow on bay Gypsy and Kathy on brown-and-white Patches."

"But what do we do?" Bob prompted.

"Wave and smile at the spectators," Linda replied. "As soon as we arrive at the judges' stand, form a line before them, salute with a wave, and I'll put Chica d'Oro into a bow. Immediately fall back into our parade formation and ride on."

Larry looked doubtful. "Wouldn't that take a lot of practice?" he asked.

"Practice would help," Linda said with a wry smile, "but since we have no time for it, just keep thinking about what we're to do and it will probably come out all right."

They were only about halfway through their meal when a neighboring camper came hurrying in to their table. "Hey," he blurted out, "good thing I heard you say you were coming here. I just saw your burro running down the street."

"Thanks," said Bob, jumping up. "We'll go after him."

Vagabond wouldn't leave without Chica Oro!" Linda cried. "She must have gone too!"

"Did you see a palomino with the burro?" asked Larry, dropping a bill on the table to take care of their meal.

"No, I didn't," the man replied. "I just noticed the jack."

"Larry and I will go after Vagabond," Bob said to Linda. "You and Kathy run back to camp and check on the palomino."

The girls hurried to the grove and saw at once that the filly was missing. None of the campers had seen anyone take her. They had heard Rango bark but thought nothing of it.

"Let's follow the boys on horseback," Linda said. "We'll catch up with them sooner."

"If we can only find Vagabond, he may lead us to Chica d'Oro," Kathy added hopefully.

Hastily the girls bridled Patches and Rocket, jumped on them bareback, and rode out of the grove. They quickly wound their way through the throngs on the main street, asking along the way if anyone had seen the palomino or the burro.

The answers were disappointing. So many people were mounted and the crowd was having such a good time that no one had noticed one more horse.

As the girls reached a side street, a thin, black-haired boy darted up to them. "You the ones looking for a palomino?" he asked. "It went there." He pointed down a narrow lane, then slipped away in the crowd before they could question him further.

Linda and Kathy stared down the narrow street, which was lined with shacks and the drooping branches of big shade trees. At the far end they saw Bob and Larry attempting to hold Vagabond. Apparently they had just caught him, for he was struggling to get away. The girls urged their horses to a gallop to join them.

"You'd better let him go," Kathy cried as they reined up, "or he'll lose Chica Oro's trail."

"Wait!" said Linda. "Chica would never run away by herself. This may be an attempt to knock us out of the competition tomorrow. Someone had better go back and guard our parade stuff. Cactus Mac may not have returned."

"That's right," Bob agreed. "Larry, you and Kathy go."

"But I think I should ride with you," Larry protested. "You may run into trouble."

"My sister had better come with me," Bob replied. "She may be able to find Chica by calling her. The filly will answer Linda."

"That's true," Larry conceded, but he looked worried as he jumped up behind Kathy on Patches and they started for the grove.

Bob held Vagabond until he was astride Rocket, then let him go. As the burro ran down the shadowy road, the Craigs followed.

Suddenly the burro stopped, uncertain about going on. Then he brayed desperately.

Bob and Linda heard no other sound, but Vagabond must have, for he started off again confidently. He turned into an alley along which there were a few ramshackle sheds.

Vagabond stopped and gave a soft bray. From one of the tumble-down buildings came an answering nicker! Linda and Bob slid off Rocket.

"Chica! Chica d'Oro!" Linda cried softly, running toward the shed.

The filly answered with a joyous whinny that directed Linda, Bob, and Vagabond to her. They fumbled in the dark for the door latch, hoping to release her.

Suddenly two figures leaped from the shadows

and yanked burlap sacks down over the Craigs' heads.

"Hey! What—" The rest of Bob's protest was lost as he fought to free himself.

Linda struggled blindly against their captors. Despite the sack over her head, she screamed, "Chica! Chica!"

Instantly strong hands clapped the rough burlap close to her nose and mouth. As she desperately pulled and scratched at the smothering hand, she realized that it belonged to a woman.

On the verge of fainting from suffocation, Linda heard the beating of hooves against the shed door, the scream of an angry horse, and then the splintering of timber.

"Watch out!" a man's voice shouted. "The horse!"

A frenzied whinny sounded over Linda's head, and she knew that Chica d'Oro was striking out with her front hooves. At once, the hands fell away from the girl's face and she heard running feet. Dropping to her knees, Linda pulled the bag from her head. The palomino's soft muzzle touched her face.

The next moment Bob was at her side. "Linda, Linda," he asked softly, "are you all right?"

"I'm fine," she answered shakily.

As he helped his sister to her feet, Kathy and Larry galloped up and dismounted.

"We decided to come back," Larry said. "I had a hunch you were riding into trouble."

"We heard Chica d'Oro whinnying," Kathy said anxiously. "What happened?"

"A couple of thugs tried to tie us up in sacks!" Bob said with a laugh.

"Chica rescued us," Linda told them, hugging her horse close. Then she turned to Vagabond. "But we wouldn't have found the pony if it hadn't been for you." She stroked the little gray burro affectionately.

"Good fellow," said Bob, patting him. Vagabond waved his long ears appreciatively.

"We'd better hurry back to camp now and see if your gear is safe," Larry said.

With Bob on Rocket and his sister on Chica Oro, they headed for the grove. Linda was silent and thoughtful as she rode along.

When they reached the main street, she whispered to Bob, "There's somewhere I want you to go with me. Let's get off here. Kathy and Larry can take the horses back."

Bob agreed and they reined up. Linda explained to the others that she had a clue she wanted to follow. "You and I started it, Kathy."

"Oh, I know what you mean," her chum said.

"Then we'll all go," Larry declared.

"Someone should check on our camp," Linda protested.

Although Kathy and Larry did not want to leave them, they saw the necessity of returning.

"I'll tell Larry your suspicions," said Kathy. "And you two be careful!" she warned sternly, as the friends parted.

"Now what is this about?" Bob asked, as Linda led the way through the crowded street toward the feed store.

"I've been thinking," his sister replied, "that the attack on us tonight had nothing to do with the parade. After all, our act is not enough of a threat to any other outfit to justify such violence."

"I've been thinking the same thing," Bob agreed.

"My assailant was a woman," Linda went on. "Suppose it was the dark-haired one who kidnapped Mary? Maybe she and her partner stole Chica d'Oro to lure me out after her."

Bob looked doubtful. "I don't see how they could be sure you would go to the sheds to find your palomino."

"I think they planted someone to show us the way," Linda replied. "We found you and Larry and Vagabond on that side street because a little boy ran up and told us my horse had gone there."

Bob frowned. "This looks bad," he said. "But why the attack on us?"

They had reached the lane alongside the feed store. Linda stopped. "Because I think I know where Mary Sutton is."

Bob stared at his sister in astonishment as she told him about the girl Kathy and she had seen at the hacienda. "If it really was Mary," she said, "the kidnappers may be afraid we saw her and that we'll report their hiding place to the police."

"The theory makes sense," Bob said seriously. "Lead the way!"

"We'd better hurry," Linda said. "If I'm right, the kidnappers will have to change their hideout right away."

She led the way through the open gate into the moonlit courtyard. They crossed swiftly and entered the deep shadows of the garden. No lights showed within the house.

"Let's go around to the back," Linda whispered. Keeping to the trees, they worked their way to the rear of the house. It also was dark.

As they watched, a dim light appeared behind the iron grille of a ground-floor window. Instantly Bob and Linda darted across the clearing, flattened themselves against the house on either side of the window, and peered in.

They saw a tall woman with dark hair and a bandage on her hand, and a large blond man with a mustache. Between them, at a small wooden table, sat Mary. She looked pale and drawn.

The man strode toward the barred window and yanked the heavy curtains almost shut. As he did, Linda noticed that the sash was open a few inches from the top.

"We've got to get out of here!" the man said. "That Craig girl and her friend may have reported to the police already."

"Whose fault is that?" the woman retorted sarcastically. "If you hadn't been scared off by the horse, we'd have had Linda and her brother right here, where they couldn't talk."

"Whose fault?" the man responded angrily. "If you'd been watching your prisoner this afternoon, she wouldn't have got out on the balcony and been seen." Then he added roughly, "Get up, Mary! We're leaving!"

The girl's voice replied faintly, "I don't feel well. I'm so hungry. . . ."

"She hasn't had anything to eat all day," the woman said. "I'll get her some supper."

"We haven't time!" came the gruff reply.

"It'll only take a minute," the woman replied tartly. "We'll really be slowed down if she faints." A moment later a light went on in the next room, showing the woman in a small kitchen.

Bob signaled to Linda and they slipped away from the window. "We must get in there and stop them from leaving," he whispered. "There's no time to go for the police."

Staying in the shadow of the house, sister and brother crept to the back door. It was locked. They hurried along the row of ground-floor windows, but each was covered with an iron grille. Silently Linda and Bob slipped around to the front door, but it, too, was locked.

"Let's go up on the balcony," Linda whispered.

Quickly they mounted the stairs and tried five bedroom windows without success. When they reached the sixth and last, Linda was tense.

We mustn't fail! she thought.

As Bob exerted his strength, the window slid open. Quickly he climbed into the dark room after his sister. Using Bob's pencil flashlight, they found their way into a hall and tiptoed downstairs to a stone-floored corridor. At the far end of it, light streamed through a half-open door.

Hugging the wall, Linda and Bob approached the room and cautiously looked in. The blond man was pacing up and down, scowling, while Mary sat by listlessly.

"Come and get the tray!" the woman's voice called from the adjoining kitchen. The man turned on his heel and strode out.

"Now!" Linda whispered to her brother.

Prisoners and Prizes · 15

The eyes of the kidnapped girl widened and her mouth flew open as Linda and Bob slipped into the room.

"Oh!" Mary exclaimed.

Linda put a finger to her lips, cautioning Mary to silence. She and her brother pressed against the wall beside the kitchen door.

In a moment, the man entered with the tray. As he set it on the table, Bob struck him a hard blow, knocking him down. At the same time, Linda turned the key in the kitchen door and locked the woman in.

"Get the police as quickly as you can!" Bob said to Linda.

As she ran to the hall door, the man leaped to his feet, pushed her aside, and fled. Bob raced after him and neatly brought the fellow down a second time. He apparently was stunned.

"You'd better get help pronto," Bob panted.

Linda dashed off. She could hear the woman pounding on the kitchen door and calling.

Ten minutes later Linda returned with two police officers, and presently two more arrived. The prisoners were handcuffed and the entire party escorted to headquarters.

As they alighted from the police car, questions were shouted at them, flashbulbs popped, and a crowd of curious people pushed and shoved to get near them. Police held back the crowd. Linda walked with her arm around Mary, who was thinner and still had on the jeans and blue-checkered shirt she had worn when kidnapped.

"Don't worry," Linda said to the trembling girl. "You're safe now."

"But there are more people in the gang," Mary said.

Inside the police station, Mary and the Craigs were hustled into the chief's private office. Mary's parents had been notified and were on their way to pick up their daughter. The grateful girl tried to thank Linda and Bob, but her eyes filled with tears and all she could say to compliment them was, "You're wonderful—just wonderful."

A lean, tall FBI man spoke up, "We think so, too, but we'd like to know the details."

Quietly Linda and Bob told the officers of their search and how they had found Mary. The girl herself had been so closely confined that she could add nothing except that her abductors were a married couple named Dolores and Sid, that they were part of a gang, and that she had also seen a heavy, swarthy-face man named Rico.

At that point another officer entered with a report that the woman, Dolores, had a past record for smuggling. She was brought in, but when questioned about the kidnapping would only say, "It was a mistake."

"Then why didn't you let Mary go?" Linda demanded.

"The boss wouldn't let us," Dolores replied. "He was afraid she'd set the police on us."

"Why did you want to kidnap me?" Linda asked.

"Boss's orders. He thought you had something of great value that belonged to him."

"A yellow clay horse," Linda said. "Where is it?"

The woman shrugged. "It has not been delivered to my husband yet."

"Then your boss will get it from him?" queried the FBI man. The woman sat in stony silence.

"Who is your boss?" the police chief inquired.

"I would not dare to say," Dolores replied, her dark eyes fearful.

"Is it C. Sello?" Linda asked suddenly.

The woman looked at the girl a long moment, then surprisingly she laughed. But she would not say another word.

Sid was brought in and questioned. He refused to admit to any charges and was taken to a cell.

In the meantime, Mr. and Mrs. Sutton arrived and tearfully showered their daughter with affection and Linda and Bob with praise.

"You've made us the happiest people in the world," Mrs. Sutton declared.

After Mary and Linda exchanged promises to visit one another, the exhausted girl was taken home by her parents.

Before Linda and Bob left the station, they called Rancho del Sol to inform their grandparents Mary had been found. It was then that they realized the rescue had been covered by radio, press, and television! They hung up in confusion.

"Guess we're famous, kid." Bob grinned.

When he and his sister finally got back to the grove, they found all the campers bursting with excitement. "We heard about you on the radio!" said one. "Tell us all the details!"

Linda and Bob told their story again, and finally the neighbors went home.

"I'm so glad it's all over!" Kathy said with a sigh of relief.

"But it's not over," Linda stated. "There are others in the gang to be captured. And we still have to solve the mystery of what is in the clay horse and where it is."

As they got ready to climb into their sleeping

bags, Linda suddenly remembered C. Sello and how strangely Dolores had laughed at the name. What was behind it? A little later Linda drifted off to sleep, but awoke as it was becoming light.

The yellow roses for the horses! Linda thought.

She awakened Kathy and after dressing, the girls hurried through the grove, where other outfits were beginning to stir. When they reached the cottage where the roses were in bloom, they saw a woman in the yard. She was delighted to sell them the flowers and proud to think that her roses would be in the big parade.

On the way back, Linda and Kathy stopped at a wagon near the entrance to the grove and bought hot chocolate and doughnuts for everyone. When Linda and Kathy arrived in camp, they found that the men had washed off all of their animals, including Rango, much to the dog's disgust.

After breakfast, the girls French-braided the red satin ribbon into the horses' manes and tails, leaving long, fluttering streamers, and fastened a rose on the top of each mane and tail. It was the perfect touch, complementing their yellow-tasseled red saddle blankets.

Linda made a flower rosette of ribbon which she fastened to Rango's collar. He looked none too pleased. And when she attempted to braid ribbon into his tail, he rebelled, going into a whirling-dervish act.

"Oh, Rango, stop that!" Linda begged. "We have no time to waste."

"You're going to spoil our outfit," wailed Kathy.

Cactus Mac strode over. "You, Rango," he said gruffly, "cut out them thar shenanigans and stand still!"

The dog looked at the foreman with uncertainty.

"You stand still now, and get on those googaws," Mac threatened. "If I can wear a sash around my middle, you can wear one on your tail."

Rango stood with the look of a martyr, and Linda finished fixing him up. Next she trimmed Vagabond's straw hat with ribbon and roses, made a couple of slits for his ears, and settled the hat on his head. He accepted it, pleased at the attention, though he knew he was being laughed at.

Linda inspected the gaily bedecked animals. "You look great. Now," she said, "it's our turn!"

In a short while the Old Sol group had dressed themselves. As the five participants gathered in front of the trailer, they made a striking picture. With his leather-tan face and graying hair, Cactus Mac looked like a real Spanish don. He turned away, embarrassed at compliments from the girls.

The various campers, now dressed for the parade, began riding out to the judging lot as Arabians, Spanish cavaliers, señoritas, charros, Indians, and plain and fancy Westerners and clowns. Horses shone and silver equipment gleamed.

There were five groups in the Family Class up for judging. The first was a man, woman, and little girl in royal blue, jeweled suits on silver-equipped Arabian horses. The child had trouble handling her mount. It kept sashaying to the side and pivoting, bringing a frown from the judges.

Next came four black steeds with the riders in black-and-white suits, then two families with unmatched horses and equipment, but wearing plain, matching Western clothing.

The Old Sol group came last, with Rango in perfect line under Cactus Mac's threatening eye. The originality of their costumes excited unusual attention, and they were the subject for many camera enthusiasts.

When the parade finally got under way, beautiful floats and several bands were fed into their positions. Linda and her companions drew enthusiastic approval from the crowd all along the route. The judges, officials, and dignitaries on the big central stand looked down the street to see who was causing the exceptional stir.

When the Old Sol group arrived at the stand, they formed the line as Linda had directed. Chica d'Oro executed a perfect bow. Vagabond waggled his hat and bent his right knee, while Rango gave a friendly bark. Then the group smoothly turned back in their parade formation and rode on. There was hearty laughter and applause from the stand.

The Old Sol group caused a stir . . .

As soon as the Old Sol exhibitors had circled back to the judging lot where the awards were to be presented, Kathy asked, "What do you think, Linda? Do we have a chance?"

"You all performed beautifully," said Linda happily. "Whether we won or not, I'm proud of you."

They moved up to a big, decorated platform where the awards were displayed. Along the edge of it stood tall mahogany trophies bearing carved clusters of cherry blossoms on the standard and topped with a golden horse statuette. On the table beside a microphone were boxes of blue, red, and yellow ribbons for first, second, and third place, and special awards of green rosettes. There was a crowd of people milling about, and police to keep order.

While Linda and her friends waited for the announcement of the winners, she suddenly spotted a small, dark man who slipped to the platform, pushed a yellow clay horse in among the trophies, and disappeared.

"That looks like my statuette!" thought Linda excitedly.

Quickly she rode toward the platform, and was almost close enough to pick up the clay horse when a heavy, swarthy man in a Spanish costume sauntered up. Quick as a wink he snatched the statuette and put it under his cape.

As he turned aside, Linda swung Chica d'Oro in

front of him, blocking the way, and called to a nearby policeman, "Help! Hold this man!"

In two strides, the officer was beside them and grasped the man. "What's the matter here?" he demanded.

Linda said that she had seen the man take the clay horse from the platform. "It looks like one that was stolen from me. I believe this man is part of a gang that kidnapped Mary Sutton." Linda explained that she was sure they were after the statuette because something valuable was hidden inside.

The policeman looked doubtful. "Let's see the horse," he said to the suspect.

Boldly the man pulled the figurine from under his cape. "I don't know what this girl is talking about. I won the horse on the spin of the wheel over at a booth."

"What do you say is in it?" the puzzled officer asked Linda.

"I don't know," she replied, "but if we could open it, you'd see I'm right."

"This is a serious charge," said the officer. "I think you'd both better come to the station to answer a few questions."

As the policeman spoke, the swarthy man began to edge away. With a fast movement Linda put her palomino behind the man, with the filly's nose to his back, and touched quick heels to her side.

Remembering the trick she had learned, Chica d'Oro gave the man a strong push, and he went sprawling to the hard ground. The clay horse shattered, and out rolled a bright gold disk!

Quickly the officer nabbed the man and blew his whistle. "You were right," he told Linda.

At the same time, Linda jumped from her horse and picked up the disk. Kathy and the men had just ridden up. They dismounted and gathered around as Linda looked, fascinated, at the solid-gold piece marked with the three crosses of Cortez.

"C. Sello!" Linda whispered. "This isn't anybody's name! It's Spanish for Cortez Seal! The gold piece must be priceless!"

"The only one of its kind," said the swarthy man softly, his eyes glittering. "There are collectors who would give almost anything for it."

"This must be part of the stolen Cortez collection that Bronco was reading about," Bob put in.

The swarthy man nodded grimly. "The most valuable piece of all," he murmured, "and now I've lost it!"

Two more policemen responded to the whistle. The small man who had left the statuette was handcuffed to one of them.

"We just picked up this fellow," the officer explained to Linda and the rest of the group. "He's one of the kidnappers. There was an alarm out for him."

The handcuffed man glared at the swarthy prisoner. "Rico, you clumsy ox! What a fine leader you turned out to be!"

"Rico!" Linda exclaimed. "He's the man who ordered the clay horse from the pottery in Mexico."

"That was the first of his many mistakes," the other man said bitterly.

"Is it my fault, Fernandez, if the pottery made two horses instead of one?" Rico retorted. "They forgot to enclose the seal in the first one. It is their mistake, not mine."

"It was your mistake to send that stupid Juan to purchase the horse," replied Fernandez. "He let the Craig girl get both of them."

"Was it Juan who broke all the statuettes in the pottery booth?" Linda asked.

Fernandez nodded wryly. "He thought maybe the seal had been put in one of the glazed horses by mistake."

"I told him to look for the curved-arrow sign on the bottom," Rico said angrily.

"And I told you we couldn't trust him, Rico," Fernandez retorted.

"Which one of you tried to poison my palomino?" Linda asked sternly.

The stocky man laughed shortly. "Juan again. When he stole the horse's head from your purse and found it did not have the seal in it, he poisoned your filly in a fit of temper."

"And he also left us the warning note?"

"He thought it would scare you off," Fernandez told her.

Rico growled. "He wasn't supposed to do that. He made more trouble than he was worth. I'll be glad to turn him in. You can find him around Olvera Street. Juan Doreno is his name."

"What about the two men who stole the horse package f.om the Scotsward mailbox?"

Rico scowled. "No more questions. I've talked too much already."

"You've told them where to find Juan," Fernandez said. "That's all they need to know. He will tell them everything else."

"We're going back to the station now," the first officer said to Linda. "Please follow us there as soon as you can. Your statement will be needed."

Linda promised and the policemen bundled their prisoners off. She and her friends turned their attention to the presentation of the awards, which had already started.

There was a smattering of applause, then the voice of the judge came over the microphone:

"Family Group."

Linda and the others exchanged looks of anticipation. As they stood tensely beside their horses, waiting, Kathy quietly crossed her fingers.

"For theme of costume, originality, and perform-ance," the judge announced, "a blue ribbon for first place and a trophy to—" he paused for dramatic effect—"Rancho del Sol!"

Linda's heart thumped in happiness, Kathy squealed, and the two girls hugged each other ecstatically. The men grinned, pleased.

"Will a member of the group please come forward to accept the award?" the judge asked.

"You go, Linda," Bob said as his sister kissed Chica d'Oro lightly on the nose.

As she hesitated, Larry said, "The act was your idea. You go!"

"Get goin'," said Cactus Mac gruffly, smothering a grin. "You can kiss everybody later."

Hastily Linda mounted and rode to the front of the platform—Vagabond following Chica d'Oro as always.

"That was a mighty fine performance, little lady," the judge commented as he handed Linda the trophy and the ribbon. As the flashbulbs popped and the crowd applauded noisily, he held the microphone down for her to speak.

"We have had a wonderful and exciting time," Linda said. "Thank you very much for the trophy It will be displayed proudly at Rancho del Sol."

As the applause broke out, Linda put Chica d'Oro into a perfect bow, and Vagabond bent his knee awkwardly to show his gratitude.

LINDA CRAIG

The Secret of Rancho del Sol

ANN SHELDON

Illustrated by St Ward

The grizzly bear turned on Linda . . .

Glossary

Arroyo Stream.

Bleachers A tier of seats in a stadium.

Bobby pin Hairgrip.

Bouillon Soup.

Broadax An axe with a broad blade used for cutting timber.

Bruin Another name for a brown bear (the word was originally used in folk tales).

Buckwheat A plant with white flowers. Its edible seeds can be made into flour.

Burro A donkey – especially one used as a pack animal.

Chuck wagon A wagon to carry provisions and cooking utensils.

Cinch Girth.

Corral A pen for cattle or horses.

Cottonwood A name given to several kinds of North American poplar. The seeds are covered with cottony hairs.

Draw A small gully.

Enchilada A Mexican dish consisting of a fried *tortilla* (pancake) filled with meat and served with chilli sauce.

Frontier pants Western riding trousers.

Ground-hitch A word used when a horse is trained to remain stationary with its reins left dangling.

Gunny A coarse fabric made from jute.

Hombre A slang word meaning "man".

Ironwood A name given to several kinds of tree, all of which have very hard wood.

Killdeer A large brown and white North American bird with a loud cry.

Lima bean Any one of several kinds of bean plant, all of which have flat pods with edible seeds.

Morgan An American breed of strong, light trotting horse.

Ornery Someone or something of a mean, nasty disposition.

Outfit Equipment belonging to a party or group.

Pinch-hit Act as a substitute.

Pinto A horse marked with white patches – i.e. piebald or skewbald.

Pumpernickel Coarse, dark bread made of unsifted rye.

Rockhound Someone who searches for and collects precious and semi-precious stones which can be cut, polished and set as gems.

Saddlebred A type of horse bred for riding.

Saddlehorn The pommel of a western saddle round which a lasso can be looped.

Scrub oak A small, shrublike species of oak.

Sourdough A type of bread made with fermented dough used as a leaven.

Spell To take turns with someone in doing a job.

Squab Any young bird – usually a pigeon.

Trail horse A horse which is able to keep a steady pace for long distances over rough ground.

Washout The washing away of earth and rocks by a sudden, strong flow of water.

Mystery Message 1

Linda ran into the ranch house living room waving a letter she had picked up from the mailbox.

"Bob," she said excitedly to her brother, who was reading, "this is addressed to you and me. It's from the Trail Blazers! Do you suppose it could be an invitation to join the club?"

"A good way to find out would be to open it," Bob replied, grinning. He was fair-haired and brown-eyed, favoring the Scottish strain of their father, while Linda had the brunette Spanish coloring of their mother.

Eagerly Linda slit open the envelope and pulled out a Trail Blazers Club 28 letterhead bordered with sketches of horses.

"This *is* an invitation to join!" exclaimed Linda joyfully. "That is, if we can qualify."

Bob beamed. "We'll work hard to. The committee doesn't take new members into the Trail Blazers every day. They've evidently been watching our riding and noted our show awards—especially yours and Chica's."

Linda smiled at the thought of Chica d'Oro, her prized golden palomino filly, whom she had trained herself.

She read on: " 'Meetings follow potluck suppers the second Thursday of each month.' What fun!"

"Thursday is the day after tomorrow," said Bob. "Say, look at the large print at the bottom of the page: "TRAIL RIDES. HORSE SHOWS. POSSE AIDES.' "

"Oh, isn't it marvelous!" Linda exclaimed. Then she frowned slightly. "Bob, do you suppose this Posse Aides category means that we'll be chasing *criminals?*"

"I doubt it. I think our part will be to track down clues to a culprit's identity, then let the sheriff do the capturing."

Sister and brother sat down to discuss the invitation in the comfortable, Spanish-style, beam-ceilinged room. It was in the Rancho del Sol, home of their grandparents, Tom and Rosalinda Mallory. Some months before, Linda and Bob Craig had lost both their father and mother in an accident in Hawaii where Major Craig had been stationed. Sixteen-year-old Linda and eighteen-year-old Bob had come to Rancho del Sol in the San Quinto Valley of Southern California to live with the

Mallorys. The young Craigs affectionately called them Bronco and Doña.

Having spent all their summers on the ranch, Linda and Bob felt at home here and loved their grandparents. To assuage their recent grief, the brother and sister had done a good deal of riding and had solved some local mysteries.

The ringing of the telephone interrupted their conversation. Linda answered.

"It's Kathy," she told Bob. Then she laughed happily. "Kathy received an invitation to join the Trail Blazers too!"

Kathy Hamilton was Linda's best friend, a happy honey-blonde of sixteen who had a pinto named Patches. Her parents owned the Highway House, a landmark on the desert highway. It combined restaurant, souvenir store, and lapidary shop. Here Mr. Hamilton cut, polished, and sold semiprecious stones. It was a mecca for local rock hounds.

Presently Linda hung up. "Kathy knows a lot about the Trail Blazers," she informed Bob. "There are sixty clubs in the group. Number 28 has the reputation for being the most active and the most fun. Number 6, the Malibu coast group, is the wealthiest and ritziest. That's the one Shirley Blaine belongs to."

"And who is she?" Bob asked.

Linda shrugged. "Kathy said Shirley is the gal I'll really have to watch out for in show contests. She's excellent, but hard to get along with. It seems that her one ambition in life is to qualify for the Olympic team and she lets everyone know it."

"Wow! That's some ambition," Bob remarked.

"And one that requires not only the tops in mounts and riding ability, but also the money to see it through," Linda reminded him. "I may never meet her, though. I'll have to qualify for the club before going against her in competition."

"Does that worry you?" Bob grinned.

"If she can beat me, it's fair enough," replied Linda with a tilt of her chin.

Again the telephone rang. Bob answered this time, saying, "Hi, Larry!" After a moment's conversation, he cried, "Great!" and nodded to Linda's question, "Trail Blazer invitation?"

Larry Spencer was Bob's friend, eighteen also, a tall, easygoing, brown-eyed youth whose father owned the leather goods and saddlery shop in the nearby town of Lockwood. Larry did not have a horse of his own, but rode one of the Rancho del Sol string.

On Thursday evening Linda and Bob drove to the Trail Blazers meeting and potluck supper in the Community Building at Tri-Canyon Junction. They carried a ham-and-lima-bean casserole and a loaf of garlic sourdough bread.

Larry was waiting outside in his jeep. "Here's one

of Mother's delicious devil's food cakes," he announced. Then Kathy arrived with a big bowl of salad.

The foursome was met by the president of the club, twenty-year-old Chuck Eller. He was a dark-haired, energetic athlete, whose commanding personality indicated the reason for the success of this particular club in the Trail Blazers.

"Hi, everybody!" he greeted them.

Sue Mason, his pretty, tawny-haired, hazel-eyed date, joined him, and took charge of the four proposed members to introduce them.

"You won't have any trouble passing the tests," she prophesied with a friendly chuckle when she left them.

It was a gala supper. Afterward, as soon as Chuck Eller had dispensed with routine business, he said, "Now we are ready to inform our four prospective members of their initiation. Our secretary will read the rules."

Sue Mason stood up with her book and began, "'All new members are required to qualify by riding and blazing a new trail to some spot of exceptional or historical interest. They must bring back a report and snapshots of the place as well as of the new trail. When approved by the initiation committee, the new members will be privileged to join in all activities and missions of the club.'"

Linda, Bob, Kathy, and Larry glanced at one another with new excitement. The members grinned approvingly and clapped.

Chuck Eller rose and announced, "We have an important new mission to accomplish. Our members have been asked by the sheriff's office to act as an auxiliary posse and to help discover who or what, rustlers or wild animals, are causing the disappearance of cattle from small outlying ranches in this area. May I see hands of those who will be able to participate in this?"

Nearly every member raised a hand.

Chuck looked pleased. "Great! You'll all receive a bulletin on this as soon as we have worked out the details."

Linda whispered to her friends, "I'd like to participate. Do you suppose we can?"

They nodded eagerly and Bob asked Chuck, "May we receive copies?"

"Yes indeed."

As soon as the meeting was adjourned, Linda suggested to her group, "How about the four of us getting together at Old Sol tomorrow to work out our initiation ride?"

The others agreed quickly and, the following afternoon, gathered on the secluded ranch patio, with its attractive redwood furniture and towering oak trees.

Rango, Old Sol's yellowish-tan, coyote-shepherd dog, lay stretched out with one eye open, and thumped his tail each time anyone spoke. He seemed aware that a riding trip was being planned, and aimed to do his best not to be left out of the fun.

Bob spread out maps of nearby sections.

"A lot of territory to choose from," Kathy remarked. "But where will we find an unblazed trail?"

"Here come two people who can help us," said Linda. "Doña and Bronco."

The fine-looking couple rode in on their horses and dismounted near the barn. Then they strode toward the patio. Both were tall and straight.

Doña Mallory, of Spanish origin, walked with a queenly gait. She was a beautiful, slender, olive-skinned woman, with dark graying hair worn in a chignon. Grandmother Mallory was always dignified and never deviated from her high ideals. Yet she joined easily in the fun and unusual situations which arose at Old Sol.

"I'm glad to see you," she said to Kathy and Larry. "We'll have tea and then suppose you tell me about your trip."

"We need advice," said Linda, as her grandmother went into the house to change from her riding clothes and ask the housekeeper to serve refreshments.

Bronco Mallory did not bother to change. He

dropped his big frame into a lounge chair. "You folks got a world-shattering problem?" he teased.

When they told him, he scratched his iron-gray hair and twirled his big sombrero in mute answer to the questions flung at him. He could think of no unbroken trail of historical interest. Doña Mallory returned, but she too could offer no solution.

At that moment Luisa Alvarez, Rancho del Sol's plump, genial Mexican housekeeper, brought out a tray of iced tea and gingerbread squares. When the nonplussed group asked if she had any suggestions, the woman shook her head regretfully.

"Problems, always problems," she muttered, turning toward the kitchen while looking over at the field where her two pet goats, Geraldine and Genevieve, were tethered. She called a cheery greeting to them in her native tongue, and waved her apron. Goat's milk was the only kind Luisa would use in her superb cookery.

"Here comes Cactus Mac," said Linda, seeing the lovable, bandy-legged ranch foreman. "Maybe he can suggest a place for us to go." She called out, "Paging Cactus Mac!"

The gray-haired man sauntered over, and with a broad smile asked drawlingly, "Who's in trouble now?"

"We all are," the young people answered.

Quickly Linda explained their problem and then

said, "Mac, you know every inch of Southern California, and about everything that has ever happened here. Where would you suggest that we ride?"

The foreman squinted his eyes in thought for a few moments, then smiled cagily. "Wal, Crespi Cove should do it. Trailer your horses over to Scotty's Steak House on Valley Highway, and leave the outfits thar. Then break a trail over the hills to the cove on the ocean. You'll find a historical marker right plumb on the sand."

"What is it?" asked Kathy excitedly.

"You'll learn when you get thar," Cactus replied and went on to the corral.

Linda laughed. "Well, I guess nothing will keep us from Crespi Cove to find out what's on that marker."

She and her friends made plans to leave early the following Monday.

"That's a long, hard ride. Take plenty of provisions," Bronco advised, and Doña added, "And blankets. It may be chilly at night."

The next morning Bronco left for a stock auction that would take him away from Rancho del Sol for an overnight stay. After Linda had said good-bye to him, she went to feed Chica. How beautiful the golden palomino was, Linda thought. The two-year-old had a white mane and tail, four white stockings, and very intelligent brown eyes.

"I'll be back to give you a workout in a little while, baby," said Linda, and hurried off to make her bed and tidy her room.

When she returned to the barn, Linda found the filly standing with her head down in one corner of the stall.

"What's the matter, baby?" the girl asked with concern. "Why aren't you out in the sunshine?"

Chica lifted her head and whinnied a weak greeting. Presuming that she had just been taking a nap, Linda saddled the horse and took her out into the adjoining ring.

Almost immediately Linda became aware that Chica was limping badly with her hind legs. Her young rider dismounted hastily and examined each hind foot. Both were clean. But Chica seemed to be in considerable pain.

Alarmed, Linda started to lead the palomino slowly back to her stall. Frantically she called, "Cactus Mac!"

He came running from the big barn, took one look at Chica, and barked, "Get the doc!"

Linda ran to the barn phone and called the veterinarian, Dr. Sawyer, in Lockwood. He reached the ranch within the hour. Linda stood by Chica petting and talking soothingly to her as he made an examination. Cactus Mac and Bob waited nearby for the diagnosis.

Dr. Sawyer examined Chica's feet and legs. Suddenly he exclaimed, "Wal, I'll be—this horse's legs have been threaded!"

"Wh-what do you mean?" gasped Linda.

"A thread has been pulled through her legs here above the hocks. It's affecting the nerves." Dr. Sawyer shook his head. "Haven't run into this for years. It was an old-time racetrack trick to put a horse out of the running. This is a criminal offense."

He went to work pulling out the threads and treating the legs with a soothing medication.

"Will Chica be all right?" asked Linda fearfully.

"She will now," declared the veterinarian. "Just give her a few days' rest. But if we hadn't found these threads, your horse likely would have gone permanently lame."

"Who could have done this?" cried Linda angrily. "And why?"

She, Bob, and Cactus Mac searched for strange horse or tire tracks that might indicate someone had ridden into the ranch from the side or back. But they could find none.

"How did the person get here? On foot?" Linda asked, but no one could answer her.

Two deputies arrived from the sheriff's office where Dr. Sawyer had stopped to report the criminal incident. At the total lack of evidence or clues, one declared, "This must have been an inside job." He turned to Cactus Mac. "You'd better make a close check of your hands."

Cactus Mac bristled. "Ain't a one o' them what's that kind o' crackpot," he retorted.

With Chica now standing quietly, and needing a rest rather than a workout, Linda went into the house. It was a custom of hers to hesitate a moment in the hallway before the large oil portrait of her great-great-grandmother Rosalinda Perez who had come from Spain as a bride with her rich young grandee husband to Rancho del Sol, a grant to him from the Spanish king.

Linda strongly resembled her lovely ancestor, having the same fine features, glossy black hair, lustrous brown eyes, and creamy complexion.

"Oh, you are so exquisite in your Spanish wedding dress!" Linda said softly.

As she stood staring at the portrait, Bob came rushing into the hall. "Better go see what's bothering Chica now. She seems upset."

Linda lost no time. She ran all the way to the palomino's stall, followed by her brother. The filly was restive and nickering nervously. She settled down immediately, however, at sight of Linda.

"It's all right, sweetie," Linda crooned. "Nothing else is going to happen to you. I'll stay right here with you day and night."

"Suppose I take the night shift," Bob offered.

At that moment Linda's eye caught sight of something wedged between the feedbox and the stall side.

She snatched it out, examined the paper, then exclaimed, "What a strange message this is!"

Stranger on the Trail 2

"A strange message?" Bob repeated, reaching for the paper in his sister's hand.

"Better be careful," warned Linda. "This must be very old, it's so fragile—and the ink is faded. I think it's part of a letter. And look!" She held out the paper for Bob's inspection. "What odd spelling!"

The Craigs read the message together:

"Family chest holds secret. Dying wishe of the mistress is for faithful servants to share the tresur."

Bob glanced up at his sister, mystified. "Say!" he exclaimed. "This is a real poser."

"It sure is," agreed Linda. "I can't imagine who left the paper here, or why, or what it means."

Cactus Mac, passing by, noted the Craigs puzzling over the scrap of paper. "What have you young 'uns got thar?" he asked, entering.

Linda showed him the old, stained scrap of paper with its mysterious message. Cactus Mac whistled.

Then he declared, "The varmint what threaded Chica must have left it here!"

Linda looked bewildered. "I don't see any connection."

"Me either," said Bob. "But there seems to be a lot happening around here that we don't understand!"

"We'd better discover fast what it's all about," said Linda determinedly.

"Check," Cactus Mac growled.

"Why do you suppose Rango didn't bark if a stranger came in?" Linda wondered. "By the way, where is he? Has something happened to *him*?"

"Not to that hound," replied Cactus with a grin. "Rango's over t' the south acreage with Bud, who's clearin' out weeds and tryin' to persuade Vagabond to haul 'em off in a cart. You know how all-fired stubborn that donk is. Won't do a lick o' work 'cept for someone he likes."

Linda smiled, recalling how Chica d'Oro had found the hapless little donkey alone in the desert one night when she and some companions were on a cattle-trailing mission. The palomino and burro had become constant companions, with Rango running a close second in their affection.

Cactus Mac scowled. "But you can safely bet your last cent it was some crackpot stranger pussyfootin' around here. 'Tweren't none o' my crew."

"At any rate," Linda said, "I'd like to show this

note to Doña if one of you will stay with Chica."

"I aim to go further," said Cactus Mac. "I'll put her in a stall in the big barn. Me or one o' the men will keep an eye onto her so's you won't have to bother."

"All right," said Linda. "Thanks."

She took the note inside the ranch house. Doña perused it with deepening perplexity. "This message is strange indeed," she remarked.

Suddenly Linda burst out, "Do you suppose the family chest mentioned in this note refers to Rosalinda Perez's?"

She and Doña went into the hall and stood by the handsome, carved, black walnut chest standing beneath the oil portrait. Inside it were Rosalinda's wedding dress and accessories.

"If the note means this chest," suggested Linda excitedly, "then the secret mentioned might refer to the jewels!" She recalled again the story of the disappearance of Rosalinda Perez's fortune in jewels.

Doña Mallory shrugged. "As you know, they are not in the chest, dear. It has been thoroughly searched many times, and even tapped for a hidden compartment."

Linda looked up at her ancestor's portrait. "If you could only tell us what you did with them!" she murmured.

The jewels had apparently been hidden at the time that Captain Frémont, in 1846, had led a march on California, which then belonged to Mexico, in an attempt to gain that territory for the United States. The Spanish ranchers, terrified by tales of the robbing and plundering by avaricious soldiers, had secreted their valuable possessions, particularly gems. Rosalinda Perez had done this also.

Soon after the war Señora Perez had lapsed into a serious illness, and had died without revealing the hiding place of the jewels. The house and gardens had been thoroughly searched by each succeeding generation occupying the ranch, but the gems had not been found.

It had long since been concluded by most of the family that the soldiers must have found the jewels and taken them. A few believed that perhaps Rosalinda had managed to send them back to her relatives in Spain.

"Do you suppose, Doña," Linda speculated, "that there actually could be a descendant of an old Perez servant who knows something about the treasure—and he's one of Bronco's new cowmen?"

"It seems improbable, after all these years," mused Doña. "But if so, he is doomed to disappointment believing the jewels are in this chest."

"Just the same," Linda said, "I think I'll go ask

Cactus Mac about the new hands." She raced outside and spotted the foreman coming from the big barn.

In response to Linda's query, he said, "No, ma'am. There ain't one of my regular bunch, old or new, who considers himself a servant like that note says. Self-respectin' cowmen, that's what they are, and if those smart-aleck young lawmen come around here again badgerin' 'em with false accusations, they'll have me to reckon with."

Bob, who had begun to mend tack nearby, spoke up. "If there is such a 'faithful servant' character, why doesn't he show himself? And what has he got against Chica?"

"I just *can't* figure out the connection," Linda said, "although the message must have been left in Chica's stall this morning when her legs were threaded."

Bob shrugged in puzzlement. "All I know is, this mystery is making me hungry." He glanced at his watch and exclaimed, "No wonder! It's half an hour past lunchtime!"

"Are you sure the outdoor bell didn't ring?" Linda asked him.

"Would I be here starving to death if it had?" Bob retorted with a chuckle.

"Not you," Linda admitted, laughing. "I'd better go see if Luisa needs any help."

Bob followed his sister into the kitchen. The

room was filled with the strong odor of burned food.

"Goodness! What happened?" Linda asked the housekeeper.

"Oh, the lunch, it is all burned, all spoiled!" Luisa lamented. "My Genevieve, for some reason she go off yesterday and not come back last night. My Geraldine is so lonesome she won't eat or drink, and does not give much milk."

Luisa was distractedly walking around in a circle with the big baking dish of scorched food in her hands.

Linda took the dish from her and put it on the drainboard. "Don't you fret about lunch," she said kindly. "I'll fix something. You go out on the patio now and cool off."

Gently she propelled Luisa toward the door. "And don't worry any more about Genevieve. As soon as Bob and I have eaten we'll ride out and bring her back. She's probably not very far away."

Somewhat calmed down, Luisa complied.

Linda and Bob ate lunch quickly. Directly afterward they went out to get horses and go after the missing goat. Linda caught a cow pony named Brownie in the field and brought him into the barn to saddle.

While fastening the girth and shortening the stirrups, she talked to Chica d'Oro, now in the protective barn stall. Instead of appearing pleased, the palomino whinnied plaintively and pawed with a forefoot. Then she reached out with her nose and gave a quick hard push to Brownie's side, making him whirl.

Linda jumped out of the way. "What's the matter?" Then she laughed. "Why baby, you're jealous!"

She went to Chica and stroked the filly's neck to calm her. "Brownie isn't replacing you, sweetie," Linda crooned softly. "He is only going to pinch-hit for you today on a short ride while your legs get well." The palomino seemed mollified and nuzzled the girl with her soft nose.

Old Bart, an Old Sol hand of long standing, came out of the feed room with a molasses cake. "You go on, now," he said to Linda. "I'll take Chica's mind off bein' left behind by givin' her a little sweeten-in'."

Linda flashed him a grateful smile and led Brownie outside, where Bob waited on his bay, Rocket. The Craigs picked up the missing goat's little tracks and followed them for some distance. They led up a draw, then disappeared.

"Oh, dear!" Linda sighed. "Where can Genevieve have gone?"

She and Bob leaned low from their horses, attempting to spot the tracks again. Suddenly a lone rider loomed up on the trail ahead of them.

In a low, concerned voice Linda said to Bob,

"Wherever did he come from?" Bob shook his head, sitting straight and alert.

The rider, who was a medium-built man of about forty, approached the brother and sister.

"Howdy!" he greeted them. "I'm Rod Coleman. I've located on a ranch near here, and am just out for a little ride to get acquainted with the valley."

His friendly manner somewhat relieved Linda of her apprehension, and she replied pleasantly, "We're Linda and Bob Craig from Rancho del Sol. We're looking for our housekeeper's goat. Have you seen a stray one?"

Coleman gave the girl a slow, broad smile and replied, "As a matter of fact, I did notice one about a mile from here. If you like, I'll ride along with you and show you the spot. Glad to have company."

"Thank you very much," said Bob. "We'd appreciate that."

The trio turned up the draw. Linda and her brother kept listening for Genevieve's bell, but failed to hear it. Finally the riders came to a cabin. It was set close against the slope, which was thickly covered with ironwood trees and blooming wild buckwheat.

Linda and Bob looked questioningly at Rod Coleman. "Is this the place?" Linda asked.

Coleman appeared baffled at the absence of the goat and replied, "That's right. Say, you might knock at the door there, and inquire."

Linda and Bob exchanged cautious glances. Bob did not dismount and knock, but rode closer. "Hello, in there!" he called out.

The cabin door opened. Framed in the entrance was a tall, uncouth, cadaverous-looking man. He stared surlily at the Craigs.

"We're sorry to bother you," said Bob politely, "but we've lost a goat. We were told it was near here. Did you notice it?"

The man ran his tongue over thin lips, and said, "Light, and come in."

"No, thank you," said Linda hastily. "We'd better keep searching for the goat."

Behind them Rod Coleman suddenly ordered, "Dismount and go in!"

The Craigs swung their horses to stare at him. Linda gasped. In Coleman's hand was a revolver, leveled on her and Bob! Every trace of geniality had left the man's face.

"Do as I say!" he ordered them. "Off your horses, and into the cabin!"

Ransacked
Ranch House 3

Shocked and amazed, Linda and Bob sat tensely on their horses. As Linda looked down the barrel of the gun which Coleman held trained on them, she tried not to tremble.

"What is this all about?" Bob demanded. "We have nothing of value on us. You must have mistaken us for someone else."

"No mistake," growled Coleman. "We're not going to hurt you. Just want to keep you here while we go to investigate something. But if you don't listen—"

"Ride out fast, Linda," said Bob quickly in a low voice, and clicked his heels to Rocket's flanks. But at that instant Rod Coleman, overhearing, fired into the air to show them he meant business.

Both Brownie and Rocket reared, then the

panicked cow pony took off on a run down the draw. Linda started to pull him in, not wanting to leave Bob alone. But she heard him yell:

"Go on! Go on!"

The next moment she also heard pounding hooves gaining on her, and Rod Coleman shouting, "*Stop!*"

When Linda did not rein in, there came a terrifying gun explosion, and the whiz of the bullet. Brownie screamed, and went down on his knees.

Linda sprang free. Almost immediately Brownie struggled to his feet, so she knew in relief that a bone had not been pierced by the bullet. She did see blood running from the cow pony's shoulder, and snatched out her handkerchief to press it against the wound.

"Easy, boy," Linda whispered. Her dark eyes flashed with outrage at Rod Coleman as he came alongside. "What kind of fiend are you to shoot a horse?" she cried.

"You do as I say, girlie, or *you'll* feel the next one!" he replied. "Get going back to the cabin and no more funny tricks."

With prickles running up and down her spine, and one hand clutching the end of Brownie's reins, Linda reluctantly obeyed. Bob was off Rocket and standing beside him. Linda, dismayed, immediately saw why he was there—the tall, gaunt man in the cabin held a rifle!

Swiftly Rod Coleman dismounted. He left all the horses ground-hitched, then pushed Bob and Linda inside the building. Bob turned furiously and struck out at Coleman with knotted fists.

With an ugly leer the other man raised his rifle menacingly and snarled, "Back off!" Linda and Bob froze.

Coleman grabbed up a length of strong cotton rope that apparently had been used for a clothesline at some time. He cut lengths from this and bound the Craigs' wrists and ankles. Now he turned to a gunrack on the way. It had been constructed of old horseshoes, bolted sideways to the wall, to hold guns or other heavy objects. Coleman tied ropes around Linda's and Bob's waists and fastened the line to the horseshoes, placing the prisoners in standing position a good six feet apart.

So Bob and I can't help each other escape! Linda thought grimly.

Rod Coleman stood before them arrogantly and said, "We'll turn you loose tomorrow. In the meantime my pal here and I are going to search the Old Sol ranch house until we find those jewels your fancy Spanish lady ancestor hid."

Linda drew in her breath. "You won't find them. They're gone."

"That's what you think. But you're wrong."

The girl's eyes flashed as a thought came into her mind. "You're the one who left that piece of an old letter in my horse's stall!" she accused.

"Now you're getting smart." Coleman chortled by way of acknowledging this.

"But why," asked Linda, "if you intended to rob the ranch house, did you leave a clue like that?"

"Just an old trick to confuse the lawmen." Coleman grinned enigmatically.

The gaunt man gave a harsh laugh. "It ought to work—or my name isn't Hank Trask—" He broke off suddenly as if he had not meant to identify himself.

"Where did you get that note about the jewels?" Bob prodded.

"Just you keep guessing on that one," Trask said with a sneer.

Linda set her jaw. "You must be the same person who threaded my horse's legs," she accused Rod Coleman.

"One and the same," he admitted with a note of swagger in his tone as if proud of his achievement. "But next time—"

"Shut up!" barked Hank Trask.

Coleman gave his pal a displeased look, but closed his lips in a hard, straight line.

"Why did you do such a heartless thing? Why?" Linda cried out. "And how did you get to the ranch?"

Coleman remained silent, except to say he had come on foot. He shoved a wooden chair in front of

Linda and Bob struggled to get free . . .

Linda, put a pan of water on it, and dumped out some crackers from a box. Then he pushed another chair before Bob and supplied it equally.

"Eat hearty!" Trask guffawed. The Craigs eyed him coldly and made no response.

The two men turned abruptly and went out, slamming the door hard after them. The strenuous jar, however, caused the door to rebound from the rusty old catch and stand open a couple of inches. It sagged badly onto the floor.

Through the crack Linda and Bob saw the men ride out, taking the Craigs' horses with them. They pulled the limping Brownie along mercilessly.

Anger flushed the faces of both brother and sister who strained desperately at their ropes. But the two soon realized with sinking hearts that they had been well secured.

Linda made a wry face at the crackers and water. "At least these men don't intend for us to die of thirst or hunger. And probably they wouldn't have shot us. We should have fought harder to get away and made a dash for it on foot."

Bob shook his head. "They weren't going to let us escape. If necessary, they would have wounded us slightly to prevent it. What I'd like to know is how Rod Coleman and Trask found out about the Perez jewels."

As a sudden thought came to Linda, she shuddered. "Bob, those awful men are headed for Old

Sol. With Bronco still away, Doña and Luisa will be alone in the ranch house. They're in danger! And we can't do one thing to help them!"

The Craigs were sunk in gloom, fears for those at the ranch racing through their minds.

"If Rango has come back to the house, he'll go straight for those men," Bob conjectured hopefully.

"But they might shoot him!" Linda answered worriedly.

"I doubt it," said Bob, trying to reassure her. "The sound of a shot would bring in Cactus Mac or any of the men who might be nearby." To himself Bob added, Those crooks might knock Rango out with a blow on the head, though.

"Oh, dear," said Linda as a new worry assailed her. "If Cactus Mac should go into the house, what chance would he have against two guns?"

"Mac has dealt with rustlers and other outlaws," Bob reminded Linda. "He won't take any foolhardy chances—count on that!"

After a few minutes of silence, Linda said, "I just cannot figure out the other mystery—why Rod Coleman tried to put Chica d'Oro out of commission."

"Right now I can't figure that out either," Bob admitted. "One thing's certain. He and his pal Hank Trask seem to be involved in more than one line of skulduggery."

The Craigs fell silent once more, their thoughts somber. As the hours passed, they caught themselves listening for sounds of the outlaws' return. No one arrived.

Darkness fell. With it came the usual night sounds—the eerie call of the killdeer, the hoot of an owl, the scurrying of small animals, and the crack of twigs under the paws of larger creatures.

Linda had half-dozed. Suddenly she gave a start. "Bob, are you awake? Could that be a wildcat I hear out there?" she asked worriedly. "It may come in and attack us!"

"I'm plenty awake," replied Bob. "It may have been a wildcat, but lucky for us the door is hanging heavy on those hinges. I doubt if a cat would be clever enough to push it open."

The Craigs kept an uneasy vigil for the remainder of the night. With the first gray light of dawn Linda exclaimed, "Maybe Coleman and Trask don't intend to come back! I'm going to call for help. Someone might be out herding." She yelled several times, but there was no response.

"I'll give it a try," said Bob, and shouted lustily.

Suddenly Linda said, "Listen! I thought I heard a dog bark."

"I did too," said Bob. "Some kid with his dog may be out rounding up strays." He repeated the call for help.

The barking became louder and nearer. Linda called excitedly. As the dog barked again, she thought there was a joyous note to it.

"Why, that sounds like Rango!" she exclaimed, and cried out, "Here, Rango! Here, Rango!"

In a few moments the familiar big yellow head appeared at the crack of the door.

"Hi, boy!" Bob grinned in relief. "Come in and get us out of here."

Getting in was no problem for Rango! He shoved his big strong paw in the crack and pushed the door back. Then he bounded inside.

"Oh, Rango!" Linda laughed. "You great big wonderful beautiful darling! Here, chew this rope off." She thrust her bound wrists toward him.

Rango went to work quickly with his teeth. Chewing a binding rope from a person or an animal was one of the early training tricks Cactus Mac had taught Rango in order to make him a good working ranch dog.

"What do you suppose made Rango come looking for us?" Linda asked.

"My guess is that Cactus Mac sent him, as soon as he found we were missing," replied Bob.

When Linda's hands were free she untied her ankles, and with Rango's further help released the rope tied around her waist and fastened to the horseshoe on the wall behind her.

Then the girl and the dog together quickly freed

Bob. He and Linda were both so cramped and sore that they could hardly move. But they massaged and flexed their arm and leg muscles until most of the stiffness was gone.

The Craigs hurriedly walked back to the ranch house with Rango following. When it came into view they approached cautiously. Everything seemed ominously quiet.

"I hope nothing dreadful has happened," Linda said worriedly.

With anxious bravado she and her brother raced into the kitchen.

"Oh!" Linda stiffened and screamed.

Doña and Luisa sat tied to chairs with dish towels, gagged. Their eyes were wells of terror. Linda and Bob hastily freed the women and asked who had bound them.

At first Luisa could only wring her hands and wail, *"Caramba!"*

Doña took a deep breath and stood up, mustering her usual dignity and composure. "What a dreadful ordeal!" she murmured. Then, before telling her story, she looked anxiously at Linda and Bob. "I'm so thankful you are back! What happened? Where have you been?"

"Tied up in an old cabin by two men who wanted to keep us away from here," Bob informed his grandmother. "We were decoyed on the trail by one of them who posed as a new rancher neighbor."

"But Rango found us," Linda added.

Doña and Luisa were horrified over what had happened, and beamed at Rango as Linda patted the big dog. Rango curved his lips in a grin and wagged his tail in happy appreciation.

"We know the names of the two men who captured us," Linda declared.

"Three men came here," said Doña. "Three masked men."

"Three?" Bob repeated in surprise. "Was one tall, and another of medium height?"

"Yes," Mrs. Mallory replied. "And the third was medium height also, but a little huskier."

"Rod Coleman and Hank Trask picked up a confederate somewhere on the way to Old Sol," Linda reasoned. "They must belong to a band of outlaws."

Bob added, "The two men we know as Coleman and Trask said they were coming here to search for Rosalinda Perez's jewels. Did they?"

"Yes," Doña replied, pained by the recollection. "Those—thieves announced they had come for the Perez treasure, and ransacked the entire house. We heard them going from room to room. I don't know what they may have taken."

Linda and Bob ran into the hall and stared in dismay at the open carved chest. The beautiful satin wedding dress and all the accessories were strewn about the floor. Linda's eyes filled with tears.

Then she and her brother gasped as they peered into the chest. "There *is* a false bottom!" Bob exclaimed. "And it has been forced open!"

"The jewels!" Linda cried out. "Rod Coleman found the jewels!"

The Captured Foreman   4

Doña, who had hurriedly joined Bob and Linda in the hallway, looked astounded.

"I never heard that there was a false bottom in the Perez chest," she declared, "or that the jewels were there. It has been thoroughly examined in the past for hidden compartments, so I am sure the gems would have been found."

Linda was not convinced that the three masked men had not succeeded in finding the jewels. "Since they had the old letter, they might have obtained further information from some source."

"That is possible," her grandmother conceded. "But I shall keep hoping the thieves went away empty-handed."

"We'll do our best to find out," Bob said grimly.

"And now"—Mrs. Mallory moved along the

hallway with quiet dignity—"I wish to make certain the vandals have not damaged our home any further."

Linda quickly put a hand on her grandmother's arm. "Oh, please, Doña, not now. You're very brave, but I know you and Luisa are exhausted from your dreadful experience. I'll make us all some hot bouillon, then won't you two go to bed and rest?"

Mrs. Mallory was finally persuaded, and Linda had the hot drink ready in a few minutes. After they had finished it, the women went upstairs.

"I'm going on a tour of inspection," Bob told his sister, "and see if anything else is missing, and if those crooks left any clues to establish their guilt."

"Good," said Linda. "Meanwhile, I'll begin downstairs and straighten up some of the jumble they made tearing this place apart."

When Bob had completed his check, he reported to Linda, "Those men sure turned things upside down and inside out. But nothing seems to have been taken except money from purses; and my collection of old coins is gone."

"What a shame!" said Linda sympathetically. "Did you find any evidence that could be used against them?"

"No. I'm going outside now and look around. And I'd like to talk to some of the ranch hands."

"I'll keep on with my job here," said Linda.

Bob went to the bunkhouse and stood inside the

door astounded. No one was there, and not a bed had been slept in, including that of Moe, the cook.

Very peculiar, Bob told himself with a frown. He wondered what had come up to keep the men and the chuck wagon out on the range overnight. They usually came in every evening.

He hastened around to Cactus Mac's private quarters and discovered that the foreman's room too had not been occupied that night. Fearful for Chica d'Oro and the other horses, Bob ran to the barn. He stopped dead in the entrance, aghast.

Slumped against a bale of hay was Cactus Mac, trussed up and gagged with a piece of feed sack. Fearing that the foreman had been badly injured, Bob hurried to his side. Cactus seemed to be merely dozing, and when Bob touched his shoulder he snapped awake.

The wiry man struggled against his bonds and made muffled sounds of anger. Bob quickly took off the gag and untied the ropes.

The foreman got up and stamped about for a few moments, berating his attackers. Then he stopped suddenly. "Say! What in tarnation happened to you and Linda?" he demanded. "Where've *you* been?"

"Trussed up like you—in an old cabin up a draw," replied Bob. "Rango tracked us down and freed us. Did you send him?"

"Nope. Never had a chance," Mac muttered.

"Guess he figured somethin' queer was goin' on here and went after you."

Bob fully relayed Doña's story. "Linda and I know the names of two of the men—the ones who tied us up. But we don't know who the third might be."

"Didn't hear any names mentioned," said Cactus. "But I saw that two were medium height, and one was tall."

Bob then asked, "Where are all the hands? None of them came back to the bunkhouse last night."

Cactus Mac frowned. "No reason for 'em to stay on the range now. I'll go check the bunkhouse."

"And I'll call the sheriff pronto," Bob said.

He started back to the house as the foreman strode away angry-faced. Bob gave Deputy Sheriff Randall complete details of everything that had happened to all of them, and the reason for the ranch house ransack. He described Rod Coleman and Hank Trask, giving their names, then told of the third man.

The officer speculated, "That third man was undoubtedly Rod's brother, Ben. They look alike, except that Ben's huskier. The Colemans and Trask are fast-buck operators who are wanted by the authorities."

"They can't be very far away yet," Bob guessed. "The men might have headed back to the cabin up the draw since they didn't know Linda and I escaped." He described the location of the cabin for Randall.

"Deputies will be sent there at once," the officer said grimly.

As Bob hung up, Linda walked in. She was astounded to hear about the empty bunkhouse and the attack on Cactus Mac. A quick look of anxiety came over her face.

"Chica!" she cried. "With all the men gone, and Cactus tied up, who knows what else Rod Coleman might have done to my palomino?"

The Craigs raced out to the barn. "Chica!" called Linda, running straight to the inside stall at the rear of the building.

The horse was not visible. A lump rose in Linda's throat. Then she saw the golden filly in a shadowy corner with her head dropped. She was sleeping.

"Chica, baby, are you all right?" her young owner asked as she opened the door and went inside.

The filly tossed up her head with a glad nicker of welcome and stepped sprightly over to Linda.

"Oh, Chica, there's nothing wrong with you!" crooned Linda joyously, hugging her around the neck. Then she turned the palomino about, looking her over carefully. "Why you're in good shape! Even your poor threaded legs seem well."

Bob, coming over to Chica's stall, said, "Colonel's

all right. I just made a check." Colonel was Bronco's chestnut Morgan. "And what do you think? Brownie and Rocket are back!"

"Coleman and Trask left them here?" Linda exclaimed unbelievingly.

"They must have."

"And they're unharmed?"

"Apparently."

"Bob, I can't understand it," said Linda. "Why do those men have a grudge against Chica d'Oro?"

"Deputy Sheriff Randall said those three men are fast-buck artists. Does that mean anything to you?" Bob asked.

"You mean someone paid Coleman to harm Chica?" Linda surmised. "But *who?*" she asked.

"I can't even make a guess," her brother answered. "But the sheriff's men are moving in on that trio of crooks. If they catch up with them and are able to make them talk, then we'll know the reason and who's causing all the trouble."

"I hope it won't be long." Linda's eyes flashed.

A moment later Cactus Mac came back into the barn. "Can't figure out what's kept my hands away," he said. "Don't believe they were run off. The lot of 'em would be a match for those three masked coyotes."

Just then he and the Craigs noticed dust whirling high on the lane leading out to the range. A rider was coming in fast.

Cactus Mac squinted into the sunlight. "That's Lanky Thompson, one o' my men!"

In a few moments Lanky slid his horse to a stop on its heels in front of the group and jumped off. "Is everything all right here?" he asked with concern.

"Ain't nothin' all right here," growled Cactus Mac. "Why you askin'? Where've you all been?"

Lanky removed his hat and took a soiled note from the crown. He explained, "A stranger rode out on the range late yesterday and gave Pinky this note signed by you, Cactus. Pinky figured the man was a new rider you'd put on."

"What's it say?" barked Cactus.

Lanky read: " 'Stay where you are until I join you. Cactus.' " He passed the paper over to the foreman.

"I never sent this note," muttered Cactus angrily. "This ain't my writin'."

"I guessed it wasn't the minute I saw the note," Lanky told him. "That's the reason I rode right in to see what was happening back here. I figured there was trouble."

"You figured right," said Bob.

"Do you know what that note-passin' joker looks like?" Cactus demanded.

"Pinky said he was medium height and stocky, with brownish hair," replied Lanky.

"Sounds like Ben Coleman, Rod's brother," Linda guessed.

"Get a fresh horse," said Cactus to Lanky, "and

go tell the men to bring the cattle close by and report in. And tell 'em any orders I give I'm a-sayin' 'em, not writin' 'em."

As Lanky went off, the foreman glanced at Linda, who was leaning wearily against the barn doorjamb. "You two better get some shut-eye," he advised.

"That's for me." Bob grinned. "I'm just about asleep on my feet."

"I *am* asleep," Linda admitted wryly.

The Craigs went quietly into the house and directly to bed. Sometime later Linda was awakened by strong sunlight and a delicious aroma. She glanced at the clock. Quarter to twelve.

"Mm-m!" Linda sniffed slowly. "I wonder what unusual dish Luisa's concocting for lunch!"

After a brisk shower and a change of clothes, Linda felt refreshed and hurried from her room. She met Bob at the top of the stairway and said teasingly, "I'll bet you're heading for the kitchen, too!" She laughed. "Only food would bring you out of bed!"

"Right!" Bob admitted, chuckling. "Come on, let's investigate."

They raced into the kitchen. Luisa, looking like her cheerful self, was at the stove stirring the contents of a huge iron kettle. From it came a tantalizing odor.

"Luisa, whatever are you making that smells so divine!" Linda exclaimed. "Is it a new recipe?"

With a mysterious smile the housekeeper gestured toward the center worktable. On it was a big basket containing a variety of vegetables yet to be peeled—tomatoes, cucumbers, cabbages, celery, and red and green peppers. Alongside was a freshly pulled pile of herbs from Luisa's garden, and boxes of spices.

"Don't tell me that's our lunch!" Linda said, astounded at the size of the kettle.

The housekeeper laughed heartily. "Not lunch."

"It smells terrific," said Bob. "How about a sample?"

Luisa laughed again and gave him a sample. "It will taste better in about four weeks," she said.

"My goodness, what *is* this recipe?" Linda puzzled, as Bob made a face and said, "It bites!"

"You ask your grandmother," the Mexican woman replied, her eyes twinkling.

Mrs. Mallory was just coming into the kitchen. She appeared rested and, to the Craigs' relief, showed no ill effects from her harrowing experience.

"Ask me what?" Doña said, smiling at them all.

"The name of the special food that's cooking in the kettle," said Bob.

"This is Luisa's famous chili vinegar," Doña informed them. "She alone knows the recipe. It has been handed down in the Alvarez family from one generation to the next. And it will be Luisa's and my contribution to the Ladies' Guild Benefit Fiesta Fair. The proceeds go to our community Children's Hospital."

"What a wonderful idea!" exclaimed Linda.

Luisa sighed. "Every year I fill more bottles, and there is never enough."

"I should think not," said Linda, "if it tastes as good as it smells."

"Do you have to cook and stir it day and night?" Bob teased.

"*Caramba!* Men!" exclaimed Luisa, throwing up her hands. "It is cooled, and strained through cheesecloth many times—that takes very long. Then it must stand in the bottles more time before using."

"I'll personally see that you and your bottles of chili vinegar arrive safely at your booth at the Fiesta," said Bob.

"*Gracias.*" Luisa beamed.

"Mind if I rustle up a piece of bread now for lunch?" he asked. "I have a powerful gnawing in my middle."

"For lunch you eat what I make for you," Luisa scolded. She opened the oven door, disclosing a baking dish of enchiladas in bubbling cheese sauce.

Doña, Linda, and Bob were soon seated in the dining room and enjoying the enchiladas and a mixed green salad. Dessert was chilled pineapple pudding.

When they had finished, Linda said, "Bob, I think we ought to start out again to look for Genevieve—although Luisa doesn't seem so upset about her today."

"She still misses the goat," said Doña. "But I called the Foster ranch, which keeps goats, to deliver a daily supply of milk here until Genevieve's return."

Mrs. Mallory's face clouded with worry. "Do you think it is safe for you two to go out again on the horses?"

"We'll be on our guard this time, Doña," Bob assured her. "And from what Randall told me, this valley will be swarming with deputies."

"I'll slip my police whistle into my pocket," said Linda. "And if I see anyone who looks even slightly like the Colemans or Trask, I'll start blowing it. That'll bring the officers fast!"

When Bob was again mounted on Rocket, and Linda on another cow pony from the work string, a chestnut named Jubilee, she asked, "Where to this time, Brother?"

"I suggest we search around all the watering spots we know," replied Bob. "It's my guess we'll find Genevieve at one of them."

"Lead off," said Linda.

They looked without luck at a couple of water holes and a big concrete trough. Then the Craigs followed a cow path to an upper range. It was impossible, however, to pick up any small goat tracks in the maze of cows' hoofprints.

Linda and Bob stopped near a bench to rest their horses. They sat down and looked admiringly at a pretty cove below, well shaded with cottonwoods and scrub oaks, and with a small stream of water trickling from the rocks on the side hill. In a few moments they became aware that the cove was occupied. Linda pointed out a man, a woman, several children, a burro, and a tarp stretched for cover.

"Gypsies!" exclaimed Bob.

"I think they're Mexicans," said Linda. "That's a Mexican blouse the woman has on." Then she added excitedly, "And look under the canvas covering—isn't that a goat?"

"It sure is," replied Bob. "Well, what are we waiting for? Let's ride down and see if the nanny answers to the name of Genevieve!"

Mama Diaz's Warning 5

As the Craigs' horses slid down the hillside, the Mexican children scampered in all directions, disappearing behind brush and boulders. The woman shielded the goat with her ample frame as she untied its frayed tether rope and pushed the animal into the dense protection of a scrub oak.

The man, hardy-looking and muscular, stood impassive, his dark eyes dull.

"Hello," Bob said. "We're from a nearby ranch, and are out hunting a lost goat. We saw the one you have here and wondered if it is yours, or if it strayed into your camp."

Linda meanwhile was gazing about, amazed at how swiftly the rest of the family had vanished. She turned to the Mexican. "Everyone is gone," she said. "What's the matter?"

A flicker of fear gleamed in the man's eyes. He shrugged, spreading his hands before him in a hapless gesture, and muttered, "No speeka English."

Linda and Bob exchanged understanding glances, and Bob repeated his questions about the goat in Spanish. He and his sister spoke the language fluently, as did each generation of Old Sol occupants.

The Mexican was staring at the Craigs, baffled, his face saddening and shoulders drooping. Speaking in his native tongue, he said, "I cannot find work. Cannot pay rent. We had to leave our little house. We have only one sack of beans and some cornmeal."

Linda and Bob dismounted, their faces filled with compassion.

"What is your name?" Linda asked.

"I am Pico Diaz, and this is my family," he said, waving a circling arm. Little, brown, round-eyed faces began to peek out from the brush. "If the goat is yours—we did not know. We did not steal it."

"Did you find the goat?" asked Linda gently.

"Not find it either," replied Diaz. "Two men who look much alike—must be brothers—came to our camp with it. They asked for a meal. The wife made beans and corn cakes for them. Then they left goat."

He clasped his hands as a momentary shine came

into his eyes. The nanny gives good milk for my little *niños*." He looked at the Craigs sadly again. "Is she yours?"

"We won't know for sure until we see her," said Linda. She called softly, "Genevieve. Genevieve."

There was an instant responsive bleating from behind the scrub oak, and Genevieve, pulling loose from the hold of Mama Diaz, came running out to Linda and Bob.

They petted her with welcoming happiness, and Linda exclaimed, "Oh, Genevieve, are we glad to find you!"

Mama Diaz came forward and stood with one hand on the goat. "You take the nanny away?" she asked despondently in Spanish. "You take milk from my little ones?"

The children gathered around the goat and fondled Genevieve. Tears moistened the eyes of several of the youngsters, who spoke up almost in chorus:

"Nanny is ours."

"We like Nanny."

"We like Nanny's milk."

While Genevieve appeared pleased to see Linda and Bob, she seemed content in her new adoring circle. Linda looked helplessly at her brother.

Bob gave his head a slight, perplexed shake, and changed the subject by asking the Mexicans, "The men who brought the goat here looked alike, you say?"

"Sí," replied Pico Diaz.

"But one was bigger," offered Mama Diaz. "They rode such nice horses, a black one and a brown one."

"The Coleman brothers, all right!" Linda exclaimed.

"You know those men?" asked Mama Diaz in surprise.

"We are pretty certain we do," Linda replied. "They're bad men." She said to Bob in English, "Now I get the picture. The Colemans took Genevieve from the ranch that night to lure you and me away. They figured on handling Doña and Luisa easily. They knew we'd go riding off looking for the goat. That's why Rod Coleman was waiting for us on the trail."

Bob's forehead puckered. "What are we going to do about the goat? We can't give her away. And if we go back and ask Luisa, these people may disappear with Genevieve while we're gone."

"I don't think so," Linda said. "I believe the Diazes are thoroughly honest. Just down, way down on their luck." She suddenly brightened. "Perhaps we could find a job for Papa Diaz!"

"That's a good idea," said Bob.

"If we tell the family that, and leave Genevieve

here, they would be sure to wait for us to come back with the good news," Linda went on.

"Terrific brainstorm, Sis! We'll do just that!" Bob exclaimed.

When the Craigs imparted this decision to the Diazes, the Mexicans' sad and tearful faces were immediately wreathed in smiles.

"We will be very good to the nanny," said Mama Diaz.

"We like Nanny!" cried the children again, hopping merrily about Genevieve.

Bob took all the money he had from his pocket and handed it to Pico Diaz. "Ride out to the store on your burro and bring back food for your family," he suggested.

With a broad smile, Pico Diaz vigorously nodded his head in gratitude, and Mama Diaz reiterated, *"Gracias! Gracias!"* and kissed first Linda, then Bob, who blushed a bright red.

The Craigs waved and set off at top speed for the ranch. As soon as they had arrived, unsaddled, and cared for their horses, Linda checked on Chica d'Oro. The palomino was still all right, but pacing restlessly against her confinement.

"Tomorrow you get out, my rambunctious beauty," Linda promised, stroking the filly fondly.

The two young people hurried toward the house. They had just reached the door when a familiar deep voice hailed them.

"Bronco!" Linda cried as her grandfather strode up to them, saying he had just returned.

After an affectionate exchange of greetings, Bob asked, "How did the stock-buying trip go?"

"Fine. Real fine," Mr. Mallory replied.

In a few minutes the entire family was convened in the living room. Luisa served mugs of cinnamon-spiced Mexican hot chocolate.

"Any news here?" Bronco asked, relaxing in his big leather chair.

Receiving no answer to his question, the rancher sat forward and looked from face to face in concern. "What's wrong? Something has happened. I can sense it."

Doña spoke up. "Linda, suppose you tell your grandfather what has taken place here, since it all started with Chica d'Oro."

"All right," said Linda, drawing a long breath. "But the rest of you please help me."

When she finished her harrowing story, Bronco's face became grim. He vehemently slapped both chair arms with his broad, hard palms, and got to his feet.

"This has gone too far! I think I'll offer my services as a deputy and hunt for those men myself!"

Doña looked at her husband admiringly but said, "Perhaps the sheriff's men have caught them already."

"May I put in the call?" Bob asked. "I want to report the Diaz story of the two men they saw."

"Go ahead."

When Bob returned, he said, "The sheriff's men haven't located the Colemans and Trask."

In the meantime Linda had told the others about the plight of the Diaz family. Now Bronco said, rubbing his hand over his thick, iron-gray hair, "I'll phone around right now—maybe I can get the man a picking job at one of the fruit ranches."

"Wonderful!" said Linda. "It would mean so much to them!"

In a short time Bronco announced that a pear-orchard owner, Ed Runcie, could use some additional pickers, and would employ the Diazes if they would be steady workers.

"I'm sure they will be," said Linda. "And the older children can help pick."

Bob got up and excused himself. "I'd better start feeding the horses."

After he had gone, Bronco turned to Linda. "Runcie is coming right over," he said. "Perhaps you and I could take him out to the Diaz camp and bring the family back to a cabin on his ranch before dark."

"Oh, yes," said Linda enthusiastically. "I'll show you the way."

When Mr. Runcie rode in, Linda and Bronco were waiting, their horses saddled. They led a

c

bareback horse on which three of the Mexican children could sit.

When they arrived at the Diaz camp, Linda was struck by how different the scene was from the one earlier in the day. The children were skipping about in happy, noisy games. Mama Diaz was singing a cheerful Mexican tune. On two planks laid across boxes was a kettle that had contained meat stew, and the remaining crumbs from a loaf of bread. Papa Diaz had apparently lost no time in bringing back food for his hungry family.

"He seems dependable," Mr. Runcie commented in a low voice. Linda had informed him, on the way, of all the details she knew concerning the Diaz family.

The three dismounted, and Linda introduced Mr. Runcie and her grandfather to the Mexicans.

"I can use pear pickers on my ranch now," Mr. Runcie told them. "Would you like a job with me?" Linda translated the message.

Pico Diaz was shocked speechless with delight for a moment, but his face mirrored his gratitude. Finally, in a voice husky with emotion, he said in broken English, "I work good."

"Fine," said Mr. Runcie. "If so, you will be kept on after the pear crop is picked. There are always other jobs around my ranch for a hard worker."

Mama Diaz clasped her hands and went into a series of joyous exclamations in her native tongue.

One of the older girls asked, "Will we live in a house again?"

"Yes," Mr. Runcie smiled. "I provide good quarters for all my workers, including clean cots for everyone."

Mama Diaz's face suddenly grew somber. She beckoned Linda aside, and said in a low tone, "I must say something to you."

Concerned by her seriousness, Linda suggested quickly, "You will ride behind me then."

The Mexicans gathered together their few possessions. Mama Diaz, holding her family's extra clothes in a bundle, mounted the plank table and managed to clamber up behind Linda on Jubilee's rump.

Three little girls were lifted by Papa Diaz onto the unsaddled horse. Bronco and Ed Runcie each took two children on their saddles.

Pico Diaz had packed their table implements inside the cooking kettle, which he held in one hand. He stepped astride the burro, then loosened Genevieve's tether rope.

"All set? Let's go!" Mr. Runcie called out, and the strange-looking caravan started off.

Immediately Mama Diaz whispered in Linda's ear, "Those two men who gave us Nanny came back. They saw the food I was cooking and asked if someone had been to see us. I told them *sí*, and described what you look like."

The woman gave a worried sigh. "At first the men acted nice. But after I told them about you and your brother, they looked mad and talked loud. They rode off fast."

Linda shuddered. The Colemans and Trask apparently had not returned to the cabin up the draw, and thus had not known that she and Bob had escaped. *Now* they've found out, she thought apprehensively.

Mama Diaz had been holding onto Linda for support. In agitation, the woman waved one hand, saying, "I am frightened they will try to do much harm to you and your nice brother."

Suddenly she started to slip sideways, and grabbed Linda tight around the waist again.

Linda said over her shoulder, "Don't worry. We will watch out for them."

At the Runcie ranch Linda took over Genevieve's lead rope, and Bronco that of the extra horse. There were no tears now from the Diazes at the prospect of losing Genevieve. The children kissed the goat good-bye, and said, "Thank you for your nice milk."

The visitors from Rancho del Sol rode off. The instant Linda and Bronco arrived home, Luisa flew outside and gathered Genevieve in her arms.

Geraldine came bounding up and bleated her welcome. The two goats butted their heads together in happy reunion.

At that moment Bob came in from the back field and said, "I think we'd better lock everything up tight around here until those crooks are caught."

"No need," said Bronco. "I'm hiring armed guards to remain on this place. A couple are going on duty tonight." He hurried into the house, phoned the deputy sheriff's office, and confirmed his arrangements for the guards.

When the family was all together again in the living room, Linda reminded Bob, "We're supposed to get started on our Crespi Cove trip tomorrow morning."

"Do go," Doña put in. "It will get you away from this upsetting situation here."

Linda was immediately aglow with enthusiasm and suggested to Bob, "How about my calling Kathy and Larry to stay here tonight so we can get an early start? I'll help Luisa pack food."

Both friends eagerly accepted. After dinner Linda brought four saddlebags into the kitchen from the barn. With Luisa's efficiency, the bags were filled with canned and dry foods and bacon. Last of all, the Trail Blazers papers were carefully tucked in.

Later the Craigs laid out the sleeping bags and horse equipment which would be taken in the cars as far as Scotty's Steak House. Horse feed was loaded into the trailer saddle compartments. One trailer was hitched to the station wagon that Bob would drive.

When Larry arrived in his car, he greeted Linda and her brother with a grin. "Looks like a real safari!"

"Packed full of adventure!" Linda retorted.

The other horse trailer was hitched to his car. A few moments afterward Kathy rode in on Patches.

"Looking for work?" Bob asked her teasingly.

"No, sir," she flashed back. "I was raised a pet!"

He helped her put Patches away for the night in the barn. By five next morning the young people were up and gathered for Luisa's hearty breakfast of sausage and waffles.

Within half an hour the group was ready to start. Rocket and Chica d'Oro were in the first trailer attached to Bob's station wagon. Kathy would ride with him. Patches and Jubilee followed in the second trailer, to be drawn by Larry's car, with Linda seated beside him.

Bronco and Doña stood waving good-bye. Between them sat Rango, thumping his tail as if aggrieved at being left behind.

As the four new Club 28 candidates drove along in the bright, crisp morning air, Linda sang snatches of popular tunes, and Larry hummed along with a half-smile on his lips. Suddenly, on the Durango Canyon Road, which dropped steeply on both sides, the couple gave horrified gasps and Larry braked to as quick a stop as he dared without throwing the horses.

The trailer ahead had lost a wheel and bumped down on one side. It was rocking and weaving perilously toward the steep embankment!

Unfriendly Bear 6

Linda and Larry sat paralyzed as they saw the trailer ahead veer crazily toward the sheer drop. The wheel had already gone over the embankment.

"Bob—Kathy—Chica—they'll be—" Linda shut her eyes as if to keep out the hideous thought.

At that moment she heard Larry exclaim, "Whew! Thank heaven!"

Fearfully Linda opened her eyes. A feeling of relief swept over her. The car and horse trailer ahead had come to a slow, bumping stop at the very edge of the cliff. Chica's stall was listing badly.

"Oh, I hope no one is hurt," Linda gasped.

She and Larry jumped out and ran to the disabled trailer. Bob and Kathy, white-faced, met them. "Are you two all right?" Linda asked anxiously.

"Sure, Sis. Just a little shaken up!" Bob assured her.

"Same for me," Kathy spoke up gamely.

The trailer was careering over the embankment ...

The boys let down the tailgate and led the horses out, turning them in a circle.

"They seem to be all right," Bob observed.

"Except they're nicked some," said Kathy.

Linda carefully scrutinized the reddening spots on Chica d'Oro and Rocket. "Not bad," she diagnosed. "I'll get out some healing powder and put it on those spots before we load up again."

Chica, apparently considerably alarmed by the shake-up, was dancing and whinnying nervously.

Linda took the filly's tie rope from Larry. "I'll walk her up and down a bit to calm her."

Bob handed Rocket's rope to Kathy. Then he and Larry went off to slide down the embankment and retrieve the wheel. When they had hauled it back up to the trailer, Bob exclaimed, "The cotter pin and nut are gone!"

Larry made a grimace and frowned. "To the best of my knowledge, a cotter pin doesn't just come out of its own accord."

The girls had returned in time to pick up the gist of the conversation. "You mean you think somebody deliberately took it off?" Linda asked.

"Yes." Bob's face flushed with anger.

"Whoever would pull a horrible prank like that?" asked Kathy incredulously.

"I'd say that this wheel business is more than a prank," stated Bob flatly. "It could have been done

74

by the same sneak who hired Coleman to harm Chica before. He would know this is her trailer because her name is on the side door."

"And it was probably done at the same time as the attack on Chica," Linda concluded. "The person wanted to be doubly sure she was harmed."

Larry was attempting to place the wheel back onto the axle. "If we can find the nut, it will probably hold the wheel on until we get to a garage."

Bob procured the repair kit and the girls searched the ground for the nut.

Kathy spoke up suddenly. "Here it is."

"Good!" said Bob and soon he and Larry had the wheel fairly secured in place. The boys borrowed a bobby pin from Kathy to replace the lost cotter pin.

Meanwhile Linda had dusted the horses' skinned spots with the healing powder. She loaded Rocket easily. But when she started to lead Chica inside, the palomino pulled back on the rope in stubborn refusal.

"Come on, baby," the girl coaxed. "We've lost too much time already." She tugged a little more forcibly on the rope, but Chica braced her legs on the pavement.

"Well!" Linda exclaimed. "Chica's never done this before." She led the filly a couple of paces, whirled her, and then ran toward the trailer. At the edge of the ramp Chica stopped suddenly and could not be budged. Larry picked up one of her forefeet and placed it on the boards. As soon as he set the palomino's other foot onto the plank, however, she backed off quickly.

"I'll try a blindfold," said Bob.

This ruse did not work, either. Chica only jumped from side to side, becoming more unmanageable.

Linda sighed. "I guess I'll just have to ride back home. The rest of you go on."

"Nothing doing!" Bob declared. "We stay together or we *all* return to the ranch until another time."

Suddenly Linda exclaimed, "I have it! You saw how Chica was thrown half down by the slant of the trailer floorboards when the wheel came off. She *might* be afraid that is how she'll have to stand in there now."

"You could be right," said Kathy slowly. "But how are we going to persuade her otherwise?"

"I know," said Linda quickly. "By putting Rocket in Chica's stall, and her into his."

They transferred Rocket. Then, with bated breath, Linda started to lead Chica into Rocket's place. The palomino walked right inside without hesitation.

"Pretty neat," said Larry. "Folks, meet the world-famous horsewoman!"

Bob grinned. "Jest bring yore hoss problems to troubleshootin' Lindy Craig!" Sobering, he asked, "Shall we go?"

When the four arrived at Scotty's Steak House, they were relieved to see a gas station a short distance farther along with a small service garage. The mechanic there assured them he would fix the trailer wheel that very day.

The Craigs and their friends arranged to leave the outfits at the garage, and started to saddle up. They attached the bags of supplies, tied the bedrolls across the horses' flanks, and after filling the canteens at the station, tied them on with the front saddle strings. Sacks containing pellet horse feed were swung over each horn along with collapsible canvas water buckets.

"Okay, let's hit the trail!" Bob urged.

The club members mounted and rode into Cabrillo Canyon beyond whose hills lay the Pacific Ocean and Crespi Cove. The riders knew they must hit a direct but unbroken route to the cove. The road they were on ended at a poultry ranch. At this point they stopped and each took a compass from his pocket.

"Cactus Mac said we were to go due west from here," Bob advised. "Everybody get your direction, and when I say point, indicate the line we should follow up the slope." He waited a couple of moments, then said, "Point!" doing the same himself.

Each initiate's finger marked exactly the same direction up the sycamore- and laurel-covered slope.

"What you might call unanimous!" remarked Linda gaily.

Laughing, the four friends started upward, but Bob halted them again at the first big sycamore. He took a roll of wide adhesive tape from his pocket, tore off a small strip, and firmly attached it to the trunk. On the tape he wrote with a black grease pencil the large, heavy letters C-H-S.

"That's for Craig-Hamilton-Spencer," he announced. "Can't do any carving. It's against forestry regulations—might kill the trees."

Larry brought out his camera. "I'd like to snap a picture here at the beginning of our trail," he said. "Look natural!"

"We'll try!" Kathy assured him. "Everybody say 'cheese.'"

As the riders proceeded, they found the going fairly easy. They all reached out and broke back the brush to establish the trail permanently. Bob left the initialed tape patches at intervals. Linda and Kathy, who both had small cameras slung around their necks, took an occasional snapshot.

In another hour they rode into pine country, and

the ground became rough with occasional mounds of huge boulders. The underbrush lessened, but there was a thick carpet of dry pine needles on which the horses' feet slipped.

"We've really hit backcountry," Bob said.

"Smells good," Linda commented, breathing deeply of the scented air.

The denseness of the forest obscured the sunlight, so Larry, who carried a supply of flashbulbs, took the pictures. The riders now had to consult their compasses frequently to keep on the right track.

Suddenly Chica stopped with her ears pricked forward. "What is it, baby?" asked Linda softly.

Signs of nervousness in the other horses caused their riders to pull them up short. Patches whirled, apparently intending to bolt back the way she had come, but Kathy held her in firmly.

Larry said in an undertone, "Look over there to the right!"

Following his pointing finger, the others saw two grizzly bear cubs playing around the base of a big pine.

"Bears, here?" gasped Kathy.

"That's sure enough what they look like!" replied Bob. "We'd better get past them as fast as we can."

But at that moment the mother bear crashed into view. At sight of the riders she reared to her hind feet and gave a fierce growl. Her jaws yawned open, baring sharp fangs.

"Have—have w-we g-got any h-honey?" stammered Kathy, frightened.

The mother bear suddenly did a curious thing. She turned on the cubs and cuffed them both up the tree.

Linda took advantage of this brief respite to pull an opened box of cookies from her saddlebag. When the grizzly turned on the riders again, growling, she threw the box toward the unfriendly beast. When it hit the ground, the cookies spilled out.

The surprised bear, sniffing sweetness, sampled a cookie. Obviously pleased, she went for the others. Instantly Bob started up and signaled his companions to follow. They rode at a good pace past the bruin, who was still eating voraciously. Not until they came to a wide stream racing over the boulders did the riders slow up, then stop.

Bob glanced around. "This must be Pesky Creek that Cactus Mac mentioned," he said.

They let the horses have a short drink, then went on, eager to get out of the woods. Soon, to their relief, they entered a clearing in which stood a crude cabin. Smoke wafted up from the chimney, and the door was open. Two mongrel dogs, which had been dozing, stood up and barked at the newcomers. A moment later an elderly man appeared in the doorway.

He lifted a hand in greeting and with a broad smile called out, "Halloo!"

"Hi!" called back the foursome, and rode up.

Bob dismounted, introduced himself and the others, explained briefly the purpose of the trail trip, and asked the old man if he would attest on the Trail Blazers' forms to their presence.

"You betcha!" exclaimed the old fellow. "Carl Johnson's my name. Now you just tie your hay burners to some branches and rest a spell while I limber up my writin' pinkies."

The young people grinned at one another and Larry asked, "Do you live here in these woods the year round?"

"That I do," replied Carl Johnson. "I work for the county watchin' out for fires, and killin' rattlesnakes and coyotes."

"But not bears," Linda declared.

The man gave her a wry smile. "You meet up with a bear?"

Together Linda and Kathy gave a colorful account of their frightening experience with the animals.

Johnson nodded. "That be Jezebel and her cubbies." He shook his head woefully. "Reckon if young people are goin' to start comin' through here, I better go out and git me a bear rug."

"But you can't shoot her now while she's bringing up a family," protested Linda.

Carl Johnson's eyes twinkled. "Didn't exactly aim

to do that. I'll just go out and run her back up to the ridge country. Bad fire there this spring drove the bears down."

"But won't she come for you with her awful teeth?" asked Kathy, aghast.

"Not when I point old Pizen there at her." He gestured to his rifle. "Jezebel's gun-shy from havin' been shot at so often—she's had her old hide nicked a time or two."

Linda said, "I didn't know there were bears in this part of California."

"Yup," replied Carl Johnson. "California was overrun with grizzlies at one time. The young *caballeros* used to go out with their *reatas* and capture the critters alive so later they could put one in a ring with a savage bull. In the old gold rush days bull-and-bear fights was right popular. 'Tweren't for the lily-livered, but there was them as figgered it was somethin' worth goin' miles to see."

Kathy shuddered. "What gruesome entertainment!" she said with distaste.

"By the way, what is the name of this creek?" Bob asked the woodsman.

"Pescado Creek," he replied.

"That isn't the way Cactus pronounced it." Bob chuckled and his companions laughed at the foreman's calling it Pesky Creek.

"Fish Creek," murmured Linda, translating the Spanish word *pescado*.

After Carl Johnson had signed the attest forms and given them to Linda, he looked at the foursome. "Now," he said, with the corners of his eyes crinkling, "I'll just fry you all up some nice bear steaks."

"Oh, no, thanks!" said Kathy quickly, growing pale. "We—we really must be getting along."

The others laughed, realizing that the good-natured old man was joking. Then he said earnestly, "I got me a right fine mess of trout this mornin'. I'd be pleased to have you help me eat 'em. A body gets tired now and then just sittin' down with his dogs."

"But wouldn't we make you short on rations?" said Linda. "How do you get supplies in here?"

Johnson beamed. "Ranger station down the creek a piece. Fire trail leads to it from the beach highway. Jeep comes up with stuff for the ranger and me."

"Then," said Linda, laughing, "we'd love to eat with you."

The others nodded. "It's past our lunchtime anyhow," Bob added. "I'm starved."

While the girls helped Carl Johnson with preparations, the boys loosened the horses' cinches. This done, Larry took several pictures of the cabin and its surroundings.

Johnson soon had a kettle of potatoes boiling in their jackets, the fish cleaned and waiting in clear, cold water to be cooked. When everything else was ready, the old woodsman shook the trout in a big sack of cornmeal and fried them on a griddle. Everyone declared the fish a treat.

The girls cleaned up after the meal while the boys checked the saddles. Then the foursome mounted, and, calling thanks, waved good-bye to their genial host and his tail-wagging dogs.

On the very next rise the riders beheld the Pacific Ocean. "How beautiful!" Kathy exclaimed. "Now that's what I call a welcome sight!"

"And a magnificent one," added Linda admiringly.

"Smell that salt air!" Bob said, sniffing. In the distance they could make out the crescent shoreline of Crespi Cove.

According to instructions the foursome was to angle slightly to the north in order to descend to the cove. They rode out of the pines and into scrub oaks, sycamores, and a tangle of light brush. The soil became loose and silty, causing the horses to slide.

Finally the riders reached the shore of Crespi Cove, a beautiful, hard-packed sandy beach rimmed with slopes. On them grew pink, lavender, and white sand plants in full bloom. From the back wall of one slope trickled a fresh spring.

The four jumped off their horses, ground-hitched them, and stretched.

"Look there!" cried Linda, pointing to a slope

against which was anchored a large, sturdy oak frame, heavily glassed. Inside on a plaque was printing.

"That must be the marker," she surmised.

The young people raced over to it and, enthralled, read the inscription:

CRESPI COVE

IN JUNE 1827 THE BLACK-BEARDED PORTUGUESE PIRATE TOMAS SOLA BROUGHT HIS PIRATE SHIP INTO THE SHELTERING HARBOR OF THIS COVE IN ORDER TO ROB THE RICH RANCHOS THAT HAD NO PROTECTING GUNS. WHEN HE CAME ASHORE WITH TWO BOATMEN IN HIS GIG HE WAS BRAVELY MET BY PADRE SANCHEZ CRESPI OF THE SAN ORTEGO MISSION, WITH A LARGE BURNING CROSS. PADRE CRESPI HAD HIS MISSION INDIANS TIE UP THE PIRATES AND TAKE THEM INTO CAPTIVITY. THE PIRATES WAITING ON THE SHIP WERE TERRIFIED AT THE SIGHT OF THE FIERY CROSS, AND WHEN THEIR LEADER PIRATE TOMAS DID NOT RETURN THEY SAILED AWAY. THE RANCHOS WERE SAVED FROM THEIR PILLAGE BY THE BRAVE DEED OF PADRE SANCHEZ CRESPI WHOSE NAME THIS COVE BEARS IN HIS HONOR.

Larry took several pictures of the marker from various angles.

By now it was late afternoon, but Linda, turning

to look out over the glorious blue Pacific and its foaming surf, exclaimed, "Let's go for a swim!"

The others agreed with enthusiasm and hurried to unsaddle the horses. Each animal was tethered to one of the big rocks on the fringing slope and rubbed down with a piece of gunnysacking. Then the boys shook out the canvas buckets and filled them at the spring. Finally, the horses were given a meal of pellet food.

The Craigs and their friends brought out their bathing suits from the bedrolls. Linda was first to run to the water's edge, and gave a little squeal as the cold water swirled over her feet.

As the next wave came rolling in, she laughed. "Here I go!" she called and dived through it before the wave broke in a high crest of foam. Linda went under the following wave neatly, then started stroking out in the exhilarating delight of a good swim.

Suddenly she felt something grab one of her ankles. The girl kicked hard to shake it off, but the grasp grew tighter. It began to pull her under! Frantically Linda wondered if she had been seized by an octopus or even a shark.

Terror gripped her as she was drawn beneath the surface, fighting desperately for her life!

A Haughty Rival 7

In that split moment everything within Linda resisted the idea of perishing underwater. Although her lungs felt as if they were about to burst, the girl's strong instinct for survival forced her to act. She mustered sufficient strength to make a barrel roll in a last hope of twisting free.

As Linda did so, she saw that her assailant was a man, tall and thin, wearing diving equipment, fins, air tank, and mask. Her one quick glance at his face behind the plastic viewplate revealed a small black mustache. She knew she had never seen him before.

It flashed through the girl's mind that he was merely a sportsman diver amusing himself at her expense. She made a final feeble struggle to break free. Surely he must see that she could not last another minute without air. But the diver did not relinquish his grasp.

Linda felt consciousness ebbing away. At the same moment she dimly perceived another form dart alongside. Her captor struck out at the newcomer with his free hand. The other swimmer veered, then made a long reach for the diver's mask.

At that, he let go of Linda's ankle and streaked away through the depths. The exhausted girl felt strong arms carrying her upward. As the two broke the surface, Linda saw that her rescuer was Larry.

He kept a supporting arm under her while she slowly took deep, gasping lungfuls of air. Finally in a weak voice she said, "Let's get to shore."

Larry nodded, keeping close as they swam in and rode a breaker onto the smooth beach. Linda sank limply to the sand.

Bob and Kathy, greatly worried, knelt by her side. "I—I'll be all right," Linda assured them with a faint smile.

"But what happened?" Kathy cried.

Larry, his face grim, explained.

"Where's the low-down sneak?" Bob exploded. "I'll—"

"I'm afraid he's out of reach by now," said Linda. She turned to Larry and asked, "When did you realize what was happening to me?"

"After I saw you dive through that second wave, I wasn't going to let you swim out any farther alone, so I started after you. I'd almost caught up when you disappeared. It was so sudden I knew something had happened. Believe me, it didn't take me many strokes to find out for sure."

"But who would have been so crazy as to hold you down like that for fun when he knew you couldn't breathe?" asked Kathy, wrapping a towel about Linda.

"I don't think it was for fun," replied Linda, rubbing her bruised ankle.

"One of the Colemans?" Bob speculated. "Out for revenge for our putting the sheriff's men on their track?"

"Not one of the Colemans," said Linda. "This diver was taller, and thin, with a small black mustache."

"It could have been a seagoing confederate of theirs," Kathy suggested.

"Right," Bob agreed. "This is an indication that we are being watched, and our comings and goings are known."

"And it had better be a reminder for us to keep close together and on our guard at all times," Larry warned.

The others solemnly nodded. "No more lone ocean plunges for me," said Linda, laughing grimly. She sat up, declaring she felt fully recovered.

"You know," said Kathy, "with what we've run

into, up against, and undergone blazing *this* trail, we ought to qualify for membership in the Royal Order of High Potentates!"

Larry grinned. "And our uniforms should be made of armor plate!"

The increased coolness of the late afternoon made the swimmers shiver. "We'd better get dressed," Kathy advised.

Afterward the boys scooped a hole in the sand and built a small fire. For a few minutes the campers stood stretching cold hands over it and enjoying the warmth.

Presently Bob asked, "What's for supper?"

"Your guess is as good as anybody's," replied Kathy. "What usually comes out of a saddlebag?"

"Beans, bacon, tomatoes," recited Larry. "Jezebel the bear got the cookies."

"You're all wrong," Linda smiled. "We are going to have an appropriate shore dinner—tuna heated in mushroom soup, and toasted English muffins to put it on, and pitted ripe olives. For dessert we'll open some cans of sliced pineapple."

"I'm ready for three helpings!" said Larry.

Suddenly Kathy whispered, "Uh-oh! Looks as if we're going to have company."

The others followed her gaze down the beach and saw a young man in a police uniform approaching. When he reached them, Bob asked, "Are we breaking regulations by building a fire?"

"No. Beach fires are permitted here in the cove," the officer replied pleasantly. "I'm Dick Ferranto of the beach patrol, just making a routine check."

Bob introduced the members of his group, then asked, "Do you know anyone who goes skin diving out here?"

"No one in particular," replied Ferranto. "The frogmen come and go to try out their flippers."

"There's a fellow somewhere out in the ocean who ought to be flipped into your jail," declared Larry. He described the mysterious diver's malicious attack on Linda.

"Very strange," Ferranto commented. "Can you give any kind of personal description?" he asked with keen interest. Linda told what she knew.

"I'll make a report of this to headquarters at once," said Ferranto, "and keep a sharp lookout for the fellow."

He turned his attention to the horses and asked, "Did you folks come far?"

"From San Quinto Valley," replied Linda, and went on to explain the purpose of their trip.

"Breaking a trail across those hills from the far valley will certainly be a great help to both equestrians and hikers," Dick Ferranto said with a smile.

"And this marker at the cove tells a really exciting story," Linda commented.

"There's an interesting sequel to it about Pirate Tomás Sola," said Ferranto.

"You mean that he escaped?" Kathy asked.

"He escaped jail," Ferranto answered, "but not by breaking out. Padre Crespi converted and baptized him. Tom, as he was then called, became one of the most energetic workers of the mission. Before that the habit of *mañana*—wait until tomorrow—was practiced so much among the workers that progress on the buildings had been slow.

"Tom was a powerful man. He hard-bossed a crew, driving them up into the Santa Monica Mountains to fell big trees and broadax them square for use at the mission. Buildings rose in short order. Later Tom Sola constructed some of the finest rancho mansions, and married Magdalena Estrada, a daughter of one of the richest grandees."

"From pirate to prince, eh?" quipped Bob, and the others laughed.

Linda said, "Our Trail Blazers organization has a club in Malibu. Perhaps you've heard of it."

"I frequently see notices of the club activities in the paper," replied Dick Ferranto. "One of the members is a society girl, and a very fine horsewoman, so her name is often in print. I have become acquainted with her, since she rides here on the beach a lot."

The visitors exchanged meaningful glances and Linda asked casually, "What is her name?"

"Shirley Blaine," replied Ferranto. His face lighted up. "Say! Here she comes now."

The Club 28 representatives looked curiously down the beach and watched the rider approach. She was on a flat saddle, cantering a beautiful chestnut Saddlebred on the hard-packed, wet sand. Shirley was a stunning blonde. Linda and Kathy were quick to note also that she wore an expensive, tailored turquoise riding habit.

"Hello, Dick," the girl said airly, riding up. She looked at the campers in their jeans and plaid shirts with haughty inquisitiveness.

"Hello, Miss Blaine," returned the officer. "Glad you rode out here this evening. Meet some of your Trail Blazers Club members from the valley." He laughed and added, "Guess you folks had better give your own names."

Linda performed the introductions, mentioning that she and Bob were from Rancho del Sol.

"Oh, from de la Sol," Shirley drawled, with a lift of her eyebrows.

Amused glances passed among the four at her affected and incorrect pronunciation of the ranch's name.

Dick Ferranto said, "Well, I have to continue my rounds," and raised a hand in farewell as he turned away.

Linda addressed Shirley Blaine pleasantly. "We're here on an initiation ride," she told her. "Blazed a trail across the hills. I suppose you went through a similar initiation."

Shirley's pretty face took on a superior look. "Good gracious, no," she exclaimed. "I wouldn't go in for anything like that. I don't care about roughing it. I'm a show-ring rider, and my top-winning reputation was quite sufficient to qualify me for membership."

Larry gave his friends a wink and said nonchalantly, "Some people have all the luck."

Shirley's eyes narrowed in anger. Quickly Linda said, "I suppose each club makes its own rules for accepting members. Tell me, don't any of yours do trail riding in accordance with the main purpose of the organization?"

"Oh, yes," replied Shirley blithely. "We have a fine chuck wagon in our club for long rides. But *I* prefer not to trail dust. And I never take care of my own horses. I have a groom for that."

She rode over by the tethered horses, scrutinizing Chica d'Oro appraisingly. Then she asked abruptly of Linda, "This is your filly, isn't she?"

"Why, yes," Linda replied, surprised. "Her name is Chica d'Oro. How did you know she belongs to me?"

"Oh, I suppose I've read it in the paper at some time." Shirley continued her critical observation of the palomino. It was evident to the others that she was fascinated. Then, to their utter amazement, she asked Linda, "What will you sell her for?"

Linda was certain that Shirley was joking and laughed. "Not for peanuts."

"How much then?" asked Shirley imperiously. "I'd like to buy your horse."

"Chica isn't for sale," said Linda softly.

"Oh, come now," exclaimed Shirley, "everything has a price. What is Chica d'Oro's? I don't intend to haggle over the cost."

"Chica isn't for sale," repeated Linda with indubitable firmness.

For a few moments marble blue eyes clashed with flashing brown ones.

Anger brought bright spots of color to Shirley's cheeks. Then she said stiffly, "You may change your mind. When you do, let me know." Without so much as a good-bye gesture, she pulled her mount around sharply and cantered off.

"Whew!" Bob exclaimed. "A real dilly of a spoiled brat! Her Saddlebred is more of a thoroughbred than she is." He made an exaggerated bow before Larry. "She's all yours, buddy boy."

"That's my dust going the other way," Larry grinned broadly.

"It sure gives me duck bumps, Linda," said Kathy worriedly, "to think of you competing against Shirley Blaine in the Trail Blazers big all-clubs show. Why, I wouldn't put it past her to pull any kind of mean trick to win against you."

Linda laughed, but with an inward troubled feeling. "I don't think she'd go that far. If Shirley should try anything unfair in the ring, she'd be disqualified, and what could she do otherwise if I'm careful? Our friend Miss Blaine apparently buys what she wants in this world. But even she can't buy Chica, so that's that!"

Bob was looking thoughtfully at the ocean. "I wonder if she knows that diving hombre?"

"Perhaps," replied Linda. "Although she obviously didn't know we were here, or who we were, until Dick Ferranto introduced us."

"We can't be too sure of that," argued Larry. "Don't forget—*someone* is spying on us."

"I thought you suspected the Colemans, who want revenge for your putting the law on their trail," Kathy said to the Craigs.

"Of course," said Linda. "And I'm positive Shirley isn't mixed up with those thieves!"

Larry changed the subject. "Right now I'd like some chow," he declared.

"Build up the fire again," directed Linda gaily, "and supper will be ready in a jiffy."

With everyone helping, the supper was soon prepared and served. After eating, the four relaxed and watched the rising moon strike a silvery path across the water.

Larry gave a low chuckle. "This reminds me of another fish dinner I've heard about."

"Give!" Kathy laughed and they all settled back to listen to one of Larry's good yarns.

"This happened up on 'the river of no return,' the Salmon River in central Idaho," he began. "A bunch of cowboys were working across the hill flushing the new calves out of the brush for branding. They'd had a hard time. It had rained some, the brush was thick, and the cows were their usual ornery selves keeping hidden. Already the crew had been out two days longer than expected. Their clothes were damp, their skin itched, and their stomachs were rebelling against Dutch-oven stew and biscuits.

"With at least two more days of work ahead of them, the trail boss called in two men, Windy and Frankie, and told them to go over to the river and catch a couple of big salmon, and not to fail.

"Happy at this respite, the two cowboys rigged up a couple of lines and rode their horses to the river. Frankie worried for fear they wouldn't be able to catch a salmon, but Windy assured him they could probably pull out a couple with their bare hands.

"At the river the cowboys baited their hooks with fat grubs they found in the shore dirt. They fished and fished without so much as getting a nibble.

"Windy concluded that they would have to find better bait, and they started looking for it. Well, Windy ran across a big black snake with a frog in its mouth.

"He grabbed the snake and eased the frog out. Then, at the reproachful look in the snake's eyes at stealing its dinner, Windy took a bottle of cough syrup from his hip pocket and poured a long drink down the snake's throat. The reptile rolled and writhed in delighted appreciation. Windy then baited his hook with the frog and immediately pulled in a big salmon.

"He and Frankie hunted for another frog, but were unable to find one. As the day wore on, Windy went back to his grub bait while Frankie kept hunting for something better. They knew one salmon wouldn't be enough for all the boys at the cow camp, and that the two who would go without would be—Windy and Frankie. Besides, they'd likely get a chapping! They felt pretty low.

"All of a sudden, Windy became aware of a tugging on his jeans leg. Thinking he had snagged it on a root, he reached down to loosen himself. And there was that big old black snake holding up another frog!"

As Larry finished his story, the others burst into laughter and Bob gave a mock groan. "For a tall tale like that—throw him in the ocean!"

At this Larry pulled off his boots and dived into his sleeping bag. "No, thanks!" he called out. "I've had my ducking for the day."

Bob yawned. "I'm going to hit the sack myself."

"Best idea yet!" Linda agreed sleepily.

The bedrolls had been arranged in a crescent around the horses so that any of the four could instantly hear the slightest suspicious sound. Within minutes after "good-nights" were exchanged, everyone fell asleep.

Linda was suddenly awakened by the bright beam of a flashlight full in her face. As she sat up with a little cry, the girl saw a figure slipping cautiously away. She hastily pulled on her boots and ran to awaken Bob.

"A man had a light on me," Linda whispered. "I see him out there. Let's try to catch him!"

Bob had his boots on by the time Linda had finished speaking, and together they raced after the skulking shape of the mysterious intruder.

Timber! 8

As the Craigs raced after the intruder they saw him scramble up the embankment and head for the rugged back country.

Suddenly Linda exclaimed, "There's someone else!" She pointed to the figure of another man who had raced from the opposite direction and was running after the first. "The Coleman brothers, I'll bet!" she added with a gasp.

"If we could only get a glimpse of their faces to be sure!" said Bob.

Then the second man shone his flashlight on the back of the other.

"That one seems thinner than either of the Colemans," remarked Linda as she climbed breathlessly.

"Maybe he's the diver," Bob suggested.

The first man, who had a good head start, was suddenly swallowed up by the dense underbrush into which he had run. Linda and Bob stopped, knowing it was useless, in the darkness, to continue their pursuit over the rugged terrain. The man with the light stopped also. Then he turned and approached the Craigs.

Linda shuddered a little as the tall, thin figure drew closer. Bob stood with knotted fists, ready to fend off any attack. In a few moments, they recognized the man as beach patrol Officer Dick Ferranto!

Relieved but surprised, Linda asked him, "Was it you who shone the light on me?"

"Yes," Ferranto admitted. "I decided to make a quick survey to satisfy myself that everything was all right. I spotted that fellow sneaking up to your camp. Unfortunately he heard my approach and slipped back into the shadows. That's when I shone my light on you to see if he had done any of you harm. Then I hurried away and tried cutting him off. But he had the jump on me."

"Did you get a look at his face?" asked Bob.

"No, I didn't," replied Ferranto. "He kept his face ducked down as he ran. But he seems to be a tall, wiry fellow—he may be the diver who held your sister underwater."

"That's what I suspect," Bob remarked. "Any news on that nut's identity?"

"Not so far," Ferranto answered. "Files are being checked, and a lead may come in tomorrow."

The three had walked back to the camp as they talked. Kathy and Larry, awakened by the sudden commotion, were standing with their boots on, waiting anxiously.

"What happened?" Kathy demanded.

"We had an intruder snooping around," Linda explained. "Officer Ferranto was checking here when he spotted the man. We all chased him—but no luck."

"Which one of our mysterious enemies do you think he is?" Kathy asked, looking about nervously.

Ferranto smiled. "Don't let this keep you folks awake," he said. "The fellow may have been just a beachcomber hunting for food or anything else of value he could pick up."

"It's a possibility," Larry remarked, but without conviction.

"Can you manage all right if I go down the beach for a while?" Ferranto asked.

"Yes," Bob replied. "We're used to looking out for ourselves."

"A million thanks for your help," Linda spoke up.

"All in the line of duty," the young officer said. "Good-night, and sleep well." He went on his way.

The horses meanwhile had become restive at the fracas, and were pawing the ground and blowing through their nostrils. Linda hurried to Chica d'Oro, stroked her neck, and talked softly until the filly calmed down. This had a soothing effect on the other animals as well.

"It looks as if someone is out to trip us up," Linda murmured to the palomino. "But baby, we're sticking together, and the troublemakers will find us a hard pair to beat!"

Chica nickered softly as she was accustomed to doing when Linda talked to her. The girl returned to her companions.

After discussing the mysterious man awhile, Kathy said, "Well, boots off, everyone, and back into the bags!"

"You all get some sleep," Larry urged. "I'm standing watch until daybreak."

"I'll spell you," Bob offered.

"I'll crawl in," said Linda, "but I know I won't be able to sleep."

Kathy yawned. "I will. But one good yell from Larry or Bob, and I'll come up fighting."

Despite Linda's prediction, exhaustion took its toll, and she dropped off to sleep. When she awoke it was morning. The boys stood by a little cook fire that they had just finished building.

Kathy still slept soundly. Impishly Linda picked up a tiny pebble and tossed it onto her friend's forehead. Kathy's eyes flew open and darted around, taking in the peaceful scene. Then she murmured, "Mm," and closed her lids again.

"No, you don't!" Linda laughed, crawled out, and shook Kathy's bag. "Up you go!" she said.

"Come on, you two cooks," called Bob. "Fire's ready and we're weak from hunger."

"Did you boys get any sleep?" asked Linda solicitously.

"We both got some—enough," Bob replied.

Kathy had emerged from her sleeping bag. She stretched, flung out her arms, and whirled in a pivot on the tabletop-hard sand. "What a gorgeous morning!" she sang. It was a bright one, the ocean scintillating under the burnished gold of the sun.

"It makes everything that happened last night seem like only a bad dream," Linda mused.

"But definitely not to be forgotten," cautioned Bob.

"Right," said Larry, "until we have our hands on a certain tall, thin fellow, and he has answered a few questions."

While the girls prepared breakfast, the boys watered and fed the horses. In a short while the campers were enjoying crisp bacon, toasted muffins, and a pot of steaming, fragrant cocoa.

"After this meal, I'm ready to take on a whole gang of intruders," declared Bob, grinning.

"They're all yours!" Kathy retorted promptly.

When the four had finished eating, they began packing up their gear for the trip home. Linda, suddenly grinning mischievously, jumped on Chica

Chica galloped into the surf . . .

bareback, and raced her toward the surf. As a big wave broke and the foaming water rolled toward the filly, she stopped so abruptly that Linda nearly went over her head. Then Chica backed almost as rapidly as she had gone forward.

Linda leaned down and said soothingly, "Okay, baby, I guess you don't want an ocean dip, but you nearly gave me one!"

Everyone laughed and felt in good spirits to start their long ride home. They saddled, fastened on the equipment, and were ready to set out when Dick Ferranto appeared.

"Glad to see you're safe and well this morning," he said.

"We're fine, thanks," Linda replied. "*Hasta la vista.*" She smiled as they waved to the officer and rode off.

They had no trouble finding the trail, since Bob had left one of his tape markers on a sycamore at the point where they had emerged onto the beach of Crespi Cove.

It was cool beneath the shade of the thickly-leaved branches of the trees. Kathy shivered and said, "I wish I had remembered to bring along some of that beach sunshine."

"Maybe we'll meet a nice warm bear," Larry teased.

Linda had been scrutinizing the ground as they rode along. Now she said, "I'm sure I see prints on this trail besides those made by our horses. Do you suppose other riders are making use of it already?"

"I hope it isn't one of our enemies!" Kathy exclaimed.

"If that is the case," Linda said, frowning, "he's ahead of us."

"Lying in wait, no doubt," concluded Kathy nervously.

Bob and Larry studied the unfamiliar horseshoe marks more closely.

"There's been one other horse along here all right," Larry declared.

"Let's not borrow trouble," Linda advised. "But we'd better be on our guard just the same."

A little distance farther along she and the others were forced to rein in. A huge fallen tree lay across their path, with great upreaching branches house-high. The tree lay in a spot where the underbrush was extremely dense. Everyone stared in awe at the tremendous trunk.

"There must have been a fury of a gale up here to blow this giant down," Linda remarked.

"But there's no other indication of a strong wind," Larry pointed out. "No broken branches lying around, or any heavy scatter of leaves."

"What could have caused the tree to fall?" asked Linda, puzzled. "It looks healthy, and it's not rotted inside."

"It couldn't have been pushed," said Kathy wryly.

"With the help of a good stout ax or saw it could have crashed," Bob speculated.

"What a shame—to cut down such a beautiful, big old tree!" Linda sighed. "Why?"

"I don't know," Bob replied. "But I guess we'll have to start cutting our way through the brush around it at one end or the other if it takes all day."

"I think we might do a quicker job by hacking the branches in the middle," Linda suggested. "Then we can jump the horses over."

"Right," said Larry. "Let's get to it."

The foursome dismounted, ground-hitched their horses, and went to work on the branches. The boys used their bowie knives on the limbs, while the girls broke away the smaller ones by hand. When they finally had cleared the section of trunk lying across the trail, the obstacle was only about two feet high.

"Go ahead, Linda," said Bob. "Chica's the best jumper. She'll be a good example for the others."

Linda lifted her palomino easily over the trunk.

"You next, Kathy," Larry said.

"I don't think so," demurred Kathy. "Patches doesn't see any sense in jumping unless there's a good reason. If the other horses are on the far side, then she'll want to follow them."

"Check," Larry agreed, and put Jubilee over the trunk.

Bob followed. Jubilee and Rocket did not execute the jump with the grace that Chica had, but, being well-trained trail horses, getting over an obstruction was all in a day's work for them.

Kathy then took Patches back a few paces for a run at the jump. Instead of taking it, the mare stopped suddenly. Kathy went flying over her head into broken-off branches on the other side of the tree.

She lay motionless.

"Oh!" Linda cried out fearfully.

Instantly she and the boys were off their horses and on their knees beside the fallen rider.

"Kathy! Kathy!" exclaimed Linda, taking her friend's limp hand. "Bob, hand me a canteen."

He quickly unscrewed the top of one and Linda soaked her yellow cotton neckerchief with the cool water, which she swabbed over Kathy's face.

The girl opened her eyes and sat up. "Ooooh," she groaned. "Did I—ever get the—wind knocked out of me!"

Bob asked anxiously, "Are you sure you're all right otherwise?"

"Sure," Kathy insisted.

"Well, you just lie back quietly for a few minutes until you feel a little steadier," Linda admonished.

Surprisingly, Kathy did so without argument.

Worried glances were exchanged among the others. On the opposite side of the tree trunk, Patches was nosing unconcernedly at the edge of the path for any tasty morsel that she might find.

"I'll bring that balky pony over in a hurry when we're ready to go on," said Bob. "Right now I think I'll investigate the base of this tree and see if it was felled." He pushed his way through the brush.

Linda meanwhile began to examine more closely the mysterious horseshoe prints. "They're smaller than those of our four horses," she commented. "But they don't go any farther on the trail. Right here the prints turn off into the woods."

Bob returned. Grimly he informed them, "The tree was felled all right."

Linda gave him a meaningful look. "Do you think it was done to stop us?" she asked.

"That's my hunch," her brother replied.

"Mine, too," Larry added.

Kathy raised herself up on one elbow. "Why would anyone go to so much trouble?" she wondered in alarm.

"And why would he want to block our path here?" Linda puzzled.

No one had an answer. "Trying to solve this riddle now isn't going to get us anywhere," said Bob finally. "We'd better keep close together. We may have company nearby."

Kathy shuddered and said in a low tone, "I almost

feel as if eyes were peering out at me from the brush."

Larry frowned. "Whoever cut down this tree obviously will go to great lengths to hamper us."

"What, actually, could he hope to gain by it?" Linda countered. "Except to delay us awhile, which is no great harm."

"I have a feeling it's an ambush," Kathy spoke up.

Bob tried to sound reassuring. "I didn't see a sign of anyone back there in the brush. Have any of you heard a suspicious noise?"

The others shook their heads.

"Evidently the tree feller was alone," Bob went on. "He must have iron muscles."

"Like those of a swimmer, for instance?" asked Linda, and glanced down at her ankle. "An underwater swimmer? The one who grabbed me surely had fingers like a vise and could wield an ax powerfully."

"Yes," said Larry, "and he could also be the prowler in our camp. But who is he, and what grudge has he against us?"

"I'm sure," Linda replied, "that the grudge is against Chica d'Oro and me. It makes me feel bad that the rest of you have to be involved."

"What do you mean?" said Larry. "We thrive on it!"

Bob clenched a fist. "One of these days that sneak

is going to get caught, and then he'll do some talking!"

At that moment Bob happened to look at Kathy, who had grown very pale. "How do you feel?"

"Like getting out of here," she replied, and Bob helped the girl to her feet.

"Everybody mount up," he said. "Kathy, you get aboard Rocket, then all of you start ahead slowly."

Bob now leaped back over the fallen tree, pulled Patches' head up, and wound her reins around the saddle horn. Her attention was caught by the departing horses, and she whinnied but did not budge.

"Guess I'll have to try stronger methods," said Bob. He dismounted, cut a small green switch from a bush, gave a war whoop, and brought the switch down across Patches' rump.

The mare leaped and fairly flew over the trunk. Like Pegasus, the flying horse, thought Bob, grinning. He scrambled over the tree trunk himself, helped Kathy onto Patches, and mounted Rocket.

The group rode along quietly, keeping alert eyes to each side. Except for a few birds rustling overhead in the branches, there was not a sound. When they came to the spot where the trail met Pescado Creek, the sun was directly overhead.

"How about stopping here for lunch?" Linda proposed.

There was unanimous assent. The riders loosened the saddle cinches and slipped off the bridles so the horses could drink and do a little grazing. Linda brought out some cans of spiced meat, pumpernickel bread, and apples.

Kathy slumped down on the mossy ground with a sigh. "Count me out. I feel a little too squeamish to eat." She smiled, but her companions noted with concern that she was still white. The weary girl lay back and, as the others ate, went to sleep.

"It might be more than squeamishness," said Larry softly. "Perhaps Kathy's suffered some injury."

"If so, we'd better get a jeep to take her out," Linda whispered.

"I doubt that even a jeep could make it on this narrow trail," replied Larry.

"If Kathy doesn't feel better," murmured Bob, "we'll both ride on Rocket, and go to that ranger station Carl Johnson mentioned. A jeep stops there."

Linda took Kathy's pulse and, looking up with a worried face, announced, "It's weak. I don't think we'd better move her yet."

The boys agreed, and the three began a long, tense vigil while trying to decide on the best thing to do.

The next few hours were anxious ones for Linda and the boys. They had decided to let Kathy sleep, and at last were relieved to note color returning to her face.

Again Linda checked her friend's pulse. "It's stronger," she announced thankfully.

Just then Kathy stirred and stretched her arms over her head.

Bob said, "Hello, Sleeping Beauty."

She opened one blue eye and winked at him. "It's an unlucky trail bunch that doesn't have one," she retorted. Then she sat up. "I feel fine—except for a certain ache in my middle from hunger. Anyone save me a crumb?"

The others laughed, exchanging looks of relief. Linda hastily spread canned meat on some slices of pumpernickel. Bob brought a cup of clear, cold creek water. Larry handed Kathy an apple.

"Anything else weird happen since I saw you last?" she asked.

"Not a thing," Linda assured her.

"We're slipping." Kathy grinned.

As she ate, Bob proposed his plan to take her to the ranger station for a jeep ride out to the valley.

"What kind of a Trail Blazer would that make me?" Kathy objected. "Thanks, but I'm back in the saddle and rarin' to ride. Honest."

"Good. Let's go!" said Bob.

They mounted and continued their leisurely pace along the trail. The young people found the fragrance of the pines and the music of the babbling creek enchanting.

"Looks as if our guardian angel has caught up with us." Kathy sighed with pleasure.

"We'd better enjoy all this while we can," remarked Larry.

"You mean, this is the calm before the storm?" asked Kathy.

"I'm no prophet." Larry grinned.

"A horseback philosopher, then?" Linda smiled.

"I haven't decided." Larry chuckled. "But I'll let you know."

When they reached Carl Johnson's cabin, Linda exclaimed at once, "Look there! A lot of fresh horseshoe prints since those we made early yesterday."

"Riders *are* using our trail already," said Bob.

"Well, three cheers for us," said Kathy. "At least we got it cut through and marked. Nobody seemed to want to stop us from doing that."

Just then old Carl came running from the cabin gripping his rifle. On recognizing his callers he immediately pointed it down and exclaimed, "By cracky! You're a right welcome sight to these old eyes."

The four dismounted and Linda said, "I see that you've had other horseback visitors already."

"Humph!" Carl grunted. "Visitors you be a-callin' 'em! Varmints, that's what they was. They cleaned me out of all my vittles."

"How many were there, and what did they look like?" asked Linda with quick interest.

"Two of 'em there was," growled Carl, "and a rough-lookin' pair. Both had dark hair and mean, dark eyes, and weren't shaved. One was short and stocky, and had a flat, broad nose. Ugly, he was. The other fellow was nearer to medium height, and took orders from the squat hombre."

"They're probably hiding out if they had to steal food," Larry deduced.

"Could be," replied Carl. "They was mighty concerned as to who made this new trail. Worried, I reckon, that they'd ridden smack into lawman territory. When I told 'em it was blazed by some young folks from the valley, they didn't appear any better pleased."

116

"It could have been those petty cattle rustlers," said Linda excitedly. "They've probably heard that members of our club are helping the posse to track them down."

"What sort of horses were the men riding?" asked Bob.

"The critters was rough-lookin' too," replied Carl. "Just a couple of jugheady, long-haired brownies."

"Let's search for clues," Linda urged. "Do you mind if we take a peek inside?" she asked the cabin owner.

"Course not," said Carl. "Them two thievin' crooks didn't bother to ask. Just barged in and cleaned me out, they did. Even took my flour."

"We don't have much food left," said Linda, "but we'll leave you what we have."

"Don't you be a-shortin' yourselves," Carl protested. "Soon as the sun gits a little lower, I'll wade downcreek and get me a nice mess of trout. Come mornin', I'll foot it to the ranger station and pick up supplies."

"We won't need the food," Linda insisted. "We'll be home by dinnertime."

She and her friends went through the saddlebags and gave Johnson the rest of the pumpernickel, a can of meat, half a pound of bacon, and several apples.

"Thanks, this'll tide me over," he said.

"Where are your dogs?" Kathy inquired wonderingly.

"I set 'em a-chasin' Jezebel and her cubbies back into the high country."

"Won't they get lost?" Kathy asked.

Old Carl chuckled. "Not those two. They'll be back when they get good 'n' ready. No need to worry. They always come back, fat and full of ginger, the rascals."

"Couldn't you have run those two thieves off with your rifle?" asked Larry.

Old Carl shook his head, scowling, and replied, "Worst luck, I'd left Pizen—my rifle—standin' up against a tree out back after I'd come from the bear chasin'. When I seen that short ruffian had a revolver pushed through his belt under his coat, I figured a few vittles wasn't worth arguin' over."

"Did you hear either call the other by name?" Bob queried.

"Nope," replied Carl. "That ugly-nosed punk jest called t'other, 'Hey you,' with him only answerin' by bobbin' his head up and down."

"Which way did they go from here?" asked Linda.

"They cut off there to the side of the cabin," Carl told her. "Said they'd better get off the trail."

The Craigs exchanged excited glances with their friends. "They surely could be the rustlers," said Linda. "Whoever they are, they're armed and dangerous. We have a good description of them and that information ought to help the authorities catch them."

The young people looked inside the cabin and around the clearing for any further clues but found none.

"It's too bad we aren't equipped to lift fingerprints," said Linda. "There must be dozens all over the cabin."

She brought the attest papers inside from her saddle pouch. Once again Carl Johnson affixed his signature to them.

"Will you be riding back through here another day?" he asked a bit wistfully.

"I'm sure we will," replied Bob. "And many of our other friends also."

"Now that will be right nice." Old Carl beamed. "A body gets a mite lonesome at times, especially when his doggies are a-traipsin'."

Linda noticed that Kathy sat at the table with her head in her hands. "Do you feel all right?" she asked gently.

"Of course," Kathy replied quickly.

"You look pretty pale again," said Bob. "Maybe this ride back is too hard for you after your spill."

"Think nothing of it," said Kathy with a forced grin. "A few hours of sunbathing will fix me up."

Her nonchalance did not fool Linda, who realized her friend should have medical attention. In a few minutes the group mounted, waved good-bye to Carl Johnson, and continued along the trail.

"At least we needn't worry about meeting Jezebel and her cubs." Bob laughed.

"That's lucky," said Kathy, "since we don't have even a cookie crumb to toss her."

When they arrived at the gasoline station, the riders found that the young mechanic had almost completed the repair work on Chica's trailer. While they waited, Linda noted with concern that Kathy appeared paler than ever and exchanged knowing glances with the others. They must get Kathy home as rapidly as possible!

"I suggest," said Bob, "that we cut off the freeway through Manzanita Canyon and take the desert road past the old borax works to Valley Boulevard, which is just about a mile from your house, Kathy."

"You'll do no such thing," protested Kathy with a spurt of spirit. "That'll make you all late getting home. I'll ride back the same way I came to Old Sol."

Linda said with forced cheerfulness, "But I'm sure the route Bob has suggested will be the nicest. I love that drive through Manzanita Canyon."

"Settled," declared Larry.

Kathy gave them a reproachful look, then sighed. "Guess I can't overrule the majority."

A short while later the mechanic announced that the trailer was ready. The travelers stored their gear in the cars and loaded the horses. To Linda's relief Chica walked in without objecting, her scare forgotten.

At Kathy's insistence, the foursome stopped at Scotty's Steak House for a snack. "You all must be starved," she said.

Linda and the boys ordered apple pie and milk. Kathy herself, however, who sometimes would get up in the middle of the night to eat a piece of pie, had only a few sips of milk. Again her friends exchanged looks of concern.

"Let's go!" Linda urged.

Outside once more, Bob pushed the gear in the station wagon to one side and unrolled a sleeping bag. "Into the sack," he commanded Kathy.

She began to object but finally shrugged with a wry smile, saying, "Honestly, I do think it will feel good to flop down."

The caravan moved at a moderate pace through Manzanita Canyon, which took its name from the red-limbed manzanita bushes banking the sides of the road. They were abloom with clusters of tiny, pinkish-white, bell-like blossoms. Above the riders here and there appeared the larger wild cherry bushes with their glossy, spiny leaves and big bright red berries, which Californians use in making wreaths at Christmastime.

Bob watched keenly for the shortcut desert road. He was relieved to find that it was still marked by a dilapidated sign at its entrance bearing the name of the borax works.

This part of the trip proved to be dreary going. On all sides as far as one could see were stretches of sand, broken only by scattered, dry scrub brush. From behind it a jackrabbit hopped occasionally.

After a while the travelers came to an apparently newly erected detour sign. They knew it was recent because paint deteriorates quickly in the hot desert air, but on this sign it was fresh and bright.

Bob stopped and came back to Larry's car. "There must have been a washout on the road ahead," he guessed.

Linda said, "Probably a cloudburst cut a deep arroyo."

"We don't have any choice but to follow the detour road," said Larry.

Linda had gone forward to speak to Kathy. The blond girl was sleeping again, but not peacefully. She was moving restlessly, and her face held an expression of pain.

Hurrying to the boys, Linda said worriedly, "We'd better get Kathy home just as soon as possible. She doesn't look well."

Bob nodded and cautioned Larry, "We'll have to take it carefully. This detour isn't more than a wide path in the sand. It doesn't appear to be used much, except by the road crew." He pointed to jeep tire tracks in the sand.

"Probably not," said Linda, "since the borax works haven't been operating for years. The road is kept open by the county because it's cross-country."

Bob returned to the Old Sol station wagon and slowly turned it into the detour. The sand was loose and deep—evidently no attempt had been made to pack it down. But by maintaining a steady, slow pace, the two cars managed to keep rolling and covered a good distance.

Suddenly the station wagon wheels commenced to spin. Instantly Bob shut off the engine. He jumped out and looked ahead.

Linda and Larry hastily joined him. "I'm stuck too," Larry stated in disgust.

Bob's face was grim. "This was no detour," he declared angrily. "The other tire marks end here. The jeep that made them apparently turned back at this spot. No wonder that detour sign looks new. It was put there on purpose so we'd get stuck in this sand!"

"Oh, how dreadful! And with Kathy so sick!" Linda cried out in despair. "But who would have known we were coming this way? We didn't decide to until we were at the service station."

Larry's eyes narrowed. "Wait a minute!" he exclaimed. "I noticed a fellow standing near our outfits at the garage. He seemed to be looking them over with interest. I thought at the time he was waiting to have his car serviced."

"But actually," Linda put in, "he may have been planning a way to stop us."

"Exactly," Bob agreed. "He easily could have overheard our plans to take the shortcut."

"What did the man look like?" Linda queried.

Larry frowned in concentration. "I hardly noticed. I do remember that he wore an open-neck T-shirt and had a hairy chest and muscular arms."

"Strong enough to cut down a tree by himself?" said Bob pointedly.

"I'm sure of it," replied Larry. "But why all these efforts to delay us?" he asked in complete bafflement.

A frightening thought widened Linda's eyes. "Do you suppose it was to keep us away from Rancho del Sol so the Colemans and Trask could ransack the house again?"

Bob shook his head. "I doubt that. They must know by this time that Bronco has armed guards on the place."

"I hope so," said Linda. "Right now we must get out of this predicament. But how?"

"A good-sized tractor would come in handy," said Larry dryly. "Maybe one of us should start walking and try to find help."

"Nobody could stand walking far in this heat," Bob objected, wiping his face with his handkerchief, "not even a horse. There's something else we can try first. It's a trick I saw a sergeant do years ago

Linda began walking in the burning heat . . .

when our dad was stationed in the Imperial Valley."

"What was it?" asked Larry hopefully.

"Let most of the air out of the tires to get traction," Bob explained, "but leave enough in to get us to a gas station."

He and Larry set about the task immediately. While they worked, Linda checked again on Kathy. Her face was slightly moist from the heat. Linda opened all the car windows for maximum circulation.

After the boys had finished their job, Bob said, "The horses will have to be taken out to lighten the load as much as possible, and led to the main road. We'll take Rocket and Jubilee out first and ground-hitch them. Linda, you hold Chica and Patches."

When the horses had been removed from the trailers, Bob and Larry started the cars. The deflated tires enabled the boys to move the vehicles inch by inch from the sand.

In the meantime Linda had caught up the tie ropes of the black and bay and, with two horses on each side, started walking. The intense heat soon made her head feel as though it were about to burst.

Bob pulled up alongside her and jumped out. "You drive now and I'll walk."

"Thanks," Linda said gratefully.

Presently they came to the detour marker. Bob laid out a blanket and pulling up the freshly painted sign, carefully wrapped it. "There might be plenty of fingerprints on this," he declared.

When the group finally reached the Highway House, Mrs. Hamilton ran out and smilingly greeted them. "Welcome home, nomads!" But immediately the slim, sweet-faced woman sobered and asked, "Where's Kathy?"

"Sleeping," replied Linda, and explained about the accident.

"Is—is she badly hurt?" gasped Mrs. Hamilton

"There are no broken bones," Linda assured her.

Mrs. Hamilton hurried to the car and opened the door. "Kathy," she called softly. "Kathy."

The girl opened her eyes. "Mother!" she said groggily. "How did you get here?"

"You're home." Bob laughed.

"Home already!" Kathy sat up suddenly. "And without anything else happening to us!"

Her three friends looked at one another but decided against relating what had happened in the desert. Kathy scrambled out. The next instant her knees started to buckle.

Bob caught her and said to Larry, "Chair service."

They clasped their hands together to make a seat and carried the girl inside the house to her room. Kathy's mother and Linda followed.

"Please call Dr. Kelly to come right out," Mrs.

Hamilton requested Linda, "while I help Kathy into bed."

The physician arrived shortly. In a little while he gave his report on Kathy to the tense group.

"She's suffering from shock," he said. "It's nothing that a week in bed and the proper medicine won't fix. There's no cause for worry," he added. "Kathy's sleeping now." Everyone drew a sigh of relief.

As soon as the doctor had left, Mrs. Hamilton turned to the Craigs. "My goodness!" she exclaimed. "I was so upset I forgot to tell you Craigs that your grandmother called. She expected you home earlier and thought perhaps you had stopped here to visit. She said someone had phoned from the Trail Blazers head office in Los Angeles that all attest papers must be in their hands by six o'clock this evening or the entries won't be valid. You'd have to wait another year before being granted membership."

Bob took a quick look at his watch. "It's five minutes to six now," he groaned.

Linda and the boys stared at one another, aghast.

"We've lost out!" Linda cried dejectedly. "We'll have to disqualify ourselves!"

Surprising News 10

It was a somber trio that pulled into Rancho del Sol and entered the house.

They were warmly welcomed by Mr. and Mrs. Mallory, but Doña's face was deeply troubled. "I am so sorry you didn't get your attest papers into the Los Angeles office before the deadline," she said at once.

"A tough break," Bronco sympathized.

For a minute there was glum silence. Linda broke it by saying, "It does seem peculiar that such a sudden, last-minute notice would be given us by what seems to be a friendly, square-shooting local group."

"It *is* odd, all right," Bob agreed.

Linda turned to her grandmother. "Doña," she said, "could you tell us what the person sounded like who phoned, and the gist of the message?"

"I believe so." Mrs. Mallory looked thoughtful. "I

remember thinking at the time that the young woman who called sounded rather giddy to be holding a responsible position at the head office of the organization."

"Why was that, Mrs. Mallory?" asked Larry.

"Because she didn't sound at all businesslike," Doña replied disapprovingly. "When I told her the Craigs were not at home, the woman announced melodramatically that your attest papers would simply *have* to be in the head office by six o'clock, or you would not qualify for membership in the Number 28 Club.

"Then, obviously curious, she asked me where you were, Linda and Bob. When I told her you had not returned from the initiation ride, I distinctly heard her give a little laugh. Although," Doña continued, "the very next second she went on in a gushing fashion to say that all the members would be so sorry not to have you join the Trail Blazers this year."

Larry and Bob paced back and forth angrily. "What creepy luck!" Larry fumed.

Linda had remained in deep thought during her grandmother's recital. Now she looked at the others speculatively. "You know, I have a feeling that woman's sympathy was put on. Furthermore, I'm sure the Trail Blazers office closes at five o'clock, so why would she have said six?"

130

"Right," Bob put in. "Besides, I never heard of any deadline regulation for our attest papers."

"Same here," Larry stated.

"That settles it," Linda said determinedly. "I'm going to phone Los Angeles. Someone may still be at the Trail Blazers office and can tell me if this whole thing is correct, or just some kind of a practical joke or hoax."

"Good idea," Bob agreed. "While you're calling, Larry and I will take care of the horses and store the gear in the tack room."

Linda's call to the head office met with no response. Next, she hunted up the home number of their secretary, and phoned. She received no answer there either.

Linda then called Sue Mason, the secretary of Club 28. Sue said she had never heard of the regulation. "It might be a new one, though, that our club hasn't been advised about. Linda," she said. "Chuck Eller is on his way over here. You'd better talk to him. I'll have him call you."

As Linda hung up, Bob and Larry came into the hall. "Find out anything?" Bob asked her eagerly.

As Linda shook her head, the phone rang and she hurriedly answered. "Oh, hi, Chuck!" Linda told him the message Doña had received.

For a moment there was absolute silence on Chuck's end of the wire. Then he exploded. "What!

Ridiculous! You bet that call was a fake!"

When Linda hung up the phone her eyes were shining. "It was a hoax," she cried joyously. "Boys, we can get our papers and pics in anytime. But the first rustler-tracking ride will take place in a few days, and the following week the big All Clubs conclave will be held. So we'd better get our qualifications down to Los Angeles—fast!"

Bob let out his special brand of war whoop, and said, "I'll deliver the papers first thing tomorrow morning."

"That's terrific news!" Larry exclaimed. "I'll take the film home and develop it tonight. Bob, stop by for the prints on your way to Los Angeles tomorrow."

Happily Linda turned back to the phone. "I'll call Mrs. Hamilton and ask her to pass the good word along to Kathy." As she finished the call, Linda gave a hungry sniff. "Mm! One of Luisa's special hams with spices. And am I starved!"

Larry grinned. "I'm glad you invited me to dinner."

The three rushed into the kitchen where Luisa stood watching over her food-laden stove.

"When do we eat?" Bob asked.

"*Caramba!*" gasped Luisa. "It is ready, waiting and waiting. I will bring the dinner in to the table quick."

"I'll help you," Linda offered.

132

In the dining room, the young people brought Bronco and Doña up to date on the events of the trailblazing ride. The Mallorys expressed great concern at the thought that someone was obviously bent on harming the young initiates, especially Linda, and her horse Chica.

"What possible motive could anyone have for doing such dreadful things!" Doña exclaimed, while her husband's face tightened in anger.

"Whatever it is," Bronco said, "I'm keeping the guard here day and night until we find out and the men responsible are captured."

Doña looked at Linda and Bob in alarm. "I am worried about your leaving here on trips," she stated.

"I promise not to go alone," said Linda. "But we must help to catch those rustlers if we expect to be good Trail Blazers."

Bob looked perplexed. "Our enemies must have another reason besides the Perez jewels for trying to annoy and even harm us. That phony call about the attest papers, for instance—I can't imagine the Coleman gang having anything to gain by that. Why would *they* want to keep us out of the Trail Blazers Club?"

"I hate to say this," Larry put in, "but it looks as though you might have two different groups to contend with."

Luisa came in to serve dessert. Noticing the

troubled expressions of those at the table, she attempted to divert them.

"Do not forget tomorrow," the housekeeper said. "It is the day of the big Santa Clarita Guild Fair—and we take my chili vinegar."

Bob regretfully explained that his trip to Los Angeles the following morning would prevent his accompanying the group.

Bronco too would be busy. "I'm sorry I can't drive you to the fairgrounds," he said. "But I guess you three ladies can manage."

His wife smiled. "I am sure we can."

Presently Larry went off in his car. Next morning Bob drove away in the pickup, leaving the station wagon for the transportation of the chili vinegar. He had with him the attest papers on which the new trail had been plainly mapped. This would be substantiated by the pictures taken en route, including the marker at Crespi Cove. Bob would stop at Larry's to pick them up.

Meanwhile Linda had found the kitchen a bustle of activity. The usual orderliness of the room was transformed into a jumble of bottles and packing cases. Luisa, who had filled the bottles the night before, was attempting to affix the Rancho del Sol labels which Doña had printed.

This was the housekeeper's big day and she was excited and nervous. The labels either landed on the bottles crooked or would not stick. Luisa threw up her hands with a volley of exclamations in her native tongue.

Linda smiled. "I'll put the labels on," she offered, "while you start filling the boxes."

Finally everything was ready, and the cases packed into the station wagon. Everyone hurried off to dress. Luisa put on a colorful native Mexican dress. Doña and Linda wore white eyelet embroidery-trimmed Spanish fiesta blouses, and stuck red roses in their dark hair.

Doña seated herself beside Linda, who took the wheel. Luisa sat in back, keeping a wary eye on her precious vinegar.

"It's a lovely sunny day for the fair," Mrs. Mallory commented as they drove off.

"*Sí,*" Luisa said happily. "It will be good for business."

Linda's eyes twinkled. Laughing, she said, "Even rain wouldn't stop people from buying your vinegar, Luisa." The housekeeper bobbed her head in delighted agreement.

Reaching the fairgrounds, the trio were directed to their booth. At once Linda and her grandmother began decorating it. They twined Spanish fiesta-red, green, and yellow crepe paper streamers around the posts, and arranged festoons across the front. Then Linda fastened on big red paper roses of Seville, which Luisa had made. Next, Luisa set up her bottles on the counter.

By the time Mrs. Mallory and Linda had finished, it was almost ten o'clock. They stood back to appraise their handiwork.

Luisa was effusive in her admiration of the booth. "It is the most beautiful here!" she exclaimed.

"*Gracias.*" Mrs. Mallory smiled.

When the gates were opened, old customers flocked to purchase the allowed quota of two bottles of vinegar to a person. Many of them said, "We don't want to miss getting our share."

"Business is really brisk this year," Linda remarked as she opened another box.

A little past noon activity dwindled, however, then ceased entirely.

"Everyone must be having lunch," Linda guessed.

Presently Mrs. Mallory went to eat with friends at a palm frond–sheltered refreshment patio. Linda purchased sandwiches, cake, and cold drinks there, and brought them back to the booth for her and Luisa. They ate quickly, expecting another rush of customers. But still no one came to make a purchase.

Luisa looked disturbed. "Why no one else buy?" she asked in a hurt voice, lovingly patting a bottle of chili vinegar. "I taste it, and taste it. It taste good like always. I think even maybe a little better."

"It's still the lull of the noon hour," Linda assured her. "Before the fair closes at midnight, you are going to wish that you had at least a hundred bottles more to sell."

Luisa sighed. "It has always been so."

At that moment a tall, thin man with a heavy mustache, bushy beard, and sideburns ambled toward the booth.

"Could be a customer," Luisa whispered uncertainly.

"Possibly," replied Linda. "I saw him talking to some people across the way, then they went off. Perhaps he runs some sort of concession and is drumming up customers."

The bearded man greeted them by inquiring affably, "Business good?"

"It has been," replied Linda. "Right now things are slow. I'm sure sales will pick up."

"Don't be too sure," the stranger warned.

"What you mean?" demanded Luisa, bristling.

The man shrugged and replied in a patient tone, "Lady, I only came to tell you there's a fellow with a booth down at the south edge of the grounds selling what he is claiming is the real chili vinegar, and telling everyone that your product is a cheap substitute."

Luisa burst out in a torrent of Spanish, then said, "He is a—a fake!"

"He certainly is, and should be stopped immediately!" exclaimed Linda indignantly. "I'll go find a fairgrounds officer at once!"

"How about coming along with me first, and I'll show you where the other booth is," the stranger offered.

"I go. I hit that man over the head with his fake bottle," Luisa said vehemently, and urged Linda to accompany them.

"Well, all right," Linda agreed. "But I must tell Doña first."

She hurried over to where Mrs. Mallory sat talking with her friends. Linda informed her in low tones of the competitive chili vinegar seller, and asked, "Would you please stay at the booth while Luisa and I go to investigate? I have a hunch he is a fraud."

"Indeed yes," replied Doña, concerned. "No wonder we suddenly lost customers."

A few minutes later Linda and Luisa, with their bearded informant, approached a small, enclosed, umbrella-type tent at the very edge of the grounds. It was a good distance from the main concessions.

"Here?" exclaimed Linda. "Why, this is no booth!"

"And where are all the customers who do not come to ours?" questioned Luisa, noticing there was no one around the tent.

"You'll see," said their guide. "Step right in."

"No, thank you," answered Linda, her suspicions immediately aroused and her palms growing clammy.

She stepped back to turn away when suddenly both she and Luisa were violently pushed from behind into the tent.

"What—!" Linda burst out, and stopped with a gasp. Confronting them, a leer on his face, stood Rod Coleman!

"Greetings," he said with an exaggerated bow.

"You!" Linda cried in shocked surprise.

Luisa's eyes were filled with fear and bafflement. "Who—who is this man?" she asked Linda.

"One of the masked men who broke into Old Sol—and also held Bob and me prisoners!" Linda's eyes blazed.

Coleman gave a harsh laugh. "You won't give us the slip so easily this time, young lady," he said ominously.

Luisa forgot her own fear at this threat to Linda and started furiously toward Coleman.

"You wicked man!" she cried. "I teach you a lesson!"

Coleman snatched a club from under his jacket. "Stop!" he commanded roughly.

Linda reached out and pulled Luisa protectively beside her.

Rod Coleman glared at them. "Don't scream for help or I'll use this!"

From Linda's past experience she did not doubt that he meant business. "What do you want, anyway?" she asked defiantly.

"You tell me where those Perez jewels are," Coleman demanded surlily.

"Why—why *you* have them," said Linda incredulously.

"There were no jewels in the chest, or the ranch house, and you know it," he growled. "The secret compartment was empty."

"If that is so," said Linda coolly, "then the old story must be true that my ancestor, Rosalinda Perez, sent the jewels back to Spain."

"Hogwash!" blurted Rod Coleman. "You know where those jewels are. You're next in line to inherit them. Talk now or we'll hold you both until you do."

"The whereabouts of the jewels is a complete mystery to me and everyone in my family," insisted Linda.

"She—she know nothing," Luisa added bravely.

"You shut up!" barked Coleman. Then he turned his head and asked out of the corner of his mouth, "All ready back there?"

The bearded man, who had remained silent at the rear of the tent, opened the back flap. An enclosed delivery truck was revealed. Linda's quick eyes also noted that one side of the man's beard was askew.

He's wearing a disguise! she thought. His beard is false and probably his mustache, too! Who can he be?

"Okay, you two!" snapped Coleman. "March!" He pointed to the truck.

140

Reluctantly Linda and Luisa walked toward the vehicle. Coleman and the other man grabbed hold of the captives and thrust them into the rear section of the truck.

"Stay put and don't make any noise," Coleman snarled, "if you know what's good for you!"

With that he slammed the panel doors shut. Linda and Luisa, clinging together, were engulfed by darkness. The next moment they were thrown to the floor as the truck started up with a lurch and drove off.

The Sheriff's Clue 11

Luisa struggled to her knees, frantically pawing at the floor of the moving vehicle and screaming.

Linda caught hold of her and gave the Mexican woman a gentle shake. "Don't, Luisa, don't!" she urged kindly. "We're going to be all right. We'll escape somehow."

Luisa ceased her wailing and slumped again to the floor. "But how we escape?" she asked despairingly.

"We'll have to figure it out," replied Linda with more assurance than she felt. "Crying won't do it."

Luisa sat up straight, her usual determined spirit returning. "So right."

The two were silent for a while, each concentrating on possible means of escape. Finally Linda leaned over and whispered, "Luisa, you start pounding on the sides of the truck—keep it up while I investigate."

The Mexican woman scrambled to her feet, rocking precariously with the movement of the truck, and shouted, "I fix heem!"

She floundered to the cab and beat her fists against the wall. Repeatedly she cried out loudly in her native tongue.

Linda understood her, of course, and wondered if the driver knew what she was saying. The truck slowed to a stop, and Linda trembled, afraid that the man was coming back to tie them up. But the vehicle went on.

It was probably a traffic light, the girl thought.

Linda's mind began to spin. There would be other stops—a chance to escape if they could only open the door! She made her way over to Luisa and in a low tone said, "Keep pounding! Keep talking! Meanwhile I'll look for a way out."

Linda crept on hands and knees to the rear of the truck. Reaching up, she felt in the darkness for a lock mechanism on the doors. Her fingers touched a catch.

Cautiously Linda tried this, and the door opened a crack. Oh, what wonderful luck! she thought.

Linda scrambled back to Luisa and whispered her discovery. "We'll have to wait for the truck to slow down," she went on, "then jump out."

"*Bueno!*" exclaimed Luisa. "I will jump like my Ceraldine and Genevieve!"

Despite herself, Linda giggled, then said seriously, "We'd better keep on talking, so the driver won't suspect anything. I'm sure he can hear what we're saying if we raise our voices."

The captives began to discuss, in loud tones, where they might be going. Linda said dramatically, "I'm afraid we'll never see the ranch again."

Luisa took the cue. "*Caramba!*" she groaned. "It is too terrible to think of!"

What seemed like hours elapsed before the truck slackened speed and stopped. "Now's our chance!" Linda hissed, pulling Luisa quickly to the rear.

The girl flicked the catch and the doors swung open, revealing a deserted road. At the same moment came the sound of an approaching train. They were at a railroad crossing.

Lucky break for us, she thought as a long freight began to thunder past. We have plenty of time.

"Jump!" Linda commanded.

Luisa obeyed, with agility surprising for one so plump. Linda followed, leaping onto the hard surface beside the Mexican woman. They fled toward a dense cluster of trees bordering the road. Linda peered out and managed to note the license number of the delivery truck, but could not get a clear glimpse of the driver. As soon as the freight had gone past, the truck started up and sped off down the road.

Suddenly the full relief at their escape hit Linda and Luisa. They hugged each other in delight. "All our talk did the trick!" Linda grinned. "That driver still thinks we're safely locked in. With the noise of the freight and his own engine, he didn't hear *us*."

Luisa laughed heartily. "Maybe he not hear so good anyhow."

"Now," said Linda, "we must find out exactly where we are and how to get back to the fair. Doña will be frantic."

Luisa looked down the strange road and said, "I not know where we are."

The two ventured out from the trees. The area seemed to be sparsely populated. There were occasional abandoned citrus orchards and wooded spots. In the distance rugged hills could be seen.

"No cars. No ride," Luisa grumbled.

"We'll have to keep walking until we can pick up one," said Linda.

Luisa sighed. "Is too much for fat lady."

"Maybe you'll lose a pound," Linda said consolingly.

"I lose, yes," said Luisa. "But walking make me hungry, so I eat it back." She laughed good-naturedly.

They walked some distance without a single car passing them. Finally they arrived at an area of small farms with a little more activity. There was a fruit and vegetable stand at a crossroads where two women had just driven up.

As they alighted, Linda said to Luisa, "I'll ask

them if they'll take us back to the fairgrounds."

"I pray they do." Luisa sighed again. "My feet hurt."

Linda hurried to the stand and approached the woman who had been driving. "Pardon me, I'm Linda Craig," she said with a friendly smile. "This is Luisa Alvarez. We were kidnapped from the Santa Clarita Guild Fair. Could you possibly return us there if you're heading that way?"

"Kidnapped!" exclaimed both women in amazement.

"How?" asked the driver dubiously.

"And why?" spoke up the other woman, obviously skeptical.

Linda briefly explained how they had been captured and forced into the delivery truck. At the end of her story both women, convinced it was true, were horrified and more than willing to help.

"Of course we'll drive you to the fair," said the owner of the car. "I've heard of a famous chili vinegar they sell there. I would like to buy some."

"Luisa makes it," Linda told them.

"You give us ride—I give you some bottles," Luisa assured the women happily.

Quickly the four climbed into the automobile. Luisa sank into the back seat with a great sigh of relief, slipped off her shoes, and wiggled her toes. "*Caramba!* This is good!" she exclaimed.

Within the hour Linda and Luisa were back at the fairgrounds. It was now late afternoon. The faces of Doña and several friends who had come to stay with her turned suddenly from deep concern to joy.

"Where have you been?" Mrs. Mallory asked Linda. "I've been very worried. I can tell by your face there has been trouble."

"A lot of trouble, I'm afraid," Linda replied. After introducing the women with her, she hastily told what had happened. Luisa interrupted now and then to say how brave "her young lady" had been.

Linda squeezed the housekeeper's arm. "*You* were wonderful—I'm sorry you had to go through such a frightening experience, but I'm thankful you were with me."

Doña expressed shock and dismay at the attempted kidnapping. "I should have realized there was something suspicious about that bearded man's story," she reproached herself.

"At least," Linda said, "I learned that Rod Coleman apparently did not locate the jewels. But he won't believe we don't know where they are."

"*Sí*, it is so," Luisa averred solemnly with a shiver. "I fear that *hombre* make big trouble—be very angry when he find out we get away."

Linda agreed. "We will all have to be constantly on our guard at the ranch and everywhere else. But what a lot I'll have to tell the sheriff!"

Mrs. Mallory explained that many people had come to the booth, reporting they had been warned by the stranger that Luisa's vinegar was spoiled. "I know now he did it to keep customers away so you and Luisa would leave to investigate."

Doña related that finally she had persuaded fairgoers that the man's story was false. "I guess word was passed around," she concluded. "As you can see, our counter is bare."

Luisa, although pleased, asked in a worried voice, "The vinegar—it is all sold? I promised some to these nice ladies for driving us."

Doña smiled. "Luckily there are a few bottles left in one of the boxes. I was so upset at your not returning, I neglected to put them out."

"I get." Luisa beamed. She brought out the remaining bottles and gave two each to the women who had brought them back. "*Gracias* for ride," she said.

Linda and Mrs. Mallory also thanked the women warmly. As soon as they had gone off, Linda said she would phone the sheriff's office.

"Yes, you must do that," said Doña. "But please return as quickly as possible."

Linda smiled and nodded. "No long trips for me this time!"

She went to the fairgrounds office and called the sheriff, giving him a full account of the kidnapping and her meeting with Rod Coleman. Linda described the false-bearded stranger and the delivery truck, reporting the license number.

"Fine work," he said. "I'm glad you got away."

The official assured Linda that he would dispatch deputies to follow the road the delivery truck had taken. In addition, other men would be sent to the fairgrounds immediately to pick up what clues they might find around the tent, and to lift imprints left by the truck's tires.

"I'll be in touch with you the minute we have any news," he promised. Linda thanked him and hung up. One of the fairgrounds officers, Mr. Donovan, who had listened with interest to the girl's report, asked her, "Just where is this tent? I don't remember seeing it."

"I'll show you," Linda offered.

She walked with the officer to the south edge of the grounds and stopped in surprise. "It's gone!" Linda exclaimed. "It was right there." She pointed to the spot.

"That figures," said Donovan. "It was apparently put up to decoy you, and taken down right afterward. I'll wait here until the sheriff's deputies arrive, and give them a hand."

Linda returned to the booth to find Mrs. Mallory and Luisa taking down the decorations. At once Linda began to help.

Doña gave her a smile. "I assume you are ready to go home, dear," she said, "or do you wish to spend the evening at the fair?"

"No, thank you." Linda half-sighed, half-laughed. "I've had enough activity for today."

"I've had enough for *all* days." Luisa groaned, pulling down streamers.

"I am happy," said Mrs. Mallory, "that our booth made better than its usual amount of money for the Guild."

"Is good." Luisa's face brightened with a broad smile.

"Chili vinegar very good," Linda said, her eyes twinkling. "Let's go home!"

Later that evening a phone call came to Old Sol from the sheriff. Linda took it.

"We've learned," he told her, "that the license of the delivery truck was issued to a Peter J. Henry of San Francisco."

Linda mulled over the name until a theory occurred to her. "Could Hank Trask, the Colemans' accomplice, be an alias of Peter J. Henry?" she asked. "Hank is a nickname for Henry."

"A good probability," the officer conceded. "I'll work on that angle."

He went on to tell Linda that no trace had been found of the bushy-bearded stranger, the truck, or its driver. "I figure that as soon as they discovered your escape, they immediately hid out in some obscure spot."

The sheriff asked Linda if she thought Trask was the driver. "I really can't say," she replied. "I never did get a good look at the man behind the wheel."

The next morning Linda and Bob went to the Highway House to pay Kathy a visit. She was resting in a deck chair on the back patio. To her friends' relief Kathy seemed a great deal better, both in appearance and spirits. Her eyes were dancing brightly, and her face had its natural warm apricot hue.

"I can't keep her in bed," lamented Mrs. Hamilton, smiling nevertheless.

Kathy grinned. "I'm rarin' to ride—any minute now!"

"Tie her down," Bob advised, and chuckled. "If she won't lie flat for the next couple of days, that is."

"Fine pal you are!" pouted Kathy playfully.

When Linda told her about the previous day's kidnapping, Kathy's face clouded over with fear. "To think of you in such danger and me here not being a shred of help!"

Mrs. Hamilton shuddered. "The whole situation is so sinister. Those awful men seem to know every move you Craigs make."

Bob's jaw tightened. "They're a foxy bunch all right, but foxes usually get trapped sooner or later."

Talk presently turned to the Trail Blazers Club 28. "Now that our papers and pictures are safely in Los Angeles," Bob said, "we should receive our certificates soon."

Half an hour later the Craigs left. That afternoon Linda worked Chica in the ring, putting her through only the exercises which she would be called upon to execute at the big show: the walk, trot, canter, reverse, figure eight, pivot, and back.

Bob had perched on the top rail of the fence to watch. "That horse is perfect, just perfect," he declared.

"Yes," Linda admitted. "But Chica d'Oro has to be better than perfect so that no matter what strange sound or sight may occur, she won't hesitate an instant in her responses to commands."

"My money is on Chica." Bob grinned. "And the hand that is guiding her."

Linda flashed him an appreciative smile, then tilted her chin and told him saucily, "Flattery will get you nowhere, buddy boy."

"Oh, no?" he retorted.

On Tuesday Linda and Bob received their handsome parchment certificates of membership in the Trail Blazers organization. Kathy and Larry phoned to say that they too had theirs.

Linda laughed gaily. "A hard-won victory," she remarked to Bob. "But worth each struggle."

"You bet," her brother agreed.

A little later Linda stood before the portrait of Rosalinda Perez as she often did when especially happy, and spoke softly in Spanish to her likeness, "I hope, dear Great-Great-Grandmother, that I may continue to live up to our name as you would wish me to do. And how glad I am that those wicked thieves did not find your beautiful jewels. You hid them well."

As often happened, Linda thought the beautiful woman smiled at her as if wanting to help.

That evening after dinner, Sue Mason phoned to tell Linda, "Be ready, all you new Trail Blazers, to start out Saturday morning on our first tracking ride. We're going after those rustlers for keeps this time. They're still hiding out and stealing cattle!"

Rustler Hunt   12

During the next three days Linda divided much of her time between working Chica d'Oro and talking on the phone. The Trail Blazers Club 28 members kept busy discussing plans for the rustler-tracking ride on Saturday. Linda relayed the various conversations to her brother, who was helping to reroof the barn. The most important was that of Chuck Eller.

"He says," reported Linda, "that two men were seen the other night right after a calf snatching. It was at a small ranch not far from the entrance to our Crespi Cove trail. But the men ran away, and it was too dark for anyone to see what they looked like."

"Those could be the two who raided Carl Johnson's cabin," said Bob. "They must still be working in that vicinity. The dense woods provide perfect hideouts."

"Perhaps we ought to pay Carl a visit first thing on our ride to find out if he has seen those men again," suggested Linda. "We might be able to pick up some good clues."

"I'll go along with that," said Bob. "Why not talk it over with Chuck? Also, ask him if he doesn't think the bunch should start out from Old Sol. We're the most centrally located."

Linda hurried off to do this, and Chuck concurred enthusiastically with her suggestions. Early Saturday morning Bob drove over to the Highway House with an empty horse trailer to get Kathy and Patches.

"Are you sure you feel up to this trip?" he asked her. "It may be rugged."

"Positive! I'm feeling great, really, and rarin' to ride." Kathy grinned. "Rustlers, here I come!"

As Bob and Kathy drove into Rancho del Sol, a big stock truck owned by the father of a member pulled in with ten horses loaded sideways, head to tail. Their riders followed in two cars, with Larry directly behind them. Chuck came next with Sue Mason and their horses. Finally, eighteen young people had gathered, chattering and laughing noisily about the trip.

"Are you sheriff's deputies ready?" the president called out with a grin.

Larry slapped one hand on an imaginary holster, whipped out an invisible gun, and pointed it toward the distant hills. "I'm a dead shot!" he announced.

Another boy, Bill Winters, bent low and made a

pretense of scrutinizing the ground with a magnifying glass. "I sure don't see suspicious boot prints," he announced. "But give me time, give me time!"

Amid the general laughter, Chuck called out, "Tallyho!"

The Trail Blazers scrambled for their cars. Linda and Bob ran back to bid good-bye to Doña and Bronco, who had come out to watch the proceedings and wish the riders luck.

"Please be careful," Doña admonished them.

Bronco added, "Keep a sharp eye out at all times."

"We'll do both," Linda promised. Rango stood beside the Mallorys wagging his tail wistfully and barking reproachfully at being left behind. "You're needed here, old boy, to act as guard and keep away intruders," Linda told him.

Cactus Mac hurried from the corral waving his big, well-worn stetson. "Bring back those *diablos*," he called to the Craigs and their friends.

The caravan moved out with Bob and Linda leading, since they knew the route. After a while the cars pulled into the wide parking area behind the service station's garage on Valley Highway. Bob introduced Chuck to the young mechanic who had fixed the trailer wheel, and the attendant agreed to keep an eye on the riders' vehicles during their absence.

Finally the Club 28 members saddled up and

started along the trail which Linda's foursome had blazed. Chuck, directly behind the Craigs, said, "I certainly recognize this route from your excellent map and pictures."

As the procession drew near Carl Johnson's cabin, his two big dogs barked excited notice of the callers' approach.

"I'm glad those animals decided to come home," said Kathy.

As before, Carl Johnson ran out of the cabin gripping his rifle. Then, seeing Linda and the others, his face broke into a happy smile and he put the gun aside. Bob introduced the elderly man to the riders, who sang out a chorus of greetings.

"Why didn't you send me a wire sayin' you Trail Blazers was ridin' this way?" Carl asked with a wry grin. "I would've hooked a whole pailful o' trout!"

"Thanks anyway," said Linda, smiling warmly. "We'll take a rain check."

"What we're really here to find out, Mr. Johnson," Bob explained, "is whether or not you've discovered anything more about those men who robbed your larder. Have you seen them again?"

Quick anger colored Carl's face. "They came back," he blurted. "I seen 'em, and I sure 'nough found out somethin'." He grinned cagily. "But them two didn't see me. I'd just come back from gettin' me a brace o' rabbits over the hill, and I seen smoke comin' out o' my stovepipe."

He winked. "I wasn't takin' any chances walkin' into the varmints, so I sneaked up Injun-style to the open window in back, and peeped in. And there was those same two grub-liners settin' down to my table scroungin' my bacon 'n' eggs."

"Then what happened?" Linda asked excitedly.

"The two galoots was hatchin' some skulduggery," Carl continued. "I heard the one call that ugly, flat-nosed coyote Max, and Max called t'other Sam. They was talkin' pretty cocky about their beef hauls—said they'd hit X next. Finished eatin' and left right off without so much as cleanin' up."

"At least," Linda remarked, "we know the men's first names, and no doubt they're the rustlers."

"True," said Bob. "Wonder what they meant by hitting X."

Larry spoke up. "I think I know. There's a ranch named the Three X just over the hill a little off the highway. I've noticed the RFD mailbox there when I've driven by. The name on it is Turnbull."

"You could be right," said Chuck. "That's in the vicinity of the last rustling activity."

"What's our next move, leader?" asked Kathy.

"We'll break up into three small groups," Chuck directed. "Each will ride in from different directions toward the outskirts of Three X, searching the woods and canyons, then converge on the ranch buildings together."

The Craigs thanked Carl Johnson for his information. "Anytime I can help pin down those varmints," he said, "let me know."

The Trail Blazers quickly formed their groups, with Chuck Eller and Sue Mason joining the Craigs, Kathy, and Larry. They all rode back to the highway and crossed it into the property of the Three X ranch. Here the three sections went their separate ways.

Linda and her fellow riders carefully looked for footprints along their designated route, and searched behind clumps of dense brush, but saw no trace of any trespassers. As Linda and her friends drew near the ranch proper, they noticed a herd of whiteface cattle peacefully grazing in a field.

When they came in sight of the buildings, Linda said in surprise, "The place seems deserted!"

"Let's ride in as slowly and noiselessly as possible behind the big barn," Chuck suggested. "We'll be pretty well obscured from view and can get a better look around."

They reined to a stop near one side of the barn and scanned the area. Then the riders exchanged startled glances upon hearing men's loud, argumentative voices inside the structure.

One was exclaiming, "You're loco, plumb loco to try runnin' off a bunch in broad daylight. I tell you we got to wait till dark."

A second voice shouted, "No such thing! Everyone's gone from here. You saw 'em all leave in the car except Mr. Turnbull and he's way off mending fence. We can cut out half a dozen fat head from the herd, and have 'em up in that brush corral of ours long before those ranch folks get back. Come on!"

The next moment the listeners heard the sound of heavy stomping toward the front of the barn.

Chuck quickly dismounted. "Let's intercept them," he urged Bob and Larry. "You girls hold the horses."

The boys hurried around in time to confront two men emerging from the wide doorway. One, short and stocky with a broad nose, was grumbling to his taller companion.

"Stop where you are, Max and Sam!" Bob commanded.

The stocky man fell back a step, astounded. "You know us?"

"We do," said Chuck, and called loudly, "*Tallyho! Tallyho!*"

The suspects turned to flee, but before they could, the three girls rode up swiftly, blocking the men's path. The boys seized the pair, and Linda tossed a coil of rope from Bob's saddle horn to them. Just as the captives were securely bound, the other Trail Blazers came at full gallop from all directions, encircling the area. With one group was the rancher who had been out mending fence and had been told by them of the club's suspicions.

"Here are the rustlers—in person," Chuck told

The Trail Blazers galloped in . . .

Mr. Turnbull as he arrived. "Max and Sam. They were all set to run off a half-dozen head of your cattle. We overheard their plan."

"I told you we should've waited till dark," whined Sam to his pal.

"Shut up!" growled Max.

"Well, I sure can't thank you young people enough," exclaimed the grateful rancher. "I'll call the sheriff pronto!" He hurried into the house.

The Craigs and their companions were highly praised for capturing the men. Within half an hour a police car pulled up and two deputies leaped out. Immediately they snapped handcuffs on the prisoners before untying them.

The men sullenly gave their full names as Max Velt and Sam Rout, and, after being advised of their legal rights, confessed to the rustling charges against them. Their shaggy brown horses were tethered in a thicket, and the officers instructed the rancher to impound them until further notice. Then the deputies sped away with their captives.

Chuck Eller turned to the Trail Blazers. "Well, old-timers, what about a rousing cheer for our new members whose clues led us to make the capture of these rustlers?"

Hats went into the air, and a loud chorus of "Hip-hip hoorays!" rang out.

Mr. Turnbull raised his stetson high and shouted, "Hooray for all of you!"

It was now past noon and Chuck asked him, "Mind if we picnic somewhere on your property?"

"I'd be honored," replied the ranch owner. "Down yonder in that clump of cottonwoods is a big water hole. Crystal-clear water too. It's a right nice place for a picnic."

They thanked him and rode to the pretty, shaded spot. The Trail Blazers had brought halters and tie ropes on their saddles. Now they unbridled the horses and secured them to trees. The long lines enabled the animals to amble about, graze, and drink. Finally the riders unsaddled their mounts and settled down on the grassy floor to eat the lunches they had brought.

"I'm absolutely ravenous!" Linda exclaimed.

Larry eyed his sandwich appreciatively. "Me too. Rustler hunting sure makes a fellow hollow inside!"

As the Trail Blazers finished eating, the rancher appeared with several huge watermelons. He cut slices of the ice-cold fruit and passed them around.

When Mr. Turnbull came to the Craigs, he remarked, "You know, I caught another pair of fellows one morning that I figured might be those rustlers. They'd been sleeping in the barn. But apparently shelter for the night was all they wanted, so I didn't call the sheriff. The men took off in a hurry, though."

"What did they look like?" Linda asked quickly.

Mr. Turnbull gave a good description: One man

was stocky and had brown hair; his companion was tall, gaunt, and bony-faced.

"Rod Coleman and Hank Trask!" Linda gasped.

"You've met up with those two?" the rancher asked in surprise.

"Yes," Bob replied, frowning. "They match the description of a couple of prowlers who broke into our ranch house."

"Well, now, I guess I *should* have had 'em picked up," said Mr. Turnbull soberly. "But I had no special reason to suspect the men. I run saddle tramps off my place every once in a while." He narrowed his eyes thoughtfully. "Come to think of it, that pair didn't look like wandering cowboys. And they did some pretty fancy talking."

"Do you remember what they said?" asked Linda.

"Partly," the rancher replied. "The bony-faced fellow called Hank Trask bragged he was a direct descendant of a servant at Rancho del Sol when the first Spanish family, the Perezes, lived there. Claimed he had some valuable family jewels due him."

"What!" Linda cried in astonishment and dismay.

Bob too was taken aback by this revelation. He explained to their host, "We live at Old Sol. My sister and I are descendants of the Perezes."

"Well, I'll be rope-tied!" Mr. Turnbull exclaimed, beaming. "I'm mighty glad I had a chance to meet you folks and alert you to those fellows."

164

"So are we," Bob declared. "Coleman and Trask will stop at nothing."

"I'll keep my eyes open in case they show up again," the friendly rancher promised. "Well, got to get to work. You young people keep on enjoying yourselves. And ride back anytime you've a mind to."

"Thank you very much," said Linda.

As soon as he had left, she went on, "Bob, that old note left in Chica's stall the day she was injured must be authentic! To think that awful Hank Trask has a claim to some of our family's jewels!"

Bob looked perplexed. "But why doesn't Trask just come forward and demand his rightful share?" he asked.

"Because," Linda conjectured, "he's in league with the Colemans, who have persuaded him to get hold of the whole collection."

"At least they haven't found the jewels yet," Bob reminded her. "And I don't think they ever will, if Rosalinda Perez sent the treasure back to Spain."

Their discussion was interrupted by Chuck Eller, who motioned the Craigs forward. The rest of the Club 28 members had formed a semicircle around their president. Silence prevailed as Linda and Bob stood facing them wonderingly.

Chuck began speaking with a broad grin. "Since all of our board members are present," he said, "and a representative number of regular members, we've just held a special meeting. There was a

165

unanimous vote to ask Linda Craig, as a delegate of Club 28, to compete in the annual contest at the big Trail Blazers show for selection of their queen."

The members clapped and cheered loudly.

"Oh!" Linda gasped. "I—I'm deeply honored—and overwhelmed. I'm not sure I can qualify." She had assumed that Sue Mason would be chosen to represent their club.

Sue spoke up promptly. "None of us has a speck of doubt. You are the best horsewoman in our group. And Chica d'Oro is the most qualified horse."

Linda blushed with embarrassed pleasure. "Well, thanks a million. Chica and I will do our very best," she said fervently.

Shortly afterward, tired, but happy at their successful mission, the riders saddled up and rode to their outfits at the gas station.

Before Kathy left for home with Bob, she murmured to Linda, "Sue Mason has a list of most of the queen contestants chosen so far. Shirley Blaine has been selected by the Malibu Club."

"That figures," said Bob wryly. "She'll be tough competition, Sis."

Linda raised her chin. "I'll be ready for her." Inwardly she was not so certain. Shirley, although frivolous and snobbish, had a reputation for being a skilled equestrienne.

A sudden thought struck Linda. My goodness!

The show is next week! I'll have to work Chica every minute I can.

Back at Old Sol, the Craigs found the household calm and undisturbed by any new incidents. Bronco, Doña, and Luisa were joyous over the capture of the rustlers and the news about Linda.

"I'm not surprised, though," said Bronco, glancing proudly at his granddaughter.

The Mallorys' enthusiasm was tempered somewhat when they learned of Hank Trask's claim to the Perez gems. Bronco frowned. "In that case, he and his Coleman cronies won't give up their search easily."

Despite this worry, Linda went to bed exhilarated over the honor of being the representative of Club 28 in the queen contest. She was too excited to sleep soundly and at two in the morning was awakened by Rango barking. She sat up.

What's going on at this hour? Linda asked herself.

She jumped out of bed, ran to the window, and peered into pitch darkness. Not even the beam of a guard's flashlight could be seen.

He must be making his rounds near the fence, Linda thought.

Rango's barking continued. It came from the front of the house. Quickly Linda put on her slippers and robe and ran into the hall. No one else was up. She hurried down the stairs. On the landing Linda froze.

Someone was tampering with the lock on the front door!

A Spiteful Hoax

13

For a few seconds Linda was frightened motionless. She heard the low voice of a man muttering about the dog's yapping.

Rango kept up his barking, which was coming closer. Frantically Linda wondered if the guard had been overpowered by this apparent housebreaker. Her heart thumping, she turned to race upstairs and awaken Bob and Bronco. At that moment she saw them coming down. Bronco signaled for her not to move and took a stand beside the light switch in the hall.

Suddenly the door was unlocked and pushed open. A tall figure entered stealthily and closed the door quickly. Rango, left just outside, gave sharp protesting yelps. Bronco snapped on the lights.

"Hank Trask!" gasped Linda.

The intruder turned to bolt outside, but Bob dashed forward and grabbed him. He struggled viciously to break free, but Bronco's strong hands also seized him. Realizing he was outnumbered, Trask ceased to resist.

Just then the door burst open and one of the guards, named Scott, entered on the run, with Rango leaping ahead of him.

"This fellow break in?" Scott asked, out of breath.

"He did," replied Bronco tersely. "Where were you?"

"Out behind the hay shed, where I found a strange delivery truck," the guard replied. "I was hunting for the driver around there when I heard Rango barking and came to investigate." He shook out handcuffs and snapped them on Trask's wrists.

Hank Trask glowered. "You've got no right to do this," he snarled. "I came here to get my inherited jewels you've all cheated me out of!"

At this moment Doña Mallory appeared at the head of the stairs. Although startled at the scene before her, the stately woman said in icy tones, "You may have a claim to the Perez jewels, but unfortunately for you and my family, their whereabouts are a complete mystery."

Trask scoffed, "You expect me to believe that?" He straightened his bony frame with a swagger, and stared about arrogantly with his piercing, light blue eyes. "You better be handing me over my share or else give me its worth in money. If not, I'll hire me a good lawyer to get my due."

"Your only due is a long jail sentence for kidnapping and housebreaking," Bronco curtly told him. "And the only kind of lawyer you'll be needing is a defense lawyer."

Linda, hoping to catch the captive off guard, said abruptly, "Your delivery truck is registered in your own name, Peter J. Henry, of San Francisco! Why the alias?"

A flicker of fear showed in Trask's eyes but he remained stubbornly silent.

Bob asked him, "Where are your friends the Colemans hiding out? If you do a little talking, things may go easier with you."

"I got nothing to say about nobody to nobody," muttered Trask, and pressed his thin lips tightly shut.

Rango had been standing in front of Trask uttering low, throaty growls. "It's all right now, Rango," said Linda, patting him. "You were a mighty good watchdog to keep trailing this trespasser and barking to waken us."

"Let's go!" Scott snapped to Trask and firmly ushered him outside.

Bronco hurried to telephone Deputy Sheriff Randall and report the capture. "We'll take good care of Trask—behind bars," Randall said emphatically. "I'll concentrate on rounding up the Coleman brothers."

That morning the family went to church in

Lockwood, then relaxed for a while on the patio.

Doña said, puzzled, "I cannot understand what possessed Mr. Trask to come here again, since he had searched our house with his partners before. It was such a reckless thing to do."

"Perhaps," said Bob, "he figured he was losing out too much by tying in with the Colemans, and wanted to have a look around here on his own."

Linda shuddered. "It seems horrible to think that any of Great-Great-Grandmother's beautiful jewels might ever be going to that dishonest man."

"Well, don't lose any sleep over it," said Bob. "The jewels evidently aren't going to anyone."

Later, Linda spent some time with Chica, brushing the palomino and talking to her.

"And now for a short workout," she said. "No tricks this week, baby. All you're going to be asked is to give a perfect performance."

She reached down and patted Chica on the shoulder. At once the filly pulled back her foot with a bent knee and went into a low bow.

"You ham!" Linda laughed, then added soberly, "But I'm glad you gave me this warning. You're such a smart horse I'll have to watch my hand during the big show so as not to give you any signals. Highly schooled stunts would go against you instead of building up points for us."

During the next two hours Linda made the filly walk, trot, canter, and gallop. At the end she hugged her. "Very good, but tomorrow you must hold your head more erect."

The following morning Linda checked the costumes she and Bob would wear in the contest. Bob was to be dressed in frontier pants of a mocha shade, brown boots, a white western shirt with a tan tie, and a white hat.

Linda's suit was kelly green with bell-bottom pants embroidered up the sides and jeweled, as was the yoke of her fringed white leather shirt. Green was the most striking color she could wear on her golden palomino. Linda would wear white boots, gloves, tie, and hat with a jeweled border and hatband. She was satisfied that everything was spotless.

"I think we'll look good," Linda concluded. "If only our performance measures up to our clothes!"

While she was giving Chica a lesson in holding up her head when standing still but not being reined up tautly, Bob was exercising Rocket in the ring. The ranch horse seemed to regard the whole procedure as a lot of nonsense—he was not going anywhere and he was not working any cattle!

"Rocket doesn't approve of this business," Bob said to his sister with a laugh. "I have a feeling we won't be very proud of ourselves."

"Well, at least you'll help fill up a couple of classes," Linda comforted him. "You know there have to be so many in a class in order to hold it."

"Anything to be obliging," Bob said. "That's us, Rocket, eh?" Rocket expressed his "obligingness" by bolting for the ring entrance.

On Thursday morning Linda received a call from the deputy sheriff's office. "Will you and your brother come to Lockwood and see if you can identify two men who have been arrested?" Randall asked.

"Yes indeed."

Excited, Linda called Bob from the corral and they drove to town. At Randall's office, in the small waiting room, the prisoners were brought before the Craigs.

"That's Rod Coleman!" Linda immediately pointed to the familiar figure of her former captor. "He and Hank Trask tied us up in the cabin."

Bob said, "I'm sure the other man is his brother Ben, from descriptions I've heard of him."

A clerk was taking notes at the desk. "Rod Coleman," he said aloud as he wrote. "Ben Coleman."

"*I* didn't say that was me," the huskier prisoner snarled.

Randall directed the clerk, "Leave it Ben Coleman."

Linda looked straight at Rod. "How do you explain your part in having me and our housekeeper kidnapped?"

"That wasn't my idea," Coleman insisted. "I was

173

just doing a job for someone else for a fee."

"For Hank Trask?" prodded Linda. "That delivery truck belongs to him. He was the driver."

The Colemans glared at her. "You don't know that," growled Ben.

"We do know it," said Bob. "The police in San Francisco sent down the registration information—including Trask's real name."

The brothers were obviously startled. Linda next questioned the prisoners about the bushy-bearded stranger who had led her and Luisa to the tent and helped shove them into the delivery truck.

"Don't know him," was Rod Coleman's sullen answer. "He's a friend of Trask's. All I ever heard is that the fellow don't have to worry about money."

"And paid you to do the job!" Linda exclaimed in disgust. "What was his motive in kidnapping us?"

The Colemans denied knowing the reason. Linda, however, overheard Ben mutter to his brother, "You were a fool to give your name to these kids in the first place."

"How was I to know they'd escape before we had a chance to find the jewels?" Rod retorted. "Anyway, we were going to change our names."

Nothing further could be learned from the men, so a waiting officer led them back to their cells.

"I think we've found out one thing," said Linda. "That bearded stranger must be the same man who paid Rod Coleman to injure Chica d'Oro, and also, he could be the mysterious diver at Crespi Cove. He has the same build."

"I'll go along with you on that theory," said Bob. "Now our only problem is to find out *who* he is, and why he did those things."

Early Friday afternoon Bob, Linda, Larry, and Kathy were ready to roll out of Rancho del Sol and head for Cowboy Park and the Trail Blazers All Clubs Show. To the two cars were attached the horse trailers. At the park the girls would use the dressing room in front of Chica's quarters, and the boys would sleep in the other trailer.

By the time the Old Sol caravan arrived at the park, outfits were coming in from all directions. The spacious area, alive with an excited bustle, was perfect for such a large gathering of people and horses.

There was a fine arena with a covered grandstand and bleachers. To one side was a grassy, dust-free, ten-acre parking lot for club contestants. In the rear of the grandstand a catering service had set up long tables, and near them a portable floor had been laid for dancing.

The foursome was greeted by Chuck Eller at the check-in gate. "Follow me," he told them, and led the way to a pleasant oak-shaded spot at the rear of the lot.

Sue Mason was there waiting. "I've been doing sentinel duty," she announced. "I really had to guard this place to hold it for you."

"Oh, thank you. It's perfect," said Linda.

Many of the people coming in for the show brought house trailers. Other participants, arriving with their families, set up tents. The horses were tied to the backs of the trailers and blanketed with day sheets to keep them clean. The Craigs and their friends went around introducing themselves to others, while the horses, affected by the air of excitement, kept whinnying back and forth.

"This is more fun than I ever could have imagined!" exclaimed Linda, stars sparkling in her dark eyes.

She and her companions remained for the alfresco supper and dancing, which most of the other Club 28 members attended. All of the queen representatives were there except Shirley Blaine. Linda found the girls to be full of fun and good sportsmanship.

"Where is Shirley?" she asked.

"I understand she's staying at a deluxe unit in the Silver Saddle Motel," one of the girls spoke up. "She's boarding her horse and groom at the fancy Sierra Stables!"

Jill Raymond, a petite girl who was the queen contestant from the Bell Gardens Club, sighed and said, "Shirley's sure to be chosen queen. With her striking looks, elegant clothes, fine trainer, trained horse, and top riding ability, how can she lose?"

Linda made no comment. Just being part of the

big show and having been chosen as representative of Club 28 meant a lot to her. Of course, she and Chica d'Oro would try to bring honor to their group by winning if possible.

The dancing concluded at ten o'clock so that participants for the following day's horse show could get their needed rest. The runoff of the various classes would start at nine in the morning.

The queens were not to participate in any of the regular events. For this reason Linda dressed in jeans and plaid shirt, then helped Kathy get ready. How attractive the blond girl looked wearing a plain burnt-orange western suit with brown boots, tie, and hat, and riding on brown and white Patches!

Larry wore tan frontier pants, a yellow plaid western shirt, and brown boots, tie, and hat. He made a fine appearance on chestnut Jubilee, as did Bob in his mocha outfit on bay Rocket.

The trio filed into the arena for the first class, the Trail Class. Unfortunately none of them performed well in overcoming the obstacles. Patches kept backing off from the gate as Kathy reached to open it. Finally the judge ordered her to ride around it. The pinto flatly refused to walk over the calfskin, and broke her ground hitch when Kathy dismounted to open the mailbox.

Jubilee accepted all the challenges, but was cautious and slow. Rocket, being a natural trail horse, took the hazards with alacrity. But when it came to the walk, trot, and canter with the group around the breaking ring, true to form he showed his disgust by frequently breaking his gait.

Only one participant of the eleven entries was without fault—a young boy with a Morgan, and he won the trophy. Bob took a third place ribbon, Larry a fifth, and Kathy did not place.

In the Western Pleasure Class, Patches worked nicely around the ring, and Kathy took second prize. Larry won fourth; Bob did not place. He was the only one of the three, however, to enter the Ring-Spearing Class, and won the trophy.

Now and then Linda would run back to the lot and check on Chica d'Oro to make sure she was not being bothered. On one of those occasions, as she walked again toward the arena to watch the last event before lunch, she came face to face with Shirley Blaine. Linda greeted the girl pleasantly and would have gone on, but Shirley stopped her.

With a cheerful smile, she said, "Why, hello there, Linda Craig. I've been looking for you. I thought we might have a little chat before we start competing against each other in the ring."

"It won't be long now." Linda smiled, inwardly surprised at the other's sudden chumminess.

Shirley shrugged and said blithely, "May the best queen win!" Then she asked, "Will you be my guest for a spin down the highway for a soda? There's a little place near the junction."

"Why, thank you, but do you think we ought to leave now?" Linda demurred.

She did not want to go with the girl. Then she reproached herself—perhaps they had misjudged Shirley. After all, Shirley might be trying to make up for her snobbishness at their first encounter.

"Oh, come on!" Shirley urged. "A couple of the other queens are going to be there. We'll relax for a bit, and come back together."

"Well-l, all right," Linda acceded finally. "But we'll have to hurry."

"I'll step on it." Shirley laughed.

She was as good as her promise, Linda discovered. Shirley kept her cream convertible at top speed. As they passed the Silver Saddle Motel coffee shop, Linda proposed, "Why not stop here? It's closer."

Shirley shook her head. "This other place is better," she stated and sped on.

During the drive Shirley had little to say. Linda made several attempts at conversation, but received only brief replies.

She's certainly changeable, the ranch girl observed wryly to herself.

Finally Shirley stopped at a small roadside luncheonette about three miles from the park. "Here we are!" she announced. The girls alighted and went inside the small restaurant.

"No one else is here," remarked Linda as they seated themselves.

"They'll be along." Shirley laughed. "I guess I drove pretty fast." The next moment she jumped up saying, "I just remembered—I want to show you some pictures! They're honeys. Order chocolate malts, will you, while I get the pics from the car?"

She hurried out to the convertible. To Linda's utter amazement Shirley hopped in behind the wheel, turned the car around, and drove off.

Linda jumped up in shocked dismay. Now she knew the reason for Shirley's affability—a means to put Linda out of the competition!

The proprietress came over. "Is something wrong, young lady?" she asked, puzzled.

"Very much!" replied Linda. "I'm stranded! Is there anyone here who would drive me to Cowboy Park?"

"Not a soul," the woman replied. "My husband always goes out with the car at this time to load up at the produce market."

Linda's mind raced. Maybe if she could reach Cactus Mac he might get her to the contest in time. "May I use your phone?" she asked. Apologetically the woman replied that there was no telephone.

Linda was heartsick. In a panic she raced out to the road and looked up and down. Not a car in sight! Frantic, she started to run.

Queens Contest 14

In Cowboy Park, Bob, Kathy, and Larry had become frantic at Linda's prolonged absence. They had searched the area thoroughly and made inquiries of many people. None had seen Linda recently.

Finally Jill Raymond, who had been away from the park for half an hour, told them, "I think I saw Linda Craig go off a little while ago with Shirley Blaine in her car."

Bob and the others were mystified. "It's hard to believe," said Kathy, "that Shirley would take a chance missing the contest."

"She isn't around either," Bob noted.

"Oh-h!" cried Kathy, worriedly. "Do you suppose the girls have been in an accident?"

"I think one of us had better hurry down to that Silver Saddle Motel," said Bob. "Maybe Shirley and Linda are there."

"You go, Bob," said Larry. "I'll get Chica d'Oro

ready in case Linda shows up. There isn't much time left before the contest starts."

Already the other queen contestants, attractively costumed, were taking their places in the arena. Bob was about to leave when Kathy exclaimed, "Here comes Shirley!"

They all stared. Shirley, resplendent in a yellow jeweled tailored suit with gold accouterments—boots, gloves, tie, and hat—was mounted on a sorrel Arabian that showed savvy and training.

Kathy ran up to her and demanded, "Where is Linda?"

Shirley raised her eyebrows and replied in a surprised tone, "You don't mean to say she isn't here!" The Malibu girl rode away before Kathy could question her further.

A group of other contestants nearby chattered admiringly. Kathy heard one say, "Isn't Shirley gorgeous? Positively dazzling! She can't lose!"

Another remarked, "She'll be our next queen—no question about it!"

Angrily Kathy ran back to the trailers, where Bob and Larry were having a hard time with Chica. The palomino was nervous and uncooperative at Linda's absence, dancing about and refusing the bit.

The call came over the loudspeaker: "Queen competitors, get ready to ride!"

Kathy was almost in tears. "Oh, Linda, where are you?"

Finally the boys were able to lead Chica d'Oro to the rear of the arena just as another announcement blared out: "Contestants ride in!"

The colorful procession of forty beautiful young women astride their fine horses started to move. At that moment a farmer's truck roared into the park road, and an excited girl in shirt and jeans jumped out.

"Linda!" shouted Bob and the others joyously. Chica gave an excited, loud whinny of greeting.

Her young owner swung into the saddle, cheeks aflame with anger. "Thanks," she gasped. There was no time to say anything more.

Bob whipped out his handkerchief and wiped the dust off one of her boots. Larry did the same for the other as she took her place in the moving line.

"Good luck!" he whispered, and hurried with Bob and Kathy for seats in the grandstand.

Inside, the queens had started around the ring. When Shirley saw Linda, she gave a perceptible start and the brilliant smile she had been affecting vanished in a look of fear. Then she tossed her head haughtily and flicked some imaginary dirt from her suit as if to remind Linda that she could not win anyhow wearing her jeans.

Linda eyed her rival steadily, and made the silent vow: I'm going to outride you, Shirley Blaine! Even if I lose on account of my clothes, I'm going to outride you.

They were going around the ring at a walk. Shirley, in her surprise upon seeing Linda, had involuntarily tightened suddenly on the reins. Her horse had made a quick little sideways step. Linda wondered if the judges had seen it.

The commands came for the trot and canter, the reverse, and walk, trot, and canter. As the queen contestants passed the grandstand, families and friends applauded for their favorite girl. But there came a general hearty handclapping from all over the grandstand when Linda went by, as if the spectators were aware that some dire occurrence had prevented her from appearing in proper attire.

Although this warmed Linda's heart, she knew that it would have no influence on the tally of the judges. Performance, conformation of horse, and costume points were all that would be considered. So far, Chica d'Oro's performance had been perfect.

Linda did not look up into the stand, since this was not supposed to be done. But she could guess that the faces of the Old Sol group wore puzzled expressions.

The contestants lined up at the far side of the arena, and the individual performances commenced. The girls rode in the order in which they had entered and were required to figure eight, pivot, and back.

Shirley was fourth. It was evident now that she was unusually tense. She held too tight a rein, which brought her horse to a standstill in the middle of its backing.

Linda and Chica d'Oro, in contrast, gave a flawless performance. The beautiful, well-trained palomino worked with ease and exactness at Linda's command.

The applause was thunderous. It meant one all-important thing to Linda—that she *had* outridden Shirley. But she knew her rival's points on costume would probably put the Malibu contestant ahead despite her one obvious fault, even possibly two.

Most of the contenders had a couple or more faults against them. Three others, besides Linda, who had performed without a demerit had not, however, given smooth performances.

Linda fought back tears. I haven't a chance against Shirley, she thought hopelessly.

There was to be a one-hour rest period before the personality tests. When Linda returned to the trailers she found Doña and Bronco there with Bob, Kathy, and Larry. "You rode like a real champ," said Bob. "And now tell us what happened. Why did you leave here?"

Briefly Linda explained, while her brother took care of Chica d'Oro. Everyone was speechless with fury and disgust at Shirley's trickery.

"She should be disqualified!" declared Bronco angrily.

Kathy, Bob, and Larry clamored to report the girl's actions to the judges. But Linda held them back.

"Please don't say anything to anybody," she begged. "The only way I want to get square with Shirley Blaine is by a fair riding contest."

Doña smiled at her granddaughter lovingly and said, "I'm proud that we have true nobility in our girl."

Linda kissed her, then said, "I'd better get into my outfit or I'll be going through the personality test still in jeans!"

"Top luck!" Bronco wished her.

Doña added, "We'll all go back to the grandstand now. I know you will perform well, my dear."

"Of course you will." Bronco gave Linda a reassuring pat.

As soon as the Mallorys had left, Kathy exclaimed, "Linda, you really must eat to put some pep into you. How do you expect to win a single point against well-fed, smug Shirley in the personality test if you're hungry, sad-faced, and angry? No argument. I'm going to get you a sandwich!"

Linda looked at Kathy and laughed for the first time in hours. "I see your point," she admitted. "I'll take your advice."

Kathy dashed to the caterer's trucks. Meanwhile Linda dressed in her sparkling green outfit and white accessories. By the time she was ready, Kathy had returned with a chicken sandwich and a glass of milk.

After she had eaten, Linda stood up and stretched. The natural sparkle had returned to her eyes and the glow to her cheeks.

"I feel like a million!" she exclaimed, looking with deep fondness at Bob and her two friends, and added huskily, "You're all so wonderful to stand by me. You know, I feel as if I just might win that personality test. At least, I'm going to try mighty hard!"

The others smiled, thinking there was a positive aura of radiance about her now.

"You can't miss, Linda," declared Larry admiringly. "You look terrific."

The call came over the loudspeaker: "Queen contestants enter!"

Linda walked with Larry, Kathy, and Bob to the grandstand. Then, while the three went up to take seats, she joined the other girls in the boxes reserved for them.

Valerie Vance, owner of a modeling school, was to be the judge for the personality contest, and Mrs. Hal Freeman, wife of one of the horse show judges, sat at a table to engage the girls in brief conversations.

Each girl was to walk for a certain distance in front of the grandstand, then turn and walk back. Next she would pose for a picture, and finally sit at the table for a few minutes talking with Mrs. Freeman.

"This is going to be lots harder than riding," murmured one of the contestants, and the others nodded in agreement.

During the test Linda held her white gloves casually in her left hand as she had once seen the wife of a commanding officer do at an important military function.

Shirley Blaine did not remove her gold lamé gloves and tightly clasped her hands together now and then. Otherwise she was well poised and outstanding in her beauty.

The applause from the grandstand was generous for even the most nervous girls. It was therefore impossible for Linda and her fellow contestants to guess how things were going.

That evening there was to be a queen's banquet for the girls and their families. At eight o'clock the announcement of the winner and her four princesses would be made, after the judges and committee had computed all of the points.

A large marquee had been erected for the banquet—featuring delicious roast squab. The girls were too excited to have much appetite, but a comedian and lively strolling musicians who had been engaged to relieve the tension largely succeeded in doing so.

At Linda's table, Kathy and the boys tried to

divert their friend by nonsensical banter. Linda laughed when Larry asked with a straight face, "Is this a coo-coo squab?" and Kathy retorted, "Anyway, it's not a cuckoo bird."

At a quarter to eight Mort Sullivan, president of the Trail Blazers organization, appeared, and immediately conversation ceased. The air became electric with anticipation. Linda's pulse throbbed rapidly and a tingle went up her spine. The judges' decision was about to be announced!

Mort began, "There is a tie between two contestants. It has been decided by the committee to break it through a horsemanship contest between the two. Will Shirley Blaine and Linda Craig please ride into the arena at eight o'clock?"

There followed a burst of excited babbling, and Shirley's mother was heard to exclaim, "Not that ranch girl in jeans! Why, I never heard of such a thing!"

Linda was stunned speechless, but Kathy hugged her, crying joyously, "You'll win! I just know it!"

Linda smiled as the others showered her with congratulations and wishes for success. Her other winning points had made up for those lost on costume!

"Well, my dear," said Doña softly, "at least *you* will be riding with a clear conscience."

"I'll get Chica d'Oro ready," Bob offered, rising.

Linda smiled. "Thank you, Brother," she replied. "You are a first-class groom, and I appreciate it. But I'd like to have a little visit with my golden girl before this particular contest."

"I understand."

Linda hurried off. The palomino welcomed her with a pleased whinny.

"Chica," said Linda earnestly, "you and I have a great challenge to meet. We'll do it, won't we, baby?"

Chica responded by whinnying again and nuzzling her mistress.

"I knew you'd agree!" Linda said and hugged the filly.

At eight o'clock the spectators were back in the grandstand. Linda and Shirley sat on their horses side by side at the arena entrance, waiting for the command to come in. Shirley appeared furious and refused to look at Linda, who wore a continuous, pleasant smile.

When the two girls were called in, they were requested to repeat their performances of that afternoon. Linda and Chica were at the peak of perfection, and made a scintillatingly beautiful picture under the bright floodlights of the arena.

Linda observed that Shirley tightened up again in her truculence, and the Arabian acted confused and hesitant a couple of times in its response to her commands. Despite this, they executed an exceptionally fine performance.

Chica performed magnificently ...

The two girls were called to the judges' box and instructed to dismount. Bob, who was standing by, took Chica, and Shirley's groom was handed the Arabian's reins. The girls remained where they were to hear the result.

Linda was outwardly calm and poised. In reality her knees felt shaky and every nerve was taut. Shirley held herself rigid, staring straight ahead.

Judge Freeman looked over his notations. Then he wrote a name on a small slip of paper and handed it to Mort Sullivan, who stood at the mike. A dramatic silence had fallen over the crowded grandstand.

The Trail Blazers president smiled at the audience, then announced, "Well, here we have the news that you've all been waiting to hear. The name of the new queen is—Linda Craig of Club 28."

The Club 28 membership went wild, and thunderous applause came from everyone else except those in the Malibu Club.

Shirley's face registered deep shock. She did not say a word to her victorious rival.

"And now the names of the princesses," Mort Sullivan continued. Shirley Blaine was named first, then three other girls.

Shirley's groom stepped over to her, and Linda heard him say in a British accent, "I did my best to help you win, Miss Shirley."

Linda studied the groom speculatively. He was tall and thin, and had a small black mustache.

Suddenly Shirley said brusquely to him, "I'm getting out of here!" She stepped into the saddle and rode quickly out of the arena.

"Miss Blaine, come back here or you will be disqualified!" called one of the committeemen. But the girl did not comply.

Mort Sullivan spoke quickly to the judge, who consulted his list to select another princess in Shirley's place. The new name announced was that of Jill Raymond, the petite black-haired girl. She jumped up and down in excitement and burst into happy tears.

The magnificent queen's trophy was presented to Linda, and an enormous sheaf of red roses placed in her arms. The congratulations and praise of all the officials were lavish, and the applause of the crowd was genuine and loud.

Trophies were also awarded to the princesses. Flashbulbs popped continuously as pictures were taken of Linda and the runners-up. Families and club members clustered about the winners.

"It's all so wonderful!" exclaimed Linda. "Like a dream. But I never could have won without Chica d'Oro's help."

Finally Doña and Bronco left to drive home. Linda, Bob, Larry, and Kathy returned to the trailers. Linda took a few seconds to show Chica the big trophy, hugged and praised her, and gave the filly a red rosebud to eat.

Suddenly the new queen turned to the others and said, "I believe I know who the mystery man is!"

"What?" Bob cried. "Sis, don't keep us in suspense!"

"Shirley Blaine's groom," was Linda's surprising answer. "He's tall, thin, has a black mustache, and I heard him tell Shirley he had done his best to help her win."

"But the English accent?" Bob protested.

"I believe he just uses that for effect," said Linda.

"We'd better hotfoot it over to the Sierra Stables before he disappears," Bob urged.

The four drove there and asked at the office for Miss Blaine's groom.

"That would be Ferd Fenwick," said the man in charge.

Linda, Kathy, and the boys quietly approached the building where the horses were kept. They slipped inside and spotted Ferd Fenwick. He was talking with several other grooms. Drawing closer, they heard him speaking.

"Just as I suspected!" Linda whispered. "Ferd Fenwick has no British accent. I'm convinced that he is the one who tried to drown me, loosened the trailer wheel, trapped us on the trail, and used the beard disguise to kidnap us at the fair!"

Without hesitation Bob called out, "Mr. Fenwick, we want to ask you some questions."

The tall man turned away from his companions and sauntered toward them. "Well, what is it?" he demanded impatiently.

Linda stepped forward and made her accusations. The groom's face contorted with rage and his lips drew back in a snarl. Suddenly he lunged at Linda as if to choke her.

An Ancestor's Revelation   15

As Fenwick lunged at Linda, Bob and Larry leaped forward to block him. The groom fought the two boys with savage thrusts. Although he was thin, the man's muscles were like steel.

Bob's fist lashed out and caught Fenwick squarely on the jaw. He staggered backward and Larry hastily pinioned his arms. Quickly Bob whipped a leather strap from a hook on the wall and tied Fenwick's wrists together.

"Ready to talk?" Bob snapped.

By now the other grooms had run over and were staring in stupefaction. "What's going on?" one asked.

"This man is guilty of attempted murder and kidnapping," Larry replied hotly. "Will you please call the sheriff?"

The man stared, dumbfounded. "Right away!" he gulped, and hastened to the office.

The other two grooms, evidently unnerved and not wishing to become involved, quickly departed. Seeing that he was trapped, Fenwick's belligerence ebbed away. He asked in a whining tone, "You going to file all those charges against me?"

"We have no choice," replied Bob sternly.

Linda faced the captive. "You may as well admit everything," she advised. "How did a fine groom like you, employed by prominent people, became associated with a man like Hank Trask?"

"Known him for years," replied Fenwick. "He used to work at the stables and would do anything to make a fast buck. I've kept in touch. He knew tricks to knock out horses. Picked them up at race tracks where he hung out a lot. I paid him to have Rod Coleman thread your horse's legs."

"But Shirley Blaine is a first-class horsewoman, and has fine horses," said Linda. "Her chances to win were good."

Fenwick gave Linda a slanting glance. "You know better. I was afraid you'd be a threat to Miss Shirley's chances in the club's horse show if you made the Trail Blazers. So I figured out various ways to prevent your becoming a member."

Kathy looked aghast. "How awful!" she cried. "Winning a contest isn't worth doing all those dreadful things."

"For me it was," declared Fenwick. "Miss Shirley has highfalutin contacts. If she'd won the competition today, she was in line to be asked to join the Olympic equestrian team. This would help *me* go on to bigger and better shows."

"In other words," Linda said in disgust, "your schemes to put me out of the running were for your own selfish ends."

Fenwick's eyes took on a maniacal glitter. "It would've been a swell deal," he said, "going along with Miss Shirley to the Santa Barbara Olympic workouts, Chicago's International show, the finals in Scarsdale, New York—and then on to the Olympic Games." The groom gritted his teeth. "I would've hit the big time—if you pests hadn't wrecked everything."

The prisoner admitted that Shirley had feared Linda's competition, but had not been part of any of the attempts to harm Linda or Chica d'Oro. The Malibu girl had mainly wanted to prevent her rival from appearing in the queens contest.

Fenwick further confessed to being guilty of all Linda's accusations, including the attempt to drown her. He had stalked the young trailblazers to the beach, carrying his skin-diving equipment. The groom had donned swim trunks, hidden behind a large rock a short distance away, and watched for his chance to harm Linda.

"Too bad you all didn't fall into that camouflaged

pit I set up near the fallen tree," Fenwick added.

"I suppose you rigged up the desert detour too," Bob said coldly.

"That's right," the groom replied insolently.

Linda next quizzed him about his tie-in with the Coleman brothers. Fenwick snorted: "Hardly knew them—they're Hank's cronies. But the one called Rod came in handy at the fair. He wanted your old family jewels enough to help me get you away. I was going to keep you locked up someplace until after the Cowboy Park show."

"You also had someone phone a fake message about closing time for the Trail Blazers entries," Linda charged.

This, however, Fenwick flatly denied. "You'll have to figure that one out," he said sullenly. Linda felt sure now that the mysterious female caller had been Shirley Blaine.

The next moment a police car roared up and several deputies jumped out. Fenwick was quickly handcuffed and, after the Craigs had made a brief statement to the lawmen, was driven off.

Linda turned to the others. "Everybody have enough excitement," she asked, "or shall I dig up some more—like finding the Perez jewels?"

Larry grinned. "No, thank you, Queen Linda! Although I'm sure you could!"

Early next morning the four new Club 28 members set out for home. They were in a festive mood, still jubilant over Linda's triumph. Upon reaching Old Sol, she was given an enthusiastic reception by everyone at the ranch.

"Yippee-ki-oo!" shouted Cactus Mac, throwing his ten-gallon hat into the air. "We're mighty proud o' our queen. And sure as shootin', you'll be winnin' another crown one o' these days on that thar purty little filly o' yours." Then he sobered. "I guess even better'n beatin' that uppity gal was catchin' those varmints."

"I'm glad," said Linda. "It worried me that I was the cause of so much trouble to all of you."

Cactus turned to Bob. "Got some good news. We just heard from the sheriff where the Colemans hid your coin collection. He's sending men to get it."

"Swell!"

Lunch was an extra-special affair, for Luisa had prepared some fine dishes for the occasion. Afterward Linda drew her grandmother aside in the hall.

"Doña," she said, "I'm still curious about the young woman who made that hoax phone call. Was there anything unusual in the way she spoke?"

Mrs. Mallory reflected for several moments. "I do recall," she replied, "the person had an odd way of pronouncing Rancho del Sol. I believe she said, 'de la Sol.'"

"I was right," Linda murmured. "Shirley Blaine *was* the culprit. But," she went on, "I won't pursue the matter. Shirley's had her punishment, I guess."

200

Doña agreed. Then, smiling, she handed her granddaughter a large, square envelope. "This came for you yesterday I have a feeling it's an invitation."

Linda noted that it was postmarked Santa Barbara, where the most famous and colorful of all Southern California fiestas is held. She observed with shining eyes the Old Spanish Days return address in the corner. Invitations, she knew, were sent only to well-screened and selected riders.

Excitedly she opened the envelope, and took out two items. One was a beautiful, formal parchment invitation to ride in El Desfile Histórico, the Old Spanish Days historical parade. There would be La Cabalgata, an equestrian promenade to socialize on horseback as in the old days, and a California Royal Rancho pageant to be presented in the Santa Barbara bowl.

The other paper was a personal letter to Linda from Anthony Trent, the parade chairman, inviting her, as a notable descendant of one of California's first Spanish families, to act as the bride in the wedding party, a most important feature of the parade.

"How thrilling!" Linda murmured, awestruck by the honor. "How wonderfully thrilling!" Then she puckered her forehead and said, "But if I accept I will have to wear a beautiful wedding dress."

Linda turned her gaze toward the portrait of

Rosalinda Perez and murmured softly, "I'll be riding with the descendants of many of the first grandee families whom you knew."

Then a striking thought came to her. Linda said slowly, "Doña, do you suppose—I might wear Rosalinda's wedding dress, if I took good care of it?"

Doña beamed lovingly upon the girl and replied, "I don't know of a more appropriate use for the dress, dear. Suppose you try it on."

"Oh, thank you!" cried Linda, and ran to the carved chest to take out the ancient gown.

She raised the heavy lid, and held up the exquisite white silk brocade and lace wedding dress with its long, tight bodice and bouffant skirt with many yards of lace flouncing. Linda gathered it in her arms and hurried to her room. Soon she returned attired in the gown.

"How do I look, Doña?" she asked breathlessly, turning slowly for her grandmother's appraisal.

Mrs. Mallory smiled warmly. "You make a lovely picture indeed. I see the bodice is somewhat long, however. It will have to be shortened."

"I'll alter it right now!" Linda ran to change and came back with her sewing basket. She sat down on the living room couch with the beautiful dress spread around her. Eagerly she ripped a well-bound seam at the waist.

Two ruby pendants and an emerald ring rolled out!

202

"Jewels!" Linda cried. "Rosalinda Perez's lost jewels!"

"How amazing!" exclaimed Doña.

Excitedly Linda ripped other seams. Each revealed jewels, until there was heaped before her a wealth of pearls, rubies, diamonds, and emeralds.

Linda, almost dazed by her discovery, said in awe, "To think that all this time they really *were* hidden in the chest!"

At that moment Bronco and Bob strode into the room and stared unbelievingly at the scene.

"Rosalinda Perez's jewels!" Linda told them, and Doña explained the find.

All four were joyful until suddenly Linda's face clouded. "That awful Hank Trask!" she exclaimed in dismay. "We will have to give him his share."

Bronco slapped his thigh. "I forgot to tell you!" he said. "I had a talk with the sheriff. It seems Trask broke down and confessed he'd faked the paper he left in Chica's stall. He had read the story of the missing jewels in the museum, saw the original letter there, and copied it. The Perez jewels belong to the Rosalinda namesakes of your great-great-grandmother."

Linda arose and went to gaze at the portrait. Smiling, she said, "How clever of you to hide the jewels in your wedding dress, Great-Great-Grandmother! Somehow you must have known we finally would discover the secret of Rancho del Sol!"